M000236259

THE RUNAWAY HEIR

The Second Book in the Fictional Retelling of the Biblical Story of

David and Michal

⳹⳺

by

Janice Broyles

THE RUNAWAY HEIR BY JANICE BROYLES

Published by Late November Literary
Winston Salem, NC 27107

ISBN (Print): 978-1-7341008-0-8
ISBN (E-Book): 9781734100815
Copyright © 2019 by Janice Broyles
Cover design by ilovemycover.com
Interior design by Late November Literary

Available in print or online. Visit latenovemberliterary.com or
janicebroyles.com

All rights reserved. No part of this publication may be reproduced in
any form without written permission of the publisher, except as
provided by the U.S. copyright law.

This is a work of fiction based on the biblical account of David and
Michal. Some of the characters and events come from the author's
imagination or are used for fictional purposes. Any brand names,
places, or trademarks remain the property of their respective owners
and are only used for fictional purposes.

All Scripture quotations are taken from the Holy Bible, King James
Version, and are used by permission.

Library of Congress Cataloging-in-Publication data
Library of Congress Control Number:2019915146
Broyles, Janice.
The Runaway Heir / Janice Broyles 1st ed.

Printed in the United States of America

DEDICATION

CɜꙄꙄ

This book is dedicated to all of my childhood Sunday School teachers.

Thank you for sharing such great Bible stories.

THE RUNAWAY HEIR

Janice Broyles

Of
Vows
And
Vices

1

CRO80

Michal

King Saul's Palace
1019 B.C.

I stared at myself through the looking glass, my lips curved in a satisfied smile. Dinah and the other attendants dressed and prepared me for the ceremony. A part of me warned myself to be careful. Mother and father were not happy at the union. But a promise was a promise, and I knew that father's reputation was in question. He could never go back on his word.

"You have yet to stop smiling these past three days." Dinah arranged the gold bangles up my arm.

"By night's end, he will be mine," I answered. "It cannot come soon enough."

The door to my private chamber swung open, and Merab, my elder sister, entered. She stopped when she saw me, pressed a hand to her heart and gasped. "Did I look this breathtaking for my wedding ceremony?"

"No," I teased. "But you were *almost* this breathtaking."

We shared a smile.

"I have not seen you this happy. Your face shines like the sun."

"Just days ago I was locked in my chambers as a prisoner and told that the love of my life would be killed by my father's hand. I am still in a bit of disbelief over the turn of events."

Merab approached me, found my hand underneath layers of

3

material, and squeezed affectionately. "Our parents have not been kind to either of us."

"Mother especially enjoyed parading us in front of a long line of suitors."

"I had it a bit easier than you." Merab frowned. "Not that it is perfect."

"Are you not happy with Adriel?"

"He is as kind as a husband could be, but it was arranged. The love will grow. I hope." My sister stared past me. I knew she thought about Benaiah, the handsome armor-bearer who stole her heart. But they never had a chance. Merab was the eldest daughter to King Saul, and Benaiah was a commoner. When she saw I watched her, she added, "I am sure there are far worse."

"I never thought that it would happen, but by some providential design, I am marrying the man I love. It is as if I must hold my breath as to not spoil this moment." My father hated my betrothed. Regardless of David's loyalty, my father saw him as a threat to his throne.

"Father did not expect that David would not only live from the task of earning your dowry but also be overly successful with the endeavor."

A laugh escaped my lips, which caused Merab to start giggling. Only my father, the king of Israel, could come up with such a disgusting request for a dowry. A hundred foreskins from our sworn enemies, the Philistines. Of course, he did not expect for my David—my handsome shepherd and Israel's giant-slayer—to make it back alive.

But he not only made it back alive, he also brought more than what was necessary to earn my hand in marriage. My father had no choice but to honor the contract.

Thus, here I stood, wrapped in ceremonial silks, the thin material laced with the finest of gold. "Was your gown so heavy? This gold is too much."

"Stop," Merab said, smoothing the layers of fabric. "The

weight is nothing when your heart is light."

"True." I smiled again at my reflection.

The door to my chamber opened as servants ushered in my mother.

The rumor throughout our land was that Queen Ahinoam was of unmatched beauty. The rumor was true. She stood in the midst of the room, completely flawless of feature and composure. Many compared her to the lovely moon goddess, Ashtoreth, but beneath that beauty lay cruelty and vanity. For that reason, among countless others, she remained the ugliest person I knew.

My skin crawled as she scrutinized me. Merab still held my hand. She squeezed it again, as if to say, *Stay calm.*

"You look happy," my mother said, with a hint of scorn.

Tread carefully, I told myself. "I am."

My mother's lips curved. "But for how long?" She stepped closer to me, her steely gaze piercing my heart. When I was younger, I longed for a mother who loved me, but that longing shriveled up when I realized my mother would never care for anyone but herself. So, it should not have bothered me that there was no warmth in her eyes, but it did.

"Can you please be happy for me?" I pleaded, even though I knew it was futile. "Today, I am marrying the man I love. The man who has completed every assignment father has placed in front of him. Despite yours and father's animosity toward him, he has shown loyalty to our kingdom, so please—"

"Happy for you?" she interrupted. "That is what you have never understood, dear daughter. You think I am cruel, but I have ever only been practical. There is no happiness. Sure, David will enjoy you for a little while, but he will tire of you. They all do. Your father used to love me. Now he has others to occupy him, and I am forgotten."

"Mother, enough," Merab said. "This is Michal's celebration. We can have practicality on the morrow. For now, let us choose to be happy, even if it is a façade for some."

5

"You seem to have forgotten that I am queen. I do not answer to you."

"It was merely a request from a daughter to her mother."

Our mother looked from me to Merab then back to me. "I never thought you for a foolish girl, Michal. But you are a most foolish girl indeed. Do not forget that this marriage was only agreed upon because you swore to your father to provide him information to condemn David when the time comes."

"You did what?" Merab searched my face.

"Even with the dowry of the foreskins, making the promise to father was the only way he would agree to the union," I said.

"And just how will the handsome lyre player take the news that his lovely wife is a trickster?" my mother asked.

"No, it is not like that. There will be nothing to report. I am certain of it." I did not add that there was nothing father could do to ever turn me from David. I only said what needed to be said to secure the union. But I could not admit that out loud. I needed to keep up appearances with my family that I planned to honor the agreement.

"This is going to end badly. Do not say that I did not warn you." The queen turned and moved toward the door. To the servants, she commanded, "Secure her veil and usher her to the courtyard."

A stillness descended on us upon her departure.

"Oh Michal," Merab whispered. "I hope you know what you are doing. Mother and father are formidable opponents."

With no one speaking another word, Dinah let the wedding veil fall into position. I could no longer see my face in the looking glass. Not that it mattered. I was no longer smiling.

2

⚬⚬⚬

David

King Saul's Palace
1019 B.C.

I reread the poem, and my fingers itched to keep going. Unfortunately, I ran out of parchment. I needed to keep busy, but there was nothing in this sparse room to keep me preoccupied.

The king kept me in an inner chamber with no windows and allowed no one to stay with me. My own troops were not allowed at the celebration. I understood the king's message without him speaking a word. I was not trusted.

Solitude did not bother me. My years shepherding often required long bouts of isolation. But at least I had the sky, my sling, and the sheep as companions.

There was a quick knock at the door before it opened. Jonathan, Prince of Israel, and one of my closest friends, peeked his head inside. "How are you doing?"

"I am ready to see my wife," I said.

"And it shall happen or I am not the eldest son of the current king." Jonathan stepped into the room. "I am here to retrieve you, but I am also here to make sure you have not changed your mind."

"I will never be worthy enough for Michal's hand, but trust me, now that her hand has been offered, my mind has thought of little else."

"I am glad that both my friend and my sister have found happy matches in each other. Besides, it is too late now. The contract has been signed."

"Praise Yahweh!" I moved quickly to the door. The time had come for me to greet my bride. As we headed down the ornate hallway, I asked, "And how is the king's temperament? I hope I have done enough for there to be peace."

Jonathan walked in silence for a moment. "We do not choose the path destiny has determined for us. I cannot tell you that the road you are on is an easy one."

"Nor for you." I knew how difficult it must be for Jonathan to know of my path to the throne, and to fully support me in the journey.

"Do you ever wish that Samuel would have poured that anointing oil on someone else's head?"

"Often." I exchanged a grin with Jonathan. "I question if the old prophet got it wrong. That I am what my father always said that I am: a lowly shepherd who picks up sheep dung with nowhere to lay my head."

"He did not see you with that sling and stone, facing the giant, nor did he see you with Goliath's sword, slicing through his own head with it."

I remembered the moment the stone went flying through the air and the small sound it made when it hit Goliath's head. His fall seemed suspended in time, as if God Himself slowed down the shifting of the sun so that I could memorize the scene. "Any confidence I have is not in myself."

"I know, which is why I like you so much. We would not be friends if you were too arrogant. We have enough of that around here." Jonathan threw his arm around me and pulled me to him while we finished the length of the great hall that led to the palace courtyard. "Now let us give you to your bride and celebrate the occasion!"

The lanterns lined the pathways of the gardens, and bonfires burned around the gathering, not that there were many. The small number in attendance were already enjoying the wine. I saw my brothers and felt my throat thicken as emotion nearly took over. For most of my life, they wanted nothing to do with me. I was the outcast of the family, born of a questionable birth. Their hatred only grew when the old prophet, Samuel, called me out from the fields and poured a horn of oil over my head. I was twelve years of age when that happened, and now, nine years later, to see them at my wedding feast felt like a miracle.

Jesse, my father, made eye contact with me. Too much had happened between us over the years, and I knew that he would never be the father to me that I had always desired and, at times, desperately needed. I still chose to smile and nod in acknowledgement that he had come to my marriage celebration. Without any reciprocation of expression, my father quickly turned away.

"Is he still not over you being the next heir to the throne?" Jonathan evidently saw my father's response to me.

"We have a complicated relationship." I tried not to think of all the times he beat me. How many nights did I go to sleep in pain with bruises on my body?

"Do not dwell on it tonight." Jonathan pointed in the other direction. I noticed Michal's maidservant, standing with others waiting to escort me to Michal. "We will be here celebrating. Go, enjoy your bride."

The small crowd quieted as King Saul stood with hands extended. The king was a warrior of a man, in height and size, commanding attention of all who came in contact with him. He used to intimidate me, but he also inspired me. I longed for his approval nearly as much—if not more so—than my own father's, but any approval with the king was short-lived. As he stood there, his gaze piercing mine, I knew that there was still only resignation. And anger. The king's expression and posture clearly indicated he was not happy with the arrangement. "The contract has been signed, and the marriage covenant is in place. Your bride is waiting."

My brothers and Jonathan called out cheers and

encouragement as I made my way to Michal's maidservants. My earlier anticipation somewhat dimmed now that I saw how unhappy the king was with the match. I warred within myself to stop thinking about the anger emanating from the king and to focus on the love of my life waiting for me to take her as my wife. But what had I agreed to? Would Michal and I constantly be under scrutiny of the king? Would he try to throw another spear at me as he did before, or would he simply continue to send me out on mission after mission until the enemy's sword found my heart?

The walk down the corridor to the wedding chambers was long and full of angst. This should be the happiest moment of my life, yet my throat felt as if it were full of sheep's wool, and sweat dripped from my forehead and through my heavy tunic. So lost in thought and worry, I nearly walked right into Merab, Michal's older sister. She waited outside the chamber door.

"Forgive me," I said. "My mind was elsewhere."

Merab kissed both my cheeks. "Welcome to the family, brother. I pray blessings upon you and this union."

I nodded and wiped at my brow.

"Protect her at all costs." Merab moved to the side, so I could enter.

The words fell like a heavy robe around my shoulders. If I truly wanted to protect Michal, why was I so selfish in marrying her? The king's animosity was apparent, and the sense of dread had replaced any anticipation. If I wanted to protect her, I should have suppressed my longings and chose her safety over our love. Yet I did not turn away. The marriage contract was signed. Michal, my lovely, beautiful princess, was mine. So, instead of answering, I opened the door and entered the chamber.

Michal, in her gold-laced garments, stopped pacing the center of the chamber. The veil had been forsaken and tossed on the floor. "David." She threw her arms around me, and in that instant, all thoughts of doubt and worry and fear melted like a candle's wax under a hot flame.

"Michal," I breathed her name and took in her scent.

We held each other with no thought of time.

Eventually, she asked, "So, is it official? Are you now my husband?"

"Yes," I said, not letting go.

"I did not want to hope until I saw you walk through the door. We have been through so much. I was almost expecting something to happen. And the wait was excruciating. I kept replaying my mother's words. But now you are here."

"What of your mother's words?" I asked, not willing to release her. Now that Michal was mine I was not sure how I would ever be able to not have her in my arms.

"Nothing of consequence. You and me. That is what matters in this moment." She kissed my neck, then brought her lips to mine.

***

"Psst."

I awoke to someone shaking me.

"Psst, David."

I opened my eyes to see Michal's maidservant, standing over me. I turned and saw Michal still sleeping beside me. "What hour is it?" I whispered. Since there was no morning light, it was far too late—or too early—to be waking me.

"My apologies, my lord," she whispered. "But Prince Jonathan needs to speak with you immediately. He said to meet him at the stables along the southern palace wall."

My first thought was to tell her to leave, then roll over and enjoy the warm blankets and my lovely wife. But if Jonathan needed to see me, and it needed to be done in secret, then there must be an important reason. "I will leave directly."

The girl nodded and left the chamber.

Michal stirred and pulled me to her. "Why are you awake?" she murmured.

I kissed her forehead. "Your brother needs to see me. I will return as soon as I can." I slid out of the blankets and threw on my tunic and trousers.

"He cannot take my husband away from our wedding chambers. It has not been the full 14 days." Michal wrapped the blankets around her and sat up. I could see her pouting even with only the moon's glow as a light.

"I promise I will return shortly. If it was anyone other than Jonathan, I would tell them to not bother me, but he would not ask me to come out if it was not important."

"And so it begins," Michal said. "My husband, Israel's fierce defender, must leave my side. But we still have one more day."

"This time together has been the best of my life." I reached for her and kissed her warm lips. "And no matter where I am, I will always be with you. We are one now."

"That will not make me miss you any less."

We knew that I would have to leave for long stretches of time. It would, unfortunately, be our norm. I commanded a thousand troops, and King Saul sent us one order after another, placing us in the thick of battle. We also knew the reason. He wanted me dead. "We do not know that Jonathan requires my service in battle. Let me meet with him, and then we can determine if we should be sorrowful or not."

"I can come with you. I always snuck around the palace in the dark when I was younger. It will get us both outside and under the stars."

"Yes." I loved the adventurous spirit of Michal, and if she wanted to join me on a walk to the stables, I would not refuse. "Let us go on a night adventure. Can you dress yourself without your maidservant?"

"Of course." Michal acted offended. "I may be a princess, but I am quite capable of dressing myself and being sneaky." She threw a wool blanket over my head then got up and dressed.

"Did I make my wife angry?" I teased.

"I'm furious," she said, tying a sash at her waist. Then she blew me a kiss. "Remind me to show you how angry I am when we return."

Once she was ready, I took her hand and led her to the chamber door.

"Should we go out that way?" she asked. "If Jonathan is meeting you secretly, maybe we should be more careful not to get caught."

"Your maidservant came through this main door. Besides, there are guards everywhere. And what do we have to hide from? We are husband and wife taking a late-night stroll."

"I like the sound of that...*husband and wife*." She kissed me.

Together we walked out the chamber and down the corridor to the palace courtyard. The fires still blazed—they would not be put out until our two-week marriage celebration was over—but no one was out except the guards along the pillars. "I wonder if my family has stayed these fourteen days," I said, as we moved quickly to the hall that led outside.

"Why would they not? The celebration offered the finest wine and the most succulent meat that they probably ever had."

"Our families are from very different worlds. And the king was not exactly welcoming."

"True. In all honesty, I do not care if everyone left after the first casks of wine were finished. Being with you is all I care about."

I kissed her hand.

"Stop for a moment," she said. "Is this not the place where I stumbled and you found me?"

"I think it is. I was practicing the lyre and praying right behind those rose bushes when I heard you crying."

"That was the first time I met that wretched Paltiel. I was so upset with my parents. I thought Jonathan was in on it, but he saw my distress and helped me change father's mind."

"And here we are," I said. "It was Jonathan that reasoned with your father to have Merab marry Adriel and not me. Your brother has been a constant ally, and I love him for it."

"It helped that you defeated Goliath and helped weaken Philistinian forces. Jonathan made sure that father honored his promise that the killer of the giant marries one of the princesses. As far as my sister goes, she also told father of my love for you."

I pulled her to me, and we kept walking until most of the paths ended, other than the one that led to the far southside stables. Having Michal by my side felt perfect. Almost perfect. I could not fully ignore the thought that it would not always be like this.

I saw Jonathan on his horse outside the stable. He had another horse beside him.

Michal and I ran the rest of the way, our hands intertwined together.

"You brought Michal," Jonathan said surprised.

"Hello to you too, brother," Michal said, slightly out of breath.

"Are we going somewhere?" I asked.

"It is a surprise," Jonathan said. "I was told to tell you nothing, other than you need to follow me."

Michal looked over at me and raised her eyebrows. "This is interesting."

"Is it bloody or unsafe for Michal?"

"I do not think there will be blood."

"Want to come?" I asked Michal.

"What a silly question." She was already at the horse. "Will you let me hold the reins?"

I helped her up and handed her the reins, then pulled myself up onto the horse.

"You can ride a horse?" Jonathan asked his sister.

"I am not very good at it, but David promised to teach me."

Jonathan acted impressed. "Women riding horses? Now, let us move. We have already wasted time."

I helped Michal with the reins as the horse headed toward the south gate directly behind Jonathan.

14

"It is your men, isn't it?" Michal asked. I could hear excitement in the words and knew she was enjoying every second on the horse.

"More than likely." I should have known that my men were not going to take the king's lack of invitation from celebrating on their own.

Once past the city gates, the horses picked up speed and headed into the outer Gibeah forests. I saw the bonfires littered across a large plain leading to the Judean foothills and heard the celebration in the distance.

"That is a lot of men," Michal said.

"Yes," I said. "These are men who swore allegiance to me."

"Then they are smart men."

Messengers must have spotted us and notified them because the cheers grew louder as we approached. Jonathan slowed, and we did the same.

I saw my childhood friend, Eleazar, on horse, approaching us. "There he is!" he exclaimed. "The married man...and his bride?"

"She wanted to come. Michal, this is my friend, Eleazar. We were shepherds together growing up."

"If I would have known a lady was coming, I might have taken a bath," Uriah yelled from the ground. The men laughed.

Shammah, my brother, approached on foot and helped Michal off the horse. "It is nice to meet the poor woman married to my ugly brother."

I slid off the horse. "Be careful what you say, Shammah. We do share the same parents," I joked.

Groups of men approached, giving us blessings and meeting Michal. They had already been celebrating for days, they said, but shared what they had left with us. Eleazar grabbed me at one point and we danced around the fire, lines of men following suit. I saw Michal standing to the side next to Jonathan, laughing and clapping along to the song.

Please, Lord, I prayed to myself. *Please, let this happiness last for as long as possible.*

But despite the loud off-note singing, God seemed eerily silent.

3

❧

King Saul

The Practice Fields outside the Palace
1019 B.C.

The young soldier handed me another spear. One of my men had painted a silhouette of a man on the outside of the large burlap sack and nailed it to an old door. But there was only one face I imagined when I flung the spear at it.

"Perfect shot," the young man said, handing me another.

"Yet, I missed." I took the next spear and threw it at the target.

"Another perfect shot," he said. "Right through the heart. You have not missed."

"I am not referring to these practice shots," I explained calmly, as if talking to a child. "I am referring to the one time I needed to hit my mark, and I failed."

You missed when it mattered, the voice hissed. I pressed my fingers to my forehead and focused on keeping the voice and the darkness that came with it at bay.

Enos, my manservant, came up behind me. "The armor-bearer you asked for has arrived."

"Good. Send him in. By the way, are the bonfires extinguished?"

"Yes, my lord. The marriage celebration is officially over. David and your daughter have left the palace and have taken up residence within the aristocrat district, per your order."

"Do not ever say his name. Understood?"

"Yes, my lord." Enos motioned another servant to bring in the armor-bearer.

A young man of my size and build approached. He had the blackest of hair and golden skin and walked with the confidence of a warrior. I was going to enjoy this conversation very much.

"My king," he said, kneeling and bowing low. "It is an honor to be called upon. How may I be of service?"

"You will be attending to the weapons tent along the Philistinian battle lines just north of Gad. You leave on the morrow." And there it was. I felt the young man's eyes flash even though he had yet to look upon me.

"The weapon's tent, sir? Surely, there is a novice armor-bearer more suited to that labor."

"And yet I just ordered you. On the morrow."

"May I ask what I have done to deserve such a demotion? I have fought valiantly in numerous battles. I have fought alongside you, and I have led hundreds of troops. There must be some mistake."

"You are Benaiah of Kabzeel, correct?"

"Yes, my king."

"Were you not the one who met secretly with my eldest daughter, Merab? I knew about your indiscretions. Do you deny it?"

Benaiah paused before answering. "I do not deny it, but that was in error. I have honored my marriage and hers. Please do not punish me for a foolish boy's improprieties."

"Oh, I am not punishing you because of that." When Benaiah did not respond, I added, "Did you not train the giant slayer?"

"David?"

"Do not say his name in my presence!"

"Yes, sir, I trained him as I was commanded. He has also fought valiantly for our cause."

"For our cause?" I grabbed the material of Benaiah's tunic and dragged him up to face me eye-to-eye. Benaiah's eyes still

18

remained downcast. "Look upon me!" I yelled, my spittle landing on his face.

He did. His eyes showed how hard it was for him to stay in submission.

"You want to fight me, don't you?"

"No, sir. I honor the king."

"Why did you train him so well?"

"I was only doing what was ordered."

I released him and picked up another spear and sent it sailing to the target. "See? Right to the heart. Nothing I throw at him works. Nothing!"

Benaiah looked from the spear to me. "His strength and fortitude do not come from my training, sir."

"All right. I will give you two options. One is that you will be the weapons cleaner from henceforward…"

"What is the other option?"

"You join that glorified shepherd's ranks, and you kill him."

Benaiah stayed quiet for a few moments. "Do I have your word that I will be protected from your hand?"

"I will make sure not one hair on that pretty head of yours gets hurt. Do we have a deal?"

"Yes," Benaiah said, and once again, bowed low.

"Good. He is still with Michal, but I am sending out orders for immediate action. Meet him at his dwelling and do what you have to do to join his ranks. Considering your past with him, and his blind trust of anyone, you should not have a problem."

"Sir? That is not the option I chose."

I lifted my chin and eyed him coldly. "What did you say?"

"You gave me two options, my king. I choose the weapons tent."

Everything around me suddenly became very quiet. Except for my mind whirling at his last words, I stayed frozen too. Finally, I asked, "Did you just say what I think you said?"

"Yes, sir, I will gladly serve under you, my king, cleaning

weapons. What I cannot do is kill an innocent man."

"An innocent man?" I grabbed another spear, thinking about the time I tried to kill David. "He is trying to take the throne. That is not innocent."

"If he wanted the throne, we would already be in battle with him. From what I see, he wants peace."

"So, you are a shepherd sympathizer. He is good. Really good. He has turned many hearts toward him. Even my family. And I am tired of it." To the guards, I said, "Take him and dump him out at the most vicious battle. He has weapons to clean."

The guards came over to Benaiah who willingly waited for them.

"By the way, you will be in the weapons tent until you die. If you choose to desert, my men have the authority to kill you instantly." I patted his bulky arm. "So glad you made the right choice."

When Benaiah was gone, I called for Enos.

"He is a shepherd sympathizer," I said.

"He is a foolish man, my lord. One day in the weapons tent and he will change his mind."

"All of these men favor him. Not only that, but they are unwilling to kill him. It is as if I am no longer king." The panic set in as I thought of the numerous ways I had already tried to kill him. "Have you requested a meeting with Samuel?"

"Yes, my lord," Enos said, no longer looking at me. "The prophet refused."

"Did you tell him that it was imperative I speak to him?"

"Yes, my lord. He said that his answer has not changed."

"Where is Abner?"

"At the Philistinian outpost where you stationed him."

"And Jonathan?"

"Now that the marriage celebration is over, he has left to join Abner."

I left Enos and headed inside. "Get my riding cloak," I

ordered to whoever listened. "And my horse. ENOS!"

"Behind you, my lord." The short man tried to keep up.

"Get me a soothsayer."

"You got rid of them. In an effort to appease the prophet."

"They did not mysteriously disappear into thin air. Find one."

I made it to the front doors of the palace, which swung open as I exited. A servant fastened my riding cloak. "Your horse is on its way, my lord," another servant said.

"How many guardsmen do you need, sir?" Enos asked.

"I go alone." Then I thought of all of David's sympathizers and scowled. "Send a messenger ahead of me. Tell Jonathan to wait and I will meet him. We will head to the conflict together."

"Yes, my lord," Enos said, turning and shouting the order.

"And I will take two guardsmen with me." Once on my horse and with the guardsmen on theirs, I rode away from the palace. To the two men with me, I said, "I have to make one stop."

As I traveled through the aristocrat district outside my palace walls, those on the streets stopped and observed. Several shouted praises for their king, but many stayed quiet.

They love their hero and hate you, the dark voice in my head murmured.

"That is not true," I said to the voice. "They love me."

"Did you say something, sir?" a guardsman asked.

I shook my head, hoping that whatever lurked within me would be quiet for the time being. The voices and shadows mostly came out at night. They tormented me, growing in number and intensity since Samuel rejected me as king. Musicians had been called to play for me during the night to quiet my inner battle, but only one had truly soothed me. David. I nearly growled out loud just thinking about him. I hated that the lowly shepherd was the only one who could silence the voices, and I hated myself for needing him.

If you were stronger, you would not need him, the voice said, still not out of my head. *You need him to slay your giants. You need*

21

him to fight your battles. You need him to sing you lullabies.

"Not true!" I yelled. Both guardsmen looked over at me. "What? Have you not observed someone talking to himself?"

We arrived outside the dwelling of Adriel and Merab. "Announce my arrival."

The guardsmen followed my directive, but I stayed seated on my horse for a moment longer, trying to shake off the isolation I felt. An entire kingdom bowed to me. I had a harem at the ready. It made no sense that I struggled with loneliness.

It is because of him. He draws the people away from you.

"Sir? Your eldest daughter receives you. She is in her courtyard."

I nodded and slid off the horse, handing the reins to one of the household servants. I entered the home and marched past the servants to the inner courtyard. As soon as I saw Merab, I said, "I should have never listened to you...or your brother."

"Father, welcome to my home." She came and kissed both my cheeks. "Let Elia offer you refreshment."

"No, I want nothing."

"What is wrong? You seem agitated."

"Because my daughter is now in the arms of a traitor...a betrayer...I should have never listened."

"Whoever slew the giant earned the hand of the princess. You were honoring your word."

"I know what I promised!" I snapped. "It should have been you. I was going to throw you at him. Until you offered to marry Adriel."

"I desired to see my sister happy. As did Jonathan. This still works out for you, father. Trust Jonathan, he is quite skilled at strategy."

"Skilled at strategy? He and the glorified shepherd are as thick as thieves."

"Jonathan is loyal to you. He does not see how his friendship with David changes that loyalty."

22

"If it was not for Jonathan and his persuading, I would have tried to kill David again. I would have brought that traitor back into my presence, and the spear would not have missed."

"What has come over you?" Merab asked. "Surely you are not already second-guessing your decision? With Michal married to David, you have him close. He is not going to act against you when he is married to your daughter."

"Have you forgotten how he betrayed me? He was my lyre-player. I even elevated him to armor-bearer. All the while he had a secret. And he was right under my nose. This is no different."

"But he did not act upon the secret. Jonathan has reminded you of this repeatedly. David has been nothing but upright and loyal to you and the kingdom. Please let your anger at him go. If you cannot do it for him, do it for Michal. She has always been close to you. That does not have to change because she fell in love."

I heard Merab's words, and a part of me understood the truth behind the words. Michal and I used to be close. She had a smile that would light up when she saw me, but then the shepherd came between us.

"She told me what she promised you," Merab said. "I know my sister. She will honor her word just as you have done."

"You truly believe that she will choose me when the time comes? I thought she loved her husband."

"Not more than she loves her father. She told me that."

My heart warmed at Michal choosing loyalty to me over her husband. "She does love me, but I have also observed how much she loves that shepherd."

"Yes," Merab said simply. "The newness of her marriage will wear off. Give it time."

I took in a deep breath, feeling better. "I have this under control."

"Now would you care for some refreshment?" Merab pointed toward the tray of figs and stew.

"No," I said, but much more good-naturedly than the

previous time. "I am meeting with Jonathan." I went to leave, then thought of my earlier meeting with Benaiah. I knew exactly what needed to be done. "You are to report to me on the goings-on of your sister and her husband. Anything to implicate him is all that is needed. If my people see him as a traitor, then they will not turn on me when their hero dies."

"Implicate him? Of what? He is loyal to you and to the kingdom."

"Do you really believe that?" I asked. "Think about it, my daughter. He hid his secret and walked among my family. My family loves him. You think that is coincidence?"

"He fights for you," she said, but it had a note of uncertainty in it.

"To keep up pretenses. He needs Jonathan supporting him. He needs Israel to believe he is the hero. All the while he undermines me. When the time comes, he will strike. It is a certainty."

"How am I to report on them? They are newly married. I am sure I will rarely see them."

"Then find a way. I am not requesting this. It is an order. If anything happens, and I find out from a source other than you, there will be consequences."

Merab's expression did not mask her disapproval. "You are ordering me to betray my sister?"

"Considering everything I have done for you, this is a simple way to repay me."

"Everything you have done for me? I am not sure I understand."

"Are you not in a marriage of position and power?"

"Yes, but I did not ask for it."

"You asked me to give Michal to David, did you not? And do you think Adriel would have married you if he knew of your indiscretions with Benaiah?" I watched the color drain from my daughter's face. "Oh, do not become upset. Your husband knows

24

nothing. I expect letters every new moon. Find something, Merab. I need something to destroy him and his reputation."

I left my daughter staring after me. Once on my horse and in route to Jonathan's location, I realized I felt a lot better. Merab would give me the information I needed to implicate the traitor. If he could keep such a secret as to being the anointed heir to the throne, then he had many more secrets. My family was not safe, nor was the kingdom.

Once everyone saw how deceptive their illustrious David was, then he would cease being their hero. And then, I could have peace.

4

⊗

Michal

King Saul's Palace
1019 B.C.

"Do I have to go?" I asked Dinah, as she finished braiding my hair. "I could send a message that I fell ill."

"If you refused the invitation, knowing your mother, she would be here banging down the door before we could exit out a back window."

I made a face to express that I was not happy.

"At least Merab was invited too. You have spent very little time with her since before the marriage." Dinah busied herself with wrapping cloths around the vats of oils and creams.

"I tried to, but the pregnancy has made her terribly cranky." I swallowed back the jealousy. I was truly happy for my sister, even if she was the grouchiest person at the present moment. I rested my hand on my flat belly and wondered if it would happen for me. Would I one day hold David's son or daughter in my arms?

"It will happen," Dinah said gently as if reading my mind. "Give it time. You have yet to be married for three full moons. You might even be pregnant now."

"The likelihood is low." I pushed myself up from a sitting position. "David has already been gone over a fortnight, and who knows when he will return."

"But he will return," Dinah encouraged.

By the time the palace guardsmen came to retrieve me and

delivered me to the palace, I was resigned that the meal with my mother would happen.

"Princess, you are late," Enos said, directing a servant to take me to mother's sitting chamber.

I refused to respond to the slight man who was a thorn in my side most of my life. Instead, I followed the servant even though I knew exactly where my mother's chambers were.

"Michal!" Rizpah, father's favorite concubine, approached. "Oh, look at you!" She kissed my cheeks. "Marriage suits you."

"It has been blissful," I said, knowing I could trust her. She and I shared an extreme dislike of my mother. Rizpah acted more like a mother on several occasions, even helping me to secure David's hand. She had the ear of my father, and having her on my side was a blessing. "I miss him though. He received orders for combat not even two moons after our marriage celebration."

"But he is yours," she said. "When he comes home, there is only one he will go to."

"True. Maybe you can see if father will allow us more time together."

"I do not know if I have the same persuasion with him as before. He has...changed." Rizpah glanced around to see if anyone was within earshot. Other than the servant waiting to escort me, we were relatively alone. "He talks to himself a lot."

"I do that sometimes."

"Let me rephrase: he talks to someone a lot, but the person is not there. He yells at the person or whatever it is. Mostly at night, but now, even during hours of the day. It is as if he is having a conversation but no one else is around."

"Does he still have spells of aggression?" I whispered, becoming more worried by the second. Somehow I knew it was all connected to David, which did not bode well.

"Yes. Not with me yet, but yes. He has become consumed with training again. Constantly throwing his spear, telling me he will not miss again."

"He is referring to the time he threw his javelin at David."

"Yes. It is all he thinks about."

Any hope I had about the possibility of my father forgetting his vendetta against my husband left like a vapor.

"I am sorry it is not better news, but I promise I am on your side."

"Maybe father will become too busy with the Philistines' advance to stay focused on David."

"And I will do my part to dissuade him of any hostility toward your husband." Rizpah rested her hands on my shoulders. "Do not lose heart. You have the man you love. Things could have turned out much worse. For now, do not worry or lament over events that have not happened."

"Thank you." I hugged her. "You are right, of course. Now, I must go and see what mother wants."

"Oh my, I am glad that I am not you."

I continued on with the servant, but Rizpah's words stayed with me. Rumors of madness had swirled around father for the last few years. I saw it firsthand, where he seemed to battle something internally. Even before he knew that David was the secret heir Samuel anointed, my father's motivation to find the usurper took over his life and influenced every decision. Finding out it was David, his beloved lyre-player, fueled his irrationality and jealousy. Yet, David vowed to me and my father that he was loyal to the kingdom and would not take the throne by force.

"You are late," my mother said, as I approached.

Merab sat on the cushions beside her and looked miserable. Her face held a deep frown, and her eyes were mostly closed.

"Mother, Merab, good to see you both." I greeted each of them and sat on the other side of mother.

"We already started eating," mother said. "Not that Merab has touched anything."

"I explained to you that I was not feeling well, yet you insisted I come," Merab said through clenched teeth.

"Aw, the joys of pregnancy," mother said, smiling as if she enjoyed watching Merab's misery. "Delight in this, daughter. Giving your husband his first heir solidifies your station in his household." She turned to me. "What of you, Michal? Do you have news?"

I allowed one of the servants to prepare my plate, then I filled my mouth with a chunk of bread dipped in lamb's juice to keep me from responding. "Mmm, this is delicious." I took another bite.

Merab grimaced and looked away. "I can hear you chewing. It is making me sick."

"Really, Michal? Newly married to a shepherd, and you have already picked up on his coarseness?"

"Is this why I was invited?" I asked, annoyed. "To be the lashing post for your words?" I sat back, refusing to eat another bite.

"No need for being so sensitive," mother said. "This meal is not all about you."

I exhaled loudly and vowed to never accept another invitation from my mother again. Even more bothersome was Merab's behavior. Sure, we used to squabble as sisters do, and Merab has always struggled with a prickly personality, but her behavior surprised me. Her arms were crossed, and she had yet to fully look at me.

"The reason I invited you both was that I have a present for each of you." She pointed toward the large shape underneath a piece of material that covered it. "This is a gift from a mother to her daughters. We may have had our disagreements, but this is tradition."

I nearly scoffed at her statement. Disagreements? She locked me in my chamber in an effort to force me into marriage with Paltiel.

Two young servants removed the material, and we were faced with a grotesque-looking teraphim. The statue gleamed in the light and seemed to be of the highest caliber stone, but its face had sharp edges, multiple eyes, and oversized features. Neither Merab nor I said anything.

"You place this by the doorway of your dwelling, and it brings home your husband safe from battle." Mother waited a moment before saying, "I am sure your silence indicates how overcome with gratitude you both are."

"Thank you for thinking of me." I wondered how to get out of such a gift. "But David does not allow pagan worship within our home."

"It is not pagan worship." Mother waved her hand as if shooing a fly. "It is a totem of protection. Surely you desire your husband to come home safe? Especially with your father's hatred of him."

"Of course," I said tightly.

"Michal can keep it," Merab said. "She needs it more than I do."

"This one is mine. I have already sent the servants to deliver one for each of you."

I tried to catch Merab's eye, but she still refused to look at me.

"Forgive me, but I am unwell. I need to take my leave," Merab said. A servant helped her stand, and I noticed the small belly already protruding from her silken wrap. She left without so much as a backward glance.

"You are not leaving so hastily, are you?" mother asked me.

"I guess not." I went back to eating. "At least she is not here to complain about my chewing."

"Oh, she is only upset because she learned of what father did to that commoner she still loves. I do not understand either of my daughters. Both are in love with men who are far beneath them."

"What commoner?" I asked, knowing exactly who.

"Do not act coy. It is annoying."

"I realize that she loved Benaiah, but that was a long time ago. Merab is happy with Adriel."

"A long time ago? She is recently married, just as you. And Merab married Adriel to release David's obligation to marry her.

The giant slayer should have married the eldest daughter. You know that."

"Yes, I know that. But she told me how happy she was with Adriel."

"She should be happy with him. He is a fine match. But Merab only married him, so that David would be free to marry you. Jonathan knew if David was no longer obligated to marry Merab, then your father would have to offer you to the shepherd. They were both very clever."

"Oh, Merab," I whispered, fully understanding the sacrifice my sister made. All her smiles were only a mask. She did not want me to feel guilty for the weight of her decision.

"There is nothing to be upset over. Adriel is a fine soldier. His ancestors are warriors, and father needed him as a general. Why are you frowning?"

"What did father do to Benaiah?" I asked, feeling sillier by the second. Of course, Merab would not have stopped loving him. Why had I been so easily fooled to believe that?

Mother popped a fig into her mouth. "He demoted him. Surely you do not think that his actions with Merab would go unpunished. She is a daughter of the king, after all."

"But I thought that is why father gave Benaiah another girl to marry. To end their relationship. This does not make sense. Benaiah has been married for two years. Why punish him now?"

Mother sighed. "If you must know, your father found out that Benaiah trained David. You know your father. He decided that Benaiah trained him too well. So, he received a demotion. Now enough of this conversation."

"Mother, please excuse me. I need to find my sister. Hopefully, she has not yet left the palace."

"You just arrived! Honestly, Michal, I am trying to put our past behind us, but you two girls are making it very difficult."

"Mother, I will try to coerce her to come back. She is upset, and you know that I can console her. If nothing else, I will return."

31

"Fine," mother said. "But if she comes back, she needs to improve her disposition. No one enjoys sour grapes."

I ran out of the room.

"Princesses do not run!" my mother yelled after me.

"Merab!" I called down the hallways.

"She exited the main doors and is waiting to be escorted home," a servant mentioned.

I barreled down the main corridor and through the main doors. Merab was stepping into the royal wagon. "WAIT!"

Merab saw me and frowned. "Leave me be, Michal. I am in no mood to be with company."

I approached her and threw my arms around my sister's neck. "Thank you," I whispered in her ear. "Thank you for all the ways you sacrificed. I did not realize until this moment everything you have orchestrated for me to be with David. I will never forget it."

Merab's body initially stiffened at the hug, but eventually, she embraced me in return. I felt the wetness of her tears on my shoulder. "Father ordered Benaiah to the weapons tent," she said, through the tears. "Why be so cruel?"

"You know why." I released her. "And I am sorry for it. All Benaiah was doing was following orders to train David. His demotion has nothing to do with you."

"He would not turn on David." For the first time this entire day, she smiled. "Father gave him a choice, kill your husband or work in the weapons tent for the rest of his life. Benaiah chose the demotion over killing an innocent man. A guardsman told me himself that Benaiah left with his head held high."

"It is not going to go away, is it?" I remembered my conversation with Rizpah. "David and I hoped that in time father would overcome this anger and jealousy, but it is only getting worse. And now father is retaliating against those who helped David in any way."

Merab's face crumbled. "Oh Michal, father visited me too.

He is looking for anything to implicate David."

"Implicate him? How?"

"Anything that shows treason or disloyalty to the kingdom. I am not sure, but I was ordered to report to father. That is why we cannot be together anymore. He has torn us apart. I cannot find out anything because I know he will find a way to get it out of me."

"He will not separate us," I said. "We are sisters first. I trust you. Father also required me to report to him. But we know that David is loyal. There will be nothing to report."

"It is not that. I cannot sit by and watch him destroy your life too. I hoped that by me marrying Adriel one of us could be happy. It is too much to bear if you suffer the same fate as me."

Merab and I hugged once more as if the embrace shielded us from our father's wrath. But we both knew that there was nothing that could protect us from that.

5

୧୫୬୦

David

From the Streets to the Palace
1019 B.C.

The steady gallop of the horse could not keep my eyes open.

"Do we need to stop?" Jashobeam poked at me with an arrow.

I sat straight up and shook myself awake. "I am fine. We have to keep moving. The king is expecting us."

"That is not what I asked," he said. "We are all exhausted. A brief rest will do us well before we come to the streets of Gibeah."

Jashobeam was the oldest of my men, and by far, one of the most protective. He was one of Saul's cast-offs, and Abner threw him with me on my very first outing after killing Goliath. What I found was that he was the fiercest, most dangerous soldier I had ever encountered. He had saved my life countless times, and I was glad for him. But he also had a hard time taking 'no' for an answer, especially when it came to my well-being.

In this moment, I was too tired to answer. I half-nodded, knowing he would handle the orders to the men, then directed my horse off the path. I rested my head on the horse and closed my eyes.

I awoke with a start, and found myself on the ground, leaning against a tree. My horse had been tied to a nearby branch. I saw Jashobeam standing over me. "Is it time?"

"If I let you, you would sleep through night and probably into the day tomorrow."

"I do not disagree." I pushed myself up from off the ground. I observed my men scattered throughout the clump of trees, sleeping in various positions. These men, numbering a hundred, were my leaders. The other troops were released to go home after victory against the Philistines. For those still with me, we were requested to present ourselves before the king to celebrate with the spoils. "How long did I sleep?"

"About two hours. We need to get moving if we are to make it to the streets by the setting sun."

Eleazar and Shammah approached.

"Did any of you men rest?" I drank from Jashobeam's wineskin.

"We set up two watches," Shammah said. "We rested first."

I rubbed my face and took in a deep breath. "This last battle was rough," I admitted. "It was really cold at night."

"Let us hope that the king will reward us for victory with some time at home," Eleazar said. "I miss my wife."

"Wake up the men, and be ready to leave shortly," I said, not wanting to bring up my wife. I thought of Michal, night and day. But I could not talk about her. I already missed her too much without saying a word.

When we made it to the streets of Gibeah, the celebration had already started. Townsfolk lined the roads to the palace. Women danced and sang while groups around them danced. The noise level increased exponentially when the crowd spotted me with my men.

"David, the hero of us all!" was soon chanted, and the words made me cringe. These people had no idea what those words would cost me. They did not understand that praises for me only added kindling to the king's jealous flames.

King Saul waited outside the palace with his chief advisors. They were much more subdued compared to the crowds on the street.

Will this be enough? I thought as we approached. *Will he see how loyal I am to him and to the kingdom?*

35

I stopped the horse and slid off, immediately focused in on the king's face. King Saul did not hide his emotions well. Only this time, his expression was guarded, and I had a hard time gauging his mood.

"There he is!" King Saul said. "My son has returned victorious once again against the Philistines."

I stood shocked. I glanced over to my men and caught Eleazar's surprised expression. "Did he just say, *son*?"

I greeted each of the king's advisers and commanders, then bowed low before King Saul.

"Stand, my son," he said.

As I did, I observed the flash of anger across his countenance briefly before being suppressed. *All is not well*, my instinct warned.

"You are once again successful, and all of Israel rejoices because of it. Come inside, and let us enjoy festivities fit for the hero of Israel!"

My men and I followed him, but throughout the night, most of us stayed on edge. I wanted nothing more than to go home to Michal. It had been over three moons since I saw her last. I barely got a taste of her as my wife before orders came that placed me and my men on the front lines.

The victory celebration went well into the night, but my heart was not in any of it. I drank only modestly but did eat my fill. The months were long on the battlefront, and a soldier's rations never felt like enough. Once I finished eating though, I longed to leave. Without release from the king, I could potentially face his wrath. I did not desire for him to see it as defiance.

The last hour before dawn, King Saul left the courtyard, which officially ended the celebration. Several of my men exchanged relieved expressions with me. Even though they could stay in the soldier's quarters near the stables, I knew everyone would go home. Which was exactly where I was headed.

"David?" Enos called out.

Jashobeam, who walked beside me, stopped along with me.

36

Ever protective, he told me once how much he despised the idea of leaving me within the palace walls. "Never forget that King Saul cannot be trusted," he told me, wagging his finger in my face.

"Your presence is requested with the king."

Jashobeam growled. "Why? Can my commander not rest his weary head?"

"Do you dare question a direct order?" Enos straightened himself up but barely reached our shoulders.

"It is not a direct order. You stated the king requested David's presence, and since I am David's second-in-command, I am requesting that David rests first."

I contemplated telling Jashobeam to stand down, but he was right. I needed rest. I needed my wife.

Enos gave a curt nod. "I will relay the message." To me, he added, "I would not get too comfortable in your bed. I am sure the request will be changed to a direct order."

Jashobeam stepped toward Enos. "You better make sure that you are dead by the time David takes the throne."

Enos's face paled. He looked over at me as if searching for confirmation or denial. I was too tired for either.

As soon as we were out of the palace, Jashobeam said, "We have a plan for this. He cannot order you to see him if he cannot find you."

"I do not think I can make it to the cave without sleep first. It is a full day's journey. Plus...my wife."

We made it outside to where several of my men waited. They were as exhausted as I was, yet their mission did not end with the battle. And they knew being at Saul's palace was dining with an enemy. An enemy I was not willing to kill.

"Shammah and Uriah, stay back with me a while longer," Jashobeam said. "Until we know that David is home. The rest of you travel with David and secure his dwelling. Any message from the king will be delivered when David has rested and invites us in."

"Can we do that?" Uriah asked under his breath.

"We will not outright defy," Jashobeam said, just as quietly. "We will act innocent and delay for as long as possible. Now let us move before Saul's manservant comes scurrying back."

"Thank you," I said to the few who stayed behind. I pulled myself up and onto my horse and let my men surround me as we left and headed to my dwelling outside the palace walls. I knew it was futile to try and resist Saul. He would order me to come to him, and I would obey. But I also knew that he would not create conflict within our own streets. He valued what people thought of him.

Once at my home and off the horse, I handed the reins to one of the men. The door opened and several servants came forward. "We heard you approach, Master David." Dinah bowed low. "We have been waiting, per Michal's request."

"Where is she?" I asked, moving toward the house.

"Waiting for you on the rooftop."

That was all the invitation I needed.

***

The dream was bloody. Michal called after me from afar, but I could not reach her. Masses of soldiers came at me from every Israeli enemy. Philistines, Amorites, Amalekites, and a host of others from unnamed legions. And I fought viciously, feverishly, slicing through soldier after soldier. The more I fought, the more the masses pressed in. I woke with a start, my hands clenched as if holding the imaginary sword. I sat up and rubbed my face, shaking off the remnants of such a nightmare.

Michal no longer lay beside me. We first slept on the roof until a light drizzle turned to a heavier rain. We made our way to our private chamber and fell asleep once again in each other's arms.

I poured water from a pitcher and drank thirstily. My heart still beat wildly. I grabbed the rolled parchment that I always kept with me but could not find the ink. I needed to write. My prayers often came out onto the parchment, and I needed to pray.

I heard the voices coming up from outside. The voices were

in a heated exchange.

"If you know that David is inside, and you are lying, the king will deal with you swiftly."

Palace guardsmen. So, King Saul did as Enos predicted. He was ordering me to come before him.

Sighing, I got up and headed to the window before any of my men could say anything. "I am right here," I said from the window. Jashobeam and others all looked up. "I will be down momentarily."

Jashobeam acted surprised. "David? I did not know you were here." Then he turned and grinned at the guardsmen.

I washed, then dressed, still feeling trepidation from the dream. Lost in my own thoughts, I did not realize Michal had entered the room.

"Why the frown?" She came over and wrapped her arms around me. "We are together. Should that not bring a smile?"

"Being with you brings true joy. Unfortunately, palace guardsmen have arrived. Your father wishes to see me."

Michal dropped her arms from my neck and frowned. "You are right. That is news deserving of a frown."

"Let us not think the worst," I tried.

She nodded. "Can you at least eat before you leave? A meal has been prepared for you."

"I will see."

"Dinah can prepare a portion for you to take with you. My husband needs to keep up his strength." She kissed me before we left the room and headed down the stone stairway.

I stopped when I saw the large teraphim beside the door. "What is that?"

"A gift from my mother. It arrived recently. I do not know what to do with it. She said it is to make sure my husband comes home from war."

"It is pagan, and it needs to go. We serve the one true God. Not this counterfeit."

"Yes, of course, but I cannot refuse a gift from my mother.

She is the queen, after all."

"Is this not the same woman who locked you in your chambers as punishment?"

"Yes." Michal sighed, "I do not want to upset you. I will get rid of it."

I moved past it to open the door. "It really is grotesque." After my troubled dream, seeing this idol only increased my trepidation.

Once I stepped outside, I heard the words I was expecting. "King Saul orders you before him. Immediately."

Jashobeam made eye contact with me and raised his eyebrows. "Sleep well?"

"I am grateful for the rest, and for the time with my wife. Thank you. Were you able to rest?"

"We each took necessary rests on rotation."

"I thought you said you did not know he was here," one of the guardsmen said.

"And I think that this conversation is none of your business," Jashobeam said through gritted teeth. "You know what I can do, Reuben. Do not question me again."

The guardsman clamped his lips together, not saying another word.

"Let me grab my riding gear, and I will be out momentarily."

"Sorry, David, the king wants you immediately. He cares not about your riding gear."

Jashobeam went to say something, but I stopped him. "That is fine. I will go."

A servant stepped out with a small basket of bread and goat's cheese.

Jashobeam pulled me aside. "I do not like this. The guardsmen say that you are to go alone. How can I protect you, if I cannot come with you?"

"It is as Eleazar often reminds me: if I am the anointed heir to the throne, then there is nothing Saul can do to stop it. Now I release you to go home to your family. You need rest too. I will notify you as soon as I can with our new orders. Something tells me that is what this is about."

"If it is all the same, I will stay here and await your return. I will visit my family after that."

I bit into the bread and agreed. "I will go and see what he requires of me."

As I traveled through the district on my way to the palace, I ate what I could of the bread and cheese. Michal was right that I needed to keep my strength. King Saul seemed determined to push me as hard as he could, but I refused to break or bend. Whatever task he lay before me, I would do it, and as long as God stayed with me, I would succeed.

Enos waited for us. "Here you are," he said. "Per the king's orders."

"Take me to him," I said simply. "I have no time for a meaningless conversation with you."

Enos's face reddened. "This way."

I noticed we walked through the main halls that led to the throne room. "Not his personal chambers?"

"No." Enos stopped at the throne room doors. "I will announce your arrival. Stay here."

I waited at the doors the rest of the day and into the evening. I understood Saul's message. I would wait for him just as he had waited for me. I was thankful that I had eaten something earlier because as the hours came and went, nothing was offered. In my head, I created and recited poetry and prayers. At one point I resorted to humming melodies to myself. Anything to keep the boredom and agitation away.

Numerous things bothered me, but I could not dwell on them. It bothered me that he kept me from my wife. It bothered me that this seemed like a big game to him. It bothered me that nothing I had accomplished was good enough. "Do not think of these things," I whispered to myself.

As evening passed into night, the doors opened. I lifted my head relieved that the time had come. Until I saw Saul sitting on his throne, a spear in his hand.

The first thought that entered my mind was *not again*.

6

⊰❦⊱

King Saul

The Palace of Gibeah
1019 B.C.

This time, I would not miss.

"Enter," I said.

Do it now, the voices said, working themselves into a frenzy.

SILENCE! I internally screamed.

"My king and father," David said and prostrated himself before me three times. Then he stood before me. "I honor you. I pray you are well."

Now! Now! Now!

But David acted ready to move on notice.

"You dare defy an order? I called for you last night!" I yelled, clenching the spear. My hand shook. My hands never shook.

"It was not defiance, my king. It was exhaustion. Please, forgive me."

"Already you elevate yourself above me. Enos told me of your men bullying the guardsmen. Do you deny it?"

"There was no bullying, sir. I only requested to rest before coming to you."

I could barely see straight. Rage blurred my vision. I forced myself to keep it contained. I could not miss this time. I could not make the same mistake again. This time the spear must pierce his heart. Or neck. Or head. As long as it killed him, I cared not where it landed. "You are hereby ordered to meet up with Abner at our northernmost camp of the Judean Mountains. You will oversee the raids of the Philistine encampments. They hide among the cliffs and ravines."

"It is an honor to serve you, my king."

"You are to arrive by the next new moon."

David bowed low.

Now. I could strike it through his spine. My hand raised.

As if sensing my thoughts, David stood straight again. "Can I play for you, sir? Let me help soothe the melancholy."

"Yes," I said before I knew what came out of my mouth. I lowered the spear to my side.

I watched as David was handed a lyre, watched as he situated himself on the floor, and watched as his fingers began to play a melody. Before I knew what was happening my breathing normalized, and the pulsing in my head subsided. I closed my eyes and listened. It had been a long time since David played his soothing songs.

The music nearly lulled me to sleep. I had waited most of the night for David to come play the lyre. My hand relaxed and the spear clattered to the floor. I jolted upright and reached for the spear. "Enough of this! I will not be made the fool." When David did not stop, I said, "I do not need you! Go!"

David paused, but he acted unsure.

"Go! I am not weak. I will not be swayed by your talents. You…you… glorified shepherd…are a traitor! You connive to steal the kingdom!"

"No," David said simply. As if desperate, he pleaded, "What more can I do to win your favor?"

"You can…*die*! Now get out of my sight!" I waited for him to turn his back. He would not be able to dodge a spear he could not see.

David slowly rose. He handed the lyre to a nervous servant, then he bowed low to me. He paused briefly, before turning to leave.

Without the soothing melodies, the voices came back with a

vengeance. *Now!*

He was nearly to the door and moving fast.

I stood, aimed, and threw it with all my might.

David ducked, and the spear hit the heavy wooden door. He turned to glare at me, and I saw the flash of anger in his eyes. He took the spear from the door and threw it across the room. "I will not fight you for the throne."

"Get out!" I bellowed, running to pick up the spear.

David stood still as if taunting me. He no longer showed fear like he did the first time I tried to kill him. This time, he seemed to wait for me to throw it again.

So, I did, yelling with all my might. He easily maneuvered away from it.

"If God wants me on the throne," David said. "There is nothing either one of us can do to prevent it."

I picked up the spear, and in my fury, broke it in half. My chest heaved from the exertion. I gathered my breath. The whole time David stood at the door, watching me. "You think you are so clever." I still felt slightly winded.

"No, my king. I am not clever. If I was clever, I would figure out a way to prove my loyalty to you and to the kingdom."

"The clever David." I refused to listen to him. "The warrior, eh? Killing all the Philistines."

"For Israel, and for my king."

"For yourself. Admit it. You are the hero. You are famous and are ready to replace me."

"No, it does not have to be this way. I want to learn and grow. There is so much that we can accomplish together."

"Together? There is no *together*."

"We fight the same enemies. Let us not fight each other. We are family."

"Because you are a trickster! You charmed your way into the hearts of my children." The defeat of my spear attack began to irritate me. Of course, David would outmaneuver me. He was much

45

younger and more agile. But I was still king. "You will pay. I may not be able to outmaneuver you with a spear, but I can do other things. I am quite capable of destroying your life."

"Please," David said again. "I do not want this for us. Let there be peace between us."

"Get out of my sight." I turned away. "And be on guard, shepherd. I will find a way to destroy you. You will not have the last word."

I studied the busted spear and gripped it tightly. Somehow I would find a way to kill him. I heard his footsteps and raised my head. He was gone.

"Enos!" I called.

My manservant rushed in. "Yes, my lord."

"It is time my daughters do what I have asked of them. They need to find something that shows he is traitorous. Something that will turn the heart of the Hebrew people."

"Yes, my lord. I will relay the message."

"One more thing. What is the name of that man who pursued Michal's hand? He tried to blackmail the queen."

"Paltiel of Gallim. He owns a vast vineyard."

"I may want to visit with him."

"Would you like me to send out a summons?"

"Not yet. Let us see how my daughters proceed with their direct orders. If Michal fails me, I know exactly what I will do to crush her and that shepherd. No one makes a fool of the king."

Of
Swords
And
Sorrow

7

⋈

Michal

The Aristocrat District of King Saul's Court
1018 B.C.

The evening air was thick, a mixture of heat and dust and despair. I kept my head low, not wanting anyone to recognize me. Even living close to the palace in the aristocrat district did not keep me from the glares of my fellow women. Glares of unspoken anger and frustration. No one dared speak against the king or royalty, but their eyes said it all.

Too many wars waged. Too many enemies surrounded us. Too many Hebrew lives taken. Too many brothers, and sons, and husbands far away from home, fighting battles they did not ask for.

And my father was too consumed with hate, fear, and jealousy to care.

As I rounded the corner, I thought of David, and my breath caught. I started coughing. The hot, heavy air made it hard to breathe.

"Here, drink this." Dinah handed me a small water jug.

I drank between coughing spells.

"We need rain," she said, fanning me with a wide palm leaf.

I nodded in agreement, but couldn't find words. I knew what I really needed was my husband. I pressed my hand to my lower belly, praying that my recent spell of coughing kept everything in place. Three days earlier I had confided in Dinah about the possible pregnancy. I made her swear to secrecy. "I'm not getting too excited

49

just yet," I had told her. Then we squealed in delight, forgetting about my comment.

She and I both knew that I had not always been regular with my monthly cycles. But this time felt different. Three moons already passed, and nothing I ate stayed down. Hopefully, when David returned, I would know for sure. I took in a sharp breath again and drank the last of the water. "Let's keep going," I said, once I felt steady. "We have already wasted too much time."

I moved quickly, following my father's men through the nearly empty street to Adriel's dwelling. Both Merab and I had refused to live within the palace walls. She and I now lived within several stones' throw of each other just outside the palace walls. But it was far enough away from our mother's constant scrutiny and our father's obnoxious displays of madness.

A heart-stopping scream ripped through the air, and I gasped and began to run.

"Be careful, princess!" Dinah called after me.

But the time had come, bless Yahweh, and I refused to miss it. Soon I would be an aunt. It did not matter that I already bore the title with all of my brothers' children. Tonight, it would be different. Tonight, I would hold my sister's infant in my arms.

Another scream hit my ears, and now that I was closer, I could hear the guttural moan that followed it. I pushed through the entryway to my sister's home. Her servants moved out of my way, as I ran up the stairs. I had to pause at the top to catch my breath. But hearing her moan louder had me moving to her.

I opened the door to the private chamber already consecrated as her birthing area. Only Elia and Tamar, the birthing nurse, were in the room with my sister. Merab's hair was drenched with sweat and stuck to her face, and she panted furiously as if her life depended upon another gulp of air. She held on to a thick rope that dangled from a rafter, her hands holding on to it so tightly her knuckles were white. Yet she still peeked through one half-opened eyelid at me and said, "About time you showed up."

I washed myself before heading over to her. "I could hear you bellowing five homes from here."

"No one should enjoy life right now while I'm in such pain." Suddenly, she tensed up, arched her spine, threw her head back and holding the rope as tightly as she could, and gave a blood-curdling scream.

"The baby has taken his time," Elia said, soothing Merab with a wet cloth to the forehead. "But soon. It should be soon."

Tamar helped Merab extend her legs as far apart as they could go. I moved to the other side of my sister and kissed her wet forehead while Tamar instructed Merab to push with the next wave of pain.

"Sister," Merab whimpered, reaching for me.

"I'm right here," I said in her ear.

I watched as her body tensed in reaction to the pain. She pushed with all she had, and I encouraged her for the remainder of the evening and well into the night.

An hour before daybreak, the cries of the newborn filled the air. "It's a boy," Tamar said, saying a chant of thanksgiving and blessing over the male child.

Merab, nearly passed out from pain and exhaustion, said, "Let me see him."

Tamar laid the infant on Merab's chest. "A nice healthy weight. All fingers and toes."

I wiped tears of joy from my eyes and kissed my sister again on her sweat-soaked forehead.

"He looks like his father, doesn't he?" Merab asked me.

I took in the sight of the child, with a head full of black hair and little fists balled together. "I can't tell. His eyes are scrunched up when he cries. When he does that, he reminds me of you."

Merab leaned back onto some cushions, the baby still on her chest. She closed her eyes and murmured, "…looks just like him…"

Tamar took the baby to clean him up while Elia tried to clean up the area underneath Merab without disturbing her too much. I

51

stayed at my sister's side until Tamar brought the baby wrapped tightly in a woven blanket to me. "Would you like to hold him while Merab sleeps? I have to clean up."

I nodded and took the child in my arms, my heart melting. His crying had subdued momentarily, even though I knew enough to know Merab would have to try and feed him soon. I studied the baby's features then kissed his forehead. I silently disagreed with Merab. The infant looked nothing like Adriel. Merab's husband had darker skin than she did, and his hair had tight curls when not pulled back. I looked from the baby to Merab and tried not to think about the thought that kept dancing in my head.

Suddenly Merab's eye flew open and she looked right at me as if reading my thoughts. We did not speak for several moments.

"You are awake," Elia said. "Good. I need to wash you up, then you will need to try feeding the baby."

Merab said nothing, only kept her eyes locked with mine.

"Elia," I said, as she neared completion. "Could I bother you for some refreshment? Merab needs some, as do I."

"Of course, let me call upon another servant to prepare a breakfast."

"She wants you to leave the room," Merab said. "She is being polite about it."

Elia raised her eyebrows then glanced over at me as if needing confirmation.

"I only want a few minutes with my sister. I did not want to be rude." I glared at Merab.

Merab rolled her eyes.

"I will see about preparing you something," Elia said, her eyes downcast.

"You have upset her." The baby curled his hand around my finger and tried to suckle it.

"So?" Merab said crossly. "She is a servant, not our equal. You mollycoddle Dinah too much."

"Elia has been with you since you were a little girl. She is your friend more than servant."

"No, she is not. She is my servant. And can be meddlesome."

"She stayed up all night with you to help deliver the baby."

"Good. That is what she's supposed to do. Now stop with the condescension and ask what you want to ask."

I heard the irritation in Merab's voice and understood that she was more cross with me than at Elia. "You know what I am going to ask," I said, more to myself.

"Why does it matter? Why do you need to know?"

I studied Merab. She looked pale, disheveled, and exhausted. "You are right. It does not matter. I do not need to know. Just get some rest."

She sighed and tried to sit up.

"No, sister, please, do not sit up. I should not have upset you after your labor. Forgive me."

She reached out her hand to me. With one arm cradling the baby, I extended the other to her. Merab squeezed my hand. "You, dear sister, are my friend. And I know that you are concerned about me, about my reputation. But I do not wish to burden you with the truth."

My mouth dropped open. When I recovered, I whispered, "Benaiah?"

Merab did not speak at first. Eventually, she said, "I am not sure, but it is possible."

"Does he know?"

Merab shook her head. "And neither does Adriel."

I stared at my sister in shock, trying to best digest the information. Merab, my most beloved sister, had committed an adulterous act. I knew she loved Benaiah, and I knew that she and Benaiah had secretly met a few times even after he had married someone else, but I never wanted to believe that she would follow through on her feelings with him. I also knew that she wanted a peaceful home with Adriel. When he was not fighting in father's army, he was kind and attentive to my sister.

53

"Please do not look at me like that. I have been faithful to my husband since the marriage covenant. It was just…one time…a few days before…I had a hard time letting go of my love for him." She glanced down at the baby, as a tear trickled down her cheek. "What am I going to do?"

I leaned over and wiped the tear from her face. "There is no way to know for sure."

"You noticed it."

"Yes, but I know your history. I am assuming you have not told Adriel about your relationship with…"

"No, of course not. I did not want to ruin what has been a peaceful marriage."

"You are not going to ruin anything. You are going to love your son, and Adriel is going to be a great father."

Elia came back into the room with a tray of breads and cheeses, along with a jug of water. As she set down the tray beside Merab, she said to me, "Dinah received a message during the night. She said it is urgent. You head home immediately."

"Whatever it is can wait." I glanced down at my nephew. "Being here is my top priority."

"It is your husband."

My head snapped up. "Is something wrong?" I was already standing and handing Merab the baby.

"I do not know. I only know what Dinah told me."

I blew a kiss to Merab before leaving the room.

Elia called out, "But you have not cleaned up yet. You must purify yourself!"

Dinah stood at the bottom of the stairs. "Is everything all right?" I asked.

"I am not sure. I only received word that he had arrived home, but I did not want to disturb the labor, and I could not enter without permission."

Dinah rambled on, but I was already out the door and running for home.

**

I stopped outside the door to catch my breath. I patted down my hair but knew that I looked awful. I had spent the entire night with my sister and had sweated the entire time in the heat of the labor room. But the thought of David on the other side of the door had me pushing the door open wide. He would not care about decorum. He would not care how I looked. That was one of the many reasons I loved him so. He loved me for me. "David," I called out.

"Up here, my love," he answered from the top of the stairs.

I ran up the steps and found him in a tunic, standing over a steaming basin.

"I was about to clean up," he said, but I did not wait for him to say anything more.

I threw my arms around him and kissed him. "My husband. I am glad you are here, and that you look well."

Without saying a word, David had already wrapped his arms around me. For several moments, there were no words. It had been too long, and we had much to say, but in this moment, closeness was all that mattered.

8

King Saul

Inside the King's Private Chamber
1018 B.C.

I lay on my back, staring at the shadows dancing across the ceiling from the flicker of the candle's flame. The shadows mocked me, whispering my fate over and over. I knew those around me now spoke of madness. Even my own family questioned my ability to rule.

And it was all because of him.

Nothing was working. Nothing.

Merab's letters were empty of implications. She lamented that it was hard to discover secrets when David was continually sent out to fight in battles. Michal said the same thing. I would keep him home more, but the Philistines were parasites who multiplied like rabbits. They were currently subdued because of David and his men. It would be so easy if he would just die by the sword. But no matter the impossible tasks, he was successful.

"Go back to sleep." Rizpah rested her hand on my chest. "You need your rest."

"I cannot sleep," I said, still watching the shadows. "They mock me."

"No one mocks you, and if they do, you will end them swiftly. Now, shush," she leaned over and kissed my cheek. "Go back to sleep. Fight your enemies in the morning."

Her gentle touch soothed me, and I closed my eyes.

I opened them to the sound of someone whispering. At first, I thought it was the shadows again, but sunlight poured through my bed chamber. No shadows in the morning light. Still, I did not move. Instead, I tried to listen to the whispers.

"…No need to wake him…"

"…you do not understand, he demanded I tell him…"

I sat up, rubbed my face, and stumbled into the open living area of my chamber. I glanced over at the musician's corner and scowled. "What is it?" I grumbled. "And why are there still cushions in the musician's area. I ordered them gone."

"Good morning, my king." Rizpah approached me, taking my hands and kissing me. "Please do not be angry. I arranged for new cushions of a different color, so the musicians would be comfortable. You still require soothing music."

I scowled and glanced back over at them. "I see him over there."

"He is not there. You have new musicians."

Not that any of them soothed me. The irony did not escape me that only David could keep the darkness and shadows away.

"Come, let us have breakfast. Would you like to eat here?"

I noticed Enos darting his eyes from my face to his feet. "What is it?" I asked, interrupting Rizpah.

But I knew what he would say before the words were out. "He has returned, my lord." Enos did not make eye contact.

"Breakfast before business," Rizpah said. "We cannot think on an empty stomach."

"Did you do as I ordered?" I tried to keep calm. I knew it upset Rizpah when I became too angry. And she was the only person I felt truly loved me.

"Yes, we upped the reward, but his men are loyal. None will fall back."

"Then we make an offer they cannot refuse. Surely someone can be bought."

Abner entered the room. "I see you have already heard that

57

his troops have returned."

"And yet he is still alive, which means that my orders were not carried through."

"David is alive, but thousands of Philistine troops are dead. It is a marvel. Not one of his men lost their lives."

"Do not say his name!" I shouted and watched as Enos and Rizpah shrank back. "I hate the sound of it!" Abner stood unflinching. "And what is a marvel is that nothing we throw at him is killing him. Nothing."

"He is fighting Israel's enemies. Let him do so. Eventually, the sword will find him," Abner stated it matter-of-factly.

"What are you not understanding?" I felt like pulling my hair out. How could Abner not see? "If he takes the throne, my entire household is dead. He will kill everyone. Including you."

"I do understand. I also understand that there is only so much we can do. He is fighting *for* us. He is killing our enemy. His popularity continues to grow. If he dies at our hand, there will be a mutiny."

"Everyone out." I pointed toward the door. I could hear the whispers in my head, and I was having a hard time suppressing them.

"Would you like breakfast," Rizpah asked, stroking my arm. "You need to eat."

For a moment, I took in the sight of her. If only things could be different. But until David was dead, I had to focus on strategy. "I will call for it when I am ready. You are released."

When she and Enos left, Abner paused at the door. "Will you not let him alone?"

"Get out," I seethed. "Do not tell me he has gotten to you too."

"Who has been at your side since we were boys?" Abner's voice was steel. "Do not question my loyalty."

"Then do not question your king. The longer he is alive, the more of a threat to my throne. To Jonathan's throne."

Abner studied me for a few moments.

"Out with it."

"I think he is a greater asset alive than dead."

"Is he a greater asset than your king? Does my sanity not measure in any of this?"

"You are consumed."

"Yes," I agreed. "When David is gone, I will have peace that the crown will stay within the House of Saul."

"We cannot let the kingdom fall over this."

"Yes. I have been saying that for some time now."

"Is the kingdom falling by his hand? No, we prosper because of him."

"Because he is purposefully swaying the people! It is his plan! How can you not see this? That is how a usurper works. And you, my family, and everyone else is falling for his trickery!"

"If I agree to his death, then could it be possible to have our king back?"

The insult brewed contempt. "Your king has not gone anywhere. And if you remember, I was counseled to let him marry my daughter. I was counseled that he would be friend and not foe. That I should keep him close."

"Yes, and if you would leave it alone, all would be fine. But it is clear that you will not leave him alone. It will continue to consume you. So, let us change the tactic."

Hope began to catch fire inside me. "What should we do?"

"Let him relax. Let him think that you are not out to get him. Let the people see their king and the giant slayer arm in arm. Once he no longer suspects any bad pretenses, we strike. Quietly. Privately."

I slowly smiled. The thought of David by my side with my sword in his heart gave me great pleasure. "Just make sure that I am the one who goes in for the kill."

"My advice is to tell no one."

"Done. There is no one I really trust." I thought of Jonathan and felt torn. As future king, he should know of this, but he had already proven where his loyalties lie. But when David died, Jonathan's heart would come back to me.

The door opened, and Jonathan entered. He was the only soul that I would ever let approach me without an invitation or acceptance. I had reasoned that as current king, my life should be no secret. I wanted him to understand the value of trust and loyalty. Now as he stood there, greeting Abner, I felt the scowl deepen on my face. "Do you knock?"

"Do I need to? Just the say the word, *my king*." He bowed low in exaggeration.

"Oh, stand straight. You are annoying me."

Jonathan straightened himself and sighed as if I exasperated him. "We have pressing matters."

"Go on."

"David's brother told me that their family continues to be taxed. I told him that I would see to it that the tax collection stops immediately, and they are restored whatever they have paid in the past year."

"Do not say his name!" I said in exasperation. "And everyone pays taxes. Just because you marry into the family, does not mean your family is excluded from advancing the kingdom."

"He was promised that he and his family would never pay taxes again. When he defeated Goliath. Remember?"

"Who is his brother?" I asked, vaguely remembering all the men from David's family at the wedding feast. They were a filthy lot. The whole crew of them. I had been too drunk to figure out who they all were.

"Shammah. He has served under you for the past five years."

"Does he serve under me now?"

"He is one of David's men."

"So, no."

"So, yes. Does David not serve under you?"

I cringed at the sound of his name. "How many of them are

there?"

"David's men?" Jonathan asked. "A thousand."

"Stop. Saying. His. Name."

Jonathan pursed his lips in frustration. "The taxes need to be paid back to them. They have freely paid, probably out of fear. Your hatred is not exactly hidden."

"How many of them are there?" I repeated the question, rubbing my temples.

"I just told you…"

"Not his men!" I bellowed. "How many filthy sons did that shepherd's father have?"

"There are eight sons," Jonathan said. "There are also a handful of daughters. Most of them have children now."

"I am impressed that you know all of this," I said, making sure he heard how unimpressed I was.

"David is my friend. We are brothers. Of course, I know. And Jesse of Bethlehem is from the tribe of Judah. They are of good blood."

I heard the admiration in my son's voice, and it made my own blood boil. "Do you know what all of those men are plotting to do? Probably right now as we speak? They are plotting to kill the king and his family, so their *good blood* can take the throne. That is a lot of men that are loyal to that traitor."

"In case you have not figured it out yet, there are a lot more than that who are loyal to David. Our entire kingdom cheers for him. They cheer for him and for Israel."

"Do you dare elevate him above me?"

"I am merely stating that right now Israel's enemies are falling at our feet. Why can't we simply enjoy the fact that we are winning?"

"By his hand," I muttered, moving to the balcony to lean against the rail. The whole situation mocked me, and I gripped the railing tightly. I studied the vast scenery, the lush hills and valleys that I had toiled to protect and preserve for decades. No one said

61

thank you. No one respected me or the sacrifices I made for them to live in peace. And I was done playing nice. If my own men could not see David as a threat, then what chance did my throne have against him? I thought of David's brother complaining about the taxes and fury clouded my vision. How dare he complain about duty to the kingdom! "Enos," I called. "Have the edict written up that frees David's family from any more taxes."

"Yes, sir."

I walked back into the sitting room. "Is that all? Any other complaints that I need to address?"

Jonathan watched me a moment with a strange countenance as if he was not sure how to answer the question.

"Go." I wanted no more questions. My plan needed to be executed, but I did not relish lying to my son. The less he knew the better. "Spend time with your wife and children."

"Oh, that reminds me," Jonathan said, as he made his way to the door. "Merab has given birth to a healthy son."

I nodded and gave a quick blessing, indicating that the conversation was over. With Enos and Jonathan gone, I said to Abner, "There's a change of plans."

"Already?"

"Did you hear my son? The shepherd's family complained. It is the start of their rebellion."

"Yes, I too found that arrogant and demanding."

"Exactly." I was surprised Abner agreed with me.

"But the plan we agreed to will take care of their arrogance and demands. Let them think all is well."

"I am tired of playing cat and mouse, where I am the mouse. It is time I show them who is king."

"I advise you to use restraint. We do not want a mutiny."

"Would there be one? You keep saying that there would be this mutiny, but heroes have fallen before. The people's hearts are fickle. Right now, the people cheer for their hero. But their hero should be their king. If they see their king kill their hero, who will they cheer for?"

"And if his supporters rise up?"

"Then they too shall fall. No one stands against their king and lives."

Abner stayed quiet.

"You told me to be the king. This. Right here. I am deciding to be king. I am the cat. That lowly shepherd is the mouse. I am going to catch him, and I am going to kill him. And I refuse to hear counsel anymore that does not support this decision."

"Then let us kill him. I still think it should be done quietly."

"No. Let the kingdom know that there is a price on his head. Now let us go hunting."

"He should still be at his home."

"That is not where I want to start. I want to teach his family a lesson. No one complains against their king and gets away with it. It will rile him up, and he will want vengeance."

"And you will be waiting."

I nearly laughed out loud at the plan. It was time. Time to stop listening to the shepherd's sympathizers. Time to get rid of this thorn in my side and show the world that no one takes my throne.

9

೦ತ೮ಾ

David

A Secluded Alcove of the Judean Mountains
1018 B.C.

I watched my wife sleep and gently tucked a few stray strands of her hair behind her ear. She did not stir. Staying up all night to help Merab deliver her first child had finally taken its toll on Michal. So, I kissed her on the forehead and left her nestled among the animal skins and woven blankets in the small cave.

"A surprise? What is the surprise?" Michal had asked with a smile.

"Since you were up all night, I can surprise you later."

"No, surprise me now!"

"There is a special place I wanted to show you. It is special to me. I thought we could have Dinah pack a meal and enjoy a small excursion."

"Yes, a million times, yes. Just let me freshen up and change skirts."

Now as I quietly dressed in a corner of the cave, I felt that familiar tug of longing. Not that it could no longer be fulfilled, but because I was gone so much it seemed as if the two of us had to steal snatches of time here and there in order to be together. Michal was already itching to have a baby and her continual complaint was that it would never happen with me gone. But as soon as I would return, there would be another assignment. It had been almost a year of marriage to Michal, but I had spent maybe a total of three moons with her. Not even consecutive.

But they had been the best days of my 22-year life.

We had yet to find any relief from the scrutiny and hostility of the king. Just this morning before we left, Jonathan had shown up at our home. The prince told me about his conversation with the king. "He is acting strange. Stranger than normal. I think he is hiding something from me. And if that is the case, then you could be in grave danger."

"Still? But my troops and I have just returned with staggering success for Israel."

"That is the problem. The more you succeed, the more the people love you."

"What is not to love?" Michal said, running her fingers through my hair, smiling tenderly at me. She then turned and greeted her brother warmly. "Thank you for protecting my husband. You are one of only a few that has the ear of our father."

"Only I am not sure that is the case any longer."

"Are you sure he is keeping secrets?" I asked.

"I cannot be absolutely positive, but I am relatively sure. This morning, I saw it. There was a secret lying behind his countenance. I wanted to come over here and let you know to be careful. Hopefully, it is nothing, and I am wrong."

"Thank you, my brother. I shall not forget your friendship. As the Lord orders my steps, He uses you to guide me."

Now as I stepped out of the cave and started gathering supplies for a small fire, I pushed all negative thoughts away. Right now, I had my wife all to myself. A smile hinted at the corners of my mouth as the cool air caressed my face. We had to travel mostly uphill to get to this spot but seeing Michal's reaction to the scenery had been worth it. As the trees cleared and opened to the private stretch of land connected to the rock wall, Michal had gasped. I took in the view, as well. Rolling hills as far as the eye could see with cragged mountain edges surrounding those hills like walls protecting a treasure. The sun spilled out from a split between one hill's ending and another's beginning, creating red, pink, and purple streaks across the sky. The enclave within a rock wall overlooked an outlying meadow close to my father's land. It was quiet, secluded, and special. Just the spot I wanted to share with her.

"It is breathtaking," she said, as I helped her down off the horse. She walked to the edge. "I wondered why our journey was mostly uphill. But this. This explains it."

I had come up behind her, wrapping my arms around her waist and gazing out across the horizon. "The earth is the Lord's and the fullness thereof. The earth and all that dwell therein."

"My husband, the poet," Michal said. She turned slightly to look back at me. "I am starting to get a complex with the number of words you write about Yahweh. Should I be jealous? Where are the words and melodies about me?"

"Do I not whisper them in your ear while in the bed?" I leaned forward and kissed her, turning her completely around to face me. Something bothered me though, scratching at the back of my mind. I stopped kissing her to survey the view one more time.

She yawned deeply. "Oh my, I am so sorry. The night's events have taken their toll."

"I am happy that you were able to be there for your sister. Children are treasures. I cannot wait until we have our own."

Michal rested her head on my shoulder. "Mmm-hmm," she murmured.

"Give me a moment to set up a comfortable spot," I kissed her forehead and left her, as I retrieved blankets and a few plush cushions from the horse. I arranged everything just inside my special cave. It was the place I had visited yearly. My own little nook in the mountain. Only Eleazar had been here with me. As boys and eventually young men, we had worked to clean it and make it roomy. Time had changed it little.

Now as I stoked the small fire and began to prepare a meal, I glanced over my shoulder at the entrance of the cave where Michal still slept. No matter how hard I tried, I could not entirely enjoy the moment. Jonathan's warning echoed in my head.

I knew that King Saul could do irrational things when he felt threatened. Marrying his daughter had done little to smooth over the tension between us. I kept hoping that the more I fought for Israel and continued to be successful, that I could eventually win his praise and approval. It reminded me of my complicated history with my own father. I could never please him either. Somehow, the praise and love I most desired from the two men who were in father-like roles eluded me.

I heard Michal shuffle out of the cave and glanced up at her. With a blanket wrapped around her and her disheveled hair framing her face, she still took my breath away. "How long did I sleep?" she asked, observing the streaks of early morning light coming from the east. "All evening and through the night?"

"Nothing wrong with sleep." I went over to her and kissed her. "And we were not always sleeping."

"True." She grinned, then looked down at her stomach. "I must admit that I am hungry. We ate together yesterday before we left, but that seems so long ago."

"Nearly a full day. Come. I am warming up lentils, and we have fruits and some goat's cheese for the bread."

"While you arrange that, I am going to get dressed." She stood on her toes to kiss me. "Do not go anywhere."

By the time Michal stepped out of the cave again, our meal was ready. "Please sit and enjoy." I stood at the cliff's edge observing the view.

Instead, she came over to me. She took my hand. "It is simply breathtaking."

"That is my father's land." I pointed out the area.

"I wish that we could receive an invitation into his home," she said. "After our wedding, I have not seen him."

"I think it is impossible for my father to simply be happy for me."

"I know the feeling."

We turned to each other and shared a sad smile.

"Let us eat. Shall we?" I asked.

But Michal's attention stayed fixed on the view. "Is that smoke?"

I looked where she pointed. I spotted it in the far distance. "It is." Something about it made the hair on the back of my neck stand up.

"Are they sacrificing? Or slaughtering a beast for a later evening meal?"

"I doubt it. Not this early in the morning. It is the same direction as my father's stables." I studied it for several minutes. Something felt off. "That is far too much." Something was wrong.

I turned to see Michal standing a few feet from me with her long, raven hair falling around her face, framing her eyes. Eyes that peered out across the horizon, studying the distance. How I loved her. For a brief moment, I was seriously torn. I could be overreacting. The stable-hands or shepherds often had flames going for countless reasons. And here stood my beautiful wife. But... I turned again and watched the smoke billow. "I should probably make sure that all is well. Since those are my father's stables."

"Yes," she said. "We can continue this another time."

"Would you like to stay and enjoy the meal? I can come back for you. I would not be gone terribly long."

"Where you go, I go. My stomach will just have to wait."

I quickly packed the few supplies I brought with us, kicking dirt into the fire to smother it. I gave Michal a small bowl of lentils to eat while I prepared the horse. Before hoisting Michal up onto the horse, she handed me a large chunk of bread with goat cheese spread across it. "Eat," she said. "Your body needs the nourishment too."

I took a big bite before straddling the beast, then ate the rest of the bread and cheese, making sure to secure Michal to me.

I moved the horse away from my secret lair and into the trees, and the two of us began to descend down the hills. I would have moved much quicker, but I would not jeopardize Michal.

"You act worried," she said, holding me tightly.

"Yes," was all I could say. I normally refused to let emotions rule over me. That was a good way to get killed. But still, I resisted my desire to make the horse go faster.

I had not realized how high up we had traveled until in a hurry to get to leveled ground. Once it was safe enough, I pushed the horse first into a steady gallop. "Are you all right?" I asked Michal. We were a way out, but from this vantage point, I could see the smoke covering more and more of the sky. Too much. It was too much.

Michal secured her arms around me. "Do not go slow on my account."

That was all the encouragement I needed. The horse raced across the outlying meadows toward what was increasingly indicating a perilous situation at the stables.

When I was within earshot, I could hear the chaos. Shouts of men trying to herd animals away from the flames and the animals themselves in distress and terror. I heard Michal's sharp intake of breath.

A shepherd saw me approaching on horse and fell on his knees in submission. Careful of Michal, I stopped the horse and jumped down. "It is only me."

"David," the old shepherd said in relief. "I thought you were more of the king's men."

I helped Michal down. When the shepherd realized who she was, he prostrated himself.

"Get up," I said. "It is only my wife. We have no pretense here. What happened?"

"They set fire to it. Looking for you." The shepherd's eyes showed fear and worry.

"And my family?" I felt the words get stuck in my throat. If they hurt them…

"Your father is shaken up but fine. Servants have escorted the household to Eliab's home. Some of your brothers are here, trying to salvage what they can. But David…they came searching for you. They said if anyone knows of your location, they must make it known. Then they did this."

"We have to save the other three stables!" Eleazar ran up to us. "We need to move!"

I had no time for anger. I only hesitated long enough to tell the older shepherd, "See that my wife gets home safely."

"No," Michal said. "I will wait here for you."

"This is dangerous," I said to her and kissed her cheek. "Please. I cannot worry about you, too. Besides, I need you to head home and be my eyes and ears. We need to find out what is going on."

She nodded. "Come home quickly. And alive."

I ran with Eleazar. "Is this one salvageable?"

"No. It's not worth our energy. We need to focus on these three."

The animals were scrambling with no order, trampling over each other. Shepherds tried to direct them, but the fire and smoke were too much. A second stable roof already smoked from the heat of the blaze. "We do not have much time. Let us secure the animals."

Borrowing a young boy's rod and staff, I worked the sheep while Eleazar directed others to protect the lambs. Here, I fell right back into shepherding. Working with patience to move the beasts along. All the while, the fire of righteous anger had been stoked inside. The king was playing dirty. How could I overcome a king intent on destroying me, especially without retaliating against him?

A loud pop exploded as the next roof ignited in flames. The animals started pushing against me, and I almost lost my balance, but patiently I whistled and sang my shepherd's song. For the entire day and well into the night, I worked with the others. We had little time to stop and refresh ourselves for the chaos had yet to quiet. Three of the four stables had been burned to the ground. The northern-most one was far enough away that it survived. I estimated that half the sheep had been saved, along with a handful of goats and mules. But many were lost or missing.

"Go home." Eleazar approached me, his face blackened from the ash and soot. "The sun is down. We can manage from here."

"This is my father's land and property. I will work beside you, just as you have worked beside me."

We searched together for missing animals, using our unique calls to summon any toward us. "The king's men did this?" I asked.

Eleazar's face appeared grim even in the dark. "Yes. The man you fight for is searching for you. I guess he means to kill you himself."

"Does he provide a reason other than despising me?"

"Crimes against the kingdom. Something about making demands of the king."

"Will he ruin his daughter trying to get to me? He has no scruples about hurting my family."

"They are safe for now, but for how long? Abner and his men already questioned them about hiding you."

"Hiding me?"

"Yes, earlier today. They came searching for you. Said that you were not at home and had taken the princess and ran."

"Is that what led to the fire?"

"What do you think?"

I stopped walking. "Michal," I whispered. "Do you think they would take her the moment she returned?"

Eleazar turned to me, his face still grave and grim. "David, it is time you realized that the king is not your friend. I know that you are holding on to some moral high ground about not wanting to hurt him, but if you don't, he will kill you first. It is time to fight."

"I do not need to fight God's battles. He is quite capable of fighting them himself."

"Until what? Until when?" Eleazar asked. "Until all who are close to you are dead? Because if he cannot get to you, then he certainly will get to others. The time for you to fight for your throne is now."

"I will fight to protect my family, to protect Israel, but I will not—I cannot—touch God's anointed. I will not take the crown like that. If Yahweh wants me to have it, He will put it in my hand."

"Then leave. Go home and make sure your wife has not been kidnapped. I will be waiting for the next order from my commander." Eleazar bowed briefly and left me standing in the dark.

"Eleazar!" I called. "Come now. Do not be like this! I am not your commander more than I am your friend! Eleazar!" I stopped yelling when I knew he would not answer in return. Feeling burdened by a heavy, invisible weight, I headed back to the one available stable to borrow a horse. But all that was available was a donkey.

10

෴

Michal

The Aristocrat District of King Saul's Court
1018 B.C.

My heart dropped at the sight of my father's men swarming my home. They stood among the small gardens that surrounded our modest, two-leveled, stone-built dwelling. Some walked the expanse of our flat roof. I swallowed hard, thinking of the last time David and I had cuddled on the roof, staring at the stars. David often liked to sleep up there. He said it reminded him of his younger years, sleeping under the stars. I often joined him, simply to be in his arms.

Abner, the captain of Israel's army and my father's right-hand man, stepped out of the doorway. A grim expression fell across his face. He nodded in my direction and walked over to assist me off the horse. He barely glanced at the servant who escorted me home.

"You smell of smoke," he said in greeting.

"Yes, my husband's family lost several barns in a fire," I said with a bite to the words.

"Is he still there?" Abner asked.

I paused, fully realizing I had just given away David's location. "Not anymore," I said quickly. To Abner and his men, my sister and I had little intelligence. We were merely girls who needed protection. Which made lying to him easy. "He sent me home and left with some men."

"On foot or by beast?"

"You expect me to answer you?" I shook my head and

73

walked past him to the house. I stopped when I felt the sharp cramp in my lower abdomen. I pressed my hand to my belly and took a deep breath. The cramp easily subsided. *Easy, Michal.* I closed my eyes and forced myself to relax as much as I could. David and I did not have time to eat much. "It is only hunger pangs," I whispered.

"You are to answer me, by order of your king." Abner approached me from behind.

"If she will not answer you, then maybe she will for me."

I opened my eyes to see my father standing in the doorway of my home, so tall that the top of his head nearly touched it. Just like David. At the thought of my husband, I took in another breath. Then I put a smile in place. There used to be a day when I was thrilled to see my father, but that was before he wanted my husband dead. "Father." I hoped I could play pretend for the sake of David's safety. "It is good to see you." I approached without invitation.

Normally, my father allowed my minor improprieties when it came to showing him affection, but now he held out his hand to stop me. "This is not an informal visit. You will address me as your king." He stepped out from the doorway, closing the gap between us. "I am still your king. Isn't that right?"

I bowed low. "You are my king and my father, and I am delighted to see you."

"She was just with David." Abner walked to the king's side.

"I have told you to never say his name in my presence," my father barked the order at Abner. I could see Abner stiffen at the tone.

"He cannot be far," Abner said.

My father turned his attention to me. "Where did he say he was going?"

"He did not tell me."

"Are you protecting him?"

"He did not tell me where he was going. He often does not give me information. He wants to spare me."

"Spare you from what?"

74

"From having to lie to you."

"You would lie to your father?"

"No...I do not know...this is confusing. Why must you pursue him? He is loyal to you!"

"Because I am protecting my line to the throne. I am protecting my family."

"But he is your family now, and he said that he will not forcefully take the throne. Why can't you believe him and leave us in peace?" The tears were there, and I knew my father would see it as weakness. But at the moment, I was so tired. Tired of my father's hatred toward my husband. Tired of us never being together because David was doing everything in his power to prove his loyalty.

"I do not expect you to understand the ways of men, but I do expect you to uphold our bargain," my father said with iron behind his words. "I told you before you ever married that shepherd that the time would come for you to choose sides. The time has come." My father walked past me to his horse. It reminded me of Beast, the horse that he rode with me when I was a young girl. A better time. A time when I looked up to and admired my father as king of Israel.

"Please," I begged, grabbing his arm before he mounted the horse. "Give us more time. If you cannot do it for him, do it for me. He is my husband."

"And I am your father," he said simply. "You do this for me, Michal, or I will cut you off."

The tears spilled down my face, and for a moment, my father's stone face melted. He closed his eyes and sighed. "This must be done, daughter. I do not act out of spite for you, but I must protect the throne. In time, I hope you will come to understand that my decisions were for my family." He mounted the horse, refusing to give me another glance.

Abner had already mounted his. "When he arrives, we are to be notified immediately. You are to tell him nothing, by order of the king."

"Why don't you let your men do it? You are keeping them

here, aren't you?"

"To make sure you follow orders. They will be here but out of sight."

"David will spot them immediately. He has been trained well, remember?"

Now my father looked at me, the coldness set on his features. "You are to do as ordered, or you will be dealt with severely."

"So, you are giving me no other option? Either I betray my husband or my father?"

"Yes. Choose wisely." My father and Abner left my courtyard with a handful of men. The rest stayed in various locations.

"Think, Michal," I whispered, as I rushed to the house. Another cramp seized my lower abdomen as I leaned against the door.

Dinah rushed in from the enclosed courtyard. "There you are. I have been sick with worry. There was no way to tell you. Michal? What is wrong?"

I pressed a hand to my belly and told myself to calm down and breathe.

"Do you need to lay down?"

I despised the thought of lying down when my husband was in such danger, but I had to calm myself. I allowed Dinah to lead me to my chaise, one of the most extravagant items I had taken with me from the palace. Father had been gifted with it from one of the princes of Egypt, and he had given it to me for safekeeping when I was a young girl.

Now I lay my head against it while Dinah slid off my sandals, washed my feet with warm water, dried them, and rested them on the lounger.

"Is it what I think it is?" she asked quietly.

"It is bad."

I felt her grab my hand. "What can I do?"

"I need to eat. I think that's why my insides keep cramping."

76

"I will bring you a warm meal."

Her gentleness mixed with the high emotions of the exchange with my father brought a new wave of tears. How could I betray David? I could not. But what did that mean? Would my father kill me? A year ago, I would have laughed at the thought. My father and I always had a strong relationship. But that was before jealousy and madness consumed him.

By the time Dinah reentered the room with a plate of warm bread and spiced stew, I had resolved myself to what needed to be done.

"Here. Eat something." She brought a spoonful of stew to my lips.

The spiced meat tickled my senses, and hunger won out. I took the spoon and ate greedily, dipping the bread in the stew's juices and devouring that too.

"I helped Master David pack enough for two meals. He mentioned that two meals were needed just in case you decided to stay longer."

"Yes, we arrived and were enjoying ourselves." I paused, feeling the emotion turn my stomach. I could not think of never feeling my husband's arms around me again. There had to be some other way. "When we awakened, David began to assemble the meal, but it was interrupted."

"Something about his family's stables? I overheard King Saul and his commander talking while they waited for you."

"They lost so much. David sent me back home because he did not want me to be unsafe."

"The king was angry when I told him that you were with Master David. He shouted at me to never say David's name again, or my tongue will be cut from my throat."

"My father threatened that this day would come." I handed the empty bowl to Dinah. "But I did not want to believe it. I did not want to believe that my own father would be so hard, especially toward someone who has fought tirelessly for this kingdom."

"What are you going to do?"

I leaned back against the chaise, staring up at the ceiling. Several different scenarios played out in my head. None of them ended well. Both David and I would have to live on the run, making the king my enemy, or I would have to surrender my beloved husband to what would be an inevitable death. "I guess that decides it."

"I do not understand."

I sat up and motioned for Dinah to draw close. I was not about to let any of my father's men hear my words. They were not in the room, but I refused to take any chances. "We are going to run."

"Should I pack your things?" Dinah whispered in return.

I thought for a moment, then nodded. "Discreetly. Only the essentials. No one can know."

"But the king? What will he do when he finds out his daughter has left with a fugitive?"

I mulled over the question, my heart breaking at the thought of betraying my father. Even though the king put me in this position, I still loved him. But I had no choice. I could never betray David. "He will know that I have made my choice."

11

෬෭෮

David

The Aristocrat District of King Saul's Court
1018 B.C.

I draped a shawl over my head as I traveled through Gibeah and tried to ignore the trepidation that knocked on my heart's door. Fearlessness was easy with God's plan clearly visible. And I could be patient. I had no problem with the king living a long and prosperous life. But somehow, I had begun walking on unchartered territory, and none of it made sense. I did not want to believe that King Saul had so fully lost his mind to think that I was the enemy, but that seemed to be the case.

After I checked on my father and family and was met with their fear and anxiety, I understood more fully Eleazar's worry and demand for action. I sought out Dodai, Eleazar's father and my childhood guardian, and explained to await word from me, and I would see that they were safe.

But first I needed to head home and make sure that Michal arrived unharmed.

The closer I got to my dwelling, the more the inner turmoil grew. Something did not sit well. I paused and took furtive glances over one shoulder then the next. The king would not want conflict on the streets, which meant if I could get inside my home, I would have some time to be with Michal and figure out a plan.

It was almost daybreak. That meant I needed to get home undetected before the sun revealed my location. I slid off the donkey and tied it to a post, slipping into a darkened corner. It would take more time, but the rest of the way would have to be done on foot.

I recited in my head words that I had scribbled onto parchment not two mornings prior.

Oh Lord, my God, in thee do I put my trust:
save me from all them who persecute me, and deliver me:
Lest he tear my soul like a lion, rending it in pieces,
while there is none to deliver…

Time worked against me, as I raced against the creeping sun pulling itself up and onto the horizon. The last year had taught me much in the art of stealth, so I knew what steps to take. I continued to move methodically from one shadow to another, remaining—at least as far as I could tell—undetected.

I ducked low behind almond trees that had been planted along the outer court walls of our home. Already the area crawled with Saul's men. If they were trying to hide, they were doing a poor job of it. There was no way I could walk right into the open and go through the front door. If I darted across my courtyard and entered through a window, it would still garner undesired attention. My disguise mattered little if I was caught outside the home. They might have orders to arrest me. Not good.

Grabbing my sling, I found a stone near my feet. Staying low, I searched for a target that would detract attention away from my home. A lantern hung over a terrace that led to one of the paths to other royal homes. Target in sight, I swung my arm and, keeping my aim accurate, released the stone. I slid back into the shadow until the second I heard the stone make contact and the lantern fall. I heard the shouts and movement, and without wasting any time, I kept the disguise in place and stayed along the outer wall, waiting for the opportunity to move. But it never came.

A lantern turned in my direction, but I stayed crouched behind a stone statue until the soldier holding the lantern moved elsewhere.

Once inside, I unwrapped the shawl, leaned against the door, closed my eyes, and drew in deep breaths. I heard Michal's footsteps above me as she walked across the floor and headed down the stairs.

"David," she whispered in relief, her face lined with worry. She ran into my arms and held tightly. "I am so glad you are all right."

I held my wife. "I snuck back into the city. The king is done with me."

"Shh," Michal said emphatically, pulling me closer as if desperate. "We do not have much time, do we?"

I hugged her not knowing what to say. "What have you heard?" I asked.

"My father was waiting for you here. It is bad. I am supposed to give you orders for your next mission. But it is a trap. His men are to notify him should you show up, and they will drag you out to face the king."

"Oh."

"I have a plan. We leave, and never come back."

My heart hurt at the thought of Michal leaving her family. She was close with her sister, and with Rizpah and some of her brothers' wives, and now if she chose me, she would have to forsake it all. "Michal, I am sorry. I do not know what to say. I need to think and develop a strategy."

"Do not say anything. Please, give me this moment. Just you and me. We will deal with everyone else later."

I had so much to do. Decisions needed to be made and acted on. But the fire at my father's stables had opened my eyes to the direness of the king's dark plans. The heavy thought emerged then and had been replaying since I journeyed to the city and snuck into my own home. How much longer would I have with my wife? How much longer before the king separated us? I felt a warning deep inside that things would get worse before they got better.

So instead of making decisions and fretting over the inevitable, I chose Michal. I kissed her right there as if my life depended upon it. Then I picked her up and carried her up the stairs.

The king and his men would have to wait.

***

I poured the water over my head and scrubbed vigorously. Even with all the servants released, I preferred to bathe alone.

"Master David?" Dinah, Michal's maidservant and the only one we kept for the night, called from the other side of the partition. "You have visitors."

"Who is it?" I felt my defenses immediately kick in. If it was Saul's men, I would climb out the window until I could talk to Jonathan. He was the only one who could talk sense into his father.

"Your second-in-command, sir."

"I am coming." I dried and dressed and headed down the stairs. "Where is Michal?" I asked. Michal's side of the bed had been empty when I woke up.

"She is visiting her sister," Dinah answered and left me alone with Shammah and Jashobeam.

"Brothers." I greeted Shammah with a kiss on each side of the face. I greeted Jashobeam in the same fashion. "How is my father?"

"He says he is fine, but we are not so easily fooled." Shammah grinned humorlessly. "He is worried and frightened."

"I will take care of my family." My words were heavy as steel. "Have no doubt."

"We know that is your intent," Jashobeam said, "but how can you guard your family when you are dead?"

"I cannot. Which means that death is not an option."

"We are glad you feel that way," Shammah nodded in agreement. "Eleazar talked to me early this morning, and then we called for Jashobeam. Time here is critical, David. It is your life or his. The choice is clear for us. We choose you."

I looked over my shoulder to make sure no servants could hear. "You are talking about an uprising," I whispered. "War would never end. Do you understand that? I already am pushing back

82

against the Philistines, and now we want another conflict?"

"The conflict is already upon you, and not of your own doing. That fire was a warning. If we do not act now, what else will he do? Who will he kill?" Shammah whispered through clenched teeth.

"If I take the throne by killing the king, the people's loyalties with lie with their king."

"The people sing your praises," Jashobeam interrupted. "You are their hero."

"People's loyalties are fickle as you well know." I looked pointedly at Jashobeam. "If he dies by my hand, I am no longer the hero. I am the murderer of the king of Israel. I cannot have that."

"They would not feel that way," Shammah said, an angry glint behind his dark eyes. "We are sure of it. We would make them not feel that way."

"And what of Yahweh?" I asked. "Would he not find me guilty of murder?"

"You have no hesitation in killing the enemy. How is this different?"

I shook my head. "It is different. God chose him just as He chose me."

"Exactly! He is the one who anointed you future king through Samuel, His holiest of prophets!" Shammah's frustration could not be contained.

"Then trust that He will make it come to pass."

"But at what expense?"

I rubbed my beard, sensing the urgency and irritation of the situation. Like a boil that continues to fester and not heal, King Saul's irrationality seemed to become angrier and angrier. What started out as a nuisance now had to be dealt with, but how? "Maybe I should try to talk to him. I am his son-in-law."

"The time for small talk is over," Shammah said. "It was over the minute he threatened your family."

I agreed. If the king insisted on pursuing me, dialogue would be pointless. "I will talk to Jonathan again. He calmed his father down last time."

"That will buy us time," Jashobeam said. "But it will not end this. You are a threat to the king and to the empire, even more so because he probably sees what we all see in you. The power of the Almighty."

The door flew opened, and all three of us jumped up ready to attack. Michal entered. My wife's eyes immediately landed on me. "We need to talk." She ordered Dinah to prepare a meal and quickly. Once Dinah had left the room, Michal walked toward us.

I saw the fear behind Michal's countenance. "What is it?"

"The guards from last night already sent a runner to inform my father that you returned. They knew when the stone broke the lantern that it was you. He has sent men to surround our house. The minute you walk out, you will be captured. My father plans to kill you himself." She covers her mouth and muffles a sob.

"Are you sure?" Jashobeam asked.

"I called upon Merab. Visited her at her place. She told me everything. Order went out this morning." She turned to me. "As I was coming back home, one of my father's messengers handed me this." Michal pulled out a directive slip from the folds of her garment. "You are ordered to leave in the morning." She handed it to me; her hand visibly shaking.

"They are drawing you out," Shammah said.

"They let us walk right up to the door," Jashobeam said.

"Because they do not want you," Michal said. "They want my husband."

"Are they not worried that we would try to rescue you out of here?" Shammah asked me.

"There must be enough men that they are not worried." I swallowed the lump in my throat and tried to think. I was trapped. Surrounded on every side. "Another game of cat and mouse."

"The time to act is now," Shammah said quietly to me.

I watched Michal as her grief slid down her face in the form of tears. "Gather the men. You know where to meet. Wait for me there." I dared not say with Michal present. I did not question her loyalty, but who knew what the king would do to her to extract information. Just the thought had fury burning inside of me. If the king laid a finger on my wife, the game would change. Simple as that.

"What of you?" Jashobeam asked. "How will you not get caught? Men should stay near to protect you."

"Thank you for considering that, but we do not want a battle here on Gibeah's streets. There would be bloodshed, and I do not want innocent lives involved. God will be with me."

The two men did not appear pleased.

I walked them to the door. "Gather your families, too. If he has truly declared my death, I am afraid that anyone associated with me might pay. I would not keep your families where they could be easily discovered."

"If we are stopped, we will say that we waited for you, but that you were not here. It will give you a little more time." The men slipped out the door.

"You are not going to wait until morning to leave, are you?" Michal asked, holding her stomach tight as if that act would contain the pain of heartache. "If you do not run for your life tonight—while having the aid of darkness—tomorrow, it will be over. You will be killed." She began to sob again. "How could he do this to us?"

I did not have the answer. I tried to prove my loyalty to the king and to the kingdom time after time. What more could I do? How many more enemies did I have to slaughter? My hands turned into fists. I needed something to punch and stone walls would not be the best choice. Instead, I ran my fingers through my hair, grabbing fistfuls and seething. Pacing back and forth only made my anger boil even more. "I am a trapped animal," I snapped. "I have nowhere to go. They might as well come in and retrieve me."

I stopped at the sound of Michal's quiet sobs. I might have my own emotions going in every direction, but I went to my wife and held her. "I have done everything I could do to prove to him how much I value him and this country. I have promised him loyalty, and I have delivered. I do not know what more I can do."

"He is a madman!" Michal wailed. "An absolute madman!"

I recalled the wild look in the king's eyes from more than one occasion. The last time he called me in to play the lyre had been another trap. Only two moons had passed since the wedding festivities when he had summoned me to play. He stood there waiting with a spear in hand. That was the last time I had been in the same room with him. All my communications these last several months had been through Jonathan or some messenger.

And I had been glad for the reprieve. I would much rather fight battles when I could fight back. But I could not—or would not—harm the king. King Saul *was* vexed by darkness, but strangely, I understood his anger. The kingdom had been stripped from him and handed over to a low-life. A shepherd. Jonathan would be an excellent king, and he was the king's firstborn. I completely understood all that, but none of this was my doing. I had not purposefully bent God's will. I had not woken up one day and decided to pursue the throne. "I will go to see Jonathan. If anyone can reason with his father, he can."

"You cannot. If you step out that door, that's it. It is over."

Dinah entered the room. "Your evening meal has been prepared."

"Bring it out then." Michal drew in a breath. "Let us try to eat something."

Grabbing my hand, she led me to our common table, sinking into the cushions surrounding it. We had been given a royal setting with seats for entertaining, but the two of us preferred the intimacy of sitting on cushions beside each other.

Despite the vulnerability and direness of the situation, my stomach growled in response to the steaming baskets of breads and fish, along with bowls of lentils. We ate quietly for most of the meal. My main objective at the moment centered on nourishment. I would not think about anything else.

Michal picked at her bread for most of the meal, eating only a few bites of anything else. "I will protect you," she said and turned to me.

"You will protect me?" I answered and swallowed the lentil stew. "I need to figure something out that does not put *you* in jeopardy." I set the bowl down and took her hands. "I do not know what I would do if something happened to you. What if he sees you as being tainted by me?"

"Listen. I know what must be done," she said adamantly. "Tonight, you are to sneak out of the house. They already know you slipped inside. That means that it will not be long before they demand you leave. When they come for you, and we both know they will, I will give them some excuse to hold them off. It will buy you and your men some time to talk with Jonathan and then escape."

"And what of you?" I shook my head. "Leave you here to deal with your father's wrath?"

"I told Dinah to pack my things. This was before you arrived. I hoped that we would be able to leave together, but now I see that I need to stay here. That is the only way it will work." Michal began tearing at her bread again. "Someone needs to know what is going on. If I get questioned, I will feign innocence. Besides, you will not be gone long. Not any longer than normal. When Jonathan talks to the king, all will be right, and you will be able to come back." She smiled at me, but it did not convince me, and I doubted it convinced her.

I rested my forehead against hers. "A part of me thinks the king is right to be so angry. When I think back to that day when the prophet poured the oil over my head, I question if he could have chosen the wrong guy."

"Then you do not see what we see. Could anyone else have killed a giant with a sling and a stone and still live to tell about it? Could anyone else escape death over and over again and win battles where it is nothing short of an act of the Almighty that you and your men are walking upright?"

I breathed in deeply and nodded. "You are right, of course. It is hard to see the goodness of the Lord when the enemy surrounds me on all sides."

"But your enemy is not in front of you."

I kissed Michal and held her, reminding myself over and over that what she said was true. Only God could allow such victory to rest on my shoulders. Not that it eliminated the threat that hovered outside. "I worry that you will be punished for being associated with me. These are strange times."

"My original plan was that you and I would run and never look back, at least until things calmed down. But that cannot happen. I see that now. Someone has to throw him off. And this is not a skill I am proud of, but I am good at acting, which is a nice way of saying that I can lie."

"I do not want to risk your safety on whether or not the king believes your deception."

"Even if he does not believe a word I say, I would still be distracting him, which helps you."

"But at what cost to you? He has already threatened you."

"I would risk everything for you," she whispered, leaning back slightly to touch my face. "I love you. And at least when we are apart, there is a hope that you are alive and that you will come back to me. If you get escorted to the palace tomorrow morning, I will never see you again." She took in a breath. "I do not think I am strong enough for that."

***

I stared at the parchment and read the words over and over until they were grafted onto the tablets of my heart. Old habits never really go away, I thought wryly, as I folded the poem among the others, tied them together with a binding string, and placed them in their spot among my supplies. I knew I had to pack light, but I also sensed that I should pack for a long haul.

I sat at the edge of a stool, reciting the words in my head. *Deliver me from mine enemies, O my God: defend me from them that rise up against me.*

"Do you have everything?"

I opened my eyes and glanced up at Michal. She stood beside her servant Dinah who awkwardly held that oblong, ugly statue with that larger-than-life face. I had demanded that she get rid of it the first time I laid eyes on it.

Dinah heaved it into the room.

"I would help you Dinah, but not with that."

"I keep it out of eyesight and only bring it out when my mother comes to visit," Michal said.

"Does the command, 'Thou shalt not make unto thee any graven image,' not mean anything to you?"

"We need it."

"No, we do not." My tone said it all.

"Not to worship," Michal said. "For this."

Dinah pulled the idol down until it lay in my spot upon the blankets on the bed. Michal took rugs and covers and strategically placed them across the graven image, so it looked like a man's form underneath. With a really ugly, larger-than-life face.

"I can see the face." I turned away.

"Wait." Michal left the room. A few minutes later, she rushed in with a goat's skin. Turning the idol so that the face pointed away from the door, she placed the goat's skin on the idol's head, giving it the appearance of hair. Michal studied her creation before saying, "It will do. With no candles lit, it will look as if you are sleeping."

"Thank you," I said to Dinah and Michal. "I appreciate you thinking of me, even if that is the ugliest thing I have ever seen."

Dinah left the room, leaving me alone with Michal. "You could have been nicer," Michal said, with her hand on her hip. "Dinah has already been threatened to never say your name or her tongue will be cut from her throat. She stays here out of loyalty to me."

"Which I am grateful for." I kissed her quickly. She opened her mouth to say something, but I did not want to argue. "I am anxious to leave. If I leave now it would give me most of the night to travel in secret."

Michal looked from the bed to me, her face furrowed in frustration. She nodded. "The back window is best. They will be watching the inner courtyard and front gardens," she said, before heading out the bedroom and toward the window to be used. "Come. I will lower you down, then your supplies."

I left the room without one more glance at the ornate idol taking my place on the bed. Once at the back window, I took Michal's hands. I could tell she was still hurt and bothered at my reaction to the teraphim. "As soon as I can, I will come home."

She nodded. "I know you cannot tell me where you plan to go, but I worry because I have no idea where you are or who you are fighting."

The sliver of moon in the sky barely provided any light, but eventually, my eyes adjusted and I saw Michal's downcast eyes. I tilted her chin up until we made eye contact. "I can tell you one thing. I think it is time I visit the prophet."

"Samuel?"

"Yes. I may go by myself, so I am not so easily found."

"What will you say to him?"

"I don't know." I searched her face. "But I need answers. Something. There is so much that I do not understand." It had been nearly ten years since I had met the prophet. I waited for an invitation that never came. Now I would go to him without one.

"Then you will come back for me?"

"I promise to return as quickly as I can. I will figure out a plan, then I will come back for you. But please know that you may have to leave everything you have ever known, and...a soldier's life is hard, Michal."

"I don't care. I can take care of myself. Besides, it will only

90

be for a little while. You are, after all, the future king of Israel."

My heart beat loudly in my chest as I saw her love for me upon her countenance. She would sacrifice everything. For me. "You have my heart."

"And you will always have mine," she said in a whispered breath.

I brought her to me and kissed her again, trying to memorize her scent and the feel of her body against mine. I was not sure when I would be back, and I did not want to admit the feeling of foreboding that had plagued my mind since the stable fires. As if as a promise to myself, I said, "No matter what happens, no matter how long it takes, I will come back for you."

And with that, I grabbed the rope, made sure that it and Michal were secured, then began to lower myself down the wall.

12

‍❦

King Saul

The Palace in Gibeah
1018 B.C.

I ran out of things to throw. My chamber lay in complete chaos. My royal garb now ripped in shreds. Servants ordered away. Only the darkness remained.

It whispered ways to kill David. As soon as Abner and my men brought him to me, it will be over. My hands trembled in nerves and excitement.

One thing was certain. I refused to listen to one more person's counsel in favor of the shepherd. My own son and daughter turned on me to support him. All Jonathan could talk about was the victorious escapades of the giant slayer. And I had yet to hear one morsel of incriminating evidence from Michal.

No more! No more worrying about decorum or about obliterating a Hebrew hero. I was the king. Not David. I had to protect my lineage. If Jonathan could not see that, then the throne did not have to be his. My wives and concubines had born many a son.

I would have no peace until my line to the throne was secured. And if Samuel—the old prophet—had something to say about it, then I would make his death happen, as well.

But it was taking too long. They should have already approached his house and brought him here.

I threw open the doors and barreled into the hall. "Where is he?"

The servants and guard jumped and scrambled away from the door.

Without waiting for an answer, I pounded down the hall in my bare feet, my tunic barely covering anything essential. But that didn't matter. I needed to pick my choice weapon. And I did not trust anyone else to do the task. *I* would pick the sword that would kill David.

Enos followed behind me. "My lord, please. Let us draw you a bath and lay out fresh garments. We can deal with David--"

"Do not say his name!" I ordered as I kept moving toward the armory. Once inside, I began rummaging through the weapons.

"Please allow me to do this for you," Enos said. "It would be an honor."

"No. Must find the right weapon to kill him."

"Your sword is in your chambers, my lord. Your son-in-law will meet a swift end with that weapon, just as countless others have."

"Do not call him that. He is no relation."

"Wh-Wh-What should I call him then, my lord? If not by his name or by his—"

"Call him dead."

The doors banged open as Abner entered.

"I've waited almost two days! Is he here?" I demanded. The voices shouted in a frenzy at the prospect of killing David. I held my hands to my ears. I could not hear Abner. The voices…were too… loud. "Stop it!" I roared.

Then there was silence.

I felt my heart pound in agitation and heard my ragged breathing as I lowered my hands. I glanced over at Abner and the other guards, all of which watched me with a measured, yet fascinated expression. "What did you say?"

"David is gone."

I blinked as I tried to process what was just said. "Gone as in

93

dead?"

"No, sir. Gone as in…gone."

The voices started to hiss and whisper his name. "Stop it!" I ordered the internal dialogue, pressing my fingers against my forehead. "How could he be gone? You said that their servants acknowledged he was there."

"Yes, and then Michal dismissed them all. All but one. She feigned ignorance."

I shook my head and started to laugh. "You believed a foolish servant?" I threw a sword at a wall laden with weapons on shelves. The noise filled the room as weapons came crashing down. "So, my daughter," I paused to laugh again. "My daughter dismissed all her servants? Why would she do that? What could she have possibly found out?"

"She visited yesterday with her sister, Merab. When she was coming back, one of my men handed her David's next commission. She acted like nothing was out of the ordinary."

"So? What happened?"

Abner took a breath and continued, "Two of his men waited for him, as well. We questioned them, and they swore that he was not there."

"You believed two men loyal to David?"

"They wore Hebrew armor," Abner said. "That means they are also under my command. If they swear by their words, I believe them."

"And you did not think that they would protect their own?"

"They are not our enemy. We continued to watch. When he never arrived, we saw suspicious movement inside. We knocked on the door and inquired after him."

"What time was that?"

"Evening."

"You waited until evening?"

"Our eyes were on the home at all times."

"Then where is he? What happened when you inquired after

him?"

"The servant girl opened the door. Led us to Michal. She said that he was sick. She even showed us where he lay."

"I guess I fail to see what this has to do with him not being here." I pointed to in front of myself. "Here. Kneeling before his king. Where I can kill him."

"We knew that you would want to see him no matter what, so we went to retrieve him this morning. I demanded Michal release him."

I moved my arms to move the story on.

"She had deceived us, sir. David had never been in the bed, only a statue with goat's hair on its head lay in his place."

I leaned against a cart and stared at the arrangement of spearheads. Michal had betrayed me? The exhaustion rested heavily on my shoulders. When had I slept last? The exertion of my tantrums had taken its toll. Not that the fury had disappeared, but it now burned with a deep intensity, leaving an intense throbbing in my chest. "My flesh and blood disappoint me," I said. "How long as he had to escape?"

"I estimate that he has been on the run for approximately 34 hours."

"So, his men, the two who swore to you that he was not there...they were lying."

Abner did not answer.

I took one of the arrowheads and maneuvered it between my fingers. "First Israel, then our own soldiers. Now my children. Is there no one who will rally behind me?" I dropped the arrowhead suddenly. "Bring Michal to the throne room. It is time she faced her king."

"We brought her back with us. We did not want to risk her escaping. We also brought the servant girl."

"Good." To Enos, I ordered, "Get me out of this tunic," then pushed my way out from the armory and toward my chambers. This time I moved with purpose. I could not let even the dark thoughts overtake me. No, I wanted to be completely sane when David and all those who were loyal to him had received their punishment. But what punishment for Michal? I had every intention of scaring her, but could I kill her? No, I easily dismissed that idea. She was worth more alive than dead. But I would see to it that she regretted choosing David over me.

As Enos and my other male attendants washed and dressed me, I stayed quiet. Why did I ever marry her to David? Had I been that moved by her tears? Now the idea seemed foolish.

Michal had dozens of suitors, many of whom would have made excellent alliances. The thought came to me like a bolt of lightning. I stood up so fast, the butler lost his balance and fell over. "That man. The one from Gallim? The one who came sniffing around with a small chest of jewels and a hundred acres of vineyard? Remember, the one who tried to blackmail the queen. He had vineyards."

"The man was slight, was he not? With pale skin and a high-pitched voice?"

"Yes." I grinned all the more. "That one. Who is it?"

"Paltiel of Gallim," Enos said and bowed low.

"Summon him here. We have a marriage contract to draw up." I liked the idea more and more. "Make the arrangements. The wedding is to happen immediately."

"And who is he marrying?"

"Michal."

Enos stopped fastening the royal robe but dared not make eye contact with me. "Sir, would not Paltiel be distressed at the prospect of Michal already being married?"

"Do not question me." I waved his hands away and finished the fastening myself, moving to the door. "Now let us go. I have a daughter waiting to greet me. And it is time she realized that she chose the wrong side."

***

This time she had no tears. She marched in with the guards, her head held high. "So, I am to be treated as a common criminal?" she asked the throne room, making eye contact with me briefly before lowering her gaze. And even that seemed forced. I could tell she would have stared me down if given the chance.

No tears this time.

I had kept her confined another day, hoping the time would let her rethink her loyalties. She was, after all, my daughter. Now as I watched her, I was surprised and irritated at her newfound confidence. Most likely a product of David's influence. One that would be stripped from her momentarily. I made eye contact with Enos who stood near the doors. My manservant gave a slight nod.

Perfect.

"Hello, daughter." I greeted her informally. "You may look upon me."

She raised her eyes. "Hello, father."

I continued to watch her. I did not want to miss one second of her reaction when the news came. "It is good to see you. Albeit, I wish it was because of better news."

Michal kept silent, only keeping her eyes fixed on mine.

"Where is he?" I asked, keeping my voice low. I did not want to stir up the darkness within.

She opened her mouth to speak, paused, and then said, "I honestly do not know."

"You allow him to escape, then cover up for him, lying to your father's men, and yet, you do not know where he is?"

"I tell you in truth. My husband did not tell me. He is a calculating man. He probably did not want to risk me telling you."

"Your husband?" I laughed at that. "Interestingly enough, I only granted you that because you swore your loyalty to me. Since your oath is no good, and you are disloyal to your father, your family, and your kingdom, the façade of a marriage is henceforth stripped from you."

There it was. Her eyes showed panic. The confidence

97

miraculously evaporated into the air. "My oath is strong. My loyalties have never wavered," she said, her voice cracking somewhat. "What have I to tell when he has been gone more days than he is been present? He stays out on his tasks longer than he should. When he comes back, he is violent. Rough with me even. The only reason why I helped him escape is that he gave me no choice."

"You expect me to believe that?" I yelled. "You mean to lie to me still? Everyone knows how much you adore him. You had a choice to hand him over to me or to let him go! You made the wrong choice!"

"He threatened me, father!" her voice shook.

I had been seated upright, my anger like a stiff rod to my back. Now I bolted up as her words hit me. Had I been too quick to judge his daughter? "Explain," I ordered, standing over her.

Michal gave no hesitation. She started, "He heard rumors that you were searching for ways to kill him— "

"How did he hear that? Did you tell him? Did your sister tell you?"

"No, father. I walked in and interrupted a heated discussion between him and his men. They urged him to leave. David threatened—"

"Do not say his name!"

"He threatened to kill me if I did not aid in his escape."

"What is his plan?"

"To follow the directives Abner gave him and to be back by the New Moon feast. He is hoping your anger will have faded by then and that he can bring back victory for Israel in honor of the king."

I noted Michal's voice had a slight hitch at the end. Like she wanted me to believe her. Unfortunately for her, it no longer mattered. I had already made a decision. "You will stay here at the palace. Preparations need to be made."

"Preparations for what?" Michal dared to ask.

Now I smiled. I imagined that glorified shepherd's face when he heard the news. "For a celebration. A marriage celebration."

"Whose marriage?"

"Yours. You will be marrying Paltiel from Gallim as soon as the New Moon feast is over."

I watched my daughter's eyes widen. "But I am already married, father."

"No, you are not. You broke our agreement, thereby nullifying the marriage."

"But, father!" she protested, panic in her words.

"Ah, where is the arrogance now, my dearest daughter?"

"But I told you—"

"Yes, David mistreated you. All the more reason for you to move on. Besides, David is a dead man. It is only a matter of time. No sense letting a flower in bloom wait until all the petals are fallen."

The guards directed Michal out, but Michal stood firm. She stuck her chin out again in defiance. Still no tears. The panic had been replaced with resolve. "I will not consummate the marriage. It is void in God's eyes because I am already married to another. And David will come and rescue me. I know it."

I walked over to my daughter until I stood right in front of her. "Good, let him come. I will be waiting. Until then, you will perform the duties of a wife to Paltiel, and I better not hear any complaint. You have already tried me enough."

Michal stared at me, blinking back any sign of emotion. Her voice did tremble as the guards began to escort her out. "Please do not do this…"

This time my heart did not soften at my daughter's pleas. My resolve did not waver. No more listening to anyone's counsel who sided with the soon-to-be dead giant-slayer. "It is already done." As they led her out, the stunned expression frozen on her face, I added, "Bring in her maidservant. Let us execute her punishment swiftly."

Michal's attention focused on me. "No," she whimpered.

"Father, no, I will do whatever you ask, but please, no. Leave Dinah alone."

"Should have thought about that before choosing the side of the enemy. I warned you that it would come to this."

One of my men led in the young woman who had served Michal for years. The young woman's dark hair had fallen from her braid and covered most of her face.

As soon as Michal saw her, she lost all composure.

"No!" she screamed, shoving all the guards and moving toward the servant. "No! I beg you!"

Michal threw herself in front of the other young woman before the guards grabbed her again and started dragging Michal away from the servant and out the door. Michal's screams were heard even when the doors slammed shut behind her.

***

His seat was empty. Second night in a row and that supposed hero had yet to show up. I gripped my goblet tightly, in an effort to keep my frustration and maddening thoughts contained. It did not help that David had run to Samuel. Michal gave us that information to save her servant girl. Not that it helped the girl. Not that it helped me either. By the time I got to Ramah, David had managed to get away. Again.

"What is wrong, father?" Jonathan asked, across from me. "We have much to celebrate." He raised his own goblet and saluted me.

I did not reciprocate the gesture. Instead, I pointed to the vacant spot. "Why hasn't the son of Jesse come to the meal?"

Jonathan set the goblet down and wiped at his mouth. I could see that the question made my son uneasy.

"First last night, now tonight? I thought maybe he was unclean, but two nights in a row? You might think he was hiding from me." I stared at Jonathan, willing him to give the right answer.

"David begged forgiveness. He requested permission to go to

Bethlehem, per his brother's request, to sacrifice there with his family."

I continued to glare at my son. "You lie." The thought shredding all decorum to tattered ruins.

"He asked for permission. To see his brothers. After all that he's done for the kingdom..."

"You!" I pounded the low table with both fists, as a hush came over the room. "You traitor! You son of a perverse woman! Do you think to fool me? That I do not know how you cover for him? You take his side to your shame and to your mother's shame!"

No one spoke or moved as if time suspended for a moment.

"I do not understand your anger at him," Jonathan eventually said, glaring at me in return. He pushed himself off his cushions and approached me. "Please, let us refrain from this conversation until we are in the privacy of your chambers."

"I care not about privacy! Each of these men should know!" I stood up to stare my son down. "He is stripping the kingdom from me! From you! From your children! As long as the son of Jesse lives, your kingdom will not be established!"

Jonathan seemed to weigh his words, once again causing silence. All eyes were on us. Even the music had paused. "It is not mine to establish," Jonathan said. "Everyone seems to understand this, but you."

The silence that followed his words seemed to echo the insult. I could barely see straight. I pointed my finger at Jonathan and ordered, "Deliver him to me at once. He. Must. Die!"

"I will not," Jonathan said with fierce resolve. "Without him, you would have already been captured and killed."

"No more traitors!" I bellowed, shoving Jonathan with all my strength. He was not prepared for the assault and stumbled back, falling onto Ishvi, his younger brother.

Jonathan regained his footing, fixing his cloak. "ENOUGH!" he bellowed in return. "I am done listening to the lunacy of a madman!"

Without thinking, I snatched a spear that rested against the wall and hurled it at my own son. "Then you can die, too!"

Jonathan dodged the spear, diving for the ground.

"Father!" Ishvi said, coming over to aid his older brother. "Jonathan is not your enemy."

My volatile emotions paused as I observed my sons. I slowly turned to see all the commanders and their guests watching the scene with a mix of fascination and horror. "Eat!" I ordered them. "This is family business."

When I turned back to Jonathan, he was standing, once again fixing his cloak. Fury was unmasked on his countenance. He approached me and said through clenched teeth, "I refuse to have any part in this." With that, Jonathan stormed out of the dining hall, stopping only briefly to stare at the spear stuck through the wall.

I guzzled the last drops of wine from my goblet and threw it down. "Somebody better find the son of Jesse."

13

∽

Michal

The Palace in Gibeah
1018 B.C.

My old private chambers had once been a place of comfort. But now it was simply a place to keep me contained. Two of father's guards stayed stationed inside the room. Neither spoke to me. I asked to see my mother, to see Merab. I asked if Dinah was still alive. But nothing.

Twice a day there was a knock at the door with a tray of food and an empty privy pot.

But it was not the lack of conversation that drove me to the brink of madness, nor was it the idea of marrying Paltiel. It was not knowing about Dinah's fate and not knowing about David that kept me from eating and from sleep. My heart broke each time I thought about what Dinah must have endured. And all because of me.

And now here I was, trapped in my old bed chamber, about to be married off to a man I despised. I reasoned that David would never allow such a charade to take place and that Paltiel would refuse to go through it, knowing David would kill him. But what if David did not know?

Or worse, what if my father or his men got to him?

"That cannot happen," I told myself while leaning against the balcony. This was how I spent most of the day, leaning out the balcony, talking to myself. "He was anointed king by the prophet. That means that he will live."

The door to my chamber opened, and mother walked in with a stream of attendants following her.

"Mother!" I exclaimed, temporarily forgetting our past conflicts. But I could not bring myself to move any closer. The attendants busily hustled around the room with mounds of silk and baskets of flowers. A large ceramic basin was brought in with several pots of steaming water. Any other words froze in my mouth.

"Daughter," she said, kissing both my cheeks. "It smells in here. How long have you been confined?"

"Thirteen days."

"Take that out of here," she ordered one of the attendants, pointing to my waste pot. "We have a lot of work to do. Now strip down and step into the tub."

"Why?"

"Because you need to bathe before your marriage ceremony."

I took a step back, shaking my head. My mother had changed little. "What don't you and father understand? My marriage contract with David is binding. I cannot do this."

"You can and you will. Just be glad that Paltiel will still have you. A marriage to any nobleman is better than dying a widow with no children."

"If something happens to David, which I doubt it will, but then within time, I will be able to marry again. But David is not dead, which makes me not a widow." I protectively placed a hand on my lower abdomen. The cramping from weeks before had abated, but I was still unsure. My belly had yet to start protruding. It felt firmer and more sensitive when I pressed against it, and my breasts continued to be tender. All the signs pointed to pregnancy, but I should have started to show by now. I wanted David's baby so badly I prayed daily. But do I tell my mother? Could it protect me from the marriage? Or would they do something to hurt the child?

"Listen," mother approached me. "I am here because your father is fond enough of you to offer a peaceful contract. But Michal,

104

know this, if you resist, you have already seen what your father is capable of. You are going to marry Paltiel today. You can do so peacefully, or we can drag you to him in chains. It will fare well for you if you follow orders."

I pressed my fingers to my temples and closed my eyes, needing to think. Every part of me screamed to fight, but what mother said was true. Father had changed. He saw me as a traitor, which means that I had limited options until David came to retrieve me. And if I was carrying David's child, I needed to be careful. I could not risk punishment. Still, the decision to go through with this fraudulent marriage to Paltiel flipped my stomach and made goosebumps sprout. "Fine," I said through gritted teeth. "But you are giving my husband no choice but to see you and the rest of King Saul's family as an enemy. It will not go well when he becomes king."

"I am not afraid of that shepherd. Now strip and let the servants clean you up."

As I allowed the servants to assist in the removal of my garments, I silently pleaded, *Please, find me and remove me from this situation. Please, David, come back to me.*

***

I stood there numb. Completely unmoving. The shock of seeing Paltiel again had worn off. Even the anger at my father no longer clouded my vision. I felt nothing. I could sense my father's steel gaze burrowing into the back of my head. Outside of the priest and a handful of servants, they were the only people present. No one else had been invited. There would be no celebration. No feast. No congratulations. My father knew how unlawful this was.

All I could think about was David. What would he do when he found out? I imagined him blazing down the paths, pushing his horse to travel as fast as it could, a look of absolute fury and vengeance on his countenance. He would avenge me.

"Michal."

I heard mother's voice. I snapped out of my fantasy and turned to her. It was hard to see with the thick veil covering my face and the tears blurring my vision.

"It is over," she said with finality. "The marriage covenant is signed."

My father left the room without so much as a backward glance.

"We have a wedding chamber prepared," my mother, said to Paltiel. "For the two weeks of private marital celebration, it is yours. I have servants assigned to you."

I looked over at Paltiel, truly noticing him for the first time today. He had changed somewhat since I last saw him over a year previously. His beard was fuller, which helped to hide his weak chin. But he still made me nauseated. Just the memory of his kiss at Merab's wedding nearly made me vomit again. Now he held out his hand to me. His clammy, nasty hand.

I did not take his hand. Then I noticed his countenance. He did not have the exuberance from years before. In all actuality, he seemed displeased. It hit me as if the cedar ceiling came crashing down upon me. "What are we doing?" I asked aloud.

"Michal," my mother's voice issued a warning.

"I am already married," I said to Paltiel. "My husband is still alive."

"Michal!"

Paltiel looked at me then at my mother. He did not even try to mask the fear.

"Their marriage contract is not binding." My mother tried to reassure Paltiel. "With David an enemy of the kingdom, it is only a matter of time." She glared in my direction. "No more outbursts from you, by order of the king and queen."

Then she left. She stopped to inform the guards that I was to enter the wedding chamber, even if was by kicking and screaming, and then she walked out just as father had. Neither one desiring to be in such an awkward situation.

Paltiel still had his hand extended, but with the queen gone, he dropped his arm. The two of us stood there, neither one of us wanting to take the next step.

"My real husband is coming back for me," I said. "And God help you when that time comes."

Paltiel did not reply, only turned and headed toward our chamber.

I took one look at the guards and knew I had no choice.

14

⚜

David

The Fields of Gibeah
1018 B.C.

I rubbed my face and sighed. I did not have time for this. My men awaited orders. My family needed to know if it was safe to stay in Bethlehem. I had a wife waiting for me.

Instead, I stayed crouched low amidst dense shrubbery awaiting word from Jonathan. After what happened with Samuel at Ramah, I had no other choice. I needed my friend's help. That meant hiding in a bush and hoping to not be found.

After fleeing my home and leaving Michal in the dead of night, I met up with my men, explained the situation, then went and sought sanctuary and counsel from Samuel. Alone.

It had been the first time I had laid eyes on him since the anointing. But I didn't know where else to go. "I have never felt more alone in my life," I wept at the prophet's feet.

"He is jealous and scared," Samuel had told me several days ago. "He knows the kingdom is no longer his, which only makes him more fiercely determined to defend it."

"But I will not take it by force," I had said.

"Of course not." Samuel's hands trembled as they grabbed mine, but his eyes were sharp. "That is why God chose you. Because He does not look at what is on the outside but what is on the inside. Your heart is after God's. As long as it stays that way, God will always be on your side."

Unfortunately, Saul found out about my visit to Samuel's and sent men to retrieve me. I had been on the run ever since.

The shrubs' branches poked at me as I tried to find a comfortable sitting spot. I closed my eyes and tried to create a new poem in my head. With being tired and hungry and wanting to go home, it was not my happiest of poems. Just thinking of Michal sent my mind reeling. What would happen if I snuck back into my house? "Michal," I whispered my wife's name and thought of better days.

Maybe Jonathan would bring some good news, and I could be done running.

I heard the *whish* of an arrow and sat up. Jonathan! The arrow had to be his, per our earlier agreement. I tensed as I heard the sound of running footsteps approaching. If Jonathan told his servant-boy that the arrow is beside him, then I knew that all was safe. If he didn't…

"Where, sir?" the boy called out.

I listened to the approaching footsteps.

"It is beyond you, son. Go, hurry and fetch it."

The words resounded in my ears as the implications became clear. *All was not safe.* I waited for the boy to leave before I gave away my location. I tried to keep my emotions in check, but I trembled from fatigue and sorrow. When the boy had been sent back to town, I stood up, every inch of me sore from staying crouched so long. But none of that compared to the pain that rippled through me.

Jonathan stood a ways off, unable to make eye contact.

"So," I said, my voice now choking back emotion. "This is it?"

"I am sorry," Jonathan said, his words filled with remorse. "I wish I brought better news."

"There is nothing I can do?"

Jonathan shook his head. Even in the early morning darkness, I could see the sorrow on my friend's face. "He is consumed. He even tried to kill me because I was defending you."

"He what? Why would he raise a hand against you? The reason he wants me dead is so that you can be the next king."

"Rationality left my father a long time ago. He did not take the news of your absence well. He accused me of being loyal to you, and when I defended you and all that you have done for the kingdom, he lost it. Threw a spear at me."

"He can no longer be persuaded?" The hopeless of the situation pressed upon my chest like a boulder of gloom.

"You deserve better than this. The only thing that keeps me from acting rashly with my father is that I know you are God's anointed. Remember that, son of Jesse. If God wills it, it will happen."

"I am not sure my next steps. Or who I should involve. If there is a price upon my head, then no one around me is safe."

"God orders your steps, David. He always has and always will. Go and keep away from my father. In time, all will come to light."

"And you? Come with me. You can lead my troops. Be my right-hand man. Anything you want, I would give it to you."

"I am my father's son," Jonathan's voice fell heavy upon me. "I am of the house of Saul. I know that what God has promised you will come to pass, but I cannot forsake my father."

I was not surprised by Jonathan's decision, but my heart broke even more. "Do you know what that means? We are no longer on the same side?"

"That is not true. I will always stand with you, but my family needs my leadership." Jonathan's voice caught. "Remember me and my family when you take the throne."

"Always. I swear an oath. I will repay kindness for kindness." Despite the despair that filled me, I fell onto the ground and bowed before Jonathan three times to seal the promise.

When I stood back up, I saw Jonathan's face contorted from sorrow. "There is more," he spoke as if saying the words hurt him.

I shook my head. "I think I have heard enough for tonight.

110

Too much sorrow fills my soul."

"It is about Michal…"

"He did not hurt her, did he?"

"No, she is fine in that regard."

I exhaled and tried to gather my thoughts. I hoped she would be willing to travel with me. I did not trust leaving her with the king. "I do not know how she will do being on the run. Maybe I can find a nice situation outside the king's grasp. Could you bring her to me? Surely you can sneak her out. One last favor for a friend?"

"I would if I could, but…She is no longer yours."

"I do not understand."

Jonathan's face showed such sorrow. He would not even look me in the eye.

"Please explain." I pushed the issue. "How is she not mine? Does the king mean to keep her from me?"

With a somber tone, Jonathan said, "My father has given her to another man. In marriage."

I felt slapped. I stepped back in shock. My Michal? "That is not possible. She is my wife. The king would never violate God's covenant between a man and his wife."

"When you are king, anything is possible." Jonathan's words were grim.

"Wh-Why? H-How?"

"As punishment to her for loyalty to you and to rob you of your love for her. Michal pledged her loyalty to the king and kingdom as a term of her marriage to you. Since she betrayed father's trust by protecting you, he has stipulated that she violated her pledge, nullifying the marriage."

"That is absurd!"

"Plus, he said you were already dead. He will not stop pursuing you until he succeeds."

I could not say anything. All words escaped me.

"If I had been there, I swear to you, I would have stopped it from happening. I had just found out upon my return."

"He has taken everything from me. My home. My country. My brother-in-arms. My wife."

"I will do anything you ask. My loyalty is to you. Please believe that. But the king will have Michal surrounded. If you make a move for her, you will be captured."

But I was no longer listening. I surrendered to every emotion I had bottled up and wept in anguish. When the anguish depleted, rage took its place. "He will not take her from me. I will go to her and take her by any means."

"Then you will play into his hand."

"So be it. I fear nothing, other than a life without my love."

"What life would you be giving her?" Jonathan tried another tactic, and it gave me pause. "Stop thinking with your emotions for a moment. She is currently safe right now. Paltiel's vineyards are vast. She will be pampered. If you can somehow push through all of my father's men to get to her and somehow make it out alive, where will you go? You have a whole army to feed and worry about."

"God will make a way."

"Maybe He already has."

I did not want to hear the words. "I must leave. Good-bye, brother."

Jonathan grabbed my shoulders. "David, trust me, my father's reign of terror cannot last forever. It is best to think things through before making a hasty decision that can lead to ruin."

I said nothing. My one thought, my only thought was Michal. Surely there had to be a way.

"Promise me, brother, that you will wait a couple days before taking action."

"I cannot do that."

"Promise me."

"And if that poor excuse of a man tries to touch my wife during that time? What then?"

"Leave that to me. I will send a threat that he will take seriously." Jonathan then asked, "Do you have your sword?"

"Yes, but it has not been properly cleaned."

"Perfect. Give it to me, and I will send it to him. That will provide you some time to talk with your men and devise a plan that does not lead to yours or her immediate death."

I knew that Jonathan had his right mind about him. I knew that my hands were tied at the moment, and taking action could be devastating for me or for Michal. So, I took the sword from its sheath, and I handed it to Jonathan. "Tell him that when I come, I will kill him. His fate is sealed." And with that, I kissed Jonathan's cheek in farewell and slipped into the fading darkness.

***

I traveled for days in a numb fog. After leaving Jonathan, I went to my family to warn them of the king's open hostility. A part of me had to fight against the bitterness. But I could not have them suffer because of the king's vendetta against me. I needed to help find a place for them, at least temporarily. Amazingly enough, I was not met with derision and confrontation. Jesse, who suffered from painful joints, said he was in no condition to move, but the entire family convinced him otherwise.

One brother asked about assembling my men and Eliab had asked about Michal, but I could not answer either of them. I only shook my head and left, telling them I would meet up with them as soon as I could.

"You have family who is on your side." Eliab rested his hand upon my shoulder.

Thoughts of his hateful words from days past filled my head.

As if reading my mind, Eliab said, "We cannot change the past, my youngest brother, but we can change in this moment. Shammah believed it almost from the very beginning. The rest of us took a little longer."

"I refuse to be bitter," I told him. "And I am grateful for the support. I pray that Yahweh protects you and the rest of the family."

What I couldn't tell them was that I did not think I could lose anyone else. I thought of Eleazar and his family, feeling deeply protective. Would I drag my men on this journey with me? It made sense that I run from Saul by myself. No one should associate with me. Anyone who did could suffer. And I refused for that to happen.

Alone I now stood in a heavy downpour outside the ancient tabernacle at Nob. The last several days had depleted me of any hope. I had traveled through towns the first day, but Saul's men were on the hunt. I wanted to go sleep in the valleys where I used to sleep, but that could bring danger to the herds and fellow shepherds.

Somehow, I found myself here. At Nob. But it was still a risk, which was why I had yet to enter. The ancient tabernacle would be safe. All the priests knew and understood who I was. Or they should. But what if? What if King Saul somehow found out that I visited here?

But hunger gnawed at me as my stomach growled. My food rations had been scarce to begin with, but they were now gone. As were most of my supplies. Weariness hung around my neck like a noose.

Necessity pushed me toward the doors. As soon as I opened them, the incense enveloped me, as did the warm, dry air. I stood—a stark contrast—dripping from the remnants of the storm outside, leaving a puddle of water at my feet.

A young priest hurried over, shutting the doors behind me. "May God be with you," he said as a welcome.

"And with you," I whispered. "I need to speak with the priest. Tell him it is urgent."

"I am son of Ahimelech, priest of the Most High. I will retrieve him."

"No need," came a solemn voice from the other side of the altar of incense. A stout man with a long beard walked hurriedly over to them. "That is all," he said to his son. I noted how the priest trembled. When his son was out of earshot, he whispered fiercely, "I saw you outside, staring at this place for some time. What are you doing here?"

I bowed. "I am David, son of Jesse, of Bethlehem. I come seeking refuge."

"I know who you are." The priest looked over both shoulders. A few priests loitered, but none were close. "You are the anointed king of Israel. What I do not know is why you are alone. Why is no one with you?"

I licked my lips and wondered if I should be honest. Should I tell him that my inner circle waited for me, but that I was on the run? Should I confess that I had decided to sneak away from everyone in order to protect them? Did the priest know that Saul was hunting for me at this very moment? I decided quickly to not put more stress upon the priest than was needed. If Saul ever questioned Ahimelech, he would not know the truth. Hopefully, that would protect him. "I came from a mission assigned by King Saul. He told me that I was to go alone, and no one was to know that I was on it."

"And what of your men? Everyone knows of the mighty warriors fighting alongside the giant slayer."

"They are not here. I am to meet them at a certain location, but first I need sustenance and a weapon. I have neither." I omitted that I still carried my sling. But I was so used to carrying a sword with the sling that I felt incomplete without one.

Ahimelech acted torn. "I do not have ordinary bread here. Only consecrated bread. Have you and your men kept yourselves from women?"

I thought of Michal. Thought of the softness of her skin, the sweetness of her scent, and nearly wept. "Yes," I barely whispered. "I have."

"Stay here," Ahimelech said. "I will be right back."

Suddenly the hair along my neckline prickled, and I furtively glanced around. My gaze landed upon another's. One behind a wood beam whose eyes stared back at me. I knew I should look away but couldn't. I felt the foreboding immediately.

Ahimelech hurried back into the room just as the man hiding behind a post hastily left. Even with the dimmed lights, I had been able to make out Doeg's features. The head shepherd and ally of Saul's who would notify the king as soon as he could.

"This is all we have." Ahimelech placed five loaves into a sack.

I needed to leave. "Thank you for your kindness." I bowed. "Oh, do you have a spear or a sword here? The mission was urgent, so I left hastily."

Ahimelech watched me for a moment. "All we have is the sword of Goliath. It is wrapped in a cloth behind the ephod. If you want it, take it. It is yours anyhow."

I saw Ahimelech appraise me with an expression of understanding. "Thank you again. I will grab it, then take my leave."

"We could provide you shelter. A warm bed."

It was tempting, but I understood the danger I put them in by staying any minute longer than needed. The only way I could keep others safe was by staying away. "I must take my leave."

"God is with you, David, son of Jesse, of Bethlehem. Remember that."

I wanted to believe it, but loneliness surrounded me on all sides. "I have been alone my entire life. I thought…hoped…that things could change."

"You have never been alone."

I stopped but did not turn around to face him. Thinking of Michal, I swallowed the lump in my throat. "Tell that to my heart."

15

ଔଞ

Michal

The outskirts of Gallim
Paltiel's vineyards
1018 B.C.

I sat on the rock at the edge of Paltiel's vineyards and stared out at the morning sunrise. It provided ample view of the hills thick with grapevines as well as the two main paths to Paltiel's home. When David came, I would be ready.

But he had yet to come.

As each day passed, more and more of my heart broke.

It felt as if I lived in some bizarre dream. None of this fit. Not only had I been taken from my love, but I no longer had my friend and confidante in Dinah. No one seemed to know what happened to her. I could not bring myself to accept the inevitable.

I heard the wagon approach but did not turn around. Paltiel would often check on me. We had yet to speak since the night of our wedding. That night, when he approached me to make his move, I boldly placed my hand on his chest and warned, "Do not touch me. It is a violation of my marriage covenant to David. If you handle me in any way, when my real husband returns, I will tell him, and I will make sure to watch as he tears you apart limb from limb."

Paltiel hesitated. I could see him weigh my statements.

"You already know that David hates you. I know my father thinks that David will die, but think about it. The king has tried to kill him for years. It has not happened yet." When I saw him not quite convinced, I added, "And I am with child. You cannot touch me."

Paltiel glanced at my belly. "If that is true, why would the king give you to me?"

"Because I did not tell them. I did not want to risk hurting the child. But it is true. Watch me bloom in the next few moons."

He took a step back and slightly bowed. "I have waited a long time for you, my lovely Michal. I do not mind waiting longer."

My mouth opened to argue, but the words halted. "Wait…what?"

"I realize the strangeness of our union. I admit that I was not entirely pleased when they summoned me to the marriage contract. The king said that David is dead to him and that you violated the marriage agreement. But I know that in such cases of love and family, that it is never that simple."

"No, it is not," I agreed. "What my father is doing is wrong."

"I do not want to be on the receiving end of the king's wrath. Or David's. Therefore, I will be patient," Paltiel said. "To the king, we are married. If David comes to retrieve you, then I will not have violated your marriage covenant with him. However, if we receive word that he is dead, our marriage will become binding."

My stomach had flipped at the thought of Paltiel consummating our marriage contract. Yet, I felt relief that Paltiel was willing to wait. I knew that meant he waited for news of David's death, but I also knew that Paltiel could require consummation at any time, even take it by force if he so chose.

Now a full moon had already passed, and still, I sat in this same spot, waiting for David. The question that ran through my mind like a river's current was: *Where is he?* Surely, he heard the news of my marriage to Paltiel.

I heard Paltiel step off the cart and approach me.

"Still no sign of him?" he asked. There was no emotion or ulterior motive behind his words, but I sensed more of a curiosity. But I refused to speak. I said my peace our wedding night and not spoken since. There was nothing left to say. I felt alone in his household. I was surprised when he introduced me to another wife and their two children. All the time he had pursued me in my father's court, he had been married. Luckily, that meant Paltiel kept busy.

Paltiel sat on another large rock off to the right of me. I felt him studying me. But my eyes did not leave the path.

"Word is he is still alone. No one goes with him."

Now I turned to him, my heart beating fast with worry. "Alone? Still?" I asked, my concern for David overruling my oath to remain silent. "Where are his men? They never leave his side."

"The king's men hunt continuously. David must mean to protect them and their families."

"But if he is alone, he is vulnerable."

"Possibly, but it also makes it easier to hide."

"David said the same thing," I admitted.

We stayed quiet. I could feel the worry begin to gnaw at me. I could not let my mind go there. David was safe. If not, I would have heard all about it. That meant that he would come for me.

"The king has ordered me to notify him at once if David comes to you."

"I am not worried," I said, even though I was quite worried. "David always finds a way to do the impossible."

Paltiel rose from the rock. "Your sister, Merab, has requested your presence. The messenger arrived as I was leaving."

"So, she found out father's treachery."

"It seems she has. Most in my village know."

I was torn. Do I go to her? "I have to be here when he arrives. I will inform your servants to invite her here."

Paltiel went to leave, only to pause. "I was wondering…"

I kept my eyes on the path. I was ready for our conversation to be over.

"I was wondering," he repeated. "Hoping that we could start over. Maybe become friends."

"That is hard to do," I admitted. "You were uncouth while pursuing me at the palace. And now you have married me, even though you know I am married to another."

"What would you have me do?" he asked. "We are both pawns of the king's whims." When I said nothing, he continued, "I did not know of your relationship with David while I sought your hand in marriage. The queen told me that you were available, and we came to an agreement."

"Yes, I remember. An agreement where you blackmailed her. Something like, 'Hand over your daughter, or I slander you to the king.'"

"Her actions were unqueenlike. I am not at fault for finding the queen in compromising situations, betraying our king."

"Then why not go to the king first. Why blackmail?"

"Because--"

"Because I am nothing more than property to you. That is why I despise you." I stopped, but the words had already escaped. I saw a flash of anger transform his face, but it disappeared. "You knew that I did not want you, but you pursued me anyway."

"I am not a perfect man, but nothing I did was improper."

"Blackmailing the queen is improper. It is morally reprehensible."

Paltiel studied me for a few moments. This time I did not look back at the path. I said words that could get me in trouble. I was almost waiting for the slap across the face. If Paltiel sent word to my father of my behavior, I did not know what would happen. But I could not play nice. Nothing about this situation was nice.

"Am I not making it up to you?" he asked. "Refraining from marital intimacy? Honoring your marriage covenant to David, even though the king ripped it up in my presence and decreed it no longer binding?" He clenched his fists. His nostrils flared, emotion evidently rising within him.

This was an attempt at peace. I understood that. I also understood that my words had angered him. I could not have

120

circumstances change between us. Until David showed up, I was at Paltiel's mercy. "Thank you for honoring my wishes to preserve my marriage to David," I said. "I know that it must be difficult. I am going through a lot right now. I will try to hold my tongue." I resisted placing my hand on my belly. Now was not the time to bring attention to my possible pregnancy.

Paltiel gave a slight nod. I was relieved at how easily he was pacified. "I will send a messenger to Adriel's and invite your sister here." He left me, sitting on the rock.

I heard him step onto the donkey-led cart and could hear as it slowly moved away and into the vineyard. But my attention was already focused on the path leading to his house. *Please, David, come to me. I am waiting.*

***

The evening came and went, and twilight descended. I had no lantern, and I had yet to eat an afternoon or evening meal. I needed to head back to the house that was not mine.

I swallowed back the despair and let the tears come. Another day without my love. Another day filled with worry, wondering where he was and if he was safe. Another day of disappointment that I still had no answers.

Torn between staying a little longer and going back while I could still see without a lantern, I decided that darkness would not be kind to me out in these fields. I stepped away from my perch on the rock and made my way through the well-beaten path I had used for these several weeks.

I saw lanterns in the distance but paused to gather some grapes from the vine. I popped one into my mouth and kept moving.

A cramp in my lower abdomen gave me another pause. Not again. There had been no cramps for weeks. I scolded myself for not bringing food with me and vowed to do so in the future. But as I continued to walk, the cramping did not dissipate. It began to intensify. I moved toward Paltiel's house, desiring to lie down, but

121

not wanting to do so out in the fields.

Another cramp twisted my insides to the point I let out a cry of pain. I pressed my hand to my belly. "No," I cried. "No. Not this. Please not this." For the first time today, I was not thinking about David. Who I needed was Dinah. She would know what to do.

The warm gush of liquid released from my womanly parts. I could not move. I crouched over, holding my belly, tears running down my face. Not like this. Not like this. I fell to my knees as sorrow overtook me. I stayed in that spot well into the night. My thighs were wet and sticky. My inner belly was on fire. I needed help but was still too far from the house.

Eventually, I heard my name being called. It was Paltiel.

"Here," I croaked, trying to call out through my grief. "Here," I said a little louder.

Soon the lantern shone upon me. "Michal?" Paltiel set the lantern down and knelt beside me.

"Blood," I said weakly.

Paltiel looked down at my skirts and uttered a quick prayer. He called out to servants. With some effort, he picked me up. A servant ran to him. "The lantern," he said. "Grab it and lead the way."

I wanted to resist, but I was too weak. I let my head fall on Paltiel's shoulder and lost consciousness.

16

☙❧

David

The Philistine Stronghold of Gath
1018 B.C.

I threw the hood over my head and moved with the crowd. Gath's streets were packed, as the heathen Philistines pushed through the morning to their destinations. Since I was filthy and wore Philistinian garb from a dead man thrown outside the city's walls, I knew I was relatively safe from detection.

Besides, who would think that the giant slayer would be among them? I could feel the weight of Goliath's sword on my back. The irony did not escape me.

I would have found it funny if not for the extreme melancholy that had fallen on my shoulders over the past fortnight.

It was my meeting with my brother, Shammah, that changed everything. He was still with our family when I sent a secret message to meet me in the dense forest of Bethlehem's border. *Tell no one*, it had read. My heart had hurt at keeping my other brothers-in-arms outside of the meeting, but I reasoned it was for their protection.

Our meeting had been brief. Mostly because Shammah informed me of such horrendous news that I had to run from him to shoulder the grief alone.

My wife. My beloved Michal. Not only taken from me and handed to another, but she had been pregnant. Our loyal spies that I had ordered to the town of Gallim to watch over Paltiel's house had sent message to my family to give to me. Michal had been with child and had lost the baby.

It had been too much. I knew Shammah would let me grieve alone, that he was not expecting me to run. But I did.

Alone. That is how God must want it. He must not want me to love. With King Saul on the hunt, everyone associated with me, just as Eleazar and others had warned, were in danger. He had taken everyone from me in one moment. My reasonable side knew that this part was my choice. My men were fiercely protective and loyal. But I cared for them too much to put them at risk of King Saul's wrath. Let them live peaceably. I had been alone my whole life. I should not have expected anything different.

Here, in this massive Philistine city, surrounded by throngs of people, speaking their language, the heavy weight of depression felt even more burdensome than before. But, hopefully, I could hide out here until King Saul gave up his pursuit.

I found the shabby inn and pushed open the door. A stale, musty odor lingered in the small room. A large man shuffled out from a back chamber. He looked me over then said in his own tongue, "What is your business?"

I had practiced my Philistinian accent and prayed that it worked. "I am inquiring about the vacant room. Jabba mentioned you had one."

He scrutinized me again. My hair was lighter than typical Philistines, but it was long and unkempt. I had made sure to cover my face with it. My eye color would give me away. Everyone within these parts knew that the giant killer had lighter-colored eyes. "Where you from?"

"Outside Ziklag." I set a heavy ingot on a small stool. "I have more." I needed him to stop studying me. "This should pay for at least a full moon."

He finally nodded and pointed up the stairs. "There is a room to the right. Do not disturb me, and we will not have problems." He took the ingot and left the room.

I walked up the stairs, opened the door on the right, and shut it tightly behind me. The room barely housed a mat on the floor. I thought of my home with Michal and gave myself a moment to imagine her in my arms. There were many times I thought about going to retrieve her. But what would we do? It would be hard to hide with a princess beside me. And what would the king do to her? No, I now knew that Jonathan had been right. She needed to stay where she was for the time being, so she could be safe. Away from me was her best option.

But oh, how I missed her.

I set my cloak down and began searching for a hiding spot. Goliath's sword needed to be protected at all costs. I would carry it around with me, but it was clearly Philistine with its markings. I found a loose board in the small fireplace. The sword did not fit. I began carving out a bigger piece of the board. A mouse skittered past. I whacked at it and kept working. After feeling satisfied that the sword was safe from discovery, my stomach growled, reminding me that I had yet to eat since this morning with the last of my rations.

Glancing at the dead mouse, I was not that hungry to make it my dinner. Instead, I tossed it out the narrow window and observed the scene below. I searched for quick escapes in case I needed it, but found that the only way out was jumping straight out the window or going through the door. I was basically stuck right in the middle of my mortal enemy.

***

I slept fitfully. The mat was useless, and the bugs kept biting. I would have gotten up and kept writing, but the last of my wood had burned out hours previously. When I did sleep, I dreamt of my wife. Mostly of her dying in my arms. I woke up from the nightmare covered in sweat.

That was when I knew someone was in my room. The sword was hidden and not by my side, but I had a small blade tied to my belt. I kept my eyes open, blinking fast to adjust to the darkness.

A heavy foot stepped forward. I saw the glint of sword being raised.

Without another passing moment, I rolled toward the attacker, reached for my blade, and sliced his leg. He howled but did not stop reaching for me. I brought the butt of the blade up to his groin and rammed it as hard as I could. As he bowled over, he grabbed me by the neck and wrapped his arm around it, cutting off my air supply. I slapped his arm, but the large man had arms like tree trunks. My blade had fallen, and I had run out of options.

"I know who you are," he whispered in his native tongue. "You killed my brother and desecrated his body. Now I am going to slice off your head and stick it on a pole for all to see, you green-eyed demon."

I used my foot to kick his wounded leg. His grip loosened only slightly, but it was enough. I kicked him again, then brought my fingers up and pushed into his eyeballs. He dropped me and kicked at me. This time I lunged at him with all my strength, knocking him to the ground. His sword clanged onto the floor beside us. But I knew that blood in the room would lead to questions. So, I pinned him to the ground, my legs holding down his arms, and wrapped my hands around his throat.

When I was sure of his death, I fell beside him as if all the energy and adrenaline had been immediately depleted.

"Close," I whispered between breathing. "Very close."

When I got my wind back, I stood up, placed my arms around his shoulders, and dragged him to the door. I paused and listened. Surely our scuffle would have awakened anyone else in the inn. I opened the door and peeked outside of it. No sound. No movement. I knew I had to do something with the body, so I dragged the man and all his girth down the stairs and all the way around to the back entry. My time was limited, and I still needed to bury him.

I found a large wooden spoon in the back chamber. With nothing else, I found a set of bushes beyond his inn and worked feverishly to make a shallow grave. I prayed, begging God to help me, reciting poetry in my head as silent prayers.

That man knew who I was with one conversation. What hope did I have? But now that he was dead, I could maybe hide in peace.

At daybreak, I dragged the man to his shallow grave, saw that it was not quite enough, and pushed to make it right. I shoved the mounds of dirt over his body and patted it down. Sweat poured off me, and I could see townspeople moving about. This would have to do.

Going back inside, I paused in the back chamber and saw a pot of broth. I took it and drank hungrily. A loaf of bread had been sliced. Flies flew around it, but I shewed them aside and ate the slices in greedy bites. Once full, I made my way up to my room, shut the door, placed a stool in front of it, and fell onto the dirty mat.

I fell asleep immediately.

17

ᚠᚠ

Michal

Paltiel's Home on the outskirts of Gallim
1018 B.C.

When I opened my eyes, Dinah stood over me. I reached for her, but she grabbed my hand and squeezed. I sat up and rubbed my eyes, wondering if I was dreaming or if my mind played tricks on me. "Dinah?"

She brought a steaming broth to me and indicated for me to drink it. She had yet to look me in the eyes.

I touched her arm. "Dinah?"

She kept her eyes downcast.

"Why are you not speaking? I thought I would never see you again."

"She is not speaking because she can no longer talk." Merab stepped up to the bed. "But I am glad to see you still have your tongue intact."

Merab sat beside me and lovingly stroked my cheek. But my attention turned back to my maidservant. She still looked like Dinah, but something had changed. Her demeanor was not her usual pleasantness. Then again, if what Merab said was true, then of course Dinah had every right to be shaken. "Is it true?" I whispered to Merab, pointing at my tongue.

"Yes, our father cut it off, and then as a wedding present to you, he is giving her back."

"As a reminder," I muttered, my heart breaking all over again for my friend.

"I was not even informed," Merab said. "About any of it."

"They kept me confined until the wedding. I could speak to no one."

"He has lost his mind. When David finds out, he is going to want vengeance."

"I think father is counting on it. He used me as a pawn against my own husband. If David comes to me, Paltiel is to notify him."

"Father does not need Paltiel to do anything but keep you here. There are spies everywhere. Trust me, if David makes a move toward you, in any surrounding area, he will be captured."

"It is good that he does not know," I said to myself. "I do not want him to find out…" I could not finish the words.

Merab took my hand. "I am sorry, my sister. You lost a lot of blood. But I am grateful Yahweh spared your life. I could not live through mine without you."

It was then I noticed the dark circles under Merab's eyes. She appeared haggard, not that I would tell her. "What about you? How are you and the baby doing?"

"My breasts hurt. Eventually, the milk will go away on its own, but it has not been enjoyable."

"You could always feed the baby."

"No. That is why we have wet nurses." Merab looked over her shoulder, then turned back to me. "I cannot believe he married you to Paltiel. I always knew father could be cruel, but you were his soft spot."

"No longer. I chose David over him. Father made sure I was punished for that mistake."

"How did you endure the wedding night? That might be why you lost this child. It is not good to do such things when you are expecting."

"We have yet to consummate the marriage."

Merab raised her eyebrows in apparent shock.

"I warned Paltiel that if he did that to me, when David came for me, he would tear Paltiel apart limb by limb, and that I would watch."

Merab covered her mouth, but a giggle escaped. "You did not say such a thing!"

"Why not? I am still married to David. What father has done is disgusting and wrong. That reminds me. How long have I been bed-ridden?"

"A little over 48 hours."

"I must get up and get dressed."

"No, you are still bleeding. You are in confinement until you are no longer unclean."

"But I must watch for him. What if he comes, and I miss him?"

"Sister…"

"Dinah," I called. "Please help dress me."

"Michal," Merab said firmly. "Stop. You need to rest."

"But David."

"Your husband is on the run for his life. He is not coming for you any time soon." Merab took my hand. "If he does, he is dead. Do you want that for him?"

"Well, no, but he promised."

"He will come for you, I am positive, but not any time soon. Father pursues him even as we speak. Rumor is that David is hiding in enemy territory."

"What?" I felt the twinges of panic. "Which enemy?"

"I am not sure. I heard Adriel talking to his men about scouting around Gath."

"The Philistines!" I covered my face.

"Father's men are not there or anywhere close. They know that they are as good as dead. Adriel was informed to tell his men to pull back."

"Which means that David is as good as dead."

"David is nothing like anyone we have ever encountered. So, do not give up hope."

"He is surrounded by enemies, Merab. Whether in the midst of the Philistines or here with his own people. He has done nothing wrong, and he is still pursued. What hope is there to have?" I fell back upon the cushions. "And now, what I had of him is gone." I touched my lower belly, which was still tender.

Merab lay down beside me, putting her arms around my waist. We used to lay like this when we were young and there were thunderstorms. Just as before, she stayed beside me until I fell asleep again.

***

I stayed confined for another full week. Merab and Dinah were with me the entire time. I asked Merab at one point if she needed to get home to the baby. She shrugged and said, "Sometimes it is good to step away. I do not want to lose myself. I am Merab first before I am a mother."

I did not understand her reasoning. I longed for a baby, but I was grateful for her presence, so I kept my opinion to myself. Yet, Dinah stayed at a distance. She took great care of me, but would not make eye contact. I noticed the scars on her wrists from the fetters, and I felt such guilt because I knew it was because of me. She stayed loyal and suffered because of it.

"Do you know why she is still alive?" Merab asked, when she saw me watching Dinah leave the room.

"It cannot simply be because father decided mercy."

"From what I have been told, Rizpah intervened."

But I was not moved. "She could have intervened before Dinah's tongue was cut out. And when I was locked in my room until the marriage, she did not come to see me at all. She was not at the ceremony either. In this war, we all must choose a side. It is unlikely she has chosen mine."

"Not that I desire to defend father's concubine, but she does not have unlimited power. And no one came to your ceremony. It was all secretive. But Rizpah convinced father to have Dinah only punished, not killed, so that she can be a spy for him in your house."

"Great," I said snidely. "So, he takes away my husband and my friend. Gives me a shell of what she once was."

Merab left for her home a few days after that conversation.

I had regained enough strength to walk to my spot at the high point of the vineyards. "Would you like to come with me?" I asked Dinah, as she finished combing and braiding my hair.

She shrugged her shoulders as if to say she did not care either way.

"You are angry with me, aren't you?" When she did not respond, I said, "I am sorry that you were punished because of your loyalty to me." I stood up and kissed her cheek. "I am glad Merab brought you to me. It has been difficult not knowing your fate or the fate of my husband."

I left her in my private chamber and entered the hall that led to backfields. Paltiel's home was large and airy. I would not admit this to him, but I enjoyed the spaciousness and the views of the vineyards. The air that came through the open verandas and porches was sweet and earthy. And it was expansive enough that my chambers were far away from his other wife and their children.

But I could not always avoid them, like this morning.

The toddler went barreling down the hall, running smack into me. He looked up at me and grinned. The poor boy would have a weak chin like his father, but his eyes sparkled, and I found myself smiling in return.

"Palti," his mother called. "Come. You do not go down this hall." She was a little woman with messy hair and a big bosom.

"It is all right," I said, as I walked him back to her.

She quickly grabbed his hand. "Do not touch my son," she said, before turning on me. "I do not want your curse upon my children."

Her words hit my heart. "You will refrain to speak to me that way. I am the daughter of the king."

"And yet you live in the house of a peasant." She continued

132

down the stairs without giving me so much as a backward glance.

Dinah stood beside me. "This is not a peasant's house," I said in defense. "Look at this place. It is nicer than the home David and I lived in." I rubbed my temples, already feeling drained. "I am cursed? Is that true?"

Dinah, for the first time in the two weeks she had been here, met my gaze. She shook her head, reached for my hand, and squeezed it.

I threw my arms around her and hugged her tightly. "But what if I am?" I whispered.

Of

Distance

And

Despair

18

❦

David

City of Gath
1018 B.C.

I scribbled furiously on the parchment. The men pounded on the door.

"Are you sure?" One of them asked.

"Yes. It is who we search for. And the dogs discovered Ladrak's body."

They kept pounding on the door.

"We know who you are," one of them said in a sing-song voice.

"Come out, giant slayer. He told us you were here," another roared in the native Philistinian tongue.

The door shook from the impact of their fists.

I reread the words. It was crazy to write a poem about God when Achish's men had discovered me. But God was all I had left. Besides, it was the only way to keep sane this past new moon, hiding in Gath.

Nothing was sane since hiding here, pretending to be someone else. My every thought turned dark and grim and bitter if I did not write. So, I wrote. A lot.

Someone slammed up against the door in an effort to tear it from its hinges. I searched for a way out, but there was none.

An idea came to my mind. Could it work?

My nerves were on edge. I needed to come up with a plan and fast. In about thirty seconds that door would be destroyed. Someone had already taken an ax to it.

Without thinking twice, I rolled up the parchment, stuffed it in a pocket, and threw myself on the floor. "God, give me strength," I whispered. Then, knowing it was either this or immediate death, I let out a shriek that would make a witch's cauldron boil. I began writhing on the floor, shrieking and carrying on like a madman.

I heard the men at the door pause.

"What's going on in there?" someone shouted.

"It's a madman!" another said in exasperation. "I thought you said this was the Hebrew who killed Goliath?"

"It is! I swear it!"

The door banged to the floor in pieces. I screamed with all I had in me and started to convulse. I felt the hands of several men pick me up. I shrieked and rolled my eyes in the back of my head, making sure to let some spit form around my mouth.

"This couldn't be him," one of them argued.

"He reeks!" another said. "Let's hurry and get him to Achish. He can decide!"

"Kill him now and get it over with!"

I uttered nonsensical words, then laughed hysterically, fighting them as they left the room. I clawed at the walls, yanked on their hair, and even tried biting them.

By the time, we arrived at their king's palace, I could hardly breathe. Acting crazy was exhausting. But I could not stop. This was the time it counted most.

They dragged me on the ground most of the way, then stopped to try to gag me with a rag. But I snarled and bit at them so much, they smacked me and hit me a few times instead.

Now at Gath's palace, I twisted and contorted, making their grips loosen. I shrieked again and began clawing the floor.

I heard commotion and voices talking. Suddenly someone hit me upside the head. My ears rang from the hit, and I bit my tongue from the impact. I made sure to let the bloody spit run from my mouth and down my beard.

"Do you take me for a fool!" Achish's voice sighed in annoyance. "You interrupt my dinner for this?" The king of Gath stepped closer to me.

I rolled my eyes into the back of my head, dribbled some spit on the floor, and then howled in a high-pitched wail.

"We have enough madmen to contend with. Why bring me another?"

"But sir, I am telling you that this is Goliath's killer. I know that face. He is the one the Hebrews have compared to their king."

I saw out of the corner of my eye that Achish was considering what the other Philistine has said. I began to talk nonsensically and then insanely laughing, yanking on my own beard.

"This could not possibly be the same man. Look at him."

I made sure to squeal in laughter and convulse on the floor for good measure.

"Get him out of here," Achish ordered in disgust. "And do not waste my time again."

The men grabbed me and dragged me out, roughly pushing against me.

"What do we do with him?" one of the Philistines asked.

"Dump him out by the city gate. The king is right. Even if he is not the Hebrew we thought he was, we still have too many crazies in this town."

I made sure to keep the act up after the long walk to one of the city's gates, after they left, and even into the night. Eventually, the nonsensical words turned to tears. Part relief—I would have died a gruesome death if Achish had believed that I was David—but mostly sorrow. How had I fallen this far? When had my home become the last place I could go and be safe? What had I done that I sat among the outcasts of a Philistine city?

The mighty giant slayer lay outside the enemy's city gate with no one to help and nowhere to go. And in that low moment, I even wondered if God had stuck around.

***

At some point, I fell asleep against the wall. The temptation to get up and leave presented itself, but I did not want to give away the disguise just yet. Several of the outcasts eyed me warily. Sleep was not in my plan, but it snuck up on me despite my intentions.

Deep into the night, a hand went over my mouth. My eyes shot open, and I reached for the weapon I did not have. I took in the sight of Jashobeam and nearly wept in relief. Jashobeam brought a finger to his mouth and motioned to follow.

I knew that being with my soldiers was life-threatening for them and their families, but at that moment, all I felt was relief at not being alone.

Jashobeam and I moved quietly outside of the city's wall toward the directions of the mountains. The two of us ran on foot well past the city without a lantern to aid us. But my eyes quickly adjusted.

Neither of us spoke as we came upon a small grouping of trees. I heard the horses before I saw them. Eleazar stepped out from behind a tree, holding the reins to three of them. He came up to me. His eyes were furious, but he nodded and handed a horse to me saying nothing. The three of us climbed on top of the horses and took off. This time I let Jashobeam take the lead.

We moved fast. As fast as possible with only the moon as a guide. I kept my eyes open for raiders or vagabonds, but the hours passed with no interruption. Right as the sun streaked the sky, the three of us on our horses burst through forest and followed a path around a creek.

Jashobeam motioned to stop. We listened for several minutes before eyeing the parameter. Eventually, Jashobeam slid off the horse and led it to the water. Eleazar followed, as did I.

As I brought my horse to the creek, I took in deep breaths of relief. I stood beside the horse and rested my head against it. Now

140

that I was out of Gath, I questioned my decision to go there alone. Surely, there was somewhere I could hide until King Saul's anger passed.

Lost in thought, I did not see Eleazar behind me until it was too late. He grabbed me and shoved me into the water. Water sloshed up my nose and into my mouth. I came up sputtering. Then Eleazar did it again. And again.

Finally, I came back up and said, "Enough!"

Eleazar picked me up by my collar and said through gritted teeth, "Do not ever leave us again. Do you understand me?"

"I was trying to keep you all safe." I had to cough out the words since I ingested a trough-load of water.

"Do not feed me lies! You ran scared. And you left us all wondering what in the world happened to our fearless leader."

I stared back at my friend. I felt ashamed. "I am not fearless," I said. "I did not want anyone else hurt. If you are associated with me, you and your entire family could die."

"I swore to you an oath." Eleazar fought back emotion. "Do you understand that? We are brothers. Always. That oath will never be broken. So, do not ever do something that stupid again." Eleazar threw me back into the water one more time. "Oh, and one more thing, you stink. Clean up before we go but make it fast. You have people waiting."

I tried to think of something to say to rid me of the shame and guilt, but no words came. Instead, I wasted no time peeling off the layers of garments and washing the filth from off me. Because of the lice, I had no choice but to take Eleazar's available knife and cut off my beard and shave my head. As I stepped out of the creek, I felt like a grimy layer of scum had been lifted like fog on a sunny morning. I noticed new garments—my garments—resting upon the horse.

Once dried and dressed, I found Eleazar and Jashobeam sitting with their backs to me, both resting against trees and eating rations. Eleazar glanced up and handed me dried meat and a half a

141

loaf of bread. Jashobeam had yet to speak to me. My heart pricked with guilt, so I made myself sit across from them.

"Your face is naked," Eleazar said.

"Bugs."

"That is what you get for living among heathen."

I opened my mouth to speak several times, but how could I explain my decision? "I am not sure how you found me, but I am grateful."

Jashobeam snorted and shook his head.

"It was your brother," Eleazar answered. "We had searched everywhere for you. We knew you could not be dead because Saul would have been shouting it from the rooftops, as would the Philistines. Shammah remembered that when you visited him right before you disappeared, you said something about that you would hide among Israel's enemies if you needed to protect others. We separated into groups, some going to Moab, others to the cities of the Amalekites. Jashobeam and I volunteered to investigate Gath. We scoped out Gath for weeks, waiting for any clue. We even disguised ourselves a few times and tried to see if we could overhear any word about you. Yesterday, we saw a group of men marching along the streets, claiming to have discovered the Hebrew hero, saying that you killed one of their men."

"It was the innkeeper," I said. "He figured out who I was and came at me in the night."

"And just like that, Israel's next king would be dead."

"I handled it."

Jashobeam looked at me, fury in his eyes. Without a word, he stood up and headed back to the horses. Eleazar gave me a look that spoke very clearly: *Make this right.*

I jumped up and followed Jashobeam. "You are angry. I understand, but I had my reasons."

"Do you?" Jashobeam turned to me, his face contorted in anger. "Do you understand how much time has been wasted searching for you? You told no one! Not your family. Not Eleazar!

Not me!" He pounded his chest. "Did you not think I had a right to know?"

"I was trying to protect all of you! If I went and hid then none of you could be associated with me. Anyone right now that is connected with me is a target and could meet their end with Saul's sword!"

"A king does not forsake his men or his country! Are you my king, or aren't you?"

The words made impact like a spear through the chest. "A king protects those he cares about," I said in a low voice. "I cannot lose anymore." I stopped before the emotion overtook me again.

"Running from your destiny is not going to make it happen. And it is not going to bring your wife back to you."

"I was only running until the king stopped his pursuit or...if he died."

Jashobeam's face did not hide his derision.

"I am still a work in progress."

"That is no excuse for stupidity."

"Duly-noted," I said. "I am filled with gratitude that you and Eleazar found me."

"You nearly died."

"I know." I felt Jashobeam's intense glare. "I am in rough shape, Jashobeam. I do not know what to do, or where to go."

"So, you chose Gath?" Jashobeam said. "Why? They have been looking for you for years."

"I am too recognized in my own land." I thought of Doeg seeing me at Nob. I did not want to risk getting discovered. "Why not hide among the enemy? That is the last place they will look."

"You have men who have sworn an oath to protect you. We cannot do that if we do not know where you are."

"I cannot defend my actions. At the time, it made the most sense, but being there alone, I realized that I must stop thinking about myself. I must think of others. My men, my people, and my wife."

"We will discuss this later. You have men worried about their leader."

"Before that," I said, pausing to consider how to phrase the next sentence. "We need to head back to Gath."

"That is not going to happen." Jashobeam pulled himself up and onto the horse.

"It is important. I hid something there that I have to recover."

"What would you hide in Philistine country?" Eleazar came over to us and did not act amused.

"Goliath's sword."

Both Jashobeam and Eleazar stared at me in shock.

"Ahimelech gave me the weapon. I needed it because I took off so fast, I had nothing. When I decided to hide in Gath, I had to hide the sword, too. They would know immediately whose it was and then it would…complicate things. So, I hid it close by. That way it would be available. In case."

Neither Jashobeam nor Eleazar said anything.

"I want that sword. With you two by my side, it can be done. I am sure of it." I pulled myself up and onto my horse. "Are you coming?" And for the first time in several moons, I felt more like myself.

19

❧

King Saul

Gibeah, under the Tamarack Tree
1017 B.C.

"Where?" I asked. "How many?"

"Only a few, my king," a young Hebrew soldier said. "Travelling away from Gath."

"Gath?" I rubbed my face and sat down. I had gathered my troops along the hillside of Gibeah in hopes that someone had news of David's whereabouts. The tamarack tree offered little protection from the sun's afternoon heat. I would not have to be here if my commanders did their jobs.

How hard was it to find him? Several moons had passed, and I was nowhere close to killing him. And that nearly drove me to the brink of madness. "Why would he be in the Philistinian town? Probably striking a deal with our enemy." The soldier did not answer. "So, tell me then. Why did you not attack him and bring him to me? Was that not the order?"

The young soldier still knelt, his face to the ground. He showed reservation in answering.

"I asked you a question."

"Who am I, sir, against David?"

I jumped up and grabbed the young soldier, dragging him to eye-level. "Who are you against your king?" I bellowed, throwing him to the ground. "You defy my orders to protect the son of Jesse?" I snatched my spear ready to hurl it through the young man's treacherous heart.

"Father," Jonathan stepped beside me. "He gave us pertinent information. He is young and immature. Worthy of punishment, probably. Worthy of death, probably not."

"Get him out of my face," I ordered as the young soldier was carried off. Then I turned quickly to my son. "Traitor," I seethed. "You are all traitors!" I yelled at the entire set of troops. "Will the son of Jesse give to you vineyards and fields? Will he make you commanders? Place you over hundreds if not thousands? Surely that must be why you all conspire against me!"

"No one's conspiring against you," Jonathan said, so no one else heard the dissent.

"None of you tell me that my own son makes a covenant with that traitor. None of you are on my side!" I yelled, throwing a pointed look at Jonathan. "None of you are helping me find him. Instead, you help him lie in wait to capture and kill me!"

Abner jogged up the hill with a herdsman with him. "Sir, this shepherd has pertinent information."

I glowered at the man, who twitched under my intense glare. "Well? What useless information do you have?"

"I saw the son of Jesse, my lord," he said as he bowed before me. "A few moons ago. He came to Ahimelech at Nob. He was inquiring of food and weapons, and Ahimelech gave him five loaves of consecrated bread and the sword of Goliath." He added quickly, "I would have brought him to you, but he left in a hurry, and I was still purifying myself and unable to leave."

"Bring me Ahimelech and his entire family of priests. I will not rest until they are in front of me." To the man still bowing, I said, "Stand up and state who you are."

"Doeg, sir." Doeg stood up but still trembled. "Your head shepherd, faithful only to King Saul."

Jonathan approached me again. I would keep my spear in place. I reasoned with myself that as soon as David was dead that Jonathan would no longer be manipulated by the son of Jesse. Still, it was hard to stare into the face of my traitorous son.

"Surely you do not believe that the priests of Nob conspire against you?" Jonathan said. "They could not turn David away. You know that. Besides, they probably have no idea what is happening to know to detain him."

Instead of addressing just my son, I shouted to the troops. "If any man is not loyal to me, then that man is dead."

***

Ahimelech knelt before me, as did his entire priesthood family. "Yes, my lord?" he said with a slight bow.

The soldiers had become eerily quiet. Even Abner stood as far away from me as possible and actually looked afraid. I found it irritating. "Why have you conspired against me? You and that son of Jesse? Hmm? Did you not give him bread and a sword? Did you inquire of God about him? Did God himself tell you that he rebels against me and waits to kill me?"

"Who of all your servants is as loyal as David?"

I had turned away from him but now whirled around ready to strike. "He conspires to kill me! So that he can take the throne!"

"Is he not your son-in-law, your bodyguard, and highly respected among your own family?"

"Leave my family out of this. Did you ask God for guidance about him?"

"Of course. But believe me when I say that we know nothing about whatever is going on between the two of you. Please do not accuse me or my family."

I closed my eyes and tried to manage the fury burning within me.

Lies, the voices whispered. *They lie. All of them lie to their king.*

No one was loyal. Everyone still revered that despicable son of Jesse. I regretted ever letting him into my household. But I could turn the tide. I could show the world my power. I had this moment.

A lesson needed to be taught to everyone that there was a civil war, and sides needed to be chosen.

Yes. Kill the priest. Kill them all. They must suffer.

I opened my eyes and zeroed in on the priest. "You are going to die, Ahimelech! You and your entire family!"

Jonathan grabbed my arm. "What are you doing?"

"Do not question your king!" I roared, yanking my arm from Jonathan's grasp.

"I will question you when it will cause your demise." Jonathan stepped so close that his face was mere inches from mine. "You cannot kill these holy men. It will be the end for you, father. God will not tolerate it."

Kill them, the voices chanted. *Kill them now.*

I shoved Jonathan. "Remember your place, or you will be next!" I turned to the priests, then said to my own men, "Surround these men and kill them!"

No one moved.

"I said kill them! They conspire against me, working hand-in-hand with that traitor, David. They helped the fugitive escape and didn't inform their king! Death to them all!"

Not one of my men stepped forward to obey the command.

"Abner!" I shouted. "Order your men to obey their king!"

Abner darted his eyes from me to Jonathan to the priests. "I...I cannot, sir. These are holy men. I...I...cannot."

"All of us realize what you refuse to see," Jonathan said, anger dripping from his words. "These are God's men. If you touch them, you will deal with God's swift hand of judgment."

I paced back and forth. The voices did not relent.

Ahimelech kept his head high, staring right at me. Not afraid. That drove me into a frenzy. No one was afraid of me anymore! "Where is that shepherd? Where is Doeg?"

Doeg stepped out from the outskirts of the assembled group. "Yes, my lord?"

"Kill them. Obey your king at once!"

Doeg briefly hesitated as he searched the faces of those around him. Then he walked toward me, hesitating briefly. I handed him a sword. Jonathan grabbed Doeg's arm. "Do not do this."

"Obey your king!" I shouted.

Any hesitation immediately left Doeg's countenance, and without another breath, turned and sank the sword deep into Ahimelech's chest.

I heard the collective gasp, but I was not giving any attention to it. I kept my eyes on Ahimelech and watched. Watched as the old priest fell to the ground in a heap. Then I watched as Doeg obeyed the rest of my command. I watched as priest after priest met their bloody end.

The darkness within me approved, but I felt a chill run up my spine that I did not like.

"There," I said, after it was done. I forced myself to ignore the trepidation that came on me suddenly. "Let us see who sides with the traitor now."

But other than the murderous Doeg, no one had stayed around to hear me.

20

CRBO

Michal

Paltiel's Home on the outskirts of Gallim
1018 B.C.

"This is where I wait for him," I said to Dinah, taking a seat on the same rock. This time I made room for Dinah to sit beside me. "It gives me full view of both paths, so I can see when he comes back to me. And he will. I do not believe what either Merab or Paltiel says. David finds a way."

I studied her for a moment. She had once again resorted to no eye contact. But now, out in the open, I began to see that it might not be anger at me that caused this disconnect. Dinah acted guilty. The more I watched her, the more she squirmed.

"You are different," I said. "I cannot imagine what you endured."

Dinah looked everywhere but at me.

"What aren't you telling me?" I asked, only to stop myself. She could no longer speak. And she did not know how to read or write. Slaves did not need that training. "Can you tell me with your hands? Make motions."

Dinah gave no response.

"You were traumatized, and I wish I could change it all. Does it feel strange? Not having a tongue there?" I paused as the sound of pounding hooves hit my ears. I turned my attention back to the paths and saw a group of men on horses traveling from a distance to Paltiel's home. "David?" I whispered, but the thought was fleeting. Israel's banners waved in the wind. "What are father's men doing here?"

Dinah stood up fast and frantically looked around as if searching for a place to hide.

"They are not coming for you," I said, trying to calm her down. "They are probably checking on me."

Suddenly she turned to me and placed her hand over my mouth. "Listen, and do not ask questions," she said forcefully.

I let out a muffled cry. "You can talk?" I asked with her hand still over my mouth. Then I furrowed my eyebrows in anger. "You can talk?" I tried again.

"Shh. It was Merab's idea. She said the less you knew, the better. But I do not see how to keep it from you. Especially now. They must be coming for me."

I tried to ask how, but her hand was securely pressed against my mouth. "I...escaped. Rizpah got the king to give me to her, and then she set me free. If his men find out that I am here, I vowed that I would not implicate her...or Merab." She moved her hand.

"You..."

"Yes."

"...can talk?"

"Yes."

"He did not cut out..."

"No. Thank the gods for Rizpah. She had already arranged this with the king, but he wanted to torment you and make you feel that I would be punished. But I am supposed to be in service to Rizpah. If he found out that I am not there, she said that she would feign innocence. Merab vowed the same thing."

"We can hide you," I said, trying to find a spot. "Just hide within the vines out here in the fields. It is a maze to get through."

"That is why I told you. I could not have you mention that I am here without you understanding the risk."

"I will say nothing."

"Let us hope that these men are here for other reasons."

"Most likely they are." I went to leave. "Stay close by while I go and investigate." Pausing, I added, "And when these men leave, we are going to discuss everything that happened."

"I promise," she said, before going in the opposite direction amidst the thick foliage of the field.

I ran down the path that led to the house. My body still felt weak, but I needed to arrive to find out any new information. So, I pushed myself to move though my muscles screamed in fatigue.

As soon as I entered the west-facing veranda, I heard my father's voice. "Where is my daughter?"

"She...She is out on her daily stroll, my king," Paltiel's voice shook.

"A daily stroll? You allow her to do that?"

"Yes, my lord. Fresh air and exercise are invigorating. I find her moods improve greatly."

"She is still in a sour disposition?"

"She misses David greatly..."

"Do not say his name!"

"My apologies."

I watched from behind a pillar as Paltiel lay prostrate in front of my father.

"Any sign that the treacherous shepherd has sought contact with her?"

"No, my lord."

"Stand up!" my father bellowed. "Address me face-to-face!"

Paltiel stood but kept his head bowed.

"Do you speak truth? If you harbor deceit about the traitor's whereabouts, I will slice you open immediately."

"N...N...No...sir, no, no, he has not...nothing. And Michal has been laid up for several days. She has neither seen nor heard from him."

I heard the soldier approach from behind me, but I had no time to move. "Your presence is required of the king." He grabbed my arm and led me into the open room. "The princess, sir."

My father turned to me, his expression full of contempt. I glared at the man I once admired and loved as my father and had to keep my fury in check.

"Will you not greet me, daughter?"

I paused and swallowed back the angry response. "Greetings, father."

"Aw, so no more pretending that you love me? It is for the best, I suppose."

The words came out of my mouth before I could stop them. "There was once a time I honored and loved you, but that was before—"

"Before what?" he asked and moved toward me. "Before that traitor tricked you!"

"No, David never tricked me. He never said an unkind word about you. Not even when you sought to kill him."

"Do not say his name!" Father's hand moved so fast, I barely registered the slap until the pain exploded across my face. I yelped and tried to move away from him. "Do not step away from me," he said. "Face me in your pride, daughter. Face me, and let me hit you again."

But I could barely understand the words because the pain had yet to subside. Mother hit me once when she discovered my love of David, but it was nothing compared to this. The force behind father's hand had the power of a warrior behind it. It reminded me of my David and the terrible abuses he suffered by the hand of his father. For some reason, that thought brought me comfort.

"FACE ME, you treacherous daughter!" he grabbed me and turned me to him.

Though my eyesight blurred from the tears, I set my gaze upon my father.

"You are to forget him, immediately," he seethed. "If you mention him in any way, it will be reported to me, and you will suffer swiftly. Paltiel has full authority to confine you for misbehavior or punish you in any way he deems fit."

I said nothing. I nearly told him how I would always love David, and that was something the king could never take from me. But I knew that inciting his wrath even more would be too much, and he may punish Paltiel and his whole household.

He released me. "I was notified that you have yet to fulfill your duties as wife. Do you deny it?"

My mind spun in several directions, not quite landing on one answer. The first thought was horror and betrayal at Paltiel for breaking his word. The next was fear that I would be forced to consummate the union in front of my father. I had yet to fully heal down below, and I would rather die a thousand deaths for my father to humiliate me in such a way. But what answer could I give? I did not know what exactly Paltiel said to betray me. "I was sick these past months. Paltiel, being the gracious husband, has allowed me time to heal and become well. But it was not out of defiance to the king."

"You are not sick," he said. "You lie."

"Ask Paltiel," I said. "He will tell you I speak in truth."

My father looked over at Paltiel who I noticed watched the scene with a mix of horror and fear upon his face. "Speak."

"Wh-Wh-What she says is true. She was sick and with child. I abstained to—"

"Stop." My father turned back to me. "With child?"

My gaze dropped. I did not want to think of the child that I would never hold in my arms.

"The infant died," Paltiel said. "And Michal lost a lot of blood. She has been on bed rest until just recently."

"The traitorous shepherd's child is dead," my father said the words in triumph. "God be praised! He does not have an heir!"

What father would rejoice in his future grandchild's death? The tears poured down my face, as I muffled my sobs. In that moment, I felt the dark feelings of hate creep into my soul.

"I order you to consummate the marriage and produce an heir," my father said to Paltiel. "Failure to do so will result in death."

154

To me, he added, "When you are tainted with Paltiel's child, let us see if David would ever want you again." He left the room, and his men followed.

No one in the room moved until the sounds of the horses were out of earshot. Paltiel released his servants before approaching me. "I said nothing," he said. "I swear to it. I do not know how he…someone here must have informed him."

I said nothing. I did not believe him. "It worked out in your favor, did it not?"

"I do not find this situation *favorable*," he said, a flash of anger shot across his countenance. "Being in the midst of the royal family feud is not favorable. Regardless of what you think, princess, I do have a life. I have property and a family already in place." His voice rose. "As I have already stated, my actions in previous years may have been selfish and underhanded, but I have tried to honor your commitment to David. And whether or not you believe me, the king did not hear about our lack of intimacy from me. Now, if you excuse me, I have work to do."

With Paltiel gone, my strength gave out, and I fell to the floor in a heap, sobbing from frustration and righteous anger. My father had me trapped, a prisoner to his will. Even if David lived through my father's pursuits, he would never be welcomed back into the country with my father in power. And by the time father died, I would already be Paltiel's claimed woman. And with that thought, the last trace of hope of David coming back for me faded into a bitter memory.

21

ᚳᚹᛖᚩ

David

A Secluded Alcove of the Judean Mountains
1018 B.C.

"David, get up. You have people here to greet you."

The voice startled me out of my sleep. I fumbled for my weapon.

"A little too late for that, don't you think?" Jashobeam said without humor. "I would have already had you filleted by now."

I rubbed my face and groaned. I had a massive headache. "I heard you approach." I threw my tunic on.

"Do not lie. It does not look good on you. And what is this?" Jashobeam kicked at the goblet and emptied wineskins.

I didn't have to open my eyes to sense Jashobeam's displeasure. But I was in no mood for it. "What does it look like?" I snapped. "I would have drunk more if I had had more supplies." Anything to take away the loneliness. Anything to dull the pain of heartache. It had been nearly half a year since I saw Michal. Full moons since I touched her soft skin and took in her scent. When I was sent on previous missions, I was also gone for months, but this time I knew that there was no going home.

Suddenly cold water came crashing down my head, and I jumped up ready to fight. I extended the sword, pointing it at Jashobeam. "Do not ever do that again."

"There," Jashobeam said, pointing his finger back at me. "There he is. I wondered what that spineless drunk had done with him."

We stared each other down.

"You are the one who dropped me off here," I said with bitterness. "So, leave me alone. Have a nice life with your family."

"Were you not the one who said this cave was your hiding place? To leave you here while we assess the situation in Gibeah?"

I *had* said that. Even though Eleazar and Jashobeam told me that I did not have to hide. That there were plenty of men who would gladly fight alongside me. But fighting led to death, and I was not too sure if I even knew what I was fighting for anymore.

"What do you expect to do? Hide until Saul dies?"

"No, I--" I could not find the words to say what I was feeling.

"Do you want us to retrieve your wife? Say the word. You will have Michal by sundown."

My heart screamed 'YES.' But I knew, just as Jashobeam did, that there would be an ambush waiting for us. King Saul wanted me to go see my wife. "It would be a blood bath."

"Then let us kill the king. The way I see it, you are choosing his life over your marriage."

"What did you say?"

"You heard me! This ends when King Saul is dead."

"I swore an oath to God. I will not...I cannot...violate that oath."

"Then you have made your decision. No need to hide in a cave and stay drunk. We have work to do. We need to continue to scout for safe ground. Your numbers continue to grow. We also need supplies and money. King Saul is no longer going to provide for your troops with you being the wanted enemy."

Once again, I felt the deep rush of despair overtake me. If only God would release me to end this conflict now. But my oath to Yahweh mattered most. Who would I be without integrity? I observed first-hand what happens when God removes His hand from a king. I could not let that happen to me. But I could not lie to myself and act as if I was not angry with the predicament. I asked God many times over the course of these long months to bring my wife to me. He stayed silent.

"Who did you bring with you?" I picked up my cloak, as rolled-up parchment fell to the ground. I went to retrieve it, but Jashobeam was faster.

"What is this?"

"More writings."

Jashobeam read from one, "*How long wilt thou forget me, O Lord? Forever? How long wilt thou hide thy face from me? How long shalt I take counsel in my soul, having sorrow in my heart daily? How long shalt mine enemy be exalted over me?*"* Jashobeam looked up with raised eyebrows.

"That one is not done yet."

Jashobeam studied another. "*I cried unto the LORD with my voice; with my voice unto the LORD did I make my supplication. I poured out my complaint before him; I shewed before him my trouble...*"*

I continued the poem while Jashobeam listened, "*When my spirit was overwhelmed within me, then thou knewest my path. In the way wherein I walked have they privily laid a snare for me. I looked on my right hand, and beheld, but there was no man that would know me: refuge failed me; no man cared for my soul. I cried unto thee, O LORD: I said, Thou art my refuge and my portion in the land of the living. Attend unto my cry; for I am brought very low: deliver me from my persecutors; for they are stronger than I. Bring my soul out of prison, that I may praise thy name: the righteous shall compass me about; for thou shalt deal bountifully with me.*" I paused. "See what happens when I am left in a cave all by myself? I write poetry and get drunk."

Jashobeam studied me for what seemed like a great length of time. "Do you believe yourself to be the next king of Israel?"

Now I was the one to laugh humorlessly. "Look at me! I am hiding in a cave, Jashobeam! Saul has stripped me of my wife and has left me without a home or country."

"You did not answer the question. Do you believe yourself to be the next king of Israel?"

I did not answer at first. Years earlier I would have said yes without hesitation. "I don't know," I said simply.

"Well, I do," Jashobeam stepped forward until he was face-to-face with me. "As do those that are outside this cave right now, as we speak. As does the current king of Israel, which is why he is pursuing you. *You* are the next anointed king of Israel. And I cannot claim to know as much about God as others, but I know that He would not want you hiding in a cave. He would want you fighting. Not necessarily with a sword, but out for all to see. That you are not guilty of Saul's accusations. That you are worthy of the kingship. It is time you gave Israel and Judah back their hero. And that is you."

"I do not want any more people getting hurt because of me."

Jashobeam shoved me hard. "Stop that! With life comes death. I would rather fight beside God's anointed than lay comfortable in my bed. As would many others. So, stop making excuses to cover the fact that you are scared. You are scared and hurt and betrayed. But you have got to shake it off and keep fighting. Consider Saul your next Goliath."

"I am not going to kill him. It is not my place."

"We can talk about that later, but that is not what I am referring to, and you know it. Where is the David that killed Goliath with a sling and a stone? Find him, and then come outside. Your parents are here, as are soldiers ready to serve under you."

"My parents?" I called to Jashobeam as he went to leave.

"Yes, David. They are without a home. Saul burned everything of theirs to the ground. You would have known that had you not run away. Oh, and Abiathar, son of the high priest, Ahimelech, is here for you. He is quite shaken."

"Oh, no." My heart dropped.

"You should probably know that Saul had every one of the priests of Nob murdered, along with their families. Murdered by a shepherd named Doeg because no one else would do it. We need to avenge their deaths. So, get out of your funk and make it quick. You have to tend to important business matters."

I watched Jashobeam exit the cave and felt as if the air had been sucked out of my lungs. My parents were homeless? How long had that been? And the priests of Nob? Ahimelech? I thought of the young priest who had first welcomed me into the sanctuary. My heart broke for those innocent holy men and their families. Had Saul no scruples? No conscience? Slowly the flame of righteous fury began to gain in strength inside me. "Doeg," I whispered in disgust. I had known that Doeg would inform the king, but I did not expect Saul to lay a hand on the priests.

I poured water in a bowl and washed my face, refreshing myself. All the while, my insides burned. When I stepped out of the cave and into the light of day, I knew that the days of acting like a madman and hiding in a cave were over. Too much time had already been wasted. I, the giant slayer, was ready to fight.

***

"Where have you been?" Shammah asked me, once I had made my way over to him. Shammah had walked ahead of the others, allowing a few minutes with me to himself.

"Gath," I replied, setting my hand on the sword of Goliath resting beside me. Shammah opened his mouth in what appeared to be the start of a tirade. "Yes, I know I should have told you. Yes, I know that I could have died. Yes, I know that if I ever do that again you will string me by my toenails."

After a pause, Shammah stepped closer and said, "You worried more than just me, brother." He glanced behind him. "You have family to think about. I know that your relationship with most of them has been rough and distant, but they are worried and are in need of help."

"I *was* thinking of them. I thought if I distanced myself then my family would be safe. I was wrong, and I am sorry." Quietly, I

160

added, "I was not thinking too clearly. I have been grief-stricken."

"As have we," Shammah said. "You are not the only one who has suffered a loss. Everything is gone. Our father's home no longer stands. The rest of the stables burned to the ground."

My heart continued to be smashed to pieces. How much had I missed while on the run? And even when I tried to protect people, like the priests at Nob and my father, horrible results occurred. The guilt that had bothered me after Eleazar and Jashobeam's chastisement now weighed even heavier upon me. I wondered what I had been thinking the day I decided to leave everything behind and hide from Saul.

I nodded still unable to put into words the remorse I felt at making such an unwise decision.

Shammah's hand rested on my shoulder. "I am sorry about what happened with the princess. I would be insulted and betrayed, as well."

"Thank you. It is not only that," I confessed. "I just…I miss her. And when you informed me that she was with child but that the infant died, I did not know how to handle my grief."

"When you become king, you will go and get her back."

I looked up and studied my brother's face. Shammah's face had hardened, his eyes clouding over. And then I knew. I understood that my entire family felt just as angry, just as betrayed. The injustices done to me had been felt by all those connected with me. It no longer mattered that my older brothers had treated me unkindly or that my father never demonstrated any affection. At this moment, my family stood with me. I hugged Shammah. "Thank you, my brother."

Now as I studied the scene before me, tents had begun being pitched all across the ledge of the mountain and scattered among the valley just below us. The animals had been shuffled into make-shift pens and fences along the valley, as well. But how long before Saul or any of his men found us? "This will not do for long." I spotted soldiers with their families. "Why did these men bring their wives

161

and children?"

"Because they have sided with you. Some have secured their families at different locations. Most did not want to leave their wives and children to deal with King Saul."

"Then we will need to find a safer location. Soon. How many men have left Saul's ranks to join with me?"

"Last count was about 400, but they are not all here yet."

"Who are 'they'? And why do they know to come here?"

"Hebrew soldiers," Jashobeam said, interrupting the conversation. Eleazar was with him. "Many served under you when you were over a thousand troops. Many were treated badly by Saul or simply have stronger loyalties to the giant slayer."

"Not all of Israel sides with Saul," Shammah said. "You would have known that if you would not have run away."

"Yes, I understand. I was wrong. You all are right. It is not going to happen again."

Uriah ran up to us. "I thought it was you!" he kissed me on one cheek and then the other. "God be with you. I am glad you are all right. I would rough you up a bit for leaving us, but I know my comrades have probably done a fair job, so I will not pounce."

"Beat on him," Eleazar said grimly. "He deserves it."

I turned to my friend. Eleazar still acted upset about the injury he received when we snuck back into Gath to retrieve Goliath's sword. I said, "I told you I would go in by myself."

Eleazar rolled his eyes. "Shut up."

Eleazar showed Shammah and Uriah where a Philistine's spear sliced through the top layer of skin on his upper arm. "Guess who hid Goliath's sword right under the Philistines' noses?"

"You got a little scratch. You will be fine."

"You got to fight some Philistines?" Uriah asked. "Not fair."

I saw my family walking toward us. Once again, I felt the guilt rise within me at running away and leaving them in the hands of a vengeful king. "Excuse me for a moment. I need to greet my father."

162

Shammah and I walked the rest of the distance to Jesse. Jesse's children flanked him on both sides. "Greetings, father," I said, as I approached Jesse. I kissed both Jesse's cheeks.

"We have nothing," Jesse said in greeting.

Before I could answer him, Eliab, who stood beside father, said, "Praise Yahweh, you are alive and well."

"Yes, and I am glad to see you in good health, too." I greeted Eliab and my other brothers and sisters, suddenly awkward over this change of dynamics. I forced myself not to think of the years of abuse and isolation I endured. None of that mattered anymore. Here, at this moment, it was clear that my family sided with me.

"Your brothers and kin extend unto you our service," Eliab said. "However, we should probably seek safety for our father."

"Of course," I said, getting emotional that my eldest brother, a strong soldier in his own might, would of his own accord join the rebellion.

Zeruiah, one of my older sisters, added, "My sons, Joab, Abishai, and Asahel want nothing more than to fight alongside their uncle and ally."

Joab, close in age to me, stepped forward and greeted me with a kiss before bowing. "I'm at your service, uncle." Abishai and Asahel followed.

I was impressed. The young men stood as tall as me with broad shoulders and strong bodies. "I am humbled, nephews," I answered. To all my family, I said, "I am humbled that all of you are here to support me. My heart is overwhelmed." I could no longer contain the emotion. "I will see to it that our parents and our families are safe. And when I become king--" I noticed that soldiers had also gathered around. Jashobeam watched me, a small smile on his face, and nodded to continue. "When I become king, that which was lost will be restored and then some. Yahweh will not forget those of you who have chosen to leave the familiar and side with the leader of a supposed rebellion. But through all of this, let no sin be committed of us. We will fight to protect God's decree, and we will fight to protect Israel from its enemies."

The soldiers shouted, as did the men of my family, and their shouts fueled my spirit. And this time, I believed my words.

22

❦

David

A Secluded Alcove of the Judean Mountains
1018 B.C.

Jashobeam, Eleazar, and Shammah, along with several other loyal men, including my nephews, sat outside the cave, surrounding me. I stood at the fire and watched it as if the answer we debated would leap from the flames.

"The Philistines are pressing in. They are already capturing some of the outlying villages," Uriah said. "We need to protect the people."

"Not to mention, they probably have a good idea that you were hiding right under their noses," Eleazar added.

"Saul is too busy chasing you to defend the land," Uriah continued.

"I agree, Uriah, but I feel an urgency to keep moving," I said. "My family needs to be taken somewhere Saul cannot harm them. They are my first priority."

"Where are you thinking?" Jashobeam asked.

"Let us head toward Mizpeh. Surely I can persuade the Moabites' king to offer sanctuary to my family."

"Especially if you offer him an alliance."

The sound of quick movement made all the men turn toward it. A young soldier stationed at one of the posts came running toward us. "Excuse me for the interruption, but there is a soldier of Saul's that is newly arrived that asks to speak to you." He looked right at me. "He is being very persistent. He says he comes in peace."

All the men stood up and flanked me. "His name?"

"Benaiah."

"Benaiah?" I repeated, surprised. "What brings him here?" I remembered my friend from my days at the palace. Much of my training came through him.

"He only says that he needs to speak with you and that he comes alone and in peace."

"Bring him to me."

"Abner's right-hand man?" Jashobeam asked while the young soldier went to retrieve Benaiah.

"Yes, but we have history. He is a fierce soldier. Taught me a lot."

"Let us hope he truly comes in peace," Joab, my nephew, said.

"I am sure he does. If he is alone, there is a reason for it." I saw Benaiah approach cautiously, so I walked toward him to close the distance. "Benaiah, my friend. Is it true you come in peace?"

"Of course, my king." Benaiah bowed low. "If you will forgive me of my past actions."

"Enough of that," I said. "We are old friends. No need for formality."

Benaiah stood upright and smiled. Then the two of us greeted each other warmly, throwing our arms around each other and kissing each cheek. "Let me look at you," Benaiah said, stepping back. "You have gotten uglier, my friend."

"Do not make me challenge you to a fight."

"The years have not been kind to me either," Benaiah said.

I saw enough of his features to agree with him, but I kept that assessment to myself. "Have you been on the front lines?"

"No, I have left the army and now have a price on my head. Saul threw me in the weapons tent for refusing to find and kill you."

"The weapons tent?" I grimaced, remembering the horror of working in such a filthy tent. "That is quite the demotion. How long have you endured it?"

"Over a year. I thought of nothing else these several moons than of joining your ranks, but I had to wait for the right moment. I have been heavily watched."

"This past year has not been good to me either," I said. "You may be choosing one nightmare over another."

Benaiah adamantly shook his head. "Fighting for Israel's next king is an honor, and I swear my loyalty to you, should you give me a chance to serve."

"Let me bring you to my men. They will have many questions." I brought Benaiah over to the men still standing around the fire and made introductions.

"A Saul deserter?" Jashobeam asked.

"Yes, sir," Benaiah answered. "I hung around too long as it was, but after Saul made it clear what his intentions were with David, I could not be there anymore. Saul demoted or threw out anyone who had had anything to do with David. Since I trained him, so that meant me."

"So, desperation brought you here? How do we know you will not run back and give your commander, Abner, information?" Shammah's jaw set in a grim line.

"How do you know anything until a person is put to the test? I am willing to be put to the test, to prove my loyalty to my friend. David knows that I have every reason to hate Saul, and I hate him even more because of what happened with Michal." Benaiah turned to me. "I am sorry for what happened. No man deserves to have his wife stolen from him."

I nodded, not wanting to talk about it.

Benaiah filled in the silence by saying, "Saul has lost his mind. He has done the unthinkable." He shook his head. "All those priests."

"We will avenge Ahimelech and his family. One of his sons escaped, and we have offered him refuge. More than that, God will not let Saul's actions go without punishment." I then said, "Let us call it a night. We leave at daybreak."

The men dispersed, Shammah offering Benaiah a place to sleep outside his tent. I knew it was more than likely to keep a watch on the newly admitted soldier, but Benaiah seemed fine to oblige.

"Hey," Eleazar said, while I listened to Shammah give Benaiah one threat after another.

Now I turned to Eleazar. "Yes?"

Eleazar bit his lip and pulled on his beard, suddenly acting unsure about something.

"What?" I turned so that Eleazar had my full attention.

"There's someone I want you to meet."

"Why didn't you bring him up here and introduce him? Besides, I trust you implicitly. If you think he is loyal, then I will not question it."

"No…no," Eleazar gathered a deep breath. "It is a woman. A young woman, actually. Very beautiful. Very kind. Soft-spoken. She would make a great wife."

My eyes widened. "Why would you think I need a wife? I have one."

"First of all, you are the next king of Israel. You are going to inherit all of Saul's concubines. Plus, the king needs to have many children. You know that. You are already close to 25. You have no children."

"Thanks for pointing that out," I said bitterly.

"You can have more than one wife. You know this. As long as Saul is alive, Michal is off-limits."

"Thanks for pointing *that* out, as well."

Eleazar set his mouth in a deep frown, acting more annoyed and talking very fast. "Her name is Ahinoam. From Jezreel. She is healthy and would be a good match. I have already talked to her father and to her. She has eagerly agreed to marry the hero of Israel. The family is noble with a vast amount of needed animals and supplies. It would be a blessing for our men to have such supplies. All you have to do is sign the ketubbah, which I will deliver, along

168

with your payment. After we secure your parents at Mizpeh, you can attend to her."

I stared out into the darkness. Flames from fires were scattered across the landscape. I sighed and rubbed my face. It would be a lie if I said I was not lonely or that I did not desire physical contact. But the thought of it felt like betrayal. I promised Michal I would come for her.

As if reading my thoughts, Eleazar said, "You do not know how long you will be away from her. And she has already married again."

"It is not legal or binding, and you know it."

"Listen, I am telling you this as your oldest friend. It is good for a man to have a wife. I am not saying that you cannot go retrieve Michal, but that is an unknown. As long as you are refusing to fight Saul face-to-face, Michal can no longer be yours. What we do know is that there is fair virgin who is more than willing to marry the giant slayer. And all of your men will benefit from such a strong union with a wealthy family. Think about it." Eleazar pushed parchment paper against my chest. "Sign the ketubbah, and I will see to it that it gets to her."

I looked down at the words of the marriage contract. I remembered when I signed the one for Michal. Suddenly, I became angry. Why did she have to go and get married again? Didn't she fight for me? Without another thought, I signed it and handed it to Eleazar. "Tell her family I will present myself after I secure my parents."

"Done." Eleazar rolled up the contract and tucked it away.

"Oh, and Eleazar?"

He looked up. "What?"

"She better not be trouble."

"She is not, my friend. Trust me, she is a good match." He left me standing outside the cave.

My insides flipped as I thought of marriage with another woman, and the intimacy that would be shared. Not from nerves or excitement, but from knowing how betrayed Michal would be when she found out. And in the darkness of the night, I found myself grieving again over what had been taken away from me.

23

⊰⊱

King Saul

The Palace at Gibeah
1017 B.C.

I leaned against a wall and only partly listened to Abner.

"If we do not act immediately, the Philistines will continue to advance against us. It's time we set our priorities straight."

"How are our priorities not straight?" I asked, catching Abner's last words. "Is it better to hand over the kingdom to outsiders while allowing mutiny to occur within our own walls?"

"But David is not acting as a threat at this point. When he does, we will act quickly," Abner added.

"Where are my sons?"

"Jonathan and Ishvi are setting up garrisons in affected or near affected regions."

I had not seen either of my sons since I ordered Doeg to kill Ahimelech months ago. Their anger, especially Ishvi's, should have been subsided by now. Neither of my sons understood that every decision I made centered on my lineage possessing the throne. If David had been captured and killed by now, it would have helped, but no. He was like a rat missing every trap laid out before him.

"We need reinforcements surrounding Bethlehem," Abner stated.

"I hate Bethlehem."

Abner looked up from his maps. "Bethlehem provides us many benefits."

I made a face. "I still hate it."

Enos entered the room. "Your daughter arrived."

I made another face. "Another nuisance. Send her to my outside chamber." To Abner, I said, "Get the reinforcements ready. We leave at daybreak."

Abner seemed pleased. "Very good."

I left the strategy room and marched down the halls toward my outside chamber. When I entered, Merab stood observing the view of the gardens. She turned, her protruding belly out-of-place on her petite frame. She appeared disheveled with dark circles under her eyes and her hair slightly unkempt. "Daughter. You may approach."

She waddled over, kissing both my cheeks. "Father. It is an honor to see you and a privilege to serve you."

"Are you unwell?" I asked.

"I am as to be expected," she said flatly. "I am married and pregnant. Again."

"Fulfilling your duties. One baby right after another shows fertility. There is nothing wrong with that."

Merab's face stayed expressionless. "You summoned me?"

"Michal has not fulfilled her duties as Paltiel's wife. Did you know this?"

"My sister is already married, and that marriage is still binding until death. I am sure that it is conflicting to both she and Paltiel."

"She is not married. I nullified the previous contract." I felt the irritation turn to anger. "She is forcing my hand. It has been several moons since I visited her, and I have yet to receive word from either Paltiel or my daughter. If I must make another trip to Gallim, they will both be sorry."

"Father, if I may speak freely?"

I grumbled to myself about wanting anything but that, still, I nodded my assent.

"It has not been enough time. Michal's body, even if she is

172

with child, may take another couple moons before producing evidence."

"You are to update me at the start of each new moon. I want to know everything." When Merab hesitated, I continued, "You will do this by order of your king. I know she trusts you."

"And you are asking me to break her trust. My beloved sister?"

"Loyalty to your king—to your father—comes first."

Merab stayed silent. Her expression did not disguise her displeasure.

Commotion from the hall distracted me. I heard Enos calling for me, "King! King Saul!" He ran past the two pillars that led to the outside chamber. "King Saul!" He panted and bowed low. "You are urgently needed. A visitor…"

"Whoever it is can wait. I will be rushed by no one."

"Samuel."

Any comeback halted on my tongue. Words escaped me. I immediately felt panic and fear.

"The prophet. He. Is. Here."

More servants rushed into the area, awaiting my command. They all acted nervous. They knew, as well as I did, that the prophet refused to visit me. Even when I tried to visit him in Ramah, he would never see me. But that was not why everyone acted fearful. They felt the judgment upon my house. Just as I did. "What are you standing here for?" I bellowed. "Attend to the priest!" I left Merab and moved quickly. "Where?"

"He has not moved from the entryway."

As I traveled down the stairs and through the halls, I could not shake the trepidation. I thought of my rash actions with the priests of Nob and immediately felt the guilt of what I did. I stopped in the middle of the hall, unwilling to move. "What does he want?" I whispered fiercely to Enos. "What did he say?"

"Nothing. Only to see you."

I swallowed back the nausea.

173

"This is what you have waited for. Years have come and gone and now the prophet returns. It is to bring you a blessing. He would not travel all this way for any other reason."

I watched Enos's face and could see that his words did not match the fear in his eyes. "You lie."

"What other chance will you have? Go to him. Persuade him."

Persuade him. Yes. I closed my eyes and sought the voices. Those dark voices that plague me night and day. But they were eerily quiet.

I mentally shook myself and moved forward. I was king. I feared nothing and no one, or so I told myself until I saw Samuel at the thick, double doors of the main entryway. He leaned heavily on his walking staff, his white hair and beard wild and unruly, but his eyes were sharp and landed upon me immediately.

Abner stood beside the prophet and appeared grim.

"Samuel." I greeted him ceremonially. "We must celebrate your return to my home."

"You killed them." Samuel stood at least a head shorter, but at the moment, seemed to tower over me. "The priests of Nob."

"They…" I glanced around to my people. Surely someone would help me explain. But no one made eye contact. "They…insulted their king by helping a traitor…and they were deceitful and kept it from me."

"You killed them," Samuel repeated. "And you will die for it."

"No," I said, fighting against agitation. "No, I will not die for it. I refuse."

"You cannot refuse death. It comes for you."

"Then speak life," I pleaded. "I have waited nearly two decades for a word from you. You speak to that glorified shepherd, but not me? Please. Lead me straight. Show me the way." I knelt before him, desiring to shake him until he blessed me.

"You are wasting your time pursuing the one destined for the

174

throne."

"I HAVE THE THRONE!" I yelled at the prophet so loudly that the words echoed in the entryway. "It is MINE."

"God has anointed another."

"No! God anointed me! I am the anointed king of Israel! Not some shepherd!"

"You cannot stop what God has ordained." Samuel leaned closer, fury behind his eyes. "And because of your evil actions against the priests and their families, not only will you die, but your sons also. Your eldest son will never take the throne."

Samuel turned and moved toward the doors. Attendants opened them and led him out.

"You do not have the last word!" I shouted, standing to my feet. "I have the last word! I am KING!"

A messenger ran past the prophet and his entourage, bowing briefly, before continuing his run through the doors. "Commander?" he panted, bowing to Abner. "Imperative news from Keilah."

I barely listened anymore. I only stared at the now closed doors, as if their slamming shut only sealed my fate.

Abner approached me. "We must move. The Philistines have invaded Keilah."

My heart pounded, as the prophet's words replayed in my head. "NO!" I shouted, pressing my hands to my temples. "I will NOT die!"

"Saul?"

"Bring him back!" I ordered Abner. I threw open the doors again and stormed out.

"Saul!" Abner jumped in front of me and faced me down. "Listen to me!"

"Did you hear him? Did you hear what he said?" I asked. "You must force him to come back and give me a blessing."

"That is what I am trying to tell you! A blessing has come from an unexpected place. The Philistines have invaded Keilah."

"Do we not have military posts there?"

"Not enough. They have been overtaken."

"How is this a blessing?" I could not muster enough emotion to care. I shouted at Samuel's carriage as it moved away. "I will NOT die!" Without another glance at Abner, I headed back inside and past the entry area. No one made a sound. I heard Abner call for me, but I did not stop.

Samuel said I would die. And that Jonathan would never take the throne. Fine. I had other sons. I could not decide to be furious or filled with anguish. So far, everything the prophet foretold had come to pass.

"Saul!"

I stopped but did not turn around. "Do not dare to call me so informally, Abner. I do not care of our past. The whole palace already questions their king."

"You are not listening, sir. I had to get your attention."

"Do what you must. Do not bore me with details."

"You are not listening," he said again. This time he walked in front of me and faced me again. "Our soldiers were overtaken in Keilah."

"Do what you must," I repeated. "Just leave me be."

"The Philistines were defeated."

"Then why bother me?"

"Because David is there with his troops. Victory came by his hand."

My left eye began to twitch. The darkness that had kept silent with the prophet now hissed in dissatisfaction.

"David and his men completely destroyed the Philistines and saved Keilah and its threshing floors."

"Why do you say his name?" Fury began to overtake the anguish. If Abner said his name one more time…

"They are still there." Abner raised his eyebrows, seeing that he got my attention. "The runaway and his men are trapped inside the city's walls and locked within its gates. The townspeople favor their king and are awaiting your arrival."

176

The magnitude of the news hit me like rain after a drought. "He is trapped."

"Yes. This is your moment."

I sighed in relief and drank in heaping gulps of air. "I will not die, Abner. I do not care any longer about that prophet. He forsook me years ago."

"Let us pay David a visit. And secure your throne."

Thinking of the prophet's words, I added, "The only one dying today is that traitorous son-of-Jesse." But even as I said the words, I already doubted their truth.

24

०३४०

David

Within the Walls of Keilah
1017 B.C.

"Where is the ephod?" I asked, trying to keep calm. The men warned me not to get involved with the city of Keilah. They said that we were not entirely safe in Judah. I agreed, but we needed supplies. I took a risk that the people still favored their hero. I reasoned that if we protected them from the surprise Philistine attack, that we would secure their allegiance. I was wrong.

"With the priest," Jashobeam said. To Joab, he continued, "Go, get Abiathar, and tell him to bring the ephod."

Joab glanced over at me. "Uncle?"

"Do you question me?" Jashobeam asked.

"It is an odd request. We are stuck within Keilah's walls and…"

"Get Abiathar," I said to Joab. "He has the ephod. And Jashobeam is your commander. Follow his directives."

Joab looked from me to Jashobeam. "Yes, uncle."

"If we get out of here alive, I am going to strangle that kid."

"He has a lot to learn," I admitted, but I could not focus on my nephew at the moment. "Let us just worry about making it out of Keilah."

"We will escape," Jashobeam answered. "If you can escape the city of Gath, then you can figure out a way to escape here."

"The difference is that I have 400 men with me here. It

makes it hard to hide or sneak out." I shook my head as if trying to get the bitterness out of it. "Who would inform the king? Especially after we saved the people from the Philistines?"

"I have told you repeatedly that people's hearts are fickle. They want security and will sell their souls to the highest bidder to get it. Do not take it to heart."

"I do take it to heart. These are my people. If they do not side with me now when I need them, then I will not have much use for them when I am king." The words sounded juvenile, but my mood had turned foul at the thought of the people of Keilah betraying those who protected them.

"King Saul has lost his mind," Jashobeam said. "The people are scared. Most here still favor you. There will always be one who is underhanded and searching for favors, but you cannot punish the masses for the one."

"We should have left yesterday. Before night fell. I was greedy, thinking only about the supplies."

"You were not greedy, David. We do need supplies. We are all living as outlaws, which means every bit of grain and every animal offered to us are commodities. We are well stocked now."

"What good is being well-stocked when we are dead?"

Abiathar entered and bowed. "I have the ephod, and I have sought the Lord."

"Leave us," I said to Jashobeam. "Tell the troops to await my command."

Ever since Abiathar found us after his family had been slaughtered by Doeg, we had formed a strong bond. We were close in age, and he reminded me somewhat of Jonathan. Ever loyal and fiercely protective. Although he could not protect me with sword, I felt comforted that he protected me with prayer.

"The Lord said to help the people of Keilah and attack the Philistines," I said.

"And just as He said, the Philistines were defeated, and the people are saved."

179

"Yet here we are. We received word that Saul is on his way, and we are trapped within these walls. I need guidance."

"Yes, what you heard is true. Saul is in pursuit."

"So, the people here are planning to hand me over to Saul?"

"Yes. We need to leave now."

"We are trapped on all sides." I fell on my knees and with Abiathar and the ephod sought guidance from the Lord.

Shammah came running up to us. "Eleazar found a way of escape. Many are loyal to you and have opened the back gates of the city's wall, but we must hurry. They do not want to cause civil unrest and face penalties when Saul arrives."

"Order evacuation immediately." To Abiathar, I said, "Let us make haste. God has provided a way out."

Abiathar agreed. "I am right after you."

Jashobeam waited for me outside the threshing floor where we had made camp. He held onto the reins of my horse. Shammah was with him. All the other men left already, leaving a trail of dust.

"Eleazar waits for us at the gate," Shammah said. "Uriah is with him. Jashobeam ordered Joab and Benaiah to travel with the men and keep those with the supplies protected."

I helped Abiathar straddle the horse behind Shammah, then I pulled myself up and onto mine. Making eye contact with Jashobeam, he said, "See? I told you we would escape."

"We are not free yet. Let us move."

Without another backward glance, I pushed the horse to go as fast as it could. I wanted out of Keilah. I wanted far away from people who wanted to betray me.

***

"Well?" Eleazar asked. "How about now?"

I sighed. "Will you leave me alone?"

"All of the men know that you will be in a much better mood afterward," Uriah said with a sly grin.

"Although I have to admit, his fighting was pretty fierce,"

180

Jashobeam joined in the teasing. "A lot of built-up tension will do that."

The men laughed while I shook my head.

"My irritability stems from the feeling of betrayal and disloyalty. Not necessarily from lack of a woman." I added testily, "You talked about it the whole way to Kir. Then after we left my parents there, you picked back up and talked it about it until we heard that the city of Keilah was in distress. And now you are talking about it again. How about if you leave me alone?"

"Are you nervous?" Shammah asked.

The men laughed again.

I actually was nervous about meeting Ahinoam. Not because of the reasons they were implying, but because of Michal. "Let us figure out where we are going to live, and then I can go claim my bride," I said without any cheer.

"We already decided on the wilderness of Ziph. The Ziphites are decent people—wanderers mostly—who do not have strong loyalties to Saul. We will be far enough away that most Israel has never even passed through that part of the desert. More importantly, we would be able to have our families move with us," Jashobeam answered.

"Which brings us back to you getting a family of your own," Eleazar teased. "Unless of course you became a eunuch and forgot to mention it."

The men laughed again.

I needed to change the subject. "We are almost to camp. We should be safe overnight, then we will pack up our belongings and family members and head to Ziph. There are wooded hills on the outskirts of it. If I am not mistaken, that will be excellent coverage."

Once the soldiers arrived and went off in different directions to their families, I signaled for Eleazar to stay behind. "I know you have been gone from your wife for some time, but I should not retrieve my bride alone."

Eleazar nodded. "Of course."

"Tell Jashobeam our plans should not take longer than a fortnight, and we will travel to Ziph, as soon as time permits. Tell him to make my nephews commanders over bands of 200 to assist in delegation."

"Of course," he repeated. "Go, get cleaned up. We will leave at sunrise."

Benaiah approached us. "I would be honored to accompany you both."

"You proved yourself in Keilah," Eleazar said. "I am not opposed." Eleazar left me and Benaiah alone.

"Why am I having such a hard time with it?" I asked Benaiah.

"Because Michal was not an arranged marriage or one of convenience. It might have been a political move for Saul, but not for you. You love her. Just as I love her sister. And I cannot tell you that love ever goes away. Time lessens the intensity and dulls the ache, but that is all."

"I thought I would be gone for only a little while, but it has been a year, and it does not look like it will be any time soon." I paused, then asked, "What of Merab? Did you two continue a relationship?"

"No," Benaiah said. "I behaved dishonorably when I was newly married, and I am sorry for it. However, once Merab married, I knew I had to move on. She already has a child and from what I hear has another on the way."

"And what of you and your wife?" I asked.

Benaiah shrugged. "She is a good woman and has given me two sons. But it was arranged, so we never had that connection that… you know what? Never mind. Talking about it does not change it. Decisions were made, and there is no going back."

"That is what I am nervous about," I admitted. "That I am going to marry this girl, and have no connection with her."

"Well, as a certain young man once told me, you can always marry another." Benaiah smiled, but it did not reach his eyes. "Go

182

on and prepare yourself. You cannot get married like that." He pointed at all of me.

I took a deep breath. "See you in the morning."

***

I entered her bed chamber while festivities carried on in the outer courts of Ahinoam's home. She had been veiled since the moment I saw her. Her veil had revealed nothing but her eyes, which I immediately observed were nothing like Michal's. I told myself that was not fair to her. I vowed that I would do better. I made a decision, and now this girl was my responsibility.

Guilt turned my stomach. Guilt and heartache.

This is part of being king, I told myself. *I must have heirs. I cannot have heirs without a wife.*

As was customary, we had been surrounded by her family and friends. Eleazar had been right about the family. They were loyal supporters of the giant slayer and were honored that I would desire a union with their daughter.

But now I was alone in the wedding chamber with her. A stranger. With Michal, we had a chance to grow our relationship before the union. This marriage to Ahinoam was foreign to me.

"How are you?" I asked, still standing near the door. She stood beside the bed, watching me with her face still veiled.

"I am fine, my lord," she said, her voice soft but shaky.

"May I get you a cup of water?" I asked, feeling thirsty myself.

Her eyes widened. "Are you thirsty? Let me retrieve one for you."

"Please," I said, as she went to move. I walked to her, touched her hand and saw how small and delicate it was. "Let me wait on you. Sit here." I ushered her to sit on the bed.

"Thank you," she said, her voice still nervous.

"Tell me about yourself," I said as I went to a table where a spread of delicacies and wine sat. I could not think of eating at the moment, so I bypassed all of that and poured two waters. I drank mine before I brought her cup over to her.

She sipped while I stood. I was not quite ready to sit on the bed yet.

"Do you have brothers and sisters?" I prompted.

"Yes," she gave a slight laugh. I observed her eyes crinkle from a smile. "I have three younger brothers whom I adore."

"I have seven brothers," I said. "And two sisters." The memory of me and Michal in the king's stables came flooding back. She had asked of my family too.

"The Lord has been good to your parents," she said.

Her voice brought me back to the present moment. I smiled at her. I liked her voice. It had yet to truly raise above a whisper, but it was soft like a high-quality silk. "You may remove your veil, if you would like."

She lifted the material from her face, and I saw a striking young woman. Yet, I still struggled with disappointment. Would I compare her to Michal for the rest of her days? I took another drink of water.

"Do you like what you see, my lord?"

"Please," I said. "Call me David."

"Will you sit beside me?"

I took a deep breath and sat down next to her, suddenly very aware of how close in proximity she was.

"May I say something?" she asked.

"Of course."

"I am honored to have the hand of David as my husband. You are already so much better than I imagined." Her face cringed in embarrassment. "I am sorry! I did not mean to imply anything negative."

"No need to apologize. I am not a beast. At least I do not think I am. Not all the time."

"I have been regaled of all the horror stories from the married women in my community. From their stories, I was a bit alarmed."

"Women telling stories of men? I cannot believe it!" I teased, but I felt as if I was floundering.

We smiled briefly at each other, not speaking for a moment. Then both of us looked away, the awkward pause growing.

What did I get myself into? I set the water down and chose the wine instead.

25

☙❧

Michal

The House of Adriel
1016 B.C.

Ashvi threw himself into my arms. "How's my little nephew?" I asked, tickling his belly. "And are you already past your second year?"

"It has been at least two moons ago," Elia said. "Thank you for coming. Merab is not herself."

I picked up a wiggling Ashvi and plastered him with kisses.

"Mimi!" he said and planted a wet kiss on my cheek.

"He is always so cheerful when you are here," Elia said.

I smiled at her but did not answer. I knew that the reason I visited so much was only partly out of concern for my sister and mostly that Ashvi was therapeutic for me as well. His innocence and sweetness helped me forget for a little bit how broken my heart was. I played with him for a few moments more before Elia took me to the inner courtyard. Ashvi ran after us, so I picked him up and carried him the rest of the way, nuzzling his neck.

"Michal arrived," Elia said to Merab.

"Good, bring us refreshments."

I stopped kissing Ashvi the moment I took in the sight of my sister. Her clothing appeared unkempt, her hair looked as if it had seen a comb or brush in at least a moon, and her pallor was pale with dark circles pronounced around her eyes. I did not say a word. I simply sat beside her, Ashvi wiggling in my lap, and held her hand.

"That bad, huh?" she asked, not looking at me.

"Have you forgotten how to bathe?" I said, trying to keep the tone light.

"I hate being pregnant." She turned to me, her face a mix of anger and exhaustion. "I have yet to eat a meal without getting sick. The only thing that brings me relief is my ginger root tea, but then it makes me have to use the pot, which means I have to stand up. And I cannot stand up. The baby sits upon my left leg in such a way that pain shoots down it when I stand upon it."

"Maybe a warm bath…"

"I do not want a warm bath," she snapped. "If I am unclean, my husband will not touch me. If he does not touch me, I will not get pregnant again. Ever."

"So, you will no longer bathe?" I asked. Ashvi reached for his mother. Merab, however, wanted nothing to do with him.

"Elia!" she yelled out. "Come and get the child!"

"He is fine. Let me hold him."

Ashvi whimpered.

"This is exactly what I did not want." Merab became emotional. She watched Ashvi cry for her with an expression of horror. "I am trapped, Michal. And I hate it. And I cannot move because I am in pain, and I cannot eat, and I cannot have peace. ELIA!"

For the first time in our relationship, I was truly worried about my sister.

Elia rushed in with a tray of refreshments, her plump face sweating profusely. "I am sorry. I hurried."

"Take the child."

"I do not mind holding him," I said, not wanting the toddler to leave just yet.

"Did you come to visit me or the child?" Merab's tone accused.

"Both," I said. Still, I handed Ashvi to Elia. "Thank you," I added and touched her shoulder. "I appreciate you taking care of my

187

sister and Ashvi."

Merab scoffed behind me. Elia pressed her lips together and nodded, quickly leaving with the boy. I turned my attention back to my sister, ready to engage in a quarrel, but saw her hands covering her face, her shoulders shaking from the silent sobs.

I left her to grab another servant. "Draw up a warm bath," I said. When I came back to Merab, I asked, "What can I do?"

"Nothing."

"Has Adriel become a bad husband?"

"He is never home. And when he is here, he wants me. And here is the result." She indicated her stomach.

"Babies are such blessings," I said softly, trying to keep my own emotion in check. "Ashvi loves you. He wants his mother."

"He does not know what he wants."

"Do not become like our mother. Please."

"Of course, I am like her! We are women! We are all trapped. Living in a man's world. Having their babies while they go out as warriors. And if another woman catches their eye, then they can have her too!" Merab stopped yelling and glowered at me. "How does it feel, Michal, to be ripped apart from your husband? You have no say. You are told who to marry, and now you are actually ordered to have Paltiel's children. Do you dare disagree with me?"

I thought of David, thought of the way he smiled at me, the way he would wrap his arms around me, the way he would tuck my hair behind my ear. "I agree with you," I said. "But I cannot...I cannot lose myself. I must stay strong."

"You still think he is returning?" Merab was quieter now as if her despair now included me.

"He promised. And I have to be ready. So, I cannot afford to lose myself."

"Well," Merab paused to rub her eyes. "Then pray for me, sister, because I am afraid that I have lost myself. I only feel darkness inside my soul. The darkness of despair. I have wondered if death would be the best way of escape."

"Merab!" I clasped her hand and brought it to my chest. "Do not talk of such things. You are a mother, and a wife, and a beloved sister! When I lost the child, you told me that you could not live this world without me. I cannot live in this madness without you. We will not talk on the matter again." But had I not contemplated the same idea?

The servant I had approached came up to us. "The warm bath is prepared."

Merab gave an annoyed expression, she opened her mouth to speak, so I quickly talked over her. "Thank you. Help me with my sister."

"I told you. I can barely walk. And I do not appreciate you undermining my wishes."

"Just as you did when you came to help me? Did I not want to get up and go, and yet you told me to stay put and heal? I am doing what is best for you, just as you did what was best for me. A warm bath is relaxing and rejuvenating, so we are going to help you get there." I motioned for the servant to stand on the other side of Merab.

"And if I refuse to get up?" she said, still grouchy.

"Then I call for more help, and we will carry you in there, but one thing is for certain. You, my sister, are taking a bath."

Merab grumbled, but she allowed me and the servant to help her up. She grimaced and gritted her teeth as she put weight on her leg.

"Put your arm around me, and your other arm around him."

Together the three of us made our way to where the steam arose from the large metal trough. "You think I am so big I need an animal trough?" Merab asked the servant.

"I did not want you to feel confined," he said. "Elia normally draws your baths. She is busy with the child."

"The child has a name," I said in irritation to him and also to Merab. "Why are you not calling him Ashvi?"

Neither answered.

Elia approached. "I will take it from here," she said to the other servant. "See to it that no one disturbs her privacy." She quickly positioned drapes around the courtyard area, while I assisted Merab in taking off her linens.

Merab occasionally moaned in pain, but as soon as Elia and I helped her into the steamy water, the moan of pain turned to one of relief. We helped her to sit down inside of it, and then she leaned back and closed her eyes.

Elia pulled a stool and sat by her head, pouring water over Merab's hair. I tried not to stare at my sister's belly, but it seemed so much larger than her last pregnancy.

"How much longer do you have?" I asked.

"At least another moon or two," Merab said without opening her eyes. She was clearly enjoying the bath, which made me smile.

"You must have two in there."

Merab grimaced. "I cannot imagine. No. I do not know what I would do."

"Give one to me," I said before I realized what I was saying. I tried to laugh it off, but the words still seemed weighty.

"Even if I have the one, you can have him." Merab's words were sleepy. "You can have the one now."

"Merab! Do not speak like that."

"Why would God do something so cruel as to withhold children from you and bestow them upon me?"

"I do not know." In all honesty, I had wondered myself.

Merab opened her eyes and turned to look at me. "Thank you for this. It does feel lovely."

"You are welcome. And we are all glad for it," I teased, but I doubted I masked my internal pain.

"It is not so far-fetched, my sister," she said, while Elia rinsed lavender oil from Merab's hair. "If Ashvi had you looking after him, he would be content, as would you. It would give you something to do, other than—"

"Waiting for my estranged husband to return?" I finished her sentence. But in that moment, I felt a little glimmer of hope. "I would not want to impose myself upon you or your children."

"I do not want them," Merab said so quietly I almost missed it. "It is not the life I desire. Adriel is never here. When he is, I will call for them."

My head began to spin. "Wait. Are you talking about Ashvi and this new baby? I do not know if Paltiel would allow me to move here."

"No, they are to stay with you. I will visit them, of course, and they will come home to visit their father, but yes, this would be such a blessing. To me and to you."

"Yes," I said fast before I could talk myself out of it. I would have to get Paltiel's permission, but I would face him and beg him if I had to. The fact was that I loved Ashvi as my own. And I needed a distraction, and someone to love. "Let me help you raise them."

***

I waited for Dinah to finish plaiting my hair. Going through the same routine with her since we were both young girls brought us a sense of normalcy. At least it did for me. She seemed eager to pick up where we left off once she was returned to me, and so we fell right back into our daily activities. It kept me from falling deep into the overwhelming grief and loneliness I felt. It still kept nipping at the edges of my mind, which was why I desired to keep living.

For David.

On this morning, I knew that I needed to hurry, so I could catch Paltiel before he left for his early rounds. "What do you think he will say?" I asked Dinah. I had told her all about Merab's offer of me watching Ashvi.

"He has been avoiding you lately, so it is hard to say."

"True." The last time we spoke was a few moons ago, after father's visit.

One of Paltiel's manservants entered the room. I found it irritating that the servants in the household did not honor my

191

privacy, but since this was Paltiel's dwelling, his rules reigned. Just the same, I sighed in exasperation. "Yes?"

"The master of the house requests your presence this morning."

Dinah and I exchanged glances. "I am on my way."

"I am to escort you."

I bit my tongue. I could not spout off my frustration because I needed Paltiel's permission to help with Merab's children. "I am ready." I followed him all the way to the back veranda. I saw Paltiel sitting atop a horse. A majestic brown horse with a dark mane and tail. And next to him, one of the servants held the reins to another horse. This one was lighter in color with patches of brown speckled across it. I could not help it. I grinned like a little girl. "Horses?" I asked, heading toward him. "I did not know you owned horses."

"They are expensive, and donkeys and mules do the job just fine when it comes to vineyards. I recently acquired these, and I thought you might desire to go for a ride with me. I need to supervise the winepress."

I barely heard his words. I was already petting the beautiful horse beside his. "Hello," I said to her. "It is female?"

"Yes. Do you know how to ride?"

"It was forbidden at the palace. I rode one with my father once, and several times with David. He would let me hold the reins."

"Would you like to learn to ride one on your own?"

"Yes. Yes, I would. Very much."

"I have been told that the horse is quite tame."

But I was not listening. A servant helped me up onto the horse. I could not straddle it the way men did. My skirts were too long and restricting. So, I let my legs dangle on the one side, the way David showed me and took the reins in my hands.

I took in excited breaths and felt, for the first time in quite a while, alive. The horse stood quietly while I petted her and told her we would be the best of friends. My excitement was barely contained.

Paltiel tried to provide some instructions, but I had already figured out how to get the horse to move forward. I laughed in glee, as she trotted along. Out of the corner of my eye, I saw Paltiel's other wife, holding two children and watching me with absolute hatred. But in that moment, I refused to dwell on anything but the beauty of the exquisite horse and the pure joy she brought me.

26

✿

King Saul

Outside of Engedi
1014 B.C.

The messenger read the report of the surrounding cities, but I wasn't listening. Instead, I leaned against an old tree and dozed. My embattled mind led to countless nights of fitful sleep and exhaustion had become a steady companion.

"Reports have confirmed that the runaway king was spotted in the wilderness of Engedi. Local farmers have confirmed it."

I opened one eye. No one said his name around me anymore, resorting to calling that traitorous shepherd 'the runaway king.' I despised it nearly as much as his name. It was a reminder that many considered him next in line. Hebrew hearts already considered him their next king, and instead of facing me man-to-man, the runaway *coward* resorted to hiding. For nearly two years, my spies searched the land, but any reports they provided of his whereabouts proved futile by the time I got there.

Jonathan answered the young messenger, "You are dismissed."

"The wilderness of Engedi is not far from here," I said with my eyes closed. I still enjoyed the fantasy I concocted in my head of all the ways to kill David. But it was hard to live in my fantasy world with my eyes open.

"Not far from here?" Jonathan asked. "You have lost too much sleep, and it has left you delirious. Continue your nap. We will head toward Gibeah at daybreak."

I heard him walk away, telling my guardsmen to make sure I rested uninterrupted. I wanted to argue, but I could not remember what I was arguing about and began dozing again. Sleep did not come to me nearly enough, so I snatched it when I could, and this time I slept hard. The darkness suddenly enveloped me, and I felt trapped inside it. If it was a dream or nightmare, it felt all too real, and I found myself gasping for breath within its confinement. *He must die*, it hissed. More voices joined in, crawling across me with their words of vengeance and hate. The darkness revealed a scene where David stood over me, my own sword in his hand. My men were all around me, but they were sleeping, all of them powerless to help me. David raised the sword and thrust it into my chest.

I sat up and gasped, clutching at my chest. I observed the setting sun and the host of Israel's army encamped around me. "How long have I slept?" I asked the men guarding me.

"Since the ninth hour of the day, sir. Roughly, three hours."

Unable to shake the agitation, I pushed myself up from against the tree. "Bring me the soothsayer. Immediately."

A messenger was sent while I paced. There once was a time I turned my nose up at witchcraft, but that was before Samuel cut me off. I would have my answers one way or another, and soothsayers did the job.

"How long does this take?" I bellowed from time to time. My mind replayed the nightmare. Over and over. The darkness from my sleep had yet to leave me. I felt my heart tighten as if being squeezed. "FIND HER!" I yelled at whoever would listen.

Eventually, Abner approached. "The witch is in your tent," he said.

I moved past him, hurriedly heading to the woman. Once inside, I felt her presence in the darkened area. I fell on my knees, my voice shaking. "I had another nightmare," I said, not even greeting her. "About him. Please. Tell me what I should do."

She came closer to me. Even though I could barely see with

195

the animal skins hanging around us, I could smell her stench draw closer. A frail, withered hand grabbed mine, and I felt the pierce of a knife into my skin. The blood dropped into a goblet. I wrapped my hand while she swished whatever mixture she had in that cup with the drops of my blood. "His hair," she ordered.

I fumbled with the tiny compartment that held David's hair from when he had defeated Goliath. I kept it around my neck as the soothsayer had instructed all those years ago. I gave it to her and waited.

Goosebumps exploded across my body at the creepiness of the exchange. No matter how many times I called upon her, I had yet to get used to the dark magic. And it made the darkness that tormented me only grow stronger. It was to the point that it had taken on a physical form that would torment me in the night, choking at my neck. Sleeping during the day helped only somewhat.

"Your nightmare is a vision," she said. "The runaway heir will stand over you with your own sword, and your men will be powerless to stop it."

"What can I do?" I pleaded. "My efforts to kill him are futile."

"You must stop at nothing!" she said through her teeth and the darkness joined in unison. "He must die or the kingdom will be destroyed. Everything you worked for…your children and grandchildren…slaughtered."

The darkness gave way to fury. It rippled through my veins.

I left the woman in the tent and marched outside, my eyes acclimating to the sudden light. "My horse," I ordered. "And get me Abner and Jonathan."

By the time Abner came over, I had already pulled myself onto the horse. "I need three thousand men. Immediately. Where is my son?"

"Sir?"

"Where is my son? I want him to join me."

"He left on a scouting mission while you slept. He should be

196

back by morning."

I heard Abner's voice, but the words kept repeating in my head. *David is in the wilderness of Engedi.* "Assemble three thousand men."

"The men are tired. We have pursued the Philistines for several moons, and they continue to gain in number. Let us replenish our resources, and then continue the fight against our real enemy."

This time I stewed over his excuses, which only added fuel to the fire. "If you had bothered to help at the very beginning…If you had banged down his door and dragged him out of his house…he would already be dead, and Israel would be free from the threat! And now, years later, that window of opportunity is gone, and you have the nerve to tell me the men are tired. You know what, Abner? I am tired. Tired. Yet, here I am, on this horse, trying to accomplish what you and my men could not do."

Abner's normally stoic features suddenly had a flash of anger. "If the situation was grave, it would be different," he said. "He poses no more threat than those sheep over there. It has been years. I thought we decided to pursue the most pressing matter."

"Yes, but now we know where that low-life shepherd and his band of misfits are. I have waited over a year to find them. And how can you say that he is not as pressing a threat? If he becomes king, what will happen to you, cousin? To your family? To all of my house? I am not only looking out for my best interests, I am looking out for yours. The soothsayer told me that my entire family would die."

Abner sighed and shook his head. "I am not disagreeing with you that the runaway heir needs to be dealt with, but right now, the Philistines continue to gain in power, especially if we do not change our tactics from defensive to offensive. Why have me run around all of Judah hunting for a man who is doing what we should be doing! Fighting for Israel! Reports show that the Philistines are being stopped at all of our outlying territories. That can be no other than Dav…the runaway heir."

"Enough! I am tired of your excuses. And he is NOT my heir!"

"Release the men."

"I have given an order!"

Abner refused to relent. "They are weary and seeing their families would strengthen their resolve, and they will appreciate the kindness of their king."

"I can barely eat, barely sleep, because all my thoughts are consumed with frustration at my failure of capturing the son of Jesse." I stopped, surprised at my honesty with Abner. "The people know I pursue him, and I am weak because I have not captured him."

Abner stayed quiet.

"See? You know it to be true."

Neither of us said anything for a moment. I could still feel the chill along my spine from the darkness and words of the soothsayer. I needed Abner on my side. The troops respected him. Obeyed him. "Am I not only asking for three thousand men? That is not even a tenth of the men. Did I not stop the pursuit to push back against the Philistines? David was right within my grasp, but I heeded your direction and protected the people of the surrounding towns of Judah."

"I will collect three thousand," Abner said, rubbing his face. "Then I am sending the others home."

"Yes. Surely there are three thousand out of our masses that will volunteer to travel with their king."

But as Abner walked away, the soothsayer's words reminded me that I was running out of time.

***

"Here." I pointed to a cave behind some sheep pens. "Let us break for a few minutes. I need to relieve myself."

I needed a moment of rest from Abner's continued diatribe about the Philistines. As I walked up a steep incline, he yelled after me, "They would have marched right through to Gibeah. Do you want the Philistines to invade your city? To capture the palace and your possessions?"

"They are not going to do that! I have it under control. I have stationed battalions and strengthened them with more troops." I went to keep walking uphill, but paused long enough to yell, "I have had it with you questioning my authority!"

"You gave me this position to lead Israel's troops and protect our land and our people. I take my duties seriously."

"And I do not?"

Abner did not answer the question. Instead, he said, "Go and relieve yourself. We have a boy to chase."

I growled at Abner and stormed up the hill. I hated when Abner referred to David as a boy. As I marched past the sheep pens and into the cave, I surveyed the surroundings before stepping inside. I felt as if someone watched me, but there was no one around save my men. The urge to urinate pushed me to act hastily. I sighed in relief as I emptied my bladder. I stopped and listened. Did someone just whisper?

I quickly finished and stepped out of the cave. Too much tormented me that now I acted as frightened as a child. *Add that to everything else*, I thought irritably.

When I reached my horse, and Abner handed me the reins, I heard someone behind me shout, "My master and king!"

I whipped around, eyes wide and searching, heart pounding, already knowing that voice.

"David," Abner whispered under his breath.

There David stood at the top of the steep hill just outside the mouth of the cave. He held his sling and was tossing a stone into the air and catching it with his other hand.

I could not reach for my spear without making any sudden moves, but my fingers itched for it. *Kill him! Kill him! Kill him!* The voices raged in my head.

Suddenly David fell to his knees and bowed. "Why, Saul?"

David called out, his voice filled with emotion. "Why do you listen to those who say I am out to get you? Do you not know me yet? Just now as I hid in the cave with my men, God handed you over to me, but I refuse to touch God's anointed. Is that not proof that I mean you no harm?"

I looked to Abner whose hand rested on his sword. "Kill him," I whispered.

"He comes in peace," Abner whispered back. "He could have killed you, but he refrained."

Chills shot through me, as I thought about the truth. Had David been in the cave? My insides began to tremble. After all the wars and battles I fought in, I never felt as vulnerable as I did at this moment. "He lies. This is our moment."

"Look at your robe as proof," David called out, as if hearing me.

I picked up the end of my cloak and saw a portion sliced completely off.

"He could have killed you," Abner whispered again.

"My men told me to do it. You were right there. All of this running would have been over, but I chose to do the right thing and honor you. I am no rebel, and you know it. I am not your enemy. And my hand will not rise up to harm you. Please end this." David added, "I pray God would set me free of you!"

Death had been right there. "Could this be my son, David?" I asked, finally able to look up and at David who now stood tall and confident on the high hill above the road. "You have done right by me," I admitted. The voices no longer harmonious. They waged with the guilt of my heart. "Why did you not kill me?"

"That is God's decision to make. Not mine."

I took in a shaky breath and wiped at my face. The guilt shoved the hatred and jealousy aside, even though they screamed the loudest. David, for whatever reason, had spared me. I thought of the nightmare, of the soothsayer's words. I squeezed my fists together, gritted my teeth, and groaned from the battling forces inside me.

David. Right here. And yet, how could I kill him when others saw his act of kindness.

"Say something," Abner said to me. "We are surrounded."

"When you become king, I implore you please do not kill my family and destroy my legacy."

"You have my word." David bowed again, sealing his vow.

I observed David's men positioned in various posts surrounding us. We would not make it out alive. I rode well ahead of most of my troops. The guilt turned to shame which morphed into embarrassment. He cut the edge of my cloak. Now all would see that God had delivered me into the hands of my hated enemy. I pulled myself onto my horse and gripped the reins tightly in every effort to not grab the spear. *Do it. Do it. Do it.* But I had enough men with me that would report David's act of kindness. I had no other choice but to leave David standing there. Alive. "Let's turn around and head back to Gibeah," I said in a low tone, still shaken by what had occurred.

Abner, thankfully, gave me my space as we traveled through southern Judah toward the palace. Each time my caravan stopped, no one spoke. Each worked silently, most trying not to even glance in my direction.

"He mocks me," I said to Abner.

"I do not think he does. He seeks peace."

"Not...David," I said through gritted teeth. I fought against the wave of emotion, but knew it was a losing battle. "God. He mocks me."

We traveled the rest of the way in silence because there was nothing more to be said.

27

⚜

David

The Wilderness of Engedi
1014 B.C.

The fire crackled and burned, as did other blazes around me, but the mood was not one of laughter and conversation. Instead, the mood stayed subdued. My men were upset at me. And I did not blame them.

Saul had been in the cave. Alone.

The same cave several of us hid in. We had heard that some farmers of Engedi gave away our location. We had to act quickly with King Saul nearly upon us. Instead of him reaching our settlement, we decided to try and meet him and discuss a truce. That way, our families would be safe should the situation not go as planned.

But it went nearly too perfect. As if on a silver platter, there he stood. Oblivious. Mine for the taking.

I finished my poem and tucked it away. I needed someone to talk to. How could I feel alone among my men? Not even Ahinoam could take away the loneliness. In many ways, the poor girl made it worse. She was not the conversationalist that Michal had been. Then again, I did not love Ahinoam. It did not help that she was a depressive sort. Complaining often of the dry heat of the wilderness. I took great care to provide comfort, especially when she had been with child. She would always be the mother of my firstborn, but she was not...Michal.

Benaiah approached. I smiled at him, hoping he came in peace. He was one who rarely complained, which I appreciated. "Hello, my friend," I said. "Would you like to sit with me?"

"Follow me," he said in a hushed tone and then walked past me without stopping. He slipped between tents, and I moved quickly, checking over my shoulder to make sure we were not being watched. If Benaiah had a reason to be secretive, then I knew enough to know there was good reason.

Without the light from the fire, it was hard to see him. He was one of the most skilled at stealth, thanks to his years of training. I refused to call out, pushing myself to use my own skills to follow him without detection from others.

Once we were outside of camp, Benaiah slowed until I caught up with him. "Danger?" I asked.

"No. A visitor."

"Oh."

We traveled on foot well past our encampment, moving quietly and swiftly into the night. Eventually, we came upon a small thicket of narrow trees. I spotted Jashobeam's shape step out from one. I knew there were others in place to protect me. Their loyalty, even when angry or frustrated, still overwhelmed me.

Once inside the thicket, I saw a small lantern being held by someone in Israeli garb. But I knew the regalia and immediately bowed. "My brother." I straightened myself and then headed toward Jonathan. We kissed each other in greeting and clasped each other's shoulders. "It is good to see you."

"And you," Jonathan said warmly.

"It has been too long."

"So, it has."

We paused. Jonathan continued, "Your men told me that you spared my father's life."

"Yes. He will not die by my hand."

"Was there no resolution? Even after you spared him?"

"No, I did not sense that. He seemed conflicted. I promised

not to lay a hand upon him or his family, but he did not seem content with that answer. I feel we are not safe to return."

"I will talk with him when I return and remind him of the gift of life you handed him. Surely he must see how you mean him no evil."

"How is your family? All of them?" I wanted to change the subject. I did not want to discuss what happened when my men were still sore about it.

"All is well within my household, though I doubt that is who we are talking about."

"How is she?" I asked, getting to the heart of the matter.

"I have been busy on the battlefront, so I have not visited with her recently. However, she writes often and tells of the joys of raising our nephews."

"She is raising children?" She should be raising our children, but I knew that saying the words would only make me feel worse.

"Yes, Merab recently birthed a set of sons, and she sent them, along with her eldest boy and the wet nurse to live with Michal. It seems that Merab is not fond of motherhood."

"Michal wanted children," I said quietly.

"And I hear you have your own to celebrate."

"Yes. A son. Another is on the way." I tried to make my words light, but I still looked away.

"Children are a blessing from God. I am glad to see you have found happiness in your exile."

Happiness? The word gave me pause. The only time I had ever truly found happiness was when Michal was in my arms. "I have learned to live life while in exile," I said carefully. "I cannot waste years out here."

"Of course not. All those who know and love you will understand."

"Has she found happiness?" I asked, searching his face in the darkness. "Has she found some semblance of a life?"

"I only know that she is caring for Merab's children. I do not know of her situation with Paltiel."

I grimaced at the name.

"I came here to warn you that my father had received word of your whereabouts, but it seems as if you have already been made aware."

"Yes. The meeting with him earlier bought us time, but we are moving out upon the morrow."

"Where will you go that he will not find you? Your army gains in numbers."

"I will hide again among the enemy if I have to…though I do not prefer it."

"I pray for you daily. And I will take up your cause with my father. I will be relentless." Jonathan added, "That is not the only reason why I am here. I seek your help."

"Anything for you, brother."

"The Philistines are closing in. They surround us on many fronts, but my father is consumed, which makes him volatile and irrational. I fear for Israel's safety."

"My men and I work tirelessly and will continue to do so, securing all the borderlands."

"I know, and I thank you, but we received word that the Amalekites are using our weakness against us by attacking in small bands."

"Provide me a location, and we will take care of it."

Jonathan did not stay too much longer. Still, we once again promised loyalty. Before leaving, he asked, "Would you like me to give her a message?"

"Yes." I paused, knowing that it would be unfair to give her hope. I was a wanted man on the run. I knew I could promise her nothing, so I changed my answer. "No, it is probably best that no message is given."

"I understand."

As Jonathan mounted his horse and left me standing amongst the trees, I heard Eleazar drop from one of the limbs before I saw him. He approached; his face sorrowful. "You could go to her, you know. This could be over. I know how you miss her."

My heart felt like a heavy weight inside me. But I made a vow before God. Either I was a man of my word, or my word meant nothing. "Do you remember when King Saul had discovered my secret? How I came to you to escape? He tried to kill me with his spear, and I barely made it out alive."

"Yes."

"And Jonathan came to see me afterward?"

"Yes."

"He could have put a sword through my heart. He is, after all, the eldest son of the reigning king." When Eleazar kept quiet, I continued, "But he did not kill me. Do you know what he said?"

Eleazar shook his head. I noticed my band of brothers slowly approach from their hiding places. All of them listening.

"Jonathan looked me in the eye and said, 'Who am I to question God? I will not touch God's anointed.'" I paused and let the words leave their impact. "How can I live with myself if I in turn lay one hand upon his father's head?"

"But he was right there," Uriah said. "I was tempted to kill him for you and take the punishment."

"I am glad that you refrained because you would have been punished, and that would have hurt me tremendously." I searched their faces. "Every day I war with myself. Every day. I left my heart in Gibeah, but still, in this one decision I have never wavered, and I never will. I will not kill the king. And if you are to stay under my command, that order applies to you. Do you think that I am oblivious to your cold shoulders? The distance you have placed between us? And still, I have not wavered. Trust me when I say that this is God's plan."

For a moment, all was still.

"I trust you," Eleazar said and squeezed my shoulder affectionately.

"I trust you," Uriah echoed.

"I trust you," Jashobeam said, as he approached from behind.

"I trust you," Shammah, Joab, and Abishai all said in unison.

Benaiah looked at everyone and nodded in agreement. "Of course, I trust you. May I add that we are in need again of supplies. Since we must leave on the morrow, let us move toward the Amalekites where we can gather the plunder."

"Each of your units device a strategy. We will meet in the morning and choose the best course."

Joab and Abishai left to their stations to secure the perimeter while the others followed me back to the camp. Noticing the shadow of a large boulder, I slowed my pace. "You may continue without me. I will stay here for a bit longer." I began searching for stones.

Jashobeam ordered a few to set up lanterns.

"I do not need them." I closed my eyes and sensed the distance between me and the boulder. I reached for my sling, placed a stone in its spot, evened my breathing, and sent the stone sailing. I heard the ping of stone against rock and allowed myself a satisfied smile. I went through my first set of stones before opening my eyes to retrieve more.

"You going to give another person a chance?" Eleazar said beside me.

"You stuck around?"

"Someone had to make sure you did not run off again."

"Ha, if anyone is running off, it would be you."

Eleazar sent a stone sailing. "Never. I will protect my best friend, even when I want to kill him myself."

"Well, get out of my way and let me practice."

"I only took one shot. You have already had five."

I stepped aside and let my friend take the next shot.

28

෴

Michal

Paltiel's Stables in Gallim
1014 B.C.

"You named the horse 'Eglah'?" Merab stayed behind me while I leaned against the wooden post to get a better glimpse of Ashvi.

Merab's oldest son, now three, sat in front of Paltiel, holding the reins of my horse, laughing with glee. "He is doing fabulously! Look at your son! He can almost do it himself."

"Are we done being outside? I am getting attacked by insects."

"Go inside," I insisted. "No one is making you stay out here."

Merab sighed. "I came over here to visit you. I will wait until you are ready."

"Tell the truth." I still watched Ashvi ride the horse in circles. "You do not wish Dinah to give you one of the petulant infants."

"All they do is cry."

"Not always. But they do feed off each other. If one is upset, the other must join in."

"Every time I visit, they are upset."

"Have you and Adriel decided upon names? I may have to come up with my own if you delay much longer."

"You? Come up with their names? Like you did for the

horse?"

"What is wrong with 'Eglah'?"

"You named her after a baby calf."

"It was David's nickname for me." I turned to look over at my sister. She looked miserable. Dressed in her finest with bangles up her arms and kohl around her eyes. Yet, the fat flies buzzed around her like she might be their next meal. "Let me get Ashvi, and we can go in for some refreshment."

"Yes, you look like you might need to freshen up."

"I am perfectly fine, thank you." I must shock her with my own appearance. My hair had been loosely braided and now strands had escaped and were blowing in the breeze. No oils or paint lined my features. No jewelry, save for the necklace David gave me as a wedding present from his mother. I was natural as I could be. At least Merab had yet to see what I had on underneath my skirts. Dinah had sewed several of my worn skirts into riding trousers that I could hide under my clothes. All I had to do once in Paltiel's stable was hike up my skirts and jump on my horse. I had yet to show Merab that I actually rode the horse like a man. It would be highly frowned upon, and I could be punished for it, but I no longer cared. The best way to ride a horse was to straddle it.

Once Paltiel observed how much I truly admired the animal, he allowed me to secretly work alongside his stable manager. That had been over a year ago. I had yet to truly thank Paltiel for this tremendous gift. I might have lost my mind while stuck inside that house. But with Merab's gift of her children and Paltiel's gift of horses, I found life again.

The horse galloped over and Paltiel handed Ashvi over to me.

"Did you see? Did you see?" the little boy asked with his arms around my neck.

"I did," I assured. "So did your mother." I set Ashvi down who ran over to Merab.

"Did you see?" he asked her.

"Yes, I did," she said while swatting at a fly. "Your father will be pleased that you are already riding a horse."

Paltiel suggested we head back. "I will take care of the horse."

I wanted to object simply because I desired to ride her myself, but I also did not want to hear it from Merab. She sounded more and more like our mother every time we visited. Outside of her aversion to horses or any outdoor activities, her interactions with the children infuriated me. She was often detached and inattentive. "Let us go refresh ourselves," I said to her. Ashvi tried to grab her hand to walk with her, but she removed it from his grasp to wave them around her head. Ashvi saw my available hand and took it.

Merab took one last withering glance at Paltiel on the horse before hoisting herself on the wagon. Ashvi and I would have walked back to the house with him riding on my back for fun, but Merab refused. Ashvi climbed on and sat beside his mother. "Do not sit so close. It is too warm out here for close contact." To me, she said, "Paltiel still lusts after you, you know."

I told the manservant to take us back to the home, then turned and shushed Merab. "Could we talk about this later?" I discreetly pointed to Ashvi.

"Why? He has no idea what we are talking about, do you?" she asked him.

Ashvi looked to me, not knowing quite how to respond. I kissed his sweaty forehead. "She teases," I told him.

We stayed quiet until we arrived outside the southside porch. Dinah and Elia approached. "Drinks," Merab ordered. "And a cool cloth. And a fan."

"Go with Dinah," I told Ashvi. "You need to cool off and drink heartily."

He ran in front of my maidservant while Merab and I rested on plush cushions on the porch. The shade provided immediate relief, and I felt the gentle breeze immediately.

"FAN!" Merab ordered to another servant. "Elia is taking too long."

One of Paltiel's men began fanning us. I smiled and thanked him.

"Is something bothering you?" I asked my sister. "You seem crankier than usual."

Merab shot me a withering look. "We just spent the late morning out in the hot sun, and I was not dressed for it."

"I thought you would want to see your son's progress on the horse."

"I will take your word from here on out."

Elia approached with a cool rag that she placed on the back of Merab's neck. "Here is your drink." She handed one to Merab and to me.

"How are the babies?" I asked.

"They sleep."

"You still have your own rooms here?" Merab ignored Elia and point the question at me.

"Yes, this place is vast, and Paltiel is accommodating."

Merab made a face that indicated she knew something.

"Out with it. Ashvi is not here now. Say your peace."

"What is there to say? He is scared witless."

"Scared? Of father?"

"Michal, when did you become so slow?"

"Save the insults, and answer the question," I said, pushing the irritation down.

"The king ordered him to consummate the marriage. Threatened death. And yet it has not happened. Who would scare him more than the king?"

"I threatened him. I told you this. And now things have changed. Paltiel wants to be friends. While David is alive, Paltiel promises to not defile my marriage with my husband."

"This is the same Paltiel who kissed you in front of the crowd at my wedding, remember? The same one who blackmailed the queen. And now, you believe that he who lusts for you daily is simply *honoring* your request? He has not changed. He is terrified. Seriously, Michal, you surprise me. You have always been the inquisitive one, and yet you live here in denial."

Merab was right. The truth hit me like an arrow between the eyebrows. Three years I lived under Paltiel's roof, and he practically left me alone. Our conversations were short and happened infrequently. "But he bought me a horse."

"Because with you lies his fate. It truly is a God-send that you are raising my children and that father is too consumed with his hate to make another visit. You and Paltiel are safe. For now. Eventually, father will find his way to you."

"Unless David kills him first."

"That will not happen. The entire kingdom speaks of David sparing the king's life."

"Yes, I heard that." I wept when I heard the news that my father was within David's grasp. It stung that David kept my father alive, even though doing so would continue to keep us apart. I had heard other rumors. Rumors of other women. But no. My heart refused to acknowledge that betrayal. David loved me. I knew it. That knowledge kept me during many a lonely night.

"It is quite evident that there is a reason Paltiel defies the order of the king. A reason that scares him even more than our father. If I were you, I would want to find out what it was."

***

I snuggled with one of the infants, freshly washed and fed by the wet nurse. Dinah approached, holding the other one. "They need names."

Dinah checked to make sure the wet nurse had left the room before answering, "Merab and Adriel will name them soon." She set the one down and came to retrieve the one in my arms. "I am glad that you are focused on their upbringing. It has brought a peace about you that is comforting."

"Merab said something today that I wanted to ask you

212

about," I whispered. "She said that Paltiel is not consummating the marriage to me because he is frightened. But that does not make sense. I would think the king would frighten him, yet Paltiel continues to honor my wishes. It is wholly possible that Paltiel has changed, right?"

"He did purchase horses for you," Dinah said. "Yet, I have occasionally observed his interactions with his other wife. He does not look at her the way he looks at you."

"She hates me," I admitted. "How have I ignored the truth staring me in the face?"

"What do you think it is?"

"If Paltiel is going against the king, there has to be a reason for it. I thought I was a good enough reason, but Merab spoke it clearly. There is only one other that it could be."

"David? But how?"

"That is the question that I need to answer."

I waited until the entire household slept, then I tiptoed past my set of rooms, through the upstairs hallways until I reached Paltiel's chamber. Paltiel did not have a strategy room like my father. He did have a large study, but the room was never used. From what I observed, Paltiel spent most of his private time within his expansive chamber.

Since this was not the palace, there were no guards, other than a few servants hired to watch the vineyards through the night. I slipped into the outer room and waited for my small lantern to illuminate the surroundings enough so that I did not knock anything over or stub my toe. The room was cluttered and smelled musty with a hint of the fermented stench of old wine. I paused and considered where to start.

Paltiel snored loudly in his sleeping chamber. Dinah told me that the servants often discussed how he could sleep through anything, so I decided to risk it and start snooping. It was time I started figuring out who the real Paltiel was, but more than that, I was desperate to find a clue about David. Anything that could point to where he was, what he was doing, and if he missed me as I missed him.

29

⊂ℬ⊱ℭ

King Saul

The Town of Ramah
1014 B.C.

The towns and villages welcomed me as I traveled through, but it seemed more raucous than respectful. I watched while crowds gathered to observe me pass.

A messenger outside of Shiloh approached my group. "A message for the king of Israel," the young man heralded.

I almost didn't permit him to tell me the news. I still struggled with what took place with David and wasn't sure I wanted to hear about the Philistines closing in on us. But everyone waited for my reply. "Go on and tell me."

"Samuel, the prophet from Ramah, is dead." The messenger bowed while on horseback.

My ears rang from the words. Samuel? Dead? "What?" I asked, glancing at my men, trying to find Abner.

"The prophet, Samuel, is dead," the messenger repeated. "The priests request to bury the body at Ramah."

"What?" I asked again, as my ears began ringing. "You must be mistaken." The noise from the crowd seemed to grow louder in my ears. "I must have misunderstood you."

The messenger repeated himself for the third time.

I held my head in my hands. I heard Abner ask for more specifics. I heard a rush of wind through my ears as if my entire world spun out of control. "No," I whispered. I needed Samuel to change his mind. I needed to hear that God would give me back my kingdom. That it would not be handed over to some glorified shepherd. "No," I said again, sliding off my horse.

"Saul?" Abner called out, but I had already pushed through the crowds, leaving my service behind me. "Saul!" Abner shouted, louder this time.

I moved quickly, pushing through the crowd. Some moved aside to let me pass, others reached out to touch me. I shoved their hands away and kept plowing through. The torment from the news ripped apart my insides. How could Samuel die? "Not yet," I pleaded. "Not yet. He has got to bless me. He has to bless my kingdom."

I reached the city gates and kept going. The town's sick and desolate called out to me. Some started to approach me.

"Stand down!" Abner commanded them, running toward them, his sword unsheathed.

Ishvi, my second eldest son, unsheathed his sword too. "Father, let us move out. We can grieve properly upon return to the palace."

"He was the one...the one who found me." I choked on my words. "My father's donkeys had taken off again, and I was sent out to find them. He anointed me king the very next day."

Abner motioned for me to come. "Let us mourn in private," he said quietly.

"What happened?" The events with David with the news of Samuel were too much. Tears wetted my beard. "God anointed me to be king, did he not? Samuel told me that I was God's chosen man. He cannot die! He must make this right!"

The crowd from the streets now crowded around us, but let them stare. All I could think about was the first time I met the prophet and the promise that came forth from his lips.

Abner and Ishvi guided me back to my horse, my guards leading the way. They helped me back onto my horse since tears compromised my vision.

Taking in a shaky breath, I wiped at my eyes and stared straight ahead. "Ramah," I ordered. "We head to Ramah. Send a messenger to the palace. My entire family needs to be there. Their caravans will need to leave almost immediately."

And then I moved with purpose, my mind replaying the many times I failed the prophet and feeling at a loss that there was no longer anything I could do about it.

***

The town of Ramah could not fit the masses who came to grieve. The priests were eerily cool around me, showing their disapproval without voicing a word. But I felt it. If my emotions weren't so raw and tumultuous, I would have handled their poorly masked disdain with a swift hand, but I could barely rise above the surface of grief's dark waters to remember to eat, let alone tackle a family of priests with little regard for me.

As the funeral continued, and the animal sacrifices made, I saw David and his grouping of warriors and their families on the south side of Ramah's tabernacle. The passing of the highly regarded priest required peace within the tribes. No internal fighting. But I still found it blatant and confrontational. They were far enough away that they could make a quick exit but close enough to be noticeable. I could easily see David's anguish, as could everyone else. David openly sobbed, as a young woman—a very pregnant young woman—comforted him.

My grief momentarily suspended as I watched the scene. Why was David grieving so tremendously? But then I knew. Because David had been anointed by Samuel, as well. Anointed to be king. Anointed to take my place. David and Samuel, from the reports, had visited several times in recent moons, as David often sought God through the old prophet. When Samuel wanted nothing more to do with me, he spent quality time with the next king in line to the throne. I scanned the large mass of people surrounding David and could feel the tendrils of anger and jealousy begin to choke my

217

soul. All of those people were loyal to David? And David had obviously remarried. I had mistakenly assumed that Michal was his weak spot. But he had used her as he had used the rest of my family. Could nothing stop him? I clenched my fists and focused on the remainder of the funeral, but my vision became blurred from seeing red.

It dawned on me that David probably only spared my life because Samuel requested it, and David respected the old prophet enough to obey him. What now? With Samuel dead, would David no longer hesitate to put his sword through my chest?

Then that meant that I was absolved of owing David my life. It had been part of David's game, to make me feel as if I owed something to that glorified shepherd.

As soon as I paid my respects and mourned the proper length of time, I would…what? Continue to hunt? I was tired of hunting.

The idea formulated immediately. There he was. Why hunt anymore when he was there for the taking. The darkness within me approved. I felt almost giddy. Ancient protocol no longer applied if the king revoked it. Which was exactly what I intended to do.

David would be dead by morning.

30

⊂ঌ৪০

David

The Town of Ramah
1014 B.C.

We could not stay long. My men were apprehensive. But Samuel was dead, and the whole kingdom seemed to show up for his burial. I reminded my soldiers of Saul's promise to leave me alone, but they refused to believe it.

"We stay at the outskirts and leave immediately," Jashobeam advised.

Throngs of people set up tents along the expanse of the valley near Ramah, bringing caravans of mourners. Did they feel the despair I felt? The gut-wrenching sorrow? Our spiritual leader gone. The same Samuel who had poured oil over our current king. The same Samuel who poured the oil over me. If I closed my eyes, I could envision it all over again. Abiathar, the young priest who had stayed with me and my troops these last few years, mourned alongside me. We tore our tunics and anointed our foreheads with ash.

Joab, my nephew who I had become close with, approached. "Uncle, your wife requests to see you."

The word 'wife' sent my thoughts in a tailspin because for just a moment I thought of Michal. I knew she was here. Somewhere in the expanse of this crowd. But I also knew it was for the best that it stayed that way. I would be tempted to kill the puny Paltiel for all to see and take Michal with me. Before I was on the run, I would have done it with no thought about the consequences. Yet, years apart had forced me to think…not as a lovesick boy…but as the future king. I could not have the people turn against me. That meant that I must play Saul's game. More than that, Ahinoam was pregnant again with our second child. I could not pine after the princess when I had a growing family. "I will go to her momentarily."

"She has come this way to see you."

"Very well then."

I sighed, leaving Abiathar still kneeling on the ground.

Ahinoam approached. "Hello, my lord," she greeted me. She still barely spoke above a whisper, and often kept her eyes downcast. "I am coming to comfort you. I feel that my time would be better served at your side."

"I appreciate your willingness to comfort me." I took her delicate hand and squeezed it gently. "But you are already doing so much caring for our son and for this little one." I placed my hand on her belly.

"Let me prepare you a warm meal," she said, as large caravans carrying carts of people stirred up dust not far from where we stood. She turned her head and coughed.

I positioned myself between her and the wagons. "I will not break my fast till the morrow, but I will visit you and Amnon then." I kissed her hand. "Where is the boy?"

"Napping. With the wet nurse."

"Please. Stay in the tent or underneath the shade of the large elm."

"We look forward to seeing you on the morrow." She reached for me and looked me straight in the eyes. "I am sorry, David, for this tremendous loss. I wish there was something I could do to comfort you."

I had a hard time masking the grief. I nodded, not wanting to talk about it. It was not fair to her that who I longed to talk to, to comfort me, was no longer mine. At least not in this moment.

It was then, I turned from her and zeroed in on the caravan

that was moving past us. And locked eyes with Michal.

Everything stopped. Everything. And she was all there was. My wife. Looking as beautiful and regal as the day I left. Jewels crowned her head, a sheer headdress revealed her raven hair, bracelets lined her arms, and the dark purple silk hugged her body perfectly. Her name escaped my lips. "Michal."

But she was too far to hear.

"Who?" Ahinoam stood beside me, trying to follow my gaze.

My heart dropped as Michal's attention turned from me to Ahinoam. I watched as her eyes dropped to Ahinoam's protruding belly.

"No," I said. "Let me explain."

"Explain what? Who are you talking to?"

I could barely register the concern in Ahinoam's voice. Because I was too caught up in the look of betrayal on Michal's countenance. "Joab!" I called my nephew.

"Yes, uncle?"

"Go to her. Explain."

"Yes. Who am I going to? What am I explaining?"

"I will handle it," Jashobeam said who no doubt understood exactly what was happening. "Would you like me to arrange something? If there was ever a time to meet, now is the time."

"Yes…no…yes."

"You are worked up," Ahinoam said.

"You are released," I said a bit sharply. "I will see you in the morning to break my fast."

Ahinoam's eyes were downcast again, and she left me, but my attention was not on her long.

I turned back to take in the sight of Michal, but she had already disappeared into the crowd.

***

I tossed and turned. Nothing appeased me. From the grief over losing Samuel to the grief over losing Michal, sleep evaded me.

Jashobeam tried to make the meeting happen, but with all the people, and Saul's men fortifying the area, it posed too great a risk. "We sent a message to her through the prince."

I knew Jonathan would make sure she received it, but it was not enough to satisfy me. My wife, the love of my life, was close.

Sitting up, I lit a candle, and finding my writing instrument, began to scribble the words furiously. My grief and anger poured onto the page. *Why God? Why has the king pursued me? Why take my wife? Why? Why? WHY?*

It was hard to see past the tears, but I did not need to see the parchment to feel the words. My heart ached onto the page. I wiped bitterly at my runny nose and kept writing.

The melancholy stayed with me as the darkest hour of the night lingered. Pages of parchment were filled and flung around my small tent. I eventually laid my head back down when the chill of intuition shot up my spine. I sat up fast and listened. A warning came to my spirit just as Abiathar rushed inside my tent. Instinct had me drawing my sword.

"It is only I, my lord." Abiathar had his hands up, as he stared down the length of the sword.

The guard followed him inside. "He rushed past me before I could hold him off."

"We must leave." Abiathar completely ignored the young man. "I have consulted the ephod. Immediately."

I was up and throwing on my tunic and girdle. "I felt it too."

Abiathar instructed the guard to pick up the parchment that littered the area. "You are to keep these," he said to me. "Do not throw away your words. Now, come."

As the guard handed me the pile of parchment, I said, "Go, and alert the others."

I looked down at all the words I wrote through the night. And God's answer was to have me run...again. "When does it end?" I asked Abiathar.

"I cannot give you a specific moment when it will be over,"

Abiathar said, resting his hand on my arm. "But David, it will be over one day, and you will be king. Do not lose sight of that."

Sighing, I turned away from him, dropped the rolled-up parchment in a small trunk, and muttered, "Let us go. I should have known that Saul would not be true to his word."

Abiathar opened his mouth to say something but closed it as I walked past him outside.

31

☙❧

Michal

The Town of Ramah
1014 B.C.

I reread the lengthy poem Jonathan's messenger delivered. I made sure my tears did not land on the parchment because I could not lose these words. The poem was beautiful and full of heartache and longing, and I felt my husband's anguish. But the tears came not from the message of the poem, but for the sight, I could not unsee.

The rumors were true. David remarried.

Another woman in his arms. Another woman giving him children.

Were there more?

I rolled up the poem and tied it in place. I wiped at my eyes and blinked back any more tears. At first, I had been angry. Angry that he did not wait for me, as I waited for him. The anger and betrayal mixed together to the point that I could not tell them apart. Dinah tried to make me feel better. All evening while others dined, I lied and said that I had menstrual cramps, just so that I could be left alone. But she stayed with me, reminding me that it was a man's world, and as future king, David could not waste all these years not bearing sons. Then my anger turned toward my father for ripping me apart from my husband.

I should be the one bearing him sons. Me. Not some other girl.

But now, none of that mattered. David was close by, and I

refused to let hurt feelings keep me from him. Even if it meant punishment. I needed to see my husband.

I changed clothes quickly, wearing clothing that a commoner would wear. The burlap and rags were itchy. I took off all jewelry, save for David's necklace. I placed a small idol from my collection onto my bedding, covering it up with animal skins. I heard Dinah enter and saw the wheelbarrow. She was coming in to help clean the contaminated materials. No man would enter my area with this excuse. The key would be to make sure that Dinah could get me out undetected.

"Are you sure you can push me?" I asked. Dinah gave me a look to show that it was a silly question. She carried far more weight in her arms than my small frame. I touched her face. "Thank you," I whispered. "I know I am asking a lot."

She nodded and looked away. Being here made her nervous. So far, my father acted as if he had forgotten all about my servant girl, which was fine by the both of us. But neither one of us wanted to bring unnecessary attention to her. "You may be dressed as a man," she whispered. "But you still look every bit a princess."

I brought the raggedy hood over my head and let it rest low on my head, then I wrapped a speckled scarf around the lower half of my face. Dinah shrugged. I quickly removed the material from my mouth and nose. "Yuck, where did you find these clothes?"

"One of Paltiel's manservants. One of the slaves wore them before giving the standard tunic."

My stomach flipped in disgust. I refused to lose my nerve. "We need to move quickly. Is the horse ready?"

Dinah nodded again, with her nerves all but bouncing off her skin. "What if you get caught?"

"I no longer care," I said if flatly, matter-of-factly. Then I kissed her cheek. "Remember, you feign innocence. No matter what. I cannot worry about you too."

She nodded.

"But we are two smart women. We will not get caught."

She did not look convinced.

"I must see him. No matter the cost. You understand that, right?"

Without waiting for a response, I climbed onto the wheelbarrow and lay on my side, bringing my legs all the way up into my chest. Dinah brought a pile of linens and dumped them on top of me. Luckily, they were mine. I still tried to find an opening from the pile to better breathe.

"Stop moving," Dinah whispered. "I am getting ready to leave your room."

Jonathan requested that his sisters stayed with him and his family within a portion of the living quarters assigned for the priests and their families. Merab chose to stay with Adriel and his men. I knew she enjoyed being the center of his universe. I also knew she enjoyed the attention of the other men, as well. The children were with them, or at least with their servants until Adriel left again. That meant that we should have easy access to outside without too much questioning.

Dinah pushed the wheelbarrow down the hall, not stopping for quite a ways. I counted doorways that I assumed we had to have passed. Eventually, she turned the wheelbarrow to the left. The wheelbarrow must have hit a protruding stone in the ground as my head smacked against it. I pressed my lips together and told myself not to move or make a sound. Soon there was another bump, and then another, and I knew she had made it to the outdoor steps.

The path became much bumpier, and there were several times I thought she might lose her grip and the entire wheelbarrow would be overturned.

I hugged my knees and prayed that we would make it to the well. Time dragged on, and I nearly threw the linens off me and jumped out. But I also knew that servants were rarely questioned when roaming the area doing their chores. My best bet was to endure the jostling of the bumpy ride and stick to the plan.

The wheelbarrow slowed then came to a stop. I stayed still

while waiting for Dinah's three taps. But they didn't come. I strained to listen, becoming more impatient by the second. That's when I heard the footsteps. Multiple footsteps. My heart beat wildly, but there was no conversation. No words at all.

Suddenly, the linens lifted from off of me, and I stared into the face of my brother.

He took one look at me and rolled his eyes. "I should have known," he whispered.

"I am going to see him," I whispered furiously. "Do not dare to stop me."

"There are commoners afoot," he said. "Vagabonds who would love to hold the princess ransom."

"Then let them. But I may not get another chance, and I am taking it."

Jonathan glared at me. "I have no time for this. David is in danger."

"What is the matter?" I sat up fast and stumbled out of the wheelbarrow. I noticed Dinah still bowed with her head lowered. "Dinah, you may leave," I told her. She stood, gave me a quick glance, and then left me.

"It is no matter for a girl." Jonathan turned to one of his men. "Take her back, and make sure she does not leave."

"NO!" I hissed. I grabbed Jonathan's arm. "Please. I implore you. Just send me on my way. I already have a horse waiting. I will not be gone long. I just...I just need to see him."

"A horse? What are you to do with a horse?"

"Ride it. I am trained to do so."

Jonathan did not mask his surprise. "You cannot go and say these things."

"We have no time to discuss this. Let me go."

Jonathan sighed. "You realize that you may not like what he has to say?"

I swallowed my emotion because I had thought of it many times. "I have to," I choked out.

"I hope I do not regret this." To his men, he said, "She will ride with me."

As we walked to the stables, someone said, "It will slow us down."

"Give me a horse," I said to Jonathan. "I assure you I can ride. Now is not the time for propriety."

We reached the stables where the king's horses stayed. I felt a chill shoot up my spine. I had planned on taking one of Paltiel's horses from our caravan, which was in the other direction. These horses were beasts. It reminded me of Beast, the horse that I grew close with while still at the palace. These horses had seen many a bloody battle.

I nearly agreed to ride with Jonathan, but I knew it would slow them down. If David was in danger, then I needed to show them that I would not keep them from their mission. My heart grew in respect and admiration for Jonathan. He loved David still. And he was willing to defy the king to protect his friend. "Thank you," I said under my breath.

Jonathan brought me to one of his trained horses. "He will be good to you," he said, petting the horse. "And he is not easily spooked." Jonathan whispered to the horse, while I petted it. "Let us make haste."

He left me with the horse. The few men with him were on their horses ready to ride. They watched me, but I could not lose my nerve and I could not waste time. Taking a deep breath, I used my arm strength to pull me up and over. It was not the prettiest mount, but I got on. The horse stayed still, as if very patient. "Thank you," I said to it, patting him.

Jonathan raised an eyebrow and seemed to take in the sight of me. "All right. No lanterns. There are enough embers still burning from fires that we should have enough light." He moved forward. "Stay close."

"I understand," I said, moving with them. I could see their hesitance. "We do not have time for hesitation. I *can* ride. Let us go."

"If anything happens, stay with her, and I will go it alone," Jonathan said to the men. I opened my mouth to say something. "The decision is final." He gave me a look that said to be silent. Then he left.

I did not wait for the other men. I kept up with my brother. At a later moment, I would have to sit back and be amazed that my brother, commander of the Hebrew army, thought enough about me to grant me this excursion. He could have ordered me back to my chamber. They could have taken me kicking and screaming. Yet, he did not.

The horses seemed to know the terrain, and Jonathan had us stick to an outside path that was out of the way but still offered some semblance of a road. The horse was twice the size of Eglah, but he was gentle and moved smoothly. If my mission was not so pressing, I would have let down the heavy hood and let the wind blow against my face. But now that we were on the move, I only had one thought...David.

The path led around the valley to the other side situated amongst forest. I knew enough of my husband to know that he preferred trees to open areas. "They are easier to climb and hide," he had explained once. His troops were expansive, covering the entire southern landscape. Did he always have this many men? And their families. The thought nearly brought upon another wave of emotion. I should have left with him. We should have run together.

And now, I shared him with another. *He is mine*, I thought bitterly.

As we drew near, Jonathan slowed, grabbed his bow and arrow, and shot the arrow up in the air and to the right of the encampment. As he put it away, he said to me, "It lets his men know that it is me."

Instead of continuing straight, Jonathan turned into the heavy brush, along the side of the path. I followed and found that he planned to go outside of David's encampment. Soon we were covered by the dense forest. I tried to adjust my eyes to the pitch darkness, but I lost my bearings.

Before I could panic, someone lit a flaming spear. That someone also sat on a horse to my left and had it pointed at my head. "Who are you?" Benaiah asked. I knew his voice and turned to look at him. "Do not face me," he ordered.

"She is with me," Jonathan said.

"She?" Benaiah asked.

Before he could say another word, I heard David's voice. "Brother."

David sat upon his horse. He and several men were all on horses, facing us. Just as this morning, he looked older and wiser. His beard had not seen a razor in many moons. His rust-colored hair had grown out in waves around his head. His eyes burned bright, and he sat on his horse with the confidence of a king. My heart longed for him so fiercely, I nearly cried out.

"I came with a warning. Be on guard. I doubt my father will follow protocol."

"Did he say that?" David asked.

"Why cannot the future king grieve in peace," a young man said to the left of him.

"One of the priests warned me." Jonathan added, "My father continues his pursuit this very night."

"Abiathar warned me, as well. I am making haste as we speak." David sounded tired.

"Who is this?" Benaiah asked, his flaming spear still aimed at my head. "Why is he not dressed in royal garb?"

I did not know if Jonathan or his men answered or acknowledged my presence because in that moment, David's eyes found mine. Without asking permission, I pulled the scarf down to my chin and then brought the hood down to my shoulders.

No one spoke.

My eyes stayed fixed on my husband.

"Michal," he said.

Benaiah lowered the spear.

"She was on her way to you. Unaccompanied."

David brought his horse toward me. I stayed frozen in that spot. Every emotion warring for control. Then he was beside me. His leg brushing against mine. He took my hand. "Michal," he said again.

One of David's men approached us atop a galloping horse. "Two come by foot. Two royal horses were abandoned several dozen cubits away."

"He is doing it alone," Jonathan said in surprise. "You need to leave. He will not be able to get to you while you are on horse."

"No," I said. "Not yet."

"Michal, he needs to leave." Jonathan's voice was firmed.

"Michal, my love." David squeezed my hand with both of his. Then he brought one hand up and cradled my face. My tears came unwelcomed. "We cannot do this here."

"Since we do not plan to kill the current king, what do we plan to do since he is nearly upon us?" The messenger asked.

David dropped his hand from my face and released the other one holding my own. "Move out," he ordered. He paused briefly to look at me one last time before leaving me in the dark forest.

I noticed Benaiah was last to leave. We made eye contact, and I observed nearly as much sorrow on his countenance as was on mine.

"Take her back to the stables, and return her to her chambers," Jonathan said to his men. To me, he ordered, "Leave. Now. And do not fight my men."

I had no more time. David's men had left, and now I needed to leave before my father discovered me. I followed Jonathan's men away from Jonathan and his armor-bearer.

Instead, I moved with Jonathan's men back to Ramah. Back to a life I never asked for. But for a moment, I was given a chance to remember my previous life. A life of love and contentment.

I waited until I was in the privacy of my own chamber to

weep bitter tears for a life I would likely never have again.

32

⚪❦⚪

King Saul

The Town of Ramah
1014 B.C.

"How did he find out?" I asked Abner. We stood just outside a thicket of trees, watching several on horses flee.

"There is no way," Abner huffed in irritation.

"I knew I should have stayed on horse. Being on foot cost us time."

"It was the only way to approach undetected. I was simply going along with the order."

"When have you ever *simply gone along with an order*? You fight me all the time."

"You woke me from a sound sleep. My thought process was to follow you along on this foolish quest to make sure you did not get yourself killed."

"You are so insulting to me. I should have you punished."

"If you must…"

"Oh, shut up. Do you think that was David on horse?"

"Of course it was. Now let us head back while there is another hour or two of darkness."

Abner and I heard the rustling of branches and the sound of hooves on the ground. He immediately stepped in front of me and pulled out his sword. "We have been spotted," he said under his breath, with no masking of the irritation.

But whoever rode the horse was not in a hurry. When it

cleared the trees, I immediately noticed the emblem of the House of Saul. I did not need to see his face to know who it was.

"Light the lantern," Jonathan said to the armor-bearer beside him.

The small light flickered, and I observed the stone face of my son. With the shadows and darkness surrounding us, it gave him a grotesque, eerie appearance. It reminded me of the nightmares I woke up to where Jonathan lay dead beside me. How could he not realize that I did all of this for him?

"What are you doing here?"

"I could ask you the same thing," he said.

I held my head high. "The king answers to no one."

"Except to God, which is why you are in the mess that you are in."

I scoffed, detesting the self-righteous tone.

"Why could he not have a few days to grieve the loss of the prophet?" Jonathan asked, his words heavily weighted with sorrow.

"Because I want it to end," I said through gritted teeth.

"It would end if you would leave it alone!" Jonathan yelled. "You could let him be, and then live the rest of your days in peace and prosperity!"

I refused to listen to any more of my son's disdain and contempt. He would never understand. My mood was sour and annoyed, and I wanted to leave immediately. To Jonathan's armor-bearer, I ordered, "Get off your horse."

The young man dismounted and handed me the reins. He bowed low. I shoved him aside and pulled myself up and onto the horse. Without another word, I left, bringing the horse to a run.

33

❦

David

The Wilderness of Paran
1014 B.C.

I watched as men set up tents and their women unloaded supplies from their caravans. It had become routine. There were only so many places I could hide with several hundred men and their families in tow. Unfortunately, for them, we never stayed anywhere for too long.

Being alone made hiding easier, but that was not an option. I already learned that difficult lesson. These warriors chose me as their king, and they would fight for me. Just the same, as I sat upon the horse, watching the scene before me, emotion got the better of me. "My men grow weary," I lamented to God. "As do I."

My emotional state had become more volatile after my encounter with Michal. I could not question my decisions because none of the events that transpired these last few years were expected. That did not matter when I saw my beautiful wife on that horse. I was tempted. For a brief moment. Tempted to forsake it all and choose her.

But there was a bigger picture, and I had a vast amount of people to think about. In that moment, there had been no time to think. No time to come up with a plan. I could have grabbed her from off that horse and taken her.

"You are thinking about her." Eleazar approached.

"What makes you say that? I am simply overseeing this set

of troops."

"And you have commanders to do that job."

"I often oversee my men. Nothing new here."

"Yes, and normally it is when you are pensive. When you are deep in thought, you watch as a way to remind you of what is at stake."

I did not respond because, although I had not thought about it like that, he was mostly right.

"She was dressed in beggar's apparel," Eleazar said.

"I know. She surprised me."

"It was a man's outfit."

"I know."

"She sat on the horse…like a man."

"I know. Decorum matters little to her. Which is partly why I love her so much. What kind of princess would dress in such demeaning apparel, only to hop on a horse and ride out in the darkness? My wife, that's who."

"A princess in love with her estranged husband. She went to great lengths. I respect that, and it saddens me."

"Yes." I swallowed back the emotion. We did not speak for several moments. "Why did I not take her?" I lamented. "She was right there. Why did I not snatch her up from off that horse?"

"I would ask if your feelings have changed for her, but I know that is not the case."

"I was in shock," I admitted. "I did not expect to see her, and then, in a moment, I had to flee."

"Is that the only reason?"

"What do you mean? What other reason could there be?"

"We are struggling here," Eleazar said. "We are continually seeking supplies. We are on the move, living along the cliffs and caves of the countryside. Remote places that are hard to live in. It is as if you are choosing her safety and comfort over either of your happiness."

"I keep hoping that something will happen. Something will

turn the tide."

"You have chosen a hard road, which reminds me. Have we inquired after Nabal? Our supplies are low."

"Yes, we should have supplies shortly. After our protection of his shepherds and sheep, I am positive he will reward us handsomely."

"Well," Eleazar said, patting my back. "I will leave you to your thoughts."

"Eleazar," I called after him. He stopped walking away and turned to me. "She was right there."

"I know. But you were not expecting it."

"This life, the one I am living now, it *is* hard."

"She understands. I am sure of it."

"No," I said, shaking my head. "She does not. I saw it in her eyes. She feels betrayed. But I must do what I must do. That is what conflicts me."

"No one said being a king was easy. It is not. There are going to be countless decisions you are going to have to make that will be upsetting to many." Eleazar paused, then asked, "Do you really want my opinion on this matter?"

"Yes. Speak freely."

"Let her go. She is from another life. One day that life will be given back to you, but not today or the foreseeable future. The longer you keep the princess as the ruler of your heart, the more anguish you bring upon yourself, and upon your current wife here who will never measure up. So, let Michal go. Saul made an unfortunate decision for you both, and what is done cannot be undone. At least not in this moment."

As Eleazar left me to myself, I allowed his words to sink deep.

Let her go.

But the words rang in my ears like an ill-tuned musical note. I was not sure letting her go was even possible.

***

I took the bucket and poured the warmed water over myself, rinsing off the remnants of soap and ash. I still did not like the idea of anyone helping me bathe.

"David?" Jashobeam called from the outside of the tent. "We have heard back from Nabal of Maon."

"Oh good. I will be right there." I tied my hair back and threw on my traveling garments. I would need to thank Nabal properly. The prominent and wealthy man would likely be more than generous in food and supplies, especially after my men helped guard over his sheep and shepherds. Vagabonds were aplenty in these parts, and Nabal often left his shepherds unprotected.

As I stepped outside, a waddling two-year-old collided with my leg. I reached down and picked up my son before the tears commenced. "Careful there, Amnon," I said, kissing the inside of the boy's neck.

The toddler squirmed and pushed against my beard.

"There he is," Ahinoam said, struggling to walk since she was full with child. "My apologies, David. Neither my maid-servant nor I can keep up with the little guy."

"This is fine," I smiled, throwing Amnon in the air, delighting in my son's squeals. "I do not see him enough as it is." My son brought me great joy, and I was grateful to Ahinoam for providing me offspring. I played with him inquiring after Ahinoam. "How are you?" I asked awkwardly. Ahinoam was lovely and polite, and I could not complain about her. But I would be lying to say that she was Michal's equal. I knew it was unfair to compare the two, but I could not help it, Ahinoam did not compare to Michal on many levels.

"I am doing as well as can be expected," she said. "I am more than ready for this next one. It has been a trying period."

"Yes," I said. This pregnancy had kept her bedridden for the first four moons.

I glanced over at Jashobeam who waited patiently with

several of the young men they sent as messengers. "I will visit you this evening, if I may, but I have to discuss some matters with Jashobeam."

"Of course," she said, taking Amnon. "I will have something prepared."

Amnon leaned across his mother, reaching his pudgy hands at me. "Papa…papa…"

I waved at my son then left him with his mother and walked over to Jashobeam. "So? What is the report? I am hoping he was more than generous."

Jashobeam acted not only displeased but outright upset. "Not at all."

I raised my eyebrows at my friend, waiting for clarification.

"He refused, sir," One of my nephews stepped forward. "He said, 'Who is this David? How do I know that he has done me any service?' He even went on to say that the country is full of runaway servants who are not deserving of good bread and wine."

My mouth dropped open. I was not expecting that response. "Surely he did not say those words. He said that?" The smile on my face from playing with Amnon had disappeared. "Please tell me you are jesting with me."

"He is like every other countryman, forgetting what you have done for the land," Jashobeam said, his nostrils flaring, his chin jutted out.

I sighed, then shook my head. "How easily people forget," I agreed, thinking about Saul who pursued me with a vengeance. By God's hand, my men and I had enough time to escape Saul from Ramah. Currently, we were stationed in the wilderness and forest of what the locals called Hakilah Hill south of Hebron, and it had bought us some time.

"We are too low on supplies to send troops out to Mizpeh," Joab said. "The bounty from there should be helpful, but we need the resources to actually get there and sustain our men for the fight."

Jashobeam affirmed Joab's statement. "Nabal's refusal to

239

help costs us greatly."

"Yes, Mizpeh will be messy." My men needed to gear up and move toward Mizpeh to help the town press back against the Philistines, who were nothing more than a boil on my backside. No matter how many of them we killed, more and more kept sprouting up. "We need those supplies."

"Taking the supplies by force will not get us the right attention. Nabal is powerful in the area and has many connections," Uriah had approached and offered his input. "Then again, he has insulted the heir to Israel's throne."

"So, do we accept the insult and find someone else with supplies, or do we go and take the supplies anyway?" Joab asked.

My irritation boiled into anger. "Why is it that when I help people, they turn around and stab me in the back?" I thought of these past years, and how tirelessly I had worked to secure Israel's borders. Only to be continually treated with contempt? "I help all of Israel and kill a giant, and what is my reward? I am robbed of my wife! I am a fugitive in my own land! My parents have to go into hiding! How many towns have I helped? How many have I kept from the siege of the Philistines? Have not all of them somehow reported me to Saul?" The more I talked, the louder my voice became, the more the anger seeped through my words. "Even the Ziphites, who have no loyalty to Saul, tattle on us out while in the wilderness of Ziph! It is never ending!"

"What do we do?" Jashobeam asked, acting as angry as I was. "Do we continue to suffer insults? Say the word."

"No," I said, as something inside me broke. All my emotions, all my hurt came to a head. Something needed to change. My decision to not kill Saul was unwavering, but from here on out, those who were not loyal to me and the continuation of the kingdom of Israel would face my wrath. "My patience has expired. Nabal is as good as dead. All of the countryside will learn that you do not insult the future king." To my nephews, I ordered, "Tell the men to gather their swords. Leave two hundred behind to protect the camp."

"Yes, sir," they said and left.

Jashobeam and I glared at each other, both angry at the same thing. "Will it ever end?" I asked my friend and advisor.

"I do not have the answer, but it is wearisome."

"It is."

"The men want a secure location to raise their families," Jashobeam said.

"I know." I pulled on my beard, weary myself. "Do you think I like the idea of my wife raising our children on the run?"

"Did they not understand what they signed up for?" Uriah asked the both of us. "Enough of their complaints! These men are warriors. Sleeping in fields, always setting up camp, this is what they do and have done. This is nothing new. At least here, we have our families. Under the king, we would leave them for many moons, all while being treated horribly."

I listened to Uriah's words and took comfort in them. "Thank you. You are right. It could always be worse."

"We gladly serve our king, which is you. This is not an easy life right now, but we know that the time will come when we will be rewarded for our service. Until then, we side with you. Anyone who complains should be silenced immediately."

I watched as Jashobeam studied Uriah. "He is right," Jashobeam agreed. "We are here at your good pleasure. I will send word to our men, reminding them of their commitment. Most of them were unwanted by the current king. They need that reminder, as well."

"First, we handle Nabal, then we can talk with our men," I said.

I moved to leave with Jashobeam, ready to find the arrogant Nabal and show him just who he was insulting, when Uriah stopped me. "A word?" he asked.

"Can we talk and walk?" I asked.

"Sure." Uriah kept up with my pace. "I know that you have strong counsel in Eleazar, Jashobeam, and others, but if I may offer some advice on an observation I made?"

"Of course. Speak freely."

"You try too hard, my lord."

His statement caught me off guard. Mostly because my focus was on getting revenge on Nabal. "Try too hard? Should I not try?"

"You are always trying to please everyone. Someone complains, and you try to fix it. But you are future king. You do not have to explain yourself so much."

We had reached my horse. I paused before pulling myself onto it. "Thank you for speaking freely. I will meditate on your words."

"I know that we do not have the history that you have with some of the others, but I am loyal to you, my king." Uriah bowed.

"You have saved my life countless times," I said. "You are my friend, Uriah. I trust you and am glad you chose my side. Now, are you coming?"

"To exact revenge upon that cowardly Nabal? Of course. I would not miss it."

Uriah left me to find his horse. For a moment, as I waited for others to join me, I contemplated the words of my men. After I ran away alone, I had tried to appease the men, and to be the leader they needed me to be. But the idea of being king still seemed a long way off.

***

By mid-afternoon the following day, we reached a ravine that would lead directly to Carmel, the land of Nabal's fields. "Show no mercy," I said to my men. "After all we did for him guarding his possessions from the wild, he insults us and refuses to honor us for our service."

"Uncle?" Joab asked from the left side of me. "Do you see that? On the other side of the ravine?"

I looked and saw a small grouping of servants on donkeys, some carrying baskets or pulling carts. "Is that a woman following

242

them?" he asked.

"Let us approach," Jashobeam advised. "It is a small group, and they do not appear threatening."

As we descended down and through the ravine, I watched as the servants and donkeys moved off to the side and only the woman on a donkey approached. Eventually, she slid off the donkey and stepped toward us. Suddenly, she fell on her knees and bowed low.

"Whoa," Joab said.

"You can say that again," Shammah said. "Who wants to bet that is Nabal's wife, and that she is smarter than her husband?"

I slowed as I approached the woman, stopping right in front of her. This entire scenario was not expected. From my men's expressions, they were just as bewildered. I slid off the horse and stepped over to her. She glanced up at me, then bowed low again. "Master, please, let me take the blame for my husband's foolishness. He is mean and a brute, but I have come to make it right."

"Please look upon me," I said, moved by her humility.

As she sat back upon her knees, I met her gaze and took in the sight of her. Since married, she had no veil, and I became enraptured by her comely face and sparkling eyes. She reminded me of Michal. "You are married to Nabal? He insulted me and my men."

"I was not there when your young men arrived, or they never would have been treated so poorly. But I am here now, and I see it as God protecting you from avenging the foolish Nabal's death. And when God further blesses you and makes you exalted over Israel, you, my master, will not have this weight around your neck."

"You know who I am?" I asked, impressed by her eloquence and persuasive skills.

"You fight God's battles," she said.

I helped her up. "It took great wisdom and courage to come out here like this."

"You have a God-protected life," she said. "I know who you are. The lives of your enemy will be tossed aside...as a stone is thrown from a sling."

"So unexpected," I said to her, a smile spreading across my countenance. "You are the blessing from God. He sent you to meet me and used your good sense to look out for me. I was blinded by my anger and would have acted rashly."

"I only ask that when God has worked things out for you that you remember me," she said.

I looked back to my men and saw they were as amazed at the beauty and resourcefulness of this young woman as I was. "I will remember you," I promised.

We stayed locked in each other's stare until she turned to her servants and said, "See to it that these men are given our gifts." She bowed again. "I must take my leave. My husband will be looking for me."

"What is your name that I might remember you properly?" I asked.

"Abigail," she said with a soft smile.

"Abigail," I said to myself as she turned her donkey around and left me staring after her.

34

❧

Michal

Paltiel's stables on the outskirts of Gallim
1013 B.C.

I brushed my horse, lost in thought. It was where I spent most my days. When I could break away from the boys, I would come out here. Not that I would ride. The last time I got on a horse to ride was the night I saw David. And that was several moons ago.

Each day passed, and I found that raising three boys took most of my time. It was best that Merab rarely came to see them. She was pregnant again—and miserable—and the boys bothered her too much. I was struggling with my own dark thoughts that I could not gather any rousing words of encouragement for her. The last time we spoke, after she spent the entire afternoon ignoring the boys all the while complaining of her fat ankles, I snapped. "It is tiring to hear you complain. You have a husband who loves you, boys who adore you, and a fertile womb. Yet, you sit and complain. If you have nothing good to say, then stop talking."

"Be careful, sister," Merab said with heavy sarcasm. "Your jealousy is showing."

"What makes it worse is how unhappy you are with all your blessings."

"And yet, I do not see it that way. I see it as I am stuck in a life I do not want. I would much rather be in your situation. Paltiel leaves you alone, and you spend your entire day, doing what you want. By the way, have you figured out why he leaves you alone?"

"It does not matter anymore," I said and ended the conversation. I had stopped investigating after my interaction with David. After seeing him with another woman. The heartbreak was so intense, it made it hard to get up in the morning or to even breathe. I forced myself out of bed for the children. They needed a mother's love, regardless of how I was feeling. And they were not receiving it from Merab. In a way, I was grateful for the three boys because they kept me from sinking into darkness and despair. They were light and life. "And you too," I murmured to the horse. "You listen to my secrets, don't you, Eglah."

My thoughts were interrupted by approaching footsteps. As I focused on Eglah again, I realized I had brushed her so much, and the brush was overrun with horsehair. "Sorry, girl," I told her.

"Michal?"

I stopped cleaning the brush at the sound of Paltiel's voice. We had barely spoken since the funeral.

"Michal," he said, now at Eglah's stall. "I knew you would be here." When I did not reply, he said, "You come here often."

With a newly cleaned brush, I went to the horse's other side and renewed the brushing.

"Your father is coming for a visit."

I fumbled with the brush and it dropped to the ground. Now I turned my attention to Paltiel. His eyes shown with the fear I felt. "Why? Did he give a reason?"

"Does he need a reason? And I think we know the reason."

"How long do we have?"

"Three days."

"We cannot say any of the children are ours," I said. "He will not believe us. They have Adriel's coloring."

"We need to tell him something," Paltiel said. To himself, he added, "There is no way I can escape punishment."

"I will tell him of my missed cycles. I have struggled with it since I was young."

Paltiel gave me a look that showed how unbelievable that

sounded.

I thought of what Merab had told me over a year ago. "Why have you not--" I stopped, unable to say the words. "It is strange for a man to simply respect a woman's wishes, and based on our previous experiences, it does not make sense. Merab thinks...well, never mind. None of this matters. Let him come." I went back to brushing the horse.

"You still do not understand, do you?"

"No, I do not," I said simply. "All I know is that four years ago, I was taken against my will and forced to marry another man, even though my husband is alive and well."

"Have I not treated you kindly?" he asked, indicating the horse.

"Yes, and I have thanked you many times. This horse, and my sister's children, have given me some semblance of a life. I would have drowned in despair otherwise." I watched as a range of emotions flooded Paltiel's features. From fear to anger to hurt and then back to fear. I picked up the brush that had fallen while contemplating his behavior. Paltiel had refused to keep his hands to himself while I lived in the palace. He blackmailed my mother into pursuing my hand in the first place, and he cared little for the fact that I quite obviously despised him and loved another. So, why, after these four years, was he respecting my wishes? Why has he defied a direct command from the king? Any man would have obeyed the order and consummated the marriage and continued in intimacy until conception took place. "What are you hiding?" I asked. "There is something you have kept from me these last few years. What is it?"

Paltiel glanced over at me, and I immediately saw the guilt in his eyes. Then he looked away without saying a word.

"What is it?" I repeated. "If it is about me, then I should know."

"Is it not always about you?" he asked, throwing his hands up in the air. "Oh, this is my reward for behaving badly toward the queen. And now I will die! Either by the current king or the future one!"

"So, David did threaten you," I said, wanting to feel the warmth from the thought of his protection. Instead, I only felt emptiness.

"Oh, he did not only threaten me. Oh, no. He sent me a gift. It was very smart. Very clever." Paltiel's voice raised in pitch, as he worked himself up. "The runaway heir sent me his sword. With dried blood still on it. His messenger told me that it would be my blood and the blood of my children on that sword, should I violate you in any way."

"He sent *his sword*?"

"Yes. And his spies check on you often. I do not know how they do it, but I find messages everywhere. Usually on small pieces of parchment with a knife holding it in place on the outskirts of the vineyard."

"All this time...?"

"And have you heard of the escapades of his pack of men? They will stop at nothing. They are little better than savages!"

"Those savages help protect the kingdom while my father loses his mind. We live in peace at the moment because of my husband and those *savages*."

"Peace? This is what you call peace?"

"Yes. My father has left us alone for years. You are rich in possessions and land. You have wives and children. You do not worry about tomorrow."

"Yes, I do. I do worry about tomorrow. The moment you moved into my home, I have been filled with worry."

"Your kindness toward me will not go without reward," I said, seeing how upset he was. Had I been that much in a fog that I failed to notice all these clues? David had been all around me, and I had failed to see it. "If he comes for me, that is. A lot has changed recently."

"Are you referring to when you rode on one of the king's horses to go see David?"

"How do you know? What are you talking about?"

"I know all about it. David sent a messenger, reminding me of my imminent death if I touch you."

"It matters little," I said. "He left me. I was ready. All he had to do was take me with him. But he has created a new life."

"Either way I wind up dead. By one king's hand or by the other. That is what you have cost me." Paltiel turned and left me with the horse.

I wrapped my arms around Eglah, but no tears came. Only frustration and anger. I had no say over my life, no real control. My father held the reins, and regardless of how hard I tried to live a productive life, to move forward, a heavy cloud seemed to hang over me that I could not escape from.

Suddenly, I felt the need to ride. "Are you ready for a ride, girl?" I asked her.

Eglah nudged me and snorted in approval.

"It *has* been too long," I said, refusing to wait for a stable hand to assist me. I prepared the makeshift saddle and straps.

Before I finished preparing for my ride, one of Paltiel's servants ran into the stable. "Princess Michal? It is Master Paltiel. He has collapsed. Servants are carrying him to the house, and a messenger has been released to find a doctor."

"Collapsed?" I stopped preparing the horse and followed the servant out of the stable. Concern trumped curiosity. Paltiel had provided me a roof over my head, and I knew it had something to do with the panic of knowing father came to visit.

The two of us ran to the house where Dinah waited for me. "Is it bad?" I asked her.

"He is barely responding."

Paltiel's other wife came rushing out of the house. "What did you do to him?" she shouted.

Her anger toward me did not surprise me. She had ignored me or glared at me with contempt since the moment I stepped into Paltiel's home. Most days, we did not see each other, but this was one out of maybe a handful of times that she directly spoke to me.

Now was not the time to deal with her irrational behavior. I moved around her and toward Paltiel's private chamber. I thought of our last conversation in the stable and felt the sharp pain of guilt. I wanted to not feel anything, reasoning that I did not ask for this situation either. But the guilt was still present.

Paltiel's manservant did not allow me into the private chamber, explaining that Paltiel was resting.

"What happened?" I whispered.

"He collapsed. One of the men he was with said that he kept pressing on his chest, trying to collect his breath."

The rest of the afternoon and evening I paced outside his chamber. Lanterns were lit within the halls as the sunset. I eventually sat on the floor and dozed through the night.

Paltiel's manservant shook me awake. I observed the early morning light. "You may go in for a few moments, but please do not agitate him. The doctor will be here on the morrow."

At his bedside, I took a moment to study the room. With candles lit, the furniture and clutter were more fully revealed. But that was not what I searched for.

"It is not in here," Paltiel said.

I turned to him and saw that he watched me. "How are you feeling? I was alarmed by the news."

"These spells come and go," he said. "They have been more frequent these last few years."

"I am glad to see that it is not as bad as I originally thought. When they said you collapsed, I thought the worst."

"It would be easier on you if I died," he said simply. "You could go back to your husband."

"I...I do not wish your death," I said, surprised by his statement.

"Do you not? I am what keeps you from David."

"If David wanted me, nothing would stop him." As I said the words, bitterness flooded out. "He did not come for me. I have been here these last several years, and instead of retrieving me, he marries another." I tried to blink back the tears, but they pushed through and trickled down my face.

"There is a reason for it." Paltiel pushed himself up to a sitting position. He held out his hand as if reaching for mine. I paused before placing my own hand in his. "He would not threaten me so if he did not plan to come back."

"Yet, here I am."

"I think he sees it as a way to protect you. Your father pursues him to kill him, and we both know that King Saul has no scruples when it comes to hurting you. At least if you are here and out of the way, the king pursues David. At least that is what makes sense to me."

I shook my head. "Do not make excuses for him."

Paltiel's other wife stepped in with a bowl of steaming liquid inside. "Please do not let me interrupt," she said, looking pointedly from me to him. "I am only here to take care of my husband. The one I do not turn away from. The one I do not feel is beneath me. I am his real wife." She set the bowl down beside him.

"Laia, please, no quarreling." Paltiel released my hand and took hers in his. "We must all find peace in this situation, even if it is challenging to do so."

"It is difficult to not be quarrelsome when she walks around your home with her nose raised as if she is something more than the discarded daughter of a mad king." The words stung, but Laia was not done. She glared at me. "Paltiel never had these bouts of chest pain until you showed up. He is trying to appease both the present and future kings and suffers relentlessly because of it."

"You act as if I showed up on purpose to make your lives miserable," I said. "I never wanted to be here. I was ripped apart from my husband."

"Then why do you stay?" Laia's voice raised. "You are free to leave. You can ride a horse like a man. Go! And leave me and family alone!"

251

"That is enough." Paltiel pressed his hand to his chest. "I cannot have this conflict right now. Both of you need to leave."

Laia kissed Paltiel's forehead, whispered something in his ear, then turned and left the chamber. Not knowing what else to say, I followed behind her. She waited for me outside the chamber door.

"You need to leave," she said.

"Where am I to go?" I asked, throwing my hands in the air. "Do you think I would stay here if I had a choice?"

"Go to your husband. Does he long for you as desperately as you long for him? He will not turn you away."

"And what of my sister's children? I am raising them now."

"Yes, that is right. You must raise another woman's children because you cannot have any of your own."

And there it was. The one reality that hurt me the most. Without my husband—my real husband—I could not have children. My insides shook, but I could not find any words to fight back.

As I pushed past her, she grabbed my arm.

"Do not ever grab me," I said. "I may be a discarded princess, but I am still the daughter of the king and the wife of the future king. You do not want to make me an enemy."

"Leave, or I tell the king about your little secret with your maidservant. I have heard the two of you talking. I know she ran away from the palace and that her tongue is supposed to be cut out. I also know that it would get you and a lot more people in trouble if the king learned of this deception." Now she smiled. "So, get out. I will even make sure your sister's children are sent home. To their real mother."

I made my way to my chambers but paused at the doorway. Dinah looked up from playing with Ashvi. She went to speak, but I shook my head. I wanted no more questions. My insides already shook from the anger and bitterness of the words spoken. Not because the words were insults, but because they were true.

Before any questions came, I left and headed to my horse. One of the servants had tied Eglah to one of the porch pillars. I lifted my skirts, revealing the riding trousers, and pulled myself onto the horse. As soon as the servant untied her, I took the reins and left the house behind.

At the trail that led to the outer vineyard, I let Eglah run. The wind whipped my face, which kept the tears from blinding my vision. Eglah and I went further than we ever had before, past Paltiel's property and along the outlying forest. Eventually, she wore herself out, so we slowed and stopped. I took in the scenery of the trees and meadows before me, but not for long. My mind went to the issue at hand.

Do I leave? I knew that traveling alone as a woman was dangerous. And what of Merab's children? They already had a mother who could not care for them. But it was the thought of David not wanting me that made me hesitate the most. What would I do if he told me he no longer wanted me?

Lost in thoughts, I almost missed the trio of horses, carrying the royal flags. I squinted at the road that led to Paltiel's dwelling. Even from my distance, I could see that horse in front was moving fast.

Father?

I turned Eglah around. "We have to move fast again."

Eglah seemed willing, so I pushed the horse to go as fast as possible. Even with Paltiel's other wife's animosity, I could not leave her to tell my father any secrets. Dinah had sacrificed too much, and I refused to lose my sole friend in this world outside of my sister. I could not allow Paltiel to face my father alone. No, I could not leave. I never asked for this life forced upon me, but there were people who needed me. If nothing else, I promised myself to do what I could to protect those who needed me most.

Any thoughts of leaving were cast off into the wind.

35

❧

King Saul

The Dwelling of Adriel
1013 B.C.

I was irritated. And there was no one to talk to about my irritation, which only irritated me more. Enos tried to soothe me with music, but it only reminded me of the only musician who could lessen the darkness and quiet the madness, so I ordered them to leave. Rizpah visited with her mother, and the other concubines bored me.

"Bring me the queen," I commanded Enos.

"My king, she visits her daughter."

I scowled. "At this early hour? Which one?"

"The eldest. Queen Ahinoam comforts her during a troubling pregnancy."

I paced my outer chamber. "Speaking of daughters, did my message get delivered to Michal?"

"Paltiel received the message. They look forward to your visit."

"How easily you lie," I muttered, remembering the severity of my last visit. "And Abner? Has he returned?"

"No, sir. He scouts the deserts for the runaway heir."

"He should be back by now. The new moon feast is nearly upon us."

"And he will, my king. As will your sons."

I stopped pacing, the agitation only becoming worse. "I must leave here. Get my horse. I will visit my eldest daughter. It has been too long since I have talked with her."

"But your wife is there…"

"So? Go, get my horse!"

"Yes, my lord." Enos bowed and left.

I waited while an attendant secured my riding cape, annoyed that I allowed Abner to talk me out of going with him. But at that moment I suffered with heat exhaustion and the comfort of the palace tempted me. At first, I enjoyed the respite. But the darkness and shadows that whispered often did not let me enjoy it for long.

With my guardsmen in tow, I set out for Adriel's dwelling. Merab married well. Adriel worked hard and pleased me greatly. That thought led me to Michal's arrangement. I did not feel guilty, only sorrow. Sorrow for what once was. The glorified shepherd, turned menace, ruined my relationship with my youngest daughter. I hoped that he would be killed quickly and my family would be restored to me. But it would happen soon. I refused to believe in any prophecy or fortune that told me otherwise. I would continue to hunt David down like a dog, then once he was found and killed, my family would come back to me. And I, being a gracious king, would welcome them back.

Once there, I waited for my guardsman to state my visit, then slid off my horse and entered the house. Adriel's servants bowed low. "I am here to visit my daughter."

No one said anything or moved.

I pointed my sword at the closest servant. "Do not make me repeat myself."

"Sh-Sh-She is not well, my lord."

"Where is the queen? Bring her to me, so that I may assess the situation."

"Th-The queen? She is not here, my lord."

"I was told she was here visiting our eldest daughter." I turned to my guardsmen, none of whom seemed to know what was going on.

"She is not here, nor has she been, my lord."

"Bring me to my daughter immediately," I snapped.

The one servant who had addressed me, stood straight, kept his eyes down, and led me to the inner courtyard. "The king of Israel calls upon you."

I saw Merab resting among plump cushions, her face pale and without paint. She turned to me and tried to stand. The servants surrounded her to help. "Leave me be!" she complained. As she approached me, I noticed how sickly she looked. "Father," she said breathlessly. "I am honored by your visit."

"What happened? Why are you sick?"

"I am pregnant," she said with a bite to her words. "Pregnancy has never been kind to me."

"Bearing children is noble and one of the few things a woman is good for."

Merab watched me and pressed her lips together before saying, "Yes, father. Would you care for some refreshment?"

"Yes," I said and moved restlessly around the courtyard. I waited until after Merab ordered her girl servant to bring trays of figs and bread, along with new wine from the wineskins. "Where are my grandsons? I would like to greet them."

"They are away."

I raised my eyebrows in surprise. "Where would they be?"

"Michal helps me raise them. As I stated, pregnancy is hard on my body. I do not have the energy or patience to have the children underfoot."

"Am I to assume that is why your letters to me have been infrequent?"

"There is nothing new to share. Michal has acclimated to life with Paltiel."

"No news about whether or not that glorified shepherd has been in contact with her."

"No, I do not believe he has. I have tried to encourage her to search for answers, so that I may have something to report. And even though I have spiked her curiosity, she has discovered nothing."

Merab's maidservant brought in trays of food and wine. I went over and popped a fig into my mouth. "Did she receive the horse?"

"Yes. She enjoys it. My eldest son, Ashvi, rides with her."

For a moment, I envisioned Michal on the horse with a young boy, showing him how to handle the reins. I found myself smiling and missing my youngest daughter simultaneously. Then I thought of who tore us apart, and the sweet memory was over. "Paltiel did not reveal to her where the horses came from?"

"No, he did exactly as you told him."

I inhaled deeply. "I know she does not realize this yet, but I am protecting our lineage from a usurper. My main regret is allowing her to marry that shepherd. That decision has cost both of us. Maybe one day she will not look upon me with such hatred."

"Let her live in peace. That is the place to start. She has a good life with Paltiel."

"She has your children, but what of her own?"

Merab's gaze dropped from mine.

"I am going to find out in two days' time. Has she disobeyed a direct order?" I felt the flicker of past anger.

"Father, it is not that simple when a woman is barren."

"Barren? She was carrying a child at one point."

"Yes, but her body would not let it grow." Merab paused, "I do know that she and Paltiel have tried. They do not wish your wrath upon them."

"So, they are, in fact, married by consummation of covenant?"

"From Michal's conversations, yes."

"She could be lying to you."

Merab looked at me in a way that expressed her disagreement. "Michal cannot lie to me. We are sisters. Besides, she does not know that you require me to report on her."

"I suppose I will find out for myself. I have a way of getting the truth out of people. Which reminds me, I need to find your mother. She said she was here, and she is not." I shook my head. "If it was the Ashtoreth shrine, she would have said as much."

"I did not realize you cared about her goings-on." Merab pressed a hand to her belly and winced as if in pain.

"When she lies about where she is going, I take it upon myself to find out. I have enough liars around me. I refuse for my wife to get away with her little excursions."

Merab suddenly yelled, "ELIA!"

"Merab?" I went to her.

"Father, stay back, the baby is coming."

Elia and another servant rushed in.

"Attend to your mistress!" I ordered. "Is there a prepared room?"

"Yes, my lord," Elia said, helping Merab out of the room.

"Someone get the midwife!" I bellowed.

Servants ran around in a frenzy.

"Father?" Merab called out.

"Yes?"

"Please bring me my sister," she said, with a whimper.

I opened my mouth to repeat the order to a messenger, but I stopped myself. The realization hit me that my daughter was not well. More than the need to deliver a baby, Merab looked like a sick soldier about to take a last breath. The thought moved me into action. I ran out of the room. "My horse!" I yelled, not waiting for anyone to open the door.

My guardsmen scurried, one quickly bringing me the horse. I pulled myself up and over and was already pushing the horse to move before the guardsmen caught up.

The journey to Paltiel's brought a flood of memories. The memories brought up emotions. I tried not to think of my last interaction with Michal. But the scene replayed in my head. Had I really slapped her?

I arrived at Paltiel's and was off the horse before it came to a full stop. "Michal!" I said to the line of servants. "I need my daughter now!"

"She is in the vineyard, my lord," a servant said, his head still bowed. "We will retrieve her."

"I will retrieve her myself," I said, climbing back on the horse. I refused to stand around and wait. As I rounded the back of Paltiel's dwelling, I took in the vastness of his vineyards. "Where would she go?" I asked anyone who was around to listen.

"I will take you, my king," one of the laborers approached on donkey. "I am heading out to the winepress right now."

"The donkey will be too slow. Point me in the right direction."

He pointed me in a direction, told me to follow the wagon trail, and sent me off. Once on the path, it did not take me long to see the winepress in the low valley. The closer I got, the more I saw the scene. Laborers had all stopped what they were doing and forming lines, but I could not place Michal. I saw a horse moving fast, coming from the east. I looked in disbelief. "Michal?"

There she was. Sitting atop a horse, riding it like a man, her hair blowing in the wind. She directed the horse to the other side of the winepress and out of my line of vision. By the time I stopped my horse in front of the laborers, Michal was walking out of the storehouse, patting her hair down. We made brief eye contact before she bowed. Her eyes used to light up when she saw me, but not in several years.

"Father," she said. "We were not expecting you for another couple days."

"Your sister. She requests your presence immediately."

Michal's head snapped up.

"The baby," I said.

"It is early, is it not?" She walked to my horse.

"She did not seem herself," I said. "Come with me. I will take you to her."

She took my hand, and I helped pull her up and onto the horse. She situated herself behind me, straddling the horse like a man and wrapping her arms around my waist. "I am ready."

We left together, and if it were not for the immediacy of Merab's situation, I would have wanted to slow down and enjoy this moment with my daughter. "I saw you riding," I said, trying to keep my tone light. "You ride it like a man."

"Yes," she said simply. "It is easier to manage the horse."

"And Paltiel approves?"

"Yes, he bought me the horse because he heard I have a fondness for them."

I smiled to myself, glad that she was enjoying the beast. I wanted to tell her it was from me. I wanted her to love me again, as she used to. But I knew that day would never come until David was dead. Just thinking of him soured my mood, but I did not want to hear the darkness. So, I enjoyed the ride with my daughter and longed for the day we could be as we once were.

Of
Tears
And
Triumph

36

☙❧

David

The Desert of Ziph
1013 B.C.

I stood outside Ahinoam's tent. My men and I rushed back to the camp at the news.

When Eleazar's wife stepped out, I looked at her expectedly. "How is the baby? How is Ahinoam?"

Eleazar's wife frowned and shook her head. "I am sorry, David," she said. "The baby was already dead. It looked like it had been dead in her womb for some time."

I covered my mouth and closed my eyes.

"The labor was hard. She lost blood, but I think she will come through."

I thought of the little baby already dead and could not keep the tears away. "Can I go in to see her?"

"You know the custom. She is still bleeding. But I think even more than that she still needs time. So, give her that."

"I want to see my son. I want to see Amnon."

"Of course." Eleazar's wife summoned a maidservant. "Bring Amnon to his father."

"The boy is sleeping," the maidservant answered.

"I will go in and look upon him," I said.

Both women looked at him as if he had lost his mind. "You cannot enter her tent," Eleazar's wife said.

"Let me through," I said, stepping into the tent anyway. I walked over to where Amnon slept, among cushions, his little thumb in his mouth. I knelt beside the small bed and wept over my lost children. Not only this one, but the one Michal had carried years prior. As the evening turned to night and my tears dried, I heard the muffled crying in Ahinoam's chamber. I knew our customs, but I did not care. I had not been there for Michal, I needed to be there for Ahinoam. I kissed Amnon, then stood up and crept to the opening that led to my wife.

For a moment, I watched her. The candles were dim, but I could easily see her staring at the side curtain, her body shaking with sobs. "Ahinoam," I whispered. Her body stopped shaking, but she did not turn to me. I entered and stayed at the foot of the bed. "I am so sorry," I said. "Is there anything I can do?"

But there was no reply.

When I left her tent and headed to my own, I stopped and fell on my knees, weeping again. I almost felt as alone as I had felt when I went into hiding by myself. How could I be surrounded by all these people and still feel as if it was me against the world? "Come to my rescue, and deliver me out of these troubles," I pleaded with God. "Come to my aid."

Instead, I struggled sleeping. I awakened up from nightmares of being chased. The last nightmare I was holding my dead child. "Amnon," I said, before waking up with a start. I pushed myself up and out of bed, washing my face with cold water. "Amnon is alive," I said to myself. "It is a dream. Amnon did not die."

"Uncle?"

I heard Joab and stepped out of my bed chamber. "Hello, nephew. I hope you slept better than I did."

"Not at all, sir. I am just arrived with word that Nabal is dead."

"Nabal? From Carmel? The one whose life we spared several days ago?"

"Yes, the very one. We heard through a message from his wife—now a widow—that he died of a heart attack."

"Abigail," I said, my heart suddenly pounding loudly. "She is no longer married?"

Joab gave me a perplexed expression. "No, sir. She is not."

Eleazar, Shammah, and Jashobeam all entered. "Did you hear?" Eleazar said in excitement. "Nabal is dead."

"This is a divine miracle," Shammah approached and kissed my cheeks. "Our shortage of supplies is soon to be over!"

"Abiathar is drawing up the marriage contract as we speak," Eleazar said. "This contract will provide much needed resources."

"I told them that you probably had a rough night," Jashobeam said. He was the only one not smiling. "This is not a good time for you."

"It is all right," I said to him. I briefly thought of Ahinoam, a girl I still barely knew, then I thought of Michal. Thought of her tenacity, her spark for life, her brilliance, her beauty. But mostly I thought of Abigail. She intrigued me, and I wanted so desperately to not feel alone. "I want her," I said before I could talk myself out of it. "Go to her immediately and offer her my hand in marriage. Tell her I want her to be my wife."

Joab nodded. "I will do so directly."

"Yes, and hurry."

Benaiah and Uriah stepped through into my tent. "Where are you headed?" Benaiah asked Joab.

"To Abigail," Joab said, sneaking a quick glance at me.

Benaiah and Uriah both looked over at me with raised eyebrows.

"Nabal died," Eleazar explained.

"I knew you liked her," Benaiah said. "But should you wait until...?"

"No, I do not want to wait. I cannot stay in grief. It will not

265

bring the baby back."

"We need supplies. This marriage would be a blessing," Uriah said with a shrug.

"Anyone else coming?" I asked and sat in my place. A young preteen boy and his sister, who had been assigned to serve my meals, began to set out a simple meal of bread and cheese—from Abigail's gift—and an assortment of figs now in season. I reached for a fig as the boy handed me a goblet of wine. "Water first."

"Saul is upon us," Jashobeam said simply. "Our scouts have observed them traveling southward in this direction. We doubt they know we're at this specific location."

"Why is that?" I asked, already feeling tense and unnerved.

"Because they are almost literally on top of us. On the other side of the mountain."

"They are probably headed to Ziph again," Benaiah said. "I did not think they would come in this direction. We are far to the west of the Ziphites."

"Which means they found out our actual location, or they are traveling through the entire expanse of wilderness to get to Ziph. Either way, they are here." I rubbed my face. The lack of sleep was catching up to me.

"They do not know our actual location. If they did, we would be dead or hostages. No, they have no idea. Which is why I advise that we act first. Take them by surprise." Jashobeam looked at me.

"And do what?" I asked.

"We kill them, David," Jashobeam said slowly. "We take every last one of them out. We win. You become king. We no longer live on the run."

"Sounds like a plan," Shammah said.

"What did I miss?" Uriah asked, coming into the tent with my other nephew, Abishai.

"We are attacking Saul and his men," Shammah answered.

"Good. About time."

"No. We are not." I glared at them all. "Let us devise a plan

266

to pack up the women and children immediately. We planned for this. Several caves will do nicely. We will take to the above hills and wait them out…"

"We are going to stuff our families in caves?" Jashobeam asked. "Do you hear yourself? Your poor wife is at death's door, and you are going to pack her up?"

"What choice do I have?"

"KILL HIM!" Jashobeam slammed his fist on the low table so hard that every dish jumped, some toppling over. "This is the second time that God has placed him within your grasp. The SECOND time. Your decision to let him live affects all of us! And our families!"

I shoved off the cushion and stood up.

"He is right," Eleazar said. "David, I understand that you do not want to take the throne by force, but these are desperate times. And what Jashobeam says is true. It seems as if God himself is placing him within your grasp. This can be *over.*"

I studied my best friend. Then I examined all of my advisors' faces. Good men. Loyal men. "I should be angry. I specifically stated that we were not to bring this up again." Jashobeam went to say something, but I shut him down. "No. Let me finish. I know what you all have sacrificed. I will never be able to repay you for it. And I am not resisting out of pride. I do understand where you all are coming from. Saul deserves to die. He is a crazy, envious, bitter old man who has wreaked havoc on my life and yours for years."

The men sighed. Several rubbed their tired faces.

"He has told all of Israel that I am a rebel, a fugitive. How easily the people's hearts have turned. Nabal, who we once helped and protected, looked down his nose at us! If it was not for his wife, I would have killed him and his whole household! No one would take the rebel leader of a pack of misfits seriously. But it is more than that. I am not God, and I will not take Saul's life in my hands. I will not do it. I will become king when the Lord determines that it's time. And not one second before. To be honest, I feel as if God is toying with me. Maybe that is not the best choice of words. Testing is a better word. I feel God is testing me."

"He is testing all of us then," Uriah said. "But we will weather this test just as we have before." He smiled at the other men. "Come now. Let us not quarrel on this again. David, our king, has spoken. Saul will live...for now. Surely he cannot live forever."

A few of the men grumbled.

"And if you are dead?" Jashobeam asked me. "What then?"

"Samuel anointed me king when I was a boy," I said. "There have been many times that I have questioned if the prophet got it right, but today, I believe he did. I am still standing, and I should have been dead countless times. I choose to trust in the Lord. I am the future king of Israel, and I choose to wait on God's timing."

The men stayed quiet for a few minutes.

"I disagree that we are a pack of misfits," Uriah said good-naturedly.

I grinned. "Have you taken a look at yourself?"

Some of the tension lifted.

"What is your plan then?" Jashobeam asked. "Send the women and children before us?"

"Actually," I said. "I think I might have a better idea."

"What's that?" Eleazar asked.

"They are on the other side of this mountain, right? Could I get there by nightfall?"

"Definitely."

"Then they have made camp for a few days, I would presume. So, I will do what I did last time. I will sneak up on him and remind him that I mean not to hurt him."

"Have you lost your mind?" Eleazar asked. "Dump yourself in the middle of the Hebrew army who all have direct orders to kill you on sight?"

"Technically, they are to capture me and bring me to Saul. I guess he wants the honors. I will go by myself."

"We're not sending you in by yourself," Jashobeam said, still grouchy. "Let us think of another plan."

"It will work!" I said. "Think about it. He turned around last time. Completely."

"Yet, he's still chasing us."

"It was Samuel's death. I know it. He probably thinks that since the prophet is dead, I have nothing to keep me from killing him."

"If only," Jashobeam muttered.

"I will go," Abishai said. He smiled at me. "We can handle it, Uncle David."

"You are barely twenty," Shammah said. "You would probably get him killed."

"Have you seen him in action?" I asked. "He will be fine. Suit up, nephew. We will leave immediately."

"Who else should go?"

"No one," I said. "If more men go with me, it will be more difficult to sneak in undetected. You stay back and get things ready. Just in case. Chances are, if he has me, he will have no need of any of you, but just the same."

"Is that supposed to encourage us?" Eleazar asked.

"I will be fine. It is like you said, God delivered him to me. So, I will remind him that I am not the enemy."

"Let me go," Uriah said. "You will need someone to scout, and I am familiar with the territory."

"All right," I agreed. "Thank you."

All the men stood up and left. Benaiah blessed me before leaving. Jashobeam grudgingly left, still irritated. Only Eleazar stayed back. "Would you like me to go?" he asked.

"No, I will be fine. The fewer people, the less chance of detection."

"They will have scouts."

"Yes, I will be careful."

"Are you sure this will work?"

"I have run out of options, friend. Hopefully, I can convince him that I pose no threat."

"You will never fully convince him."

"I only need to convince him this time. If nothing else, it gives us a chance to escape without incidence."

"Then what?" Eleazar said, tiredly.

"I will think of something."

"Then God be you."

"As you told me all the days of our youth…He is," I said. And I hoped with all my heart that He was.

***

Abishai, Uriah, and I huddled together, looking down at Saul's army.

"This almost seems too easy," Uriah whispered. "I do not see any movement at all."

"Well, we did wait until the dead of night."

"No," Uriah said. "There is always someone up. Scouts, guards, prostitutes."

"Prostitutes?" Abishai whispered. "How come we do not keep prostitutes in our camp?"

"Are you serious?" I stopped scoping out the scene to glance over at my nephew.

"No?" Abishai answered, looking at Uriah for help.

"Don't look at me, kid," Uriah chuckled. "You are on your own."

"So, here is the plan," I said, still whispering. "I will go down and see if I cannot do what I did before. Cut the hem of his robe, or maybe take his spear or something. Then I will head back here."

"Sounds good," Uriah said.

"Who comes with?" I asked. "I will need another set of eyes."

"I will go," Abishai said.

"Uriah, if anything happens down there. Rescuing us is not

270

your mission. Your mission is to get back to camp and stay low."

"My mission is to get back to camp, round up the 600 able-bodied soldiers, and come back ready to kill."

"Do not kill Saul," I ordered. "Besides 600 against what looks to be a couple thousand is no match."

"Gideon only had 300 men and look at what he accomplished. Besides, your band of misfits has killed a whole lot more than a couple thousand in one sitting."

"Let us hope it doesn't come to that." I motioned for Abishai to move. We both stayed low and climbed down several sets of hills that surrounded the landscape. I stopped and listened, as did Abishai. But there was no sound of movement. Only a small breeze and the distant sound of a crackling fire inside Saul's camp. "Saul is right in the center of camp, so we will have to not make a sound as we approach," I whispered in my nephew's ear.

"This is it, uncle! The time to act is now! I can see him sleeping from here. See his spear at his head? One move and that is through his heart. I do not need more than a second to do it."

"No. We stick to my plan."

We furtively moved past tents and snoring soldiers, but nobody so much as twitched. I paused just outside of the few surrounding Saul. All of them, even Abner, acted deep in sleep. "Take the spear and the jug," I mouthed to Abishai.

Taking both the weapon and the water jug, Abishai tip-toed over Saul's guards and around them, but none stirred. I would not have believed it if I hadn't been there to experience it. When we made it outside the camp and up the first hill, Abishai started to laugh. "That was incredible. Nobody moved."

I looked back at the camp. "That was God. It had to be." I thought about my men and how easily it would have been to be done with it all. I shook my head.

"What?" Abishai asked.

"Somethings I do not understand."

When we reached Uriah, he looked us both over. "That was

quick. A little too quick."

"The whole camp was asleep," Abishai answered him. "Every single person."

Uriah made eye contact with me, and I knew exactly what he was thinking. Then he shrugged and said, "You are my king, and I will not question your decisions. At least not out loud."

"Good," I said. "Because at the moment, I am questioning my decisions for the both of us."

"What now?" Abishai asked. "Go back to our camp with his things?"

"You two go off aways, so you have a quick exit." Before either of them could say anything, I ordered, "Move. Leave his things."

Once they left, I turned to Saul's camp and shouted, "HEY, ABNER!" I paused, then called again, "Abner! How long must I call you before you decide to wake up?!"

I heard Uriah and Abishai snickering behind the bushes. They evidently did not go too far.

Movement in the camp began in waves. I watched as Abner pushed himself up next to the fire, searching for where the voice was coming from. "Who's talking to me? Show yourself!"

"Is that how you keep your king safe? Fall asleep? Did you not even assign any guard to stand watch? And now look what I have…the king's spear and water jug. You should lose your job over this."

"That is David," Saul said, already standing. "Isn't that right, my son? Coming at me again without my knowledge?"

"But not for your life," I answered. "I came to ask, why do you still pursue me? Am I nothing but a flea, yet you waste all this time and energy chasing after me? How do you explain that? Once again, I have proven that I am not your enemy. Is this not enough? Can you not leave me alone in peace? If God wants me dead, He does not need your help doing it. Do not continue to tarnish my legacy by believing rumors and spreading them."

Saul ran his hands through his hair, pausing them to press his temples. He turned to Abner and they communicated quietly. I could not hear them from where I stood. I watched as men woke up and some started toward me. I was still far enough away, but my heart still beat loudly in my chest. Saul turned in my direction though he still acted unsure as to where I was. "You are right, again! Come down here and let me honor you. I am done playing the fool. I am done."

The words did not ring true. I did not believe him for one second. "Let the Lord see that he delivered you unto me today, yet I honored His anointed and did not harm you. Here is your spear," I thrust it into the ground. "Send one of your servants to retrieve it."

Then I moved quickly into the darkness, distancing myself from soldiers who drew too close. I motioned for Uriah and Abishai to get up, and together we headed back to camp. Most of the way Uriah and Abishai laughed about the apparent victory, but I mostly stayed quiet, hoping that my actions would at least buy them enough time to find somewhere else to live.

But weariness descended upon me as I realized that I had run out of places to hide.

37

CℨℰↃ

Michal

The Dwelling of Adriel
1013 B.C.

I did not need to take a look at Merab to smell death in the room. It smelled of excrement, blood, and despair.

"She has lost so much blood," Elia said, not holding back emotion.

I stood in place unable to move. *Not my sister. Please, God, do not take her from me.*

"Michal?" Elia gently touched my arm. "She continually asks for you."

I walked past the curtain that had been erected, only to immediately halt at the sight. My stomach rolled. The amount of blood nauseated me.

"There is one more that needs to come out," the midwife said, grimly. "His head is stuck."

Merab whimpered, and my gaze fixed on hers. She was so weak, she could not move, so I went to her and sat beside her head. I picked her head up, kissing her sweaty forehead. I wiped her face and kissed her again. "You are all right," I said, wanting desperately to believe it. "I am here. You need to push the baby out."

"Stuck," she said, too weak to form a complete sentence.

"We tried to stand her up, which often helps, but she is too weak."

I could see the worry on Tamara's face.

"I have her loosened enough. One more push and I can hopefully grab ahold of the baby's crown."

"Hear that?" I said to my sister. "You are almost done."

Merab whimpered, and with a sudden burst of strength, wrapped her arm around me. I helped her sit up partly. "Up," she said. "Stand me up."

I ordered Elia and two other servants to assist. Merab moved like a rag doll, but by some miracle, we women got her standing. Tamara laid out several large sacks on the floor underneath Merab. Her weight was too much for me, but I refused to let my sister down.

"The next wave is coming," Tamara said, feeling Merab's swollen belly. "Squat, and push as hard as you can, and I will do what I can to catch the baby."

Merab's fingers squeezed me so hard as her next wave of labor came that her nails dug through my skin. I gritted my teeth and forced myself to help hold her up as she squatted and pushed simultaneously. Her wail shook my insides, and I felt the trickle of my own blood go down my arm from where she dug her fingers in.

"There he is," Tamara said.

Merab's legs gave out, as the other women and I dragged her back to her bed. I took a cool rag to Merab's head, while the other women tried to clean up the blood. "You did it," I said, kissing my sister's head. But Merab was unresponsive.

"Come on, little one," Tamara said, gently slapping the newborn, then cleaning out his mouth. Suddenly the baby's body jerked, and he coughed out a wail that pierced the room. "God's blessings upon you. It is another son!"

"Did I hear that there was another baby?"

"Yes, he came out nice and easy, but then the distress came. The wet nurse has him. Would you like to see him?"

"In a little bit," I said, turning back to my sister.

Something was wrong. Her head lay at an odd angle. "Merab?" I felt her chest for signs of life. "Merab?" Panic fell on me like hot lava. I shook her. I lightly tapped her cheek. "Merab?"

Tamara came up from behind me. "Let me have a look."

But I did not listen. "Merab, say something. I know you are tired. Flutter your lashes. Here, here is my hand." I tried to hold her hand, but it was limp. Lifeless. "Merab!"

Suddenly, two servants had me by the shoulders and were moving me away from my sister.

"No." I struggled against them. "No! Merab? Do not leave me! Merab!"

"Let Tamara help," Elia said.

But one look from the midwife told me all I needed to know. My sister was dead.

38

❦

David

Outside Gad
1013 B.C.

Most of camp was packed up with portions of it already on the move when Uriah, Abishai, and I returned.

"How are my wife and Amnon?" I asked Eleazar, who stood with at least a dozen of our warriors. I noticed my tent still stood erected, but the tents for Ahinoam and her maidservants had been taken down.

"She is well enough," Eleazar said as if choosing his words. "The women went on ahead with 200 soldiers closer to Jeshimon and more into the forest. It will not do for long-term, but it will work until we come up with a more permanent solution."

"How did it go?" Jashobeam approached and asked. "Uriah said that it was as still as a dead man's heart."

"Yes, Uriah tells you correctly. I was able to move in and out of the camp nearly effortlessly. Abishai and I took the king's spear and water jug, and then we were a safe distance I called out to him and asked him to stop this game of cat-and-mouse."

"It worked," Abishai said. "They did not follow us."

"It is a temporary fix," I said, not masking the gloom that had befallen me since our return.

Eleazar stayed quiet.

"I was tempted," I said to my old friend. "For a brief moment, I thought of all of you. I thought of the sacrifices we have made. How easy it would have been. I knelt beside the sleeping king and thought, *Why Lord, are you doing this? Why give him to me when I know that I must protect him?"*

"And did God answer?"

"He was as silent as Saul's camp."

"So?" Shammah and several others now surrounded me. "Where are we going? Where can we hide outside of Saul's grasp?"

I sighed. I had an idea. One that I began mulling over through the night as we headed back to our camp, but there were too many variables.

"You have an idea, but we will not like it," Jashobeam said, reading me perfectly.

"Just say it," Eleazar said. "We do not like most of what comes out of that mouth."

"Gath," I answered before Eleazar finished speaking.

"What was that?" Eleazar asked. "Did you say--?"

"Gath. Yes, I did."

"The Philistines?" Abishai's eyes widened and his mouth fell open.

"You were unsuccessful at hiding yourself," Jashobeam said. "And you think you are going to hide 600 soldiers, not counting their families?"

"I am not planning on hiding anyone. What would happen if I offer my services to Achish?"

"What services?" Uriah asked. "Like soldier services?"

"Like mercenaries," Jashobeam said, still watching me. "The king of Gath would love to have someone like David on his side."

"All of us are deadly," I said. "Not just me."

"So, you would offer all of our services to the Philistines? The very people we have been fighting against for the past several years?" Shammah looked at me as if I had lost my mind.

"And if we kill our own people?" Jashobeam asked. "Have you thought of that?"

"Yes, I have, but there is a way we could avoid doing that."

278

"We cannot kill our own people, just as we cannot kill Saul." Shammah placed his hands on his hips, shook his head, and laughed. "This is crazy, David. Even for you."

"The Philistines have many enemies other than Israel. We could focus on them. Chances are we would not have to touch any Hebrew."

Once again, no one spoke. The men acted tense and unsure. *How much longer, Lord?* I thought. *How much longer must I push these men to the brink of exhaustion and death?*

"I think it is a decent idea," Benaiah said, stepping forward. "Saul will not pursue us if we are in Philistine country. We are already soldiers, and many of the Philistine enemies are ours, so I do not see why we are acting squeamish about this."

"Because it is the Philistines," Shammah said.

"This is not the first time a rebellion hid within the walls of the enemy, and it will not be the last. Many of Israel's forefathers dwelled among the enemy and were protected." Benaiah did not back down from Shammah.

"You were not with us when we sliced off 200 foreskins," Shammah said. The others around him agreed. I could see several were becoming agitated. "You do not realize how much they hate us. Especially David."

"We are dead here, but we have a chance there. It is a sound political move. Achish desires David dead, but I wager what he desires even more is for David to be on his side."

"If we could have handled Saul, none of this would be needed," Jashobeam said with a sigh.

"Why are you bringing that up again? David has repeatedly asked us not to. Do you support David or not?" Benaiah yelled.

Jashobeam whipped around on Benaiah and grabbed him in a chokehold. "Do not ever question my loyalty again, or that day will be your last. Just because we do not see eye-to-eye does not mean I would not follow him to the depths of hell. Which is pretty close to where we are at."

But I knew what was coming before Jashobeam did. Benaiah was highly trained and simply knocked Jashobeam's legs out from under him. Jashobeam fell with a thud, and Benaiah within that same second was on top of him, pinning him down. "Never do that again," Benaiah said. "And for someone who is loyal to David, you certainly never shut up about your complaints."

Jashobeam spit in Benaiah's face and used the opportunity to bring his legs up and wrap them around Benaiah's neck. The two wrestled along the ground. "Enough," I snapped. "We are not the enemy. We will not fight amongst ourselves."

Shammah grabbed Benaiah, and Eleazar grabbed Jashobeam.

Benaiah wiped off his face. "You spit on me," he said in disgust.

Jashobeam smirked at him. "Keep talking, and I will do it again." He maneuvered out of Eleazar's grasp and glowered at me. "Let us go pay a visit to King Achish. And may God protect us from the enemy's hand. And from each other."

***

"This could go terribly wrong," I heard someone whisper from behind me. I chose to ignore it. Mostly because I had thought the same thing.

Jashobeam, Shammah, and Uriah went ahead of us to parlay with the king of the Philistines, King Achish. We thought it too dangerous for me to go with them out in the open. My head was wanted throughout the land. The last thing I needed was to kill Philistines on the way to seek a truce with their king. Which meant only an invitation from King Achish would work.

Three days had passed since they left, and I was trying not to worry. What if the king took one look at my men and slaughtered them? It would be a declaration of war, which was the last thing I needed. I was already warring with an undesired enemy. Abiathar prayed with me and counseled me these last few days, consulting the ephod, and encouraging me that this was the right path.

But weariness tormented me. Here I was right back to the Philistines.

"Uncle David, someone is coming," Abishai said, bringing me out of my thoughts.

I focused my attention where Abishai pointed. I saw the three men approach on horseback. "It is them." I breathed a sigh of relief. At least they were not dead. "Let us hope they come with good news."

When the three men got close enough, I saw their grim expressions. My hope dissipated. "First, and foremost," I said to them. "I am glad to see that you are well. We have anxiously awaited your arrival."

The men around me chanted a blessing.

I continued, "I take it from the dour expressions that I do not have an invitation."

"Oh, you do," Uriah said. It was a surprise to see him so grim-faced. He normally stayed the most optimistic out of the men. "But they mean to kill you."

"Achish seemed quite eager to meet with you," Shammah added. "I believe it was sincere. His lords, however, they wanted to kill us on the spot. Uriah overheard part of their discussions with Achish."

"They spoke very fast," Uriah said. "But I know Philistinian phrases well enough to piece together their plan."

"They released us to bring you to them. They plan to accept the peace treaty to get you there. The lords want Goliath's brothers to be there." Shammah looked pointedly at me. "To take turns."

"Jashobeam? What say you?" I asked. I knew he hated the idea to begin with, but he had yet to speak since they returned.

He took in a breath, glanced over at Shammah and Uriah, then said, "What they say is true. I saw it on the lords' faces. They want no peace with you."

"Is there no way?" Benaiah asked.

The men who surrounded me began to talk among

themselves, which quickly spread the word through the ranks. "Where do we go from here?" someone asked.

Jashobeam held up his hand to silence the men. To me, he said, "Just because the lords want to kill you, does not mean that we reject the idea."

Shammah shook his head. "Let me say that the three of us do not necessarily agree."

"What are your thoughts?" I asked my brother.

"It is risky. Too risky. The thought of them going near you to harm you in such a way sends chills down my spine. I do not like the idea of putting you in a situation where we will be surrounded on all sides with men who want to take turns slicing you into pieces."

I saw the emotion on my older brother's face and nodded in understanding.

"Then we think of another way," Eleazar said. "Protecting David is our mission above all else, so let us break for camp and then come up with another plan of action. There are many undiscovered caves in the Judean Mountains. All is not lost. God will provide a way."

"Jashobeam and Uriah do not agree with me," Shammah answered Eleazar.

Eleazar raised his eyebrows in surprise. I, too, was surprised. Jashobeam was against the idea from the very beginning. "What has changed your mind?" Eleazar beat me to the question.

"Achish's desire to conquer far outweighs his need for revenge," Uriah answered first. "I saw it in his eyes, as he listened to his men. The lords were discussing ways to kill you, but there was a glint in his eyes that showed something else."

"It is as Uriah says," Jashobeam grudgingly agreed. "I saw it too. He was seeing conquests and victories."

"It is too risky," Shammah said again.

"Achish wants Israel most of all," Jashobeam said. "Having Israel's hero switch sides will be too much for him to refuse."

"He was practically salivating. Told us to bring you at once.

That the truce will stand as long as an agreement is made."

"If I am within his camp, an agreement may be forced upon me," I said. "But I never expected it to be easy."

"There are plenty of undiscovered caves," Eleazar said to only me. "You do not have to do this."

"We have lived in caves for the last couple years," I said. "Let us see what Achish says."

"And what of Shammah's concerns?"

"A friend once told me that there was nothing King Saul could do to stop God's will from happening. Do you remember that?"

"Yes," Eleazar said simply.

"We either believe that, or we do not, my friend."

"Then God be with us because I am accompanying you."

***

"I cannot believe my ears," Achish said in broken Hebrew. "David, the one and only, who we have been looking for eight years, is standing before me, asking for a truce." Achish paced in front of me, Jashobeam, Uriah, Eleazar, and Shammah. The rest had stayed back to await word. Achish took his sword and pointed it at my chest. "Tell me again why I do not want to slice you right here."

"Because you need me," I said, refusing to look away. They may have forced me and the four others on our knees, but all four of us stared down the King of Gath. The lords of Gath sat forward, anticipating the violence. I could feel their hatred. They talked to Achish in their native tongue, and I understood enough to know they awaited command from their king to kill. So, I kept my eyes on Achish and prayed that God was with me. "I will fight for the Philistines. I know we share common enemies. They will not stand a chance against me and my men. All we ask is for a town of our own. A place where we can lay our heads in peace."

"And the king of the Hebrews has not provided that?" Achish asked. When I did not respond, he continued, "Are you not the

Hebrew hero? Did you not kill our giant?"

I heard the hissing of men around me.

"I would think that you would be like a god among your people."

I did not desire to speak out against Saul, so I simply kept my eyes on Achish.

"He hunts you like a rat, does he?"

"I am at your service, my lord. That is all that matters. My men and I are fierce, and we will be at your command. Your enemies will fall at our feet, and the world will sing the praises of Achish and the Philistine army."

Achish glanced over at his guards, an impressed smile. But his lords were not having it. "Let me at him," one said in their tongue.

I could feel the tension between the four men beside me. I knew that they had several plans ready to be carried out should this not go as planned.

Achish answered his men, "If we kill him, there are warriors like him that will see this as an act of war."

"Was it not an act of war the countless times he killed our men?"

"But Saul's hatred of him works to our advantage. Do you not see? With David busy keeping our enemies at bay, Israel will not have their hero. I think I like this. We send these scoundrels off to do our dirty work. It saves Philistine lives, and if David and his men die?" Achish shrugged. "It is no loss to us."

To me, he said, "The Geshurites have been nothing but trouble, as have the Girzites and the Amalekites. You raid those three providences, bring me back all beasts and belongings, and I will give you Ziklag."

"Consider it done," I said, in Achish's Philistinian tongue.

Achish grinned and walked over to me, helping me stand up. "You and I," he said. "We make better allies than enemies. Now we no longer have the giant, but we have the one who slew him. Even better!" He slapped me on the back and kissed me hard on the cheek. "Now go settle in, and give me a detailed report when the assignments are complete."

After the Philistine guards saw us out, we quickly left the palace and moved outside its walls. When we were out of eyesight and earshot, Eleazar leaned against a stone wall and took deep breaths.

I refused to let my resolve falter, but I still asked, "Are we all good?"

None of the four answered. Instead, Shammah asked, "What in the world did we just sign up for?"

"You heard him. We will do his dirty work," I said, not any happier. "I do not like it, but at least our families will be safe in Ziklag. It is a nice piece of land."

"How long do you plan to be allied with Achish?" Jashobeam asked as we continued forward through Gath's streets.

"We are both serving a purpose for each other. That is all. Let us keep it at that for right now." I had to breathe through my mouth, the stench on the streets of Gath was overpowering.

"Gah," Shammah covered his nose. "Let's hope Ziklag does not stink this badly."

Two men plowed through us. Both of the Philistines eyed us with steely appraisals.

"I hope we know what we are doing," Jashobeam muttered.

I did not bother to respond. Because I simply did not know the answer. I did not relish the thought of following Achish's rash orders, but until Saul's death, I had limited options.

We traveled outside the city gates, not far from where I had slept a couple years back. We moved quickly to where our messengers waited with their horses.

"Should we tell them to meet us at Ziklag?" Jashobeam was asking.

"Yes," I answered. "Achish said to settle in before we began our raids." To the messengers, I said, "Ziklag is about right in the middle of the mountains, south of here and north of Beer-Sheba."

"Yes, I am familiar with the location," one the young men said.

"Good, direct our caravans to head in that direction. We will follow too and assist right behind you."

"Yes, master." Before leaving with the other messengers, he said, "Oh, and Joab has returned with Abigail. She has agreed to the marriage covenant and is in waiting."

Even with the trepidation still lingering, Eleazar looked at me and raised his eyebrows at the news. Shammah, Uriah, and Jashobeam did not mask their smirks. "That is pleasant news," Shammah said.

My first thought was one of hope. Maybe now I would not feel so alone. "Well, gentlemen," I said, trying to not show how eager I was. "What do you say we go check out our new home?"

We pulled ourselves onto the horses and headed south to Ziklag.

39

⋙⋘

Michal

Paltiel's Home
The Outskirts of Gallim
1012 B.C.

"You need to eat something," Dinah said, setting down another tray of food. The previous one from the morning remained untouched.

I did not respond.

"You look unwell," she tried again. "A warm meal will replenish your strength."

The infant squirmed in my arms, searching for his next meal. "He needs to feed," I said, handing him over to Dinah.

I did not need to look at her to know she was worried. My maidservant took the baby and left to find the wet nurse.

Paltiel rode up to the open porch with Ashvi and his other son riding with him. Since Merab's death, Paltiel had tried to keep peace in the house and was extremely kind to Merab's sons. Adriel had signed himself off to war and had not visited them since my sister's funeral. Ashvi and the two toddlers called Paltiel an endearing term 'Papi,' and he did not seem to mind.

The boys were the only reason I kept breathing. They were little remnants of my sister, and I could not surrender to the darkness I felt within myself.

"Mimi!" Ashvi slid off the horse and came running over. "Papi says I can help him in the vineyard!"

I smiled as he hugged my neck. "Wonderful. You can pick special grapes for our meals."

"I think your father has arrived," Paltiel said, approaching us. "There are horses here with royal flags."

Not now, I thought, closing my eyes.

"He has left us alone," Paltiel said quietly. "That has been a relief."

"I deserve to mourn in peace," I said, kissing Ashvi on the cheek and telling him to go wash his face.

"Do you think it is because you turned your mother away?"

"I did not turn her away," I said. "I merely did not offer for her to stay. There is a difference. In just that one meal I shared with her after Merab's passing, she made everything about her."

"You turned Rizpah away, as well."

"I did not turn her away."

"You did not come in from outside to receive her."

"I was busy with the horse." In all actuality, I was sitting on the large rock where I used to sit and wait for David to show up. I found myself walking back to that same spot simply because I wanted peace. I could cry and remember my sister without interruption. "What do you want me to say? I just cannot pretend anymore. I am so tired."

A servant stepped onto the porch. "Prince Jonathan is here to see you."

"My brother?" I asked, surprised. I saw him briefly at Merab's funeral, but I kept mostly to myself and stayed indoors grieving in private.

Jonathan followed the servant onto the porch. "Our prince. What an honor for this visit," Paltiel said, bowing briefly before snapping his fingers and ordering immediate refreshment.

But Jonathan's gaze locked with mine. "I would ask how you are doing, but your appearance says it all."

I looked away. Just seeing the empathy and grief behind his eyes, nearly made me break down. My composure was already fragile.

Paltiel left us on the porch. Neither Jonathan nor I said anything for some time. He leaned over the platter of food Dinah had left for me and started eating. More platters came as servants brought tray after tray of breads, wine, and cheeses. Figs and dates were mixed with a plethora of grapes and poured out over the large bowl and onto another tray. Jonathan busied himself while I looked on. "How can you eat so?" I asked, amazed.

Jonathan paused to glance in my direction. "I am hungry. You should eat too."

"I do not want anything."

"Starving yourself will not bring Merab back."

"I know that," I said testily.

"And you need your strength."

"For what?" I snapped. "What reason? Give me one."

"The boys."

"They do not need me to eat. I have an assortment of servants and wet nurses that do a fine job."

"They want you."

"No, they want their MOTHER!" I yelled. My vented anger surprised me, although Jonathan acted unruffled.

"You have been their mother long before Merab died," Jonathan said. He stayed calm and continued eating a chunk of cheese. "And they need you."

I scoffed, but my bottom lip trembled.

"She is not coming back," he said again, gentle but firm. "Life is a gift, Michal. And you have been given not just the gift of your life, but the lives of those five boys."

I wiped at my eyes, but the tears did not stop. "My life ended several years ago. I have been simply existing."

Jonathan sat across from me and took my hand. "Then what a waste of a life."

My head shot up, and I glared at him. "I do not need condescension. I will not have it, brother. You have no idea--"

"No idea, what?" Jonathan interrupted. "That father ruined your marriage to David? That you have been estranged from your husband while he runs and tries to protect not just his life but the lives of his soldiers and their families? You are not the only life that suffers. Do you know that David and his men must up and move every several moons, sometimes sooner? They live in caves, or in remote locations where there is little to no vegetation. They must rely on spoils from war or upon the good graces of the local countrymen. Feeding over a thousand mouths is no easy feat."

"He has his new wife to help him," I said, the bitterness seeping out.

"His second wife is a young woman who came from a wealthy family. It was a business transaction, so he and his men could have sheep and goats."

"I came from the wealthiest of families! He could have come back for me! I do not want to hear excuses. I do not want to hear that I need to move on with my life. My heart has been ripped out of my chest and trampled on again and again."

"As I have already stated, you are not the only one who suffers." An angry glint flashed across my brother's countenance. "I had to choose between standing beside my lunatic father or beside my brother and friend. I thought that if I stayed with our father that I could talk with him and try to get him to change his mind. Instead, I have watched these years slowly tear his sanity apart. When I meet up with David, I see a man who bears the weight of our people upon his shoulders. Every action he does must be weighed and calculated. He loves the Hebrew people. He loves the king. Twice, our father could have been killed by him, but David chose to honor his covenant over his comfort. We *all* suffer, Michal."

I said nothing.

"Sitting around waiting for a future that may never happen is a complete and total waste of time." He dropped my hand and stood up again. He went to the edge of the porch and studied the scene. "This is beautiful country. What I would do to leave the battlefield

290

and enjoy the life you have been given."

"Is it life where there is no love? I do not love Paltiel. And now I do not have my beloved sister."

"Stop," Jonathan scolded me. "Paltiel is far from perfect, and he is not David, but he has housed you and supported you. You have acted like a spoiled child for almost seven years when you have all this." He extended his arms.

"Do you not remember how uncivilized Paltiel was before I married David? He tried to blackmail mother! The only reason why I am left alone here is that David threatened to rip him apart once he is seated on the throne. Self-preservation is what has allowed me such freedom."

"Exactly, so why grumble and complain? You have your horses, and you have five handsome sons. Look upon their faces and remember your sister. But continuing to act so immaturely tarnishes her memory." He came over, bent down to where I sat, and kissed my cheek. "I must leave. There is a large Philistine advance, and we must go and push back before they tear down our fortified walls."

"Is David not out there? How are they able to advance?"

"David and his men reside in Ziklag."

"How?" I asked, standing up for the first time since morning. My heart began to pound in my chest. "Is he captured?"

"No, they live there as a form of payment. From King Achish."

"I do not understand. What is the Philistine king paying them for?"

"They work for him now."

"They fight against us?" I covered my mouth in shock.

"No, David refuses to touch the Hebrews, but by fighting the Philistines' battles against other enemies, it has allowed them to gain in numbers and strength. I would be lying if I said this advancement did not worry me. We are already losing men in high numbers."

For the first time since his visit, I saw the worry on my brother's face. "Can we win?" I asked. "We always win. The

291

Philistines have yet to completely defeat us."

"But that was when we had David and his mighty men fighting along the outskirts of our land. But because of our father's hatred and jealousy, David had no choice. There was nowhere else for him to go where he and his men could live with some semblance of peace." Jonathan smiled sadly and repeated, "You are not the only one who suffers. We are all pawns, Michal. I just…I just need to know that you will be all right."

I heard the somber tone and knew what was implied. "Do not sound so final. You will come back. You will fight valiantly, and you *will* come back. *Promise me.*"

"I cannot make such a promise. What I can promise is what I have always promised. That I will fight for my people. When the God of the heavens determines that my fight in this life is over, then it will be so."

I shook my head vehemently. "Stop talking like this. I have never heard you without hope. If I promise to have hope, then you must promise to have it too."

Jonathan reached out, wrapping his arms around me. I hugged him in return, the tears not yet abated. When he released me, he said, "I need to know that my beloved sister will continue living. I need to know that you will be all right." Jonathan's eyes became wet. "One of us has to make it."

"But I am not all right," I said, in full transparency. "I do not have the strength."

"Then find it. You, my sister, who rides horses like a man, who raises children who are not her own, who sneaks out in the middle of the night in servant's garb in an effort to steal a moment with the runaway heir, you are one of the strongest, most fierce people I know."

Hearing such kind words was like drinking cool water on a parched day. It refreshed my soul. "I learned from the best."

We shared a small smile. Jonathan hugged me again, kissed my cheek, and whispered, "Forgive him," before leaving me alone on the porch.

But to whom was he referring? David? Our father? Paltiel?

Each of those men brought pain and hurt to my heart. Each for different reasons. I nearly ran after him and asked, but knowing my brother, I wondered if he had meant them all.

40

∞

King Saul

The Streets of Gibeah
1012 B.C.

I went for a stroll around the garden. Alone. I checked behind me where my guards watched the garden entryway, and walked quickly, deep among the floral bushes and trees. I pushed through the darkness with no lantern as an aid until I felt the vines along the farthest wall.

I paused as more guards chatted above me at the top of the enclosure. Creeping along the wall, my hand came across the small door that led to the town. It was a small escape door that I had never used. Until now.

One more check over my shoulder before I knocked once, then twice, then once more. The same knock repeated back to me. Taking out the heavy key, I unlocked and opened the door and pushed through thick canopies of greenery before shutting the door behind me and letting the greenery fall back into place.

Someone tapped me on the shoulder, making me jump. "Do not do that again," I hissed at Enos.

"Sorry, my lord, I only wanted you to know I brought the things you requested."

"Good." I glanced around. We were deep in a patch of forest that surrounded the southern portion of the palace. Without another thought, I took off my royal garb and emblems and, taking the commoner's clothes from Enos, dressed in the disguise. "Does this work?" I asked Enos.

"Yes, my lord, no one will recognize you. At least I do not think they will. To be honest, I cannot see."

I rolled my eyes and sighed. "Stop calling me lord and king, for the time being. That will give it away."

"Yes, my lo--. Yes."

"So, you are sure about this woman?"

"Yes. Most of the charmists and those who dabble with familiar spirits are completely out of your cities. But this one is sneaky. Baker by day, witch by night."

"Good. Lead the way. I do not have much time." The Philistines were closing in fast, already piling up in Shunem. Their sheer mass of an army reminded me of when they brought Goliath. The trepidation brought on by this Philistine army only surpassed the trepidation I had before when Goliath taunted us. That time, almost eight years ago, Israel had been saved because of that no-good shepherd. Now that traitor fought on the enemy's side. That thought alone made me growl in disgust. "If only I had killed him that night he took my spear."

"A life for a life," Enos answered, already knowing to what I referred.

"He was toying with me!" I raised my voice. Then, whispering fiercely, I added, "If I would have killed him, he would not have gone over to the Philistines and traded our secrets for protection! I always knew he would turn on his people. But he once again toyed with my mind. Made me feel relieved that he kept me alive when he deserved to die for sneaking up on the king!"

When I first heard that David lived among the Philistines, I wanted to jump on a horse and continue to chase him down. Samuel would have been so disappointed! I thought that it would bring the power of God back into my own life. I longed for the insanity and demanding voices to stop in my head. But no. None of the prophets had heard from the Lord for me. Not even when I begged them for an answer on what to do with the advancing Philistine army. "Do I fight? Should I stay back? What do I tell my soldiers?"

But the priests and counselors stayed silent.

"Why will you not answer me?!" I had shouted at the priests. "I am even leaving the traitor alone. He lives among the enemy, so I have turned him over to God. Does not that justify me? Even a little?"

"We have prayed and inquired after the Lord," one of the priests said. "But He is not speaking. He has departed from you and your leadership."

That was just fine. I would go directly to another source.

A cart attached to a donkey waited for us. One of my other manservants held the reins. We climbed onto the bench with me in between the two servants. "How far is it?" I asked.

"Not too far. She is at Endor."

We rode in silence the entire trip. Most of the village roads were deserted at the late hour. A few stray drunks teetered from one side of the road to the other, and a stray cat or dog would shriek or bark, but nothing out of the ordinary. I still held my head in my hands. The headaches never fully went away anymore. The voices had intensified since the night David snuck into my camp. The voices were in a frenzy when I heard David's voice through the darkness. *Kill him. Kill him. Kill him.*

Their message had slightly changed since then. *Kill yourself. You are worthless. You should have never been king. You are spineless.*

We reached a corner residence that housed a small bakery in the front. *Honey cakes for the weary traveler.* A small handmade sign etched onto wood was nailed to a crooked door. "Around back," Enos whispered.

We went together around the corner to a back door. I reared back in disgust at the waste pile outside the door.

"Come in," a woman said before Enos could knock.

We stepped inside the dimly lit room, and goosebumps shot all through me. Something was not right about this place. The air lay thick with a pungent, musky odor. I could hear the scurrying of rodents. And my dark thoughts seemed to awaken inside of this place. "I need you to make contact with a spirit," I said quickly, talking myself out of leaving with no answers. "I have money for the trouble."

"Do you not know that King Saul has kicked out all the soothsayers and wizards of the land? Do you wish me harm by coming in here tonight?"

"No, I swear no harm will come to you."

She sat down at a low table. "Who do you want me to conjure up?"

"Samuel."

The woman's head snapped up. "The prophet from Ramah?"

"Yes."

She took a withered bird's feather, dipped it in ink, and dropped her head like a rag doll. Without looking up, her hand began to feverishly jerk along the parchment, as if controlled by something else. She whispered an unknown dialect, her body unmoving except for the one hand scribbling ferociously on the weathered parchment. She gasped and sat straight up, staring at me, clearly possessed. "You are Saul!" Then she hissed, pointing the bird feather at me. "Trickery! TRICKERY!"

"Do not be afraid of who I am," I said. "Just tell me what you saw."

Her head snapped at an unnatural angle as her eyes rolled into the back of her head, her voice whispered its ancient tongue.

The darkness enveloped me, and I began to tremble at whatever spirits had been ushered into the room. It surrounded me just like in my nightmares. I wanted to order it to stop...all of it...but I had no other choice. This was my only help. My only hope.

The shadows took on forms of their own and began to mock me. I closed my eyes, but they were in my head, as well. I faintly heard Enos talking to me, asking me if I was all right. His terror hung on each word.

"I see gods coming up from the ground," she breathed. "An old man comes forth. He wears a mantle."

"Samuel," I cried, falling onto the filthy floor and bowing low. I began to sob. "Make the voices stop. Make the darkness flee."

"Why have you bothered me?" the woman said in an unearthly voice.

I shook from fear. "Please, Samuel, it is me, Saul. The Philistines are upon me, you are gone, and God does not answer me when I pray. Please tell me what I am to do."

"Why ask me? I am the one who told you that God had departed from you. You have become his enemy. He has ripped the kingdom from you and handed it to David. You who have a disobedient heart will be handed over to the Philistines tomorrow. You and your sons will join me on that day."

"What? Not death!" Fear gripped me like an entity with strong hands and arms. "NO!" I cried out, sobbing and suddenly convulsing. "NO! Samuel, please, no!" I pulled at my hair as if the outward pain would make the inside battle less consuming. "It cannot end this way."

"Here, help me get him up," the woman said, completely of herself.

I quieted down and saw that the woman no longer sat at the table, but had crouched next to me.

"Come now," she said. "Let me get you something to eat."

"No," I said, shaking my head. "I want nothing. Just leave me alone."

"Master, please eat something," Enos also had crouched beside me.

I leaned on my manservant and stood up until my trembling legs gave out. Enos sat me on the narrow bed, along the wall.

"You are weak, sir. Let the woman put a hot meal in your belly."

My stomach gnawed at me, and I agreed. The normalcy of sipping on soup somewhat helped.

"Let us leave," I said, shakily standing and exiting the backroom. I needed out of there. "To the palace," I said. By the time we arrived at the palace, my disguise had been discarded, but I had yet to cleanse myself of the stench.

I didn't say anything to anyone. Instead, I made my way to my private chambers.

Enos was on my heels. "Would you like a bath, my lord? Some music? A meal?"

"Rizpah," I said. "Get her."

Enos left me, and I went to the balcony, tearing off the rest of my garments.

"Burn those," I said to the servant laying out another ensemble. He took the pile on the floor, and I quickly threw the clean tunic over my head. Looking back over the balcony again, my skin still crawled from whatever spirits that witch had ushered in. The doom was palpable. I could feel it upon me. "You determine your own fate," I said out loud. "You do not have to believe some stupid woman's folly. She probably lied for the money."

Rizpah entered my chamber and smiled warmly at me. "My love," she said. "Where did you go?" she asked, as she came to me and kissed me.

"It is of no matter," I said. Still, I took her in my arms and embraced her.

"You are shaking," she said. "Talk to me. Let me soothe you."

"You are the only one who has not forsaken me."

"That is not true," she said gently. "Your sons stand by you. Do they not fight Hebrew battles?"

I thought of the witch's words and shivered. "The queen is never around. She lies about where she goes. Merab is dead. Michal is lost to me. The priests will not speak to me. My sons fight for Israel, not for their father." My voice shook. I did not want to show weakness, but the thought of my family not by my side broke me. "I did all of this for them. And I failed."

"You have not failed."

"David wins. I am in ruins. Tomorrow I die."

"We will not talk of such things."

I allowed Rizpah to comfort me, but my heart hurt as the voices paraded my failures in my head.

Enos knocked and opened the outer chamber door. "My king?" he called. "Urgent message from Abner."

I knew it would not be good. I clutched Rizpah as if holding on to her would keep away fate.

The messenger approached, bowed, and held out the rolled parchment. "You are needed immediately, sir. The Philistines push us into the mountains. They have strongholds. Abner has ordered more men on the battlefront. Your sons are there, fighting steadily."

I knew before I opened the parchment. "What is the location?"

"Mount Gilboa."

The witch's words had yet to leave me, but I knew that I could not stay back when my sons needed me. In this, I could show them how I have always fought for them. "Suit me up," I ordered Enos.

"Sleep tonight, my lord, and leave at sunrise."

"I gave you an order." I kissed Rizpah and held her for a moment more, memorizing her scent. "I must leave."

"I will pray," she said.

All I could do was think about if tomorrow was my last day alive.

41

ॐ

David

Ziklag
1012 B.C.

I yanked on the ropes, pulling the donkeys forward. "Is this the last of them?" I asked my nephew.

Joab wiped at his brow. "I am not sure."

"What do you mean you are not sure?" I asked under my breath, so the Philistine stable manager did not hear.

"No one is answering me. All they do is argue. It is chaos. This is the last from Benaiah's troops. I am pretty sure on that."

"What of Eleazar's?"

"I have yet to see them."

"Did their spoils not come through?" I asked, searching for my friend.

Jashobeam rode up to us. "All is accounted for."

"Eleazar's troops turned in their spoils?"

"Yes," he said. "I ordered troops to head to Ziklag while we finish up here."

"Thank you," I said with relief.

King Achish was true to his word and used us for his raids and plunders, so much so that keeping track of all the spoils proved challenging. My troops were exhausted and most of my commanders were displeased with me. It did not sit right with many of my men that we worked for the Philistinian king.

The stable manager handed me a sack of coins. He grunted in

my direction, and then turned and walked away.

"Hey," I called out. "This is not the agreed-upon terms."

"All of our resources are being used up at Mount Gilboa," he said. "That is all I have, so that is all you get."

"Then give us our ration in sheep and goats. I have an agreement with the king."

"And he is off fighting your people," the stable manager came back to me. "But do not worry, all will be right soon. Reports are that the Hebrews fall in droves."

Frustration and fury mixed together, and I reached out, grabbing him in a chokehold. "We. Have. An. Agreement. I act honorably, and I expect to be treated the same. We have returned all the spoils. Now I can stand here holding your neck until you die, or you can count up the animals and hand them to us."

Through his gasping, he gave a slight nod. I released him, and he fell to the ground.

As he went to retrieve the animals, I told Joab to assemble the troops who remained. "We will need to move the sheep quickly, so tell them to be prepared." I noticed Jashobeam watching me. "I know," I grumbled. "I should have handled it better."

"What I was thinking was why you did not let me handle it for you? Go," he said. "I will finish up here."

I went to disagree, but I found that I was relieved that he offered. I patted him on the shoulder and walked to my horse.

The soldiers would not stop bickering. I decided to follow the last set of troops because it was better than listening to the griping.

None of the men were happy. I knew that. King Achish sent them from one raid to another. And it was never easy. Killing insubordinate men was one thing, but killing women too shattered the soul.

I would be lying to myself if I said I was not upset at God. How long did I have to suffer? How long did I have to watch my men suffer simply because they chose to support me? It was not that

Ziklag itself was bad. The area was fertile with crops and mostly stocked with stable animals. But it was the phantom shackles around our wrists that reminded us of our lack of freedom that bothered us the most. The shackles might have been only imaginary, but every soldier under me knew that we were the mercenaries to the Philistines. It was a heavy price, and I watched daily as it ate away at the conscience of my men.

Now the Philistines had decided to wage an all-out war against Saul and Israel. They had wanted me to fight, only to decide they could not trust me. That I would turn on the Philistines in the heat of battle. That worried me. How much longer before the Philistines decided they were done with me and my men?

I wished I could go back to Saul and talk things out, but Saul had shown more than once that any dialogue was over.

At least we were done raiding for a few moons. It would depend on how long the battle with Israel lasted. For now, all I wanted to think about was visiting Amnon and Ahinoam and then spending the night with Abigail and my new son, Daniel.

Even with my growing family, I felt alone. Ahinoam had completely shut me out, especially after she was introduced to Abigail. It reminded me that a time was coming where I would have to have a conversation with Michal. I hoped that reconciliation was possible, but with each passing moon, as the years slipped away from us, the hope of reconciliation faded. Guilt ate at me. People were unhappy, and it was my fault. I could have ended this a few years back when Saul was in the cave. I could have marched into Paltiel's home and demanded my wife. I would already be king.

My decision to be honorable had cost me.

Yet, in the middle of my wilderness, along came Abigail. Abigail was different from both Michal and Ahinoam, but I knew that would be the case the second I laid eyes on her. She was serious and respectful and wise beyond her years. Our initial union brought about my second son, Daniel. But he was a sickly baby and demanded Abigail's attention. The intensity of my initial attraction to her slowly waned. I respected and admired her, and when we did speak I enjoyed our conversations. Despite her intelligence and beauty, I questioned in my heart if what I really desired was all the resources and riches she brought to the marriage covenant. And I disliked myself for it. Because at the heart of the matter, it was not the fault of Ahinoam or Abigail that my heart belonged to another. No matter how hard I tried to not think about Michal, she had a way of slipping into my dreams.

"David!"

I stopped daydreaming to see who called me by name. Joab, on horse, sprinted toward me. "Come quick!" he urged, all color drained from his face. "Hurry! Come to Ziklag!"
He turned the horse and sprinted back in that direction.

The panic showed up immediately. "Stay the course," I commanded the men, and then I brought my horse to a sprint. "Please not another challenge," I prayed. I kept praying as I pushed the horse to move faster. Suddenly, the words suspended on my tongue.

The entire town of Ziklag had been turned to ash and smoldering flame.

Everything destroyed.

"Oh God, please, no," I said, my stomach rolling. "No." I pushed the horse to go fast again until I arrived. I slid off the horse before it came to a complete stop. My tents...burned to nothing. My family. "Abigail?" I yelled. "Ahinoam?" I ran between the damage of all the tents to where the stables would have been. But they were nothing but charred remains too.

Everything taken or burned. I turned in slow motion, taking in each catastrophe. Whoever came, spared no one.

The wailing began. An eerie sound coming from a leveled village. Soldiers seeing the scene now running on foot to their home to see if by miracle their family had been spared.

"They are gone," Eleazar approached me. He would have been one of the first ones on the scene since he had traveled in front.

Now his eyes were bloodshot, snot dripped from his nose, a sob escaped his lips. "My wife. My five children."

I shook my head, my own lips trembling, but I could not find any words.

"It is your fault," Eleazar said. "All of this." he points around us. "Is on you!"

He grabbed my collar and shoved me over and over again, his tears seeping into his beard. "You..." he shoved. "Our families were supposed to be safe," he shoved. "You never listen!" he shoved one last time.

I regained my balance while my friend fell on his knees, his body shaking from the sobs.

"You killed them!" Shammah ran at me, tackling me to the ground.

I let Shammah hit at me. I covered my head to protect myself from the blows, remembering the beatings from my father. A part of me wanted to feel the pain. Pain felt better than anguish.

"Stop it!" I heard Jashobeam approach and throw Shammah from off me. "This solves nothing!"

"It is his fault!" Shammah said. "Would he listen to us? Does he listen to us? Never! You know it, too. How many times did you try to reason with him, Jashobeam? How many times?"

"Now Philistine enemies have become ours," Eleazar said, his voice still shaken.

I sat up and saw that the men—most of the 600—were all headed over to us. Many in tears. Some in shock. All angrily glaring at me.

But my children were gone, too. Amnon and Daniel. I covered my ears not wanting to imagine their screams or cries for help. Unable to shoulder any more grief or torment, I ran past the men, past the ravaged dwellings, past the angry glares. I ran past the cactus and desert brush, tripping, falling, getting back up and continuing to run until I could no longer take in a breath. I fell on my knees, my head to the ground while I gulped in large quantities of air.

"God!" I wailed to the heavens. I yelled until my head pounded from a lack of oxygen. "Why?!?" I pounded the earth again and again, lamenting at the loss of all that my soldiers and I held dear. "I did not ask for this!" I threw my head back and bellowed. "I did not ask to be king! I did not ask to be on the run for these eight years! I did not ask for any of this! Why torment my soul? Why?" But no more words came.

I stayed in the desert and wept. Wept and prayed. The day turned into evening, which turned into night. My head still lay upon the earth. I knew the nocturnal birds and creatures were emerging from their lairs, but all I could do was lay on the ground and relive moments of my life.

Suddenly, words tumbled out of my mouth from a prayer I wrote years earlier: "*Save me, O God, by thy name, and judge me by thy strength. Hear my prayer, O God, give ear to the words of my mouth. For strangers have risen up against me, and oppressors seek after my soul. He shall reward evil unto mine enemies: cut them off in thine truth. I will freely sacrifice unto thee: I will praise thy name, O Lord; for it is good. For he hath delivered me out of all trouble: and mine eye hath seen his desire upon mine enemies.*"

Saying the words out loud calmed me, and my breathing returned to normal. Suddenly, a thought came to me, as if planted inside my brain. It pushed me to an upright position.

Where is the evidence of their death? The thought asked.

When towns or clans are raided, bodies litter the area. Even with the burning of the tents and stables, the smell of burnt human flesh is impossible to mask. There would have been evidence, but I do not remember seeing any.

They live. This time a gentle voice spoke directly to my heart.

I immediately stood up and felt the first flickers of hope. My thoughts focused on my next steps. Everything became clear, as I realized what should be done. I walked back to Ziklag, praying

306

continually. When I arrived I saw many men gathered around a fire, trying to heat up some rations and discussing what should be done to me.

"He has failed us," someone grumbled. "Everything we have sacrificed, and now we have nothing."

"Something must be done," said another.

I stayed hidden, not wanting another fight. I found Abiathar, my friend and priest, sitting on a stump, facing the forest. Surely, he would see me. "Do you have the ephod?" I whispered, trying not to draw attention to myself. I knelt beside him and bowed my head. "I would like to inquire of the Lord."

"Of course. I have been waiting for you to return." Abiathar retrieved it from under his cloak. "My trunk escaped the flames with very little damage."

By now, someone had spotted me and alerted the others. My advisors slowly made their way to me. The light from the bonfires showed that our battle was not quite finished. Eleazar and Shammah would not look at me. But I could not focus on them just yet. With the priest there, I inquired of God, "Should I pursue whatever troops did this to us? Will I be successful?"

Abiathar closed his eyes in prayer, his hands outstretched. "Pursue. You will be successful, and you will recover all that has been taken."

I breathed a sigh of relief and nodded. "I felt the same thing while praying in the desert," I said to the priest. "I wanted to make sure."

"God has never left your side," Abiathar said, eyes still closed. "Do not dismay for you will be victorious."

I stood up and surprised Abiathar by hugging him. "Thank you." To Jashobeam, I said, "So, what is the consensus? How am I to die?"

"Right now the vote is to stone you, but to be honest, everyone is too exhausted to lift a rock." Jashobeam appraised me, then asked, "So, what is our next move?"

"We pursue who did this."

"We do not know who did this," Joab, my nephew, said. "We have quite a few enemies."

"Yes, but God will reveal it to us. What evidence have we collected?"

Abishai, my other nephew, stepped forward. "They traveled southward, and I believe that our families are captive...not dead... That is good, right?"

"Thank you," I said to my nephew. "I thought the same thing. Most attackers do not take the dead bodies with them. There would be some evidence to suggest that there was a slaughter. Glory to God, there is an absence of that evidence."

A couple dozen men surrounded me, and I heard their assent.

"That is enough hope for me. Let us water and feed the horses, and ourselves, and then let us leave immediately. We need to gain ground. Those who are too weary to make it can stay behind. No questions asked."

With the directive, most of the men got to work. Some were truly weak or injured, and I assured them that we would do our best to bring back all of the captives.

As morning light broke across the eastern sky, I rested alongside my horse, encouraging myself in the Lord. I knew the men moved as fast as they could, so I forced myself to wait until Jashobeam said that it was time to leave.

Abishai ran up to me, handing me a water jug. "Uncle, we found someone on our way to the brook. Come, come."

I took the water jug and guzzled, then followed my nephew to an open field near the water. Jashobeam knelt beside what appeared to be a young, dark-skinned man. "We have fed him and gave him water," he said. "He says he did not eat or drink for three days and nights."

"Who are you?" I asked. "Do you belong to someone?"

"I am from Egypt, but I serve an Amalekite. We invaded a portion of Judah, south of Caleb, and then burned Ziklag to the ground."

I felt the anger already building. The Amalekites! "Can you tell us where they were going?"

"If you promise to keep me alive and not to hand me over to my master, I will show you where they camp."

"I swear by God that you will not die, nor will I hand you over to your former master."

The Egyptian young man gave a slight nod. "Then let me direct you."

To Jashobeam, I said, "Tell the men to gird themselves and sword up. It is time to get our families back."

42

❧

King Saul

Mount Gilboa
1012 B.C.

"We cannot keep up with the wounded," Abner said. He stood beside me, along with Jonathan, and my other two sons, Abinadab and Melchishua, and several other commanders.

"It seems the more we lose, the more they gain," Jonathan said. "But we have no choice but to push back. Turning around will only give them the go-ahead to gain control over the surrounding areas."

"Where are their commanders? The Philistines run around unorganized when their leaders are dead."

"That is what I was thinking," Jonathan said. "But that puts us right in the midst of enemy lines. It is possibly a death sentence."

"Then we do not do it," I said, the chills shooting up my spine.

"I am going to do it," Jonathan said. "I volunteer. It is the only chance we have. Our outlook is bleak, but this could work. And if God goes before me, as He has in times past, then I will be successful."

"And if He does not?" I asked. "I cannot lose my heir."

"I am not the heir to the throne," Jonathan said. "And I am not asking permission. I am going to go and fight. And if it is my time to die, then I hope that I can at least take out a couple of their commanders in the process."

"We have men for this job," I said, raising my voice.

"I will go with you," Abinadab, my other son said. "Saul's sons are not cowards. I am not going to stand aside like with Goliath. This time, I fight."

I watched Jonathan nod. Melchishua agreed to go too.

"No, my sons, I beg you. You are my legacy. Please, I will go. You all stay back." My knees started to shake. The voices began the chant: *you will die, you will die, you will die.*

"We must make a decision," Abner said.

"The decision is made." Jonathan grabbed his helmet. "Let us go along the sides where the weakest men are. If we can get to trees, then we can climb them."

I reached for Jonathan's arm. "Son."

Jonathan looked at me, and I saw it in his eyes. He knew. "You will die."

"It is a sacrifice I make for Israel."

"Then I will go too. I never miss," I said, refusing to think of the times I did, in fact, miss.

My sons and I left the tent and moved to our troops awaiting word. Jonathan explained the plan and ordered them to go before to take out the weakest positions. "I am not going to lie. This is dangerous. We need to get in the midst to take out their commanders. The only way that can happen is to kill those that surround them."

"We do this for Israel," someone said.

I heard another ask if David and his men were coming to help. As I stood among my men, the scales of deception that had covered my eyes seemed to fall off, and I faced the truth. If I had never pursued David, the Philistines would have never gained such a foothold.

"We move out," Jonathan said, bringing me out of my thoughts.

We pulled ourselves onto our horses while the troops marched before us.

"We will have to approach on foot soon," Jonathan said. They will easily spot us."

As we made our way through our camp and through the valley of the previous days' battles, I saw the mounds of men, many of whom had already been decapitated. My stomach flipped.

Jonathan motioned for us to stop. Normally I would not let him lead, but my mind was frozen. "We have to move on foot now. Men need to travel in twos. Crouching when necessary."

Our group followed instructions and started moving through the tall brush, trying to move undetected. The day came and went, and most of it was spent crawling on our bellies. Battles waged to the east of us and all day we heard the victory cry of the Philistines.

We were nearly upon the outer groupings changing weapons.

"Now," Jonathan ordered.

I watched as our men attacked one set of men, trying to still be as undetected as possible. Then I noticed the surroundings. Various trees littered the landscape. "They are hiding," I said. "It is a trap."

I tried to get Jonathan's attention, but they had already crouched into the grasses again. I crawled fast. "They see us!" I said, barely above a whisper.

Suddenly, arrows flew at us from various positions.

"Ambush!" Jonathan said. "We do not deviate. The commanders are close."

Arrows hit our men, but with us still crouched, the bush hid us. Unfortunately, we also could not see the Philistines on foot heading to us. We heard them at the same time.

"Fight!" Jonathan yelled, suddenly standing and maneuvering with great skill and strength. To me, he ordered, "Stay down!"

But as I watched my sons fight while the arrows flew, I refused to let them fight my battles alone.

A spear pierced Abinadab through the throat.

"No!" I yelled, jumping up and running over to my son.

Jonathan knocked me down. "Stay low!" he ordered, standing back up and running toward those who came at us. He, along with his armor-bearer, killed the slew of Philistines in his path. But the arrows were great in number.

I held Abinadab, but it was too late.

Melchishua shouted, "We must retreat. They expected this."

The Philistines outnumbered us, and those who remained would not be able to fight them all.

Jonathan said, "We will not retreat. We must gain better footing. More groups come. Let us move toward that section of trees."

"They will be there," I said, still crouched. "We are very much surrounded."

"We have a mission. Crawl back to safety if you must."

I knelt frozen, holding my dead son, the words of the witch taunting me. "I must fight," I said, crawling in the direction of our men. Jonathan, with his armor-bearer, and Melchishua, with his, along with those not hit yet, fought fearlessly, taking out Philistines while avoiding arrows.

But the masses, like ants, moved toward my men...my sons.

And I was paralyzed with fear.

Suddenly an arrow ripped through Jonathan, and I watched my eldest son fall to the ground.

"NO!" I cried, standing up and running to him.

Our men fell one after the other.

Melchishua fought several before a sword sliced through him.

"Please, no. Oh God, no. Not my sons!" I cried. I found Jonathan.

He gasped. "Go...go..."

"Move!" my armor bearer shouted. "They are upon us!" The armor-bearer pushed at me until I began to run in retreat. My feet moved, but my heart grieved.

Three of my sons: Jonathan, Abinadab, and Melchishua all

dead. I slowed, the grief making me short of breath. "To the trees!" the armor-bearer yelled.

I was almost there. As I threw myself down and into the forest, I felt searing pain rip through my body. "I'm hit! I'm hit!"

The armor-bearer took in a breath. "Hold still. I need to pull the arrows out."

"How many?" I panted, trying to push past the pain. My vision blurred from it. I cried out as one ripped out of my flesh. "No more!" I begged. "No more. This is it."

"What can I do, sir?" the armor-bearer asked. "You have two more that have struck you through."

I thought bitterly of the witch's words. "I am…to die."

"Let me get you help."

"N-N-No, just take your sword and end it. Please do not let these uncircumcised heathens find me and torture me."

"I cannot. You are my king."

"It must end." I fumbled for my own sword, hearing the approaching march of the enemy. "Get out of here," I said to my armor-bearer. When I saw the young man wanting to question me, I ordered, "GO! I command you! Save yourself!"

I took one look at my own sword and thought of everything I should have made right. Gritting my teeth, I knew that it could have turned out so much better, but I did not let my mind go there. Instead, I situated the sword between two rocks, and closing my eyes, fell onto it.

And for once, the voices were silent.

43

❦

Michal

Paltiel's Home in Gallim
1012 B.C.

I pushed Eglah to run as fast and as far as she could. The wind stung against my tears.

The words replayed in mind.

King Saul has fallen. His sons: Jonathan, Abinadab, and Melchishua have fallen, as well. The message has been delivered to Ishvi, King Saul's surviving son. Queen Ahinoam requests your presence as soon as possible for the mourning period.

Paltiel had placed his arm around my shoulder as he chanted a prayer. All I remember after that was walking away and to the stables.

Now, I moved through the Gallim countryside, down familiar meadows and vineyards, feeling so very alone. The grief physically hurt. My stomach stayed in knots, my hands trembled from clutching the reins so tight, and my heart ached like an arrow had pierced it.

Eglah slowed, and I knew she needed a rest. We came to the top of a rolling hill that we had stopped at several times before. It overlooked the expanse of Paltiel's vineyard. His home was a little dot in the distance. My dwelling for the past seven years.

I bent down and hugged the horse, but the tears were gone. The ache remained.

Memories of my childhood flooded my mind. Sneaking around with Merab, eating the honey cakes Jonathan would save for me, my first horse ride with my father. Better, happier times. Before I knew betrayal, misery, and heartache.

I stayed out in the open air until the sun started to descend into the western sky. I remembered Jonathan's words to me the last time we met. *I need to know that my beloved sister will continue living. I need to know that you will be all right.*

"He knew," I said to the horse. "He did so much to protect me. To protect David."

David.

He would be heartsick at the news. But…was he king? Was it that simple?

Surprisingly, I felt no surge of joy or excitement. I felt more hesitation and awkwardness. What did this mean? Would he come for me, and if he did, what would happen?

He had other wives, and they had children. My husband now had a family, and it did not include me.

You are one of the strongest, most fierce people I know. Jonathan told me that before he left to go fight in a battle he would never return from. I could not allow those words to return void.

I took in a deep breath, scanned the beautiful view in front of me, and said out loud, "So, be it." I would take one moment at a time. To honor my brother and my sister, I vowed to live. Besides, I had five sons to raise, and I would remind them of the legacy of our family.

And if David came for me? Well, I would face that day when it happened.

My way back to Paltiel's dwelling was much slower, as I let my mind continued to work out a plan. The darkness and grief were right there at the edges, but I focused on my surroundings and my plans for tomorrow.

At the stable, I dismounted Eglah and walked her back to her stall. Laia, Paltiel's wife, stepped out of the stall. She did not make eye contact.

"Are you waiting for me?" I asked, while helping a stable

316

hand feed and water the horse.

"Y-Yes," she said, with some hesitation.

"Out with it," I said, brushing my hands on the sash around my waist. "I do not want to be bothered with your poison, so say what you must and be gone."

"Is he coming for you?"

"Who?" I asked, knowing exactly who she meant.

"Is David...King David...coming for you? He is the next king, correct?"

I stepped out of the stall, closed the heavy wooden gate, and latched it closed. "I do not know," I said simply.

"Is Paltiel in danger? He seems worried."

"No, he is not in danger. I will defend him to David when the time comes. Paltiel has his challenges, but he has been upright and has taken care of me these past several years."

Laia nodded as if somewhat satisfied. She paused, before asking, "Do you really hike up your skirts when you ride?"

The question took me by surprise. "Yes. It is near impossible to ride a horse without freedom of movement."

I started to walk away but stopped. I noticed that she asked with curiosity, not contempt. Laia currently looked upon Eglah with a sort of fascination.

"Have you ever ridden a horse?" I asked.

"No, but I have watched you. At first, I was alarmed at such a lack of propriety. Women are not to ride horses like men, but—"

"Would you like to?"

Laia turned to me and raised her eyebrows in such a way that I did not know if she was angry-shocked or excited-shocked.

"You do not have to," I said quickly. "I would never push you to do something you do not want to do, but it sounded like you might be interested."

"Yes," she said. "I have wanted to ask for some time, but I did not think you would after my horrible words to you."

"If you want to learn, I am happy to teach you. You will love it, just as I do."

"Do you think the horse will kick me off?"

"I will teach you how not to have that happen. Eglah here is patient. She will be a good place to start for you."

And for the first time in the seven years I lived in Paltiel's house, Laia, his wife, smiled at me. "I have not been this excited in a long time. I must ask Paltiel, but he has mentioned for me to come and ask you, so I believe that he will agree to it."

"After the mourning period is over, we will begin," I said, finding myself delighting in being a teacher.

"Oh, and Michal? I wanted you to know something." Laia paused again. "I am only bringing this up because I can only imagine the pain you are in right now. The horses were a gift from your father."

"A gift? I thought Paltiel—"

"The king ordered Paltiel to say that they were from him. He said something about it being a gift for the marriage. I found out because, well, I was in a jealous rage, so Paltiel told me in secret. The king wanted you to be able to pass the time here, and he told Paltiel that you were not to know that they were from him."

"Surely, you are mistaken. My father and I have been at odds for these past several years. He has said and done unthinkable things."

"Sometimes men do not know how to show their love. Or to apologize. I would wager that both of those reasons played a role."

I tried not to think about the angry interactions between my father and me. For the last couple years, I had been so angry and hurt at him. "He took me from my husband," I said, my eyes welling up with tears.

"I know. I just thought you should know that maybe, in his own way, the king loved you."

The emotions I had mastered on the ride back started to show themselves. "He does not get to do this," I said, more to myself than to Laia. "He does not get to love me, not after he ruined my life. And he does not get to die before I can tell him how I feel!"

I felt Laia's arm awkwardly around my shoulders. "I should not have told you," she said. "I only wanted you to think warmly of your father."

"Excuse me, miss?" a stable boy approached. "You are being summoned. By the queen herself."

I groaned. "Not now."

"I was told it is urgent."

I blinked back any more tears, not wanting to fuel my mother's dramatic gestures of grief. I paused before walking away. "We will pick up our conversation soon," I said to Laia.

Dinah waited for me outside the stables. "She noticed me."

I knew she referred to my mother, but I did not see the point in being nervous anymore. "She is a widow now. Do not worry."

"She still has some power, especially with her connections."

"Dinah," I stopped to take her hands. "My father is dead, and with that, is any threat to your life."

"But the way she looked at me just now. I am not comfortable." Dinah appeared visibly shaken.

"All right. I will not call for you. Go to my chambers and await news that she is gone."

"You are to go to the palace for the mourning period. That means I am to follow you. There are many still loyal to King Saul."

"Please stop worrying," I snapped. I pinched the bridge of my nose. "Have I not always protected you? I will continue to do so."

Dinah gave a stiff nod but did not appear convinced.

"You have nothing to worry about," I said, a bit gentler. "Your biggest threat is gone, and I will handle my mother."

I left Dinah and took a deep breath before entering Paltiel's home. Even after all these years, I could not bring myself to call it mine. It was his, and I was here occupying space. Outside was different. The vineyards, the rolling hills, the valleys were a part of me now.

Mother looked nothing like a grieving widow. She had yet to change into her mourner's apparel. She still held herself with the utmost composure and air of superiority, but when our eyes met, I saw not only sorrow, but fear. It was then I noticed that she had not traveled alone. "Rizpah?" I asked, shocked to see the two of them together.

"Already she does not greet me," Mother said.

"I am surprised, is all." I went and greeted my mother, then did the same to Rizpah. I could tell from the dark circles under Rizpah's eyes and the lack of color upon her cheeks that she struggled greatly with grief.

"What brings you both here? I am to leave for the palace on the morrow."

Both women glanced at each other before looking back at me.

"Have you heard from David?" Rizpah asked. "Does he yet know?"

"I have not been in contact with him for years. You know that."

"She does not realize the severity of this," Mother said to Rizpah.

"I am standing right here."

"Your husband is going to assume his place on the throne," Mother said, and I heard the fear laced with her words. "These are dangerous times for us, Michal. He will either take your father's concubines for himself or worse yet."

"He could kill us all," Rizpah said.

"David would not do that." Still, the thought of him taking all those women for his harem made my stomach roll.

"These are different times than of your youth," Rizpah continued. "David is the anointed heir to the throne. That means that he is going to deal swiftly with any and all threats."

"Which includes Saul's children and grandchildren."

"Your half-brothers and half-sisters are in very real danger."

320

Rizpah became choked up. "My own two sons—"

I took Rizpah's hand and squeezed. "Do not talk like that. All is well. David was a kind, attentive husband. I cannot see killing an entire household."

"It is the way of men, especially those who have their eyes set on the throne."

"The new king eliminates potential threats. David could see Saul's family as potential threats." Rizpah fought back emotion.

I remembered the vow David said that he shared with Jonathan years before. He told me that he vowed to protect Jonathan's family no matter King Saul's actions. But did that account for Jonathan's extended family too?

"We believe that if you came back to the palace permanently that it would help when David comes for the throne," Rizpah said. "Your mother thought to bring me here to encourage you to come with us, not just for mourning."

"I knew you would never listen to me," Mother said.

"I cannot leave here," I said. "I have my five sons, and this is their home. I also have my horses, and--" I paused. I nearly said, "And it's my home."

"You and Ishvi are all I have left," Mother said quietly as if it hurt her to say the words. "Three of my sons died with my husband. I know that things have not always been good between us, but I have always loved you. I need you now. Your brother needs you now. Already the advisers are in conversations to place him on the throne. You need to be there."

"No," I said, the old wounds showing their ugliness. "You do not want me there because you love me. You want me there because you see me as some protection from David. What makes you think he will not come for me in the same way? We are estranged. He has remarried and has families with those women. I am a nobody. Someone from his distant past that is no longer relevant." The words hurt as I said them because they were true.

"And what of me?" Rizpah asked. "I have helped you in

321

many ways. Will you not do this for me?"

"If it was not for Rizpah, your maidservant would be dead, or at the very least, mute. This is where family loyalty comes into play." Mother's features had once again turned cold. "You need to choose sides."

"Leave Dinah out of this. She did not deserve such a horrible fate, nor does she now. As for choosing sides, last time I did that, it did not work well for me."

"We are the House of Saul," Rizpah said, lifting her chin. "It is in your blood. You are King Saul's daughter, princess of Israel."

"It is time you chose your father's side," Mother added.

I needed to think. I promised them that I would arrive at the palace in three days' time for the mourning period and that I would think about the rest. Mother hugged me awkwardly, but Rizpah's hug lasted much longer.

"I want to believe the best in David," she said. "But, Michal, I do agree with your mother on this one. Years have passed, and David and his men are a mighty force to reckon with. When they find out, they will be here, and anyone from Saul's house could get slaughtered."

I opened my mouth to refute her, to tell her that David would never do that. Until it dawned on me how little I knew about my husband now. I only knew that he fought on the side of the Philistines. My David, or at least the David I had fallen in love with, would have never done that. So, I simply nodded and kissed her cheek, realizing that I had no idea who he was anymore.

44

ﮪﮪ

David

Ziklag
1012 B.C.

The Amalekites lay slaughtered at our feet. It had been no contest. The fury and grief ripped through the treacherous Amalekites like an unexpected hurricane on a calm sea.

Once the enemy was defeated, we quickly went and released our families.

As soon as I found Abigail and Ahinoam, I fell onto my knees, hugged and cried for them both, then hugged and cried over my children. My heart released some of the guilt of the Amalekite raid, but not all. I still had to grapple with the fact that my men could not take much more.

I assigned troops to oversee the women and children back to Ziklag. I then assigned troops to loot the camp and take back everything they could find of value. Other troops were in charge of all the animals. It was not long before the caravans were underway and headed back to our camp.

At least our spirits were lighter and not as full of gloom. I sat on my horse and traveled, overseeing the safe passage of the families. No way would I let them out of my sight. At least not tonight.

We made camp twice, in order for the women and children to rest, but in three days, we arrived at Ziklag.

The 200 who stayed at Ziklag to recuperate saw me returning

with the plunder and ran toward us cheering.

"Success!" I yelled to them.

Abishai on his horse galloped over to me. "The men want to know if those that stayed back will reap any of the spoil? Many do not feel they should."

"We do all the work, and they get the rewards?" One of the men traveling by foot said.

"That is no way to talk," I said. "After what we have been through? We are all brothers. And brothers share in the blessings." I looked over at Abishai and said, "Spread the word, all soldiers partake in the plunder. Also, make sure that Judah receives part of the plunder, as well, as a token of peace and renewal."

"Good idea," Eleazar said, coming up on my other side.

I nodded in his direction but did not say anything. The air between us felt different. I was not sure how to make it right.

"I am sorry I took my worry and frustration out on you," Eleazar said.

"Everything you said had truth in it."

"No, it did not. How were you to know that the Amalekites would sneak in on us in retaliation?"

"But if I would have killed Saul," I started. "I know you feel that way. I missed two opportunities to end it."

"True," Eleazar admitted. "But I do see your reasoning. Which is why you will make a great king." Eleazar reached over and squeezed my shoulder. "I would have never let them stone you. For the record."

I laughed. "Good."

Once in Ziklag, temporary provisions needed to be made, but everyone did their part to erect shelters, build tents, start the evening meal and draw water from the brook for washing and drinking. By the time I rested my head, after kissing my sons good night, it was far into the night. Once my eyes closed though, I slept hard.

***

The scene was familiar. A host of men rose up in battle, and I fought. Only this time I fought my people. Hebrews. They mocked me, pushed at me, called me names, and then lunged at me with their swords. "Stop it!" I yelled. "I do not want to fight you."

"David!"

I heard her voice and pushed past men to find her.

"David!" Michal called again.

"Michal!" I yelled.

I followed her voice, trying to maneuver through the Hebrew army without killing them, but bodies still fell to the ground as if I had no control over my hand and sword. I found her kneeling, blood covering her garments, so much so that I could not distinguish another color. Her family lay around her: Merab, Jonathan, her other siblings, and Saul. She rocked back and forth, holding her father.

"What happened?" I asked, kneeling in front of her.

She stopped wailing to look at me. Her eyes were not filled with the love and warmth of our past. They were cold and dead. "You killed them," she said, stonily.

Before I could defend myself, I heard my name. "Master David?"

I awoke with Michal's cold glare piercing through my heart. I peeked one eye open. "Yes?" I asked, my voice dry.

"There is a messenger here, sir. From the Israeli battle lines."

If I was not fully awake before, I was at that moment. I had yet to fully shake off the remnants of the horrible dream. "All right. Give me a few minutes."

I stood up from the ground and stretched my back. They had built a tent for me, and they had even recovered enough materials to make beds and assemble them, but there was not quite enough to go around. I made sure my wives and sons had them, which left me with several animal skins and blankets. I slept so hard, I obviously did just fine, even though my back was feeling it at the moment.

Pouring water from a jug and into a basin, I cleaned myself as best I could, and put on a fresh tunic from someone else's supplies. The lightness of the previous evening was now gone. A heaviness descended upon me that I could not shake off. I suddenly, desperately missed Michal. The thought of her not loving me made me physically sick to my stomach. Her love had been the burning embers that kept my fire from fading. I knew she was not happy with me, and I knew she probably had questions, but the dream was so real that I felt a foreboding that things would never be right with her. I again found myself asking God when it would ever be over.

When I stepped out of the tent and into the morning air, my eyesight immediately zeroed in upon a nervous man, who looked like he stepped out of mud and into the daylight. He held a bag and clutched it as if his life depended on it.

When he saw me, he immediately fell to his knees and held out the linen sack.

"Who are you?"

"I have escaped from the camp of Israel. My lord, it is bad. The Israelites have fled, and that is the few who did not die."

I closed my eyes, the nightmare still fresh, and felt grief all over again.

"I am sorry to report that King Saul and his son, Jonathan, have fallen in battle. They are dead."

I opened my eyes, furrowing my eyebrows. "What did you say?"

"Forgive me, my lord. I do not want to bear the bad news, but the king is dead."

"And Jonathan? Please tell me I misunderstood you."

"Jonathan is dead too." The messenger bowed low to the ground.

"Do not sport with me," I said, my heart catching at the thought of my friend and brother, Jonathan, dying by the hand of the Philistines. The same Philistines I worked under. "How do you know for sure? He is probably fine. He is a valiant soldier. Braver than all."

"I was there, sir. He fought courageously. I saw Jonathan

326

fall…and…and… I saw King Saul badly wounded. He begged me to kill him to end his misery. What could I do but honor his wishes." He opened up the sack. "I took the crown and royal bracelet as proof, sir." He held them out for me to see.

I stared at the crown and bracelet, not wanting to believe the evidence in front of me. "If I had been there," I said, then stopped myself. Instead, I stepped back, and in mourning, rent my tunic in half. Others around me did the same thing. All fell silent as the weight of the words heavily hung in the air.

I excused myself and stepped back inside my tent. My breathing ragged, my heart torn to shreds, I pressed against my chest and mourned the loss of my friend. And even though Saul had treated me so horribly, I mourned the king of Israel for Michal's sake. I hoped that the Philistines had not recovered his or Jonathan's bodies.

"David," Eleazar called from outside. "Are you all right?"

"No," I answered, but stood up and washed my face and stepped outside anyway.

This time all of my trusted advisors and family members stood close by. All of them looking expectantly at me. All of them in mourning, but all of them with hope in their eyes.

"Is it finished?" Eleazar asked.

Jashobeam took the crown and royal bracelet from the messenger and brought it to me. Then he knelt before me. "Long live, King David!"

Each person followed suit. Men stepped out of tents and made their way over, all kneeling before me.

"Long live, King David!" Jashobeam shouted again.

"Long live, King David!" the men replied.

I tried to keep calm, but there was so much emotion running through my veins, I did not know to laugh or cry. All the years of running, all the years of fearing for my life, all the years of worrying about the safety of my men and their families, of worrying about my own family…and yet, it was over.

And what of my past life? It had been ripped from me and Michal. Now as I stood, still in shock, still not-quite-believing, I wondered if the crown had come too late to salvage that relationship. Now I had a nation to lead, and a people to protect.

Jashobeam handed me the crown and bracelet.

I took the royal items not quite sure what to do. The two pieces felt foreign in my hands. Then I looked over at Eleazar, who was kneeling along with everyone else, and answered his question. "Yes, my friend. It is finished."

Eleazar nodded. "Then what is next?"

I thought about my answer for a moment. I would have to punish the messenger for daring to lay a hand on God's anointed, but after that, there was only one other thing that kept replaying over and over in my mind. I lifted my head, scanned the crowd, and said, "My brothers, it is time we go *home*."

The End of Book Two

Author's Notes

David's story comes straight from the Scriptures. However, many of the events of the books in this series are created from the author's imagination. If it happened in the Bible, the author took great care in making sure those events happened on these pages. That said, there is so much that happened behind the scenes of Scripture, that those backstories manifested into what you have read on these pages. Here are some answers to your burning questions.

How long was David on the run?

David received King Saul's crown at Ziklag around the age of 30. This means that he was on the run approximately eight years.

What was Michal and Paltiel's situation really like?

There is no mention in Scripture about Michal and Paltiel's situation other than when Abner comes to retrieve her (that scene is in the third book). Taking that scene into account, it can be inferred that Michal found some semblance of life there. Much of the events in these first two retellings come from Jewish history, which explains that their marriage was never consummated and that David's sword had something to do with it.

Why did Merab die? Was that Biblical?

Merab's unfortunate death was Biblical, as was Michal's raising of the five boys. How Merab died is not specified in Scripture, and therefore, creative license was taken.

Why didn't David take Michal with him?

This question gets asked a lot. The simplest answer is that they probably thought that he would not be gone long. King Saul had animosity toward David for a couple years before this event, and

Jonathan had always been able to reason with his father. Once on the run, David must have found out that Michal had been given to Paltiel in marriage. This would have been a huge insult to David, and it completely changed the trajectory of their lives.

Why did David marry two women while on the run?

In our modern times, David's decision to marry two women while on the run is an ultimate betrayal to Michal. In ancient times, the world was different, and he had a few very practical reasons to do so. First, once he realized that King Saul would not stop until he was dead, David had to provide for those men and their families who joined forces with him, easily over a thousand people. That means that they needed resources and supplies. Marriages to these women provided necessary assistance. Secondly, kings fathered many children. Times were volatile, and death always threatened (whether from sickness or war). The more children a king had, the better chance his lineage would continue on the throne. With Michal and David separated, David could not waste those fertile years without fathering children.

Why didn't Jonathan join forces with David? Why did he choose his father when he knew it wouldn't end well?

Love. Honor. Tradition. Loyalty. These are the words that come to mind when thinking about Prince Jonathan. The Bible mentions him often as a man of integrity and honor, as well as a man of faith and courage. He could have chosen to stay with his father simply because he was King Saul's eldest son, and he was loyal to his family. He was possibly worried about his father with his worsening condition. More than likely, Jonathan probably thought that he could be the voice of reason with his father and assist in reconciling King Saul with David. It is important to remember that while he loved David as his own brother, he loved his father too. Considering how honorable Jonathan was, it is easy to see him desiring peace between the current and future kings.

Did David have such a close bond with his mighty men?

Yes, the Bible speaks of the close bond with these men. Scripture also discusses how weary the men were in Ziklag. Many other portions of their interactions were grounded in the Bible. However, their personal backstories (such as Eleazar and David's childhood friendship) were creatively developed to further this retelling.

Did Michal really love horses?

Michal's love of horses, albeit a great story-builder, is completely fictional. There is nothing in Scripture to indicate this.

Did King Saul really lose his mind?

It is important to note that King Saul was not a stupid man. He was intelligent and calculating and had many successes for Israel. However, he was rash and often cruel (remember the scene with the killing of the priests). The Bible indicates that King Saul suffered from rages and irrational behavior. David's lyre-playing and singing helped to soothe him. His jealousy, however, only fueled his insanity, as did Samuel's (and God's) rejection of him as king.

Why would God put David through so much?

One can only study Scripture and reasonably speculate God's motives. Here are some considerations: if God would have placed David on the throne too early, David would not have been successful. We know that throughout Scripture, God always cultivates a relationship with His chosen. David's relationship with the Almighty grew throughout his years on the run because David had no one else to turn to. As far as separating David and Michal, which seems cruel, it could be that God was protecting David from the pagan idols and rituals that the Bible indicates Michal eventually embraced (you will read more about this in the next book). That may not be the nicest answer, but God is all about covenant and relationship. And although Michal is one of the author's favorite characters, she may have been more a hindrance to David's relationship to God.

***

If you have more questions that you would like answered, check out the author's website at www.janicebroyles.com, and email her your questions. And make sure to read the third book to the David saga, *The Anointed Heir*, due out in 2020.

Acknowledgements

Once again, I find myself at the end of a book I created, and I am overwhelmed with gratitude at those who helped get me here. Writing a book, especially one that requires meticulous research, is an arduous journey. I am appreciative of those who read chapters and offered expert advice, and those who simply supported my dream and listened to me ramble on about David and Michal.

Thank you to my family and for all the ways you support me. A special thank you to my friend and critique partner, Rachel Anderson, for reading the opening chapters with a critical eye. Thank you to Late November Literary for providing me this opportunity to publish my work, and thank you to the many businesses that help bring books to fruition and into bookstores.

Last, but not least, all glory belongs to God. I have learned and grown in my faith while writing these books, and I am forever in awe of His goodness and mercy.

Made in the USA
Columbia, SC
20 April 2021

35835592R00202